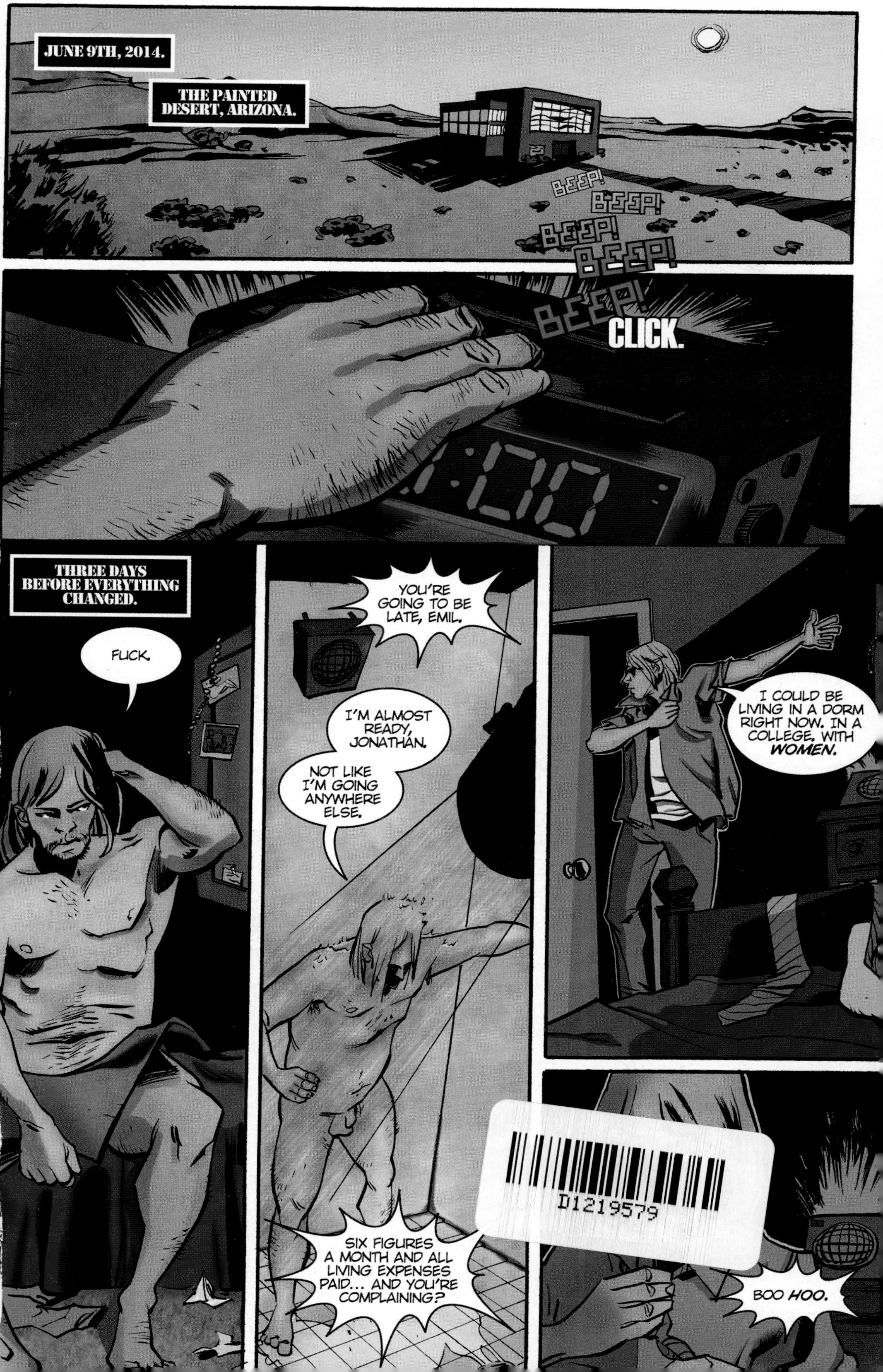
JUNE 9TH, 2014.
THE PAINTED DESERT, ARIZONA.
BEEP! BEEP! BEEP! BEEP! BEEP!
CLICK.
THREE DAYS BEFORE EVERYTHING CHANGED.
FUCK.
YOU'RE GOING TO BE LATE, EMIL.
I'M ALMOST READY, JONATHAN.
NOT LIKE I'M GOING ANYWHERE ELSE.
I COULD BE LIVING IN A DORM RIGHT NOW. IN A COLLEGE. WITH WOMEN.
SIX FIGURES A MONTH AND ALL LIVING EXPENSES PAID... AND YOU'RE COMPLAINING?
BOO HOO.

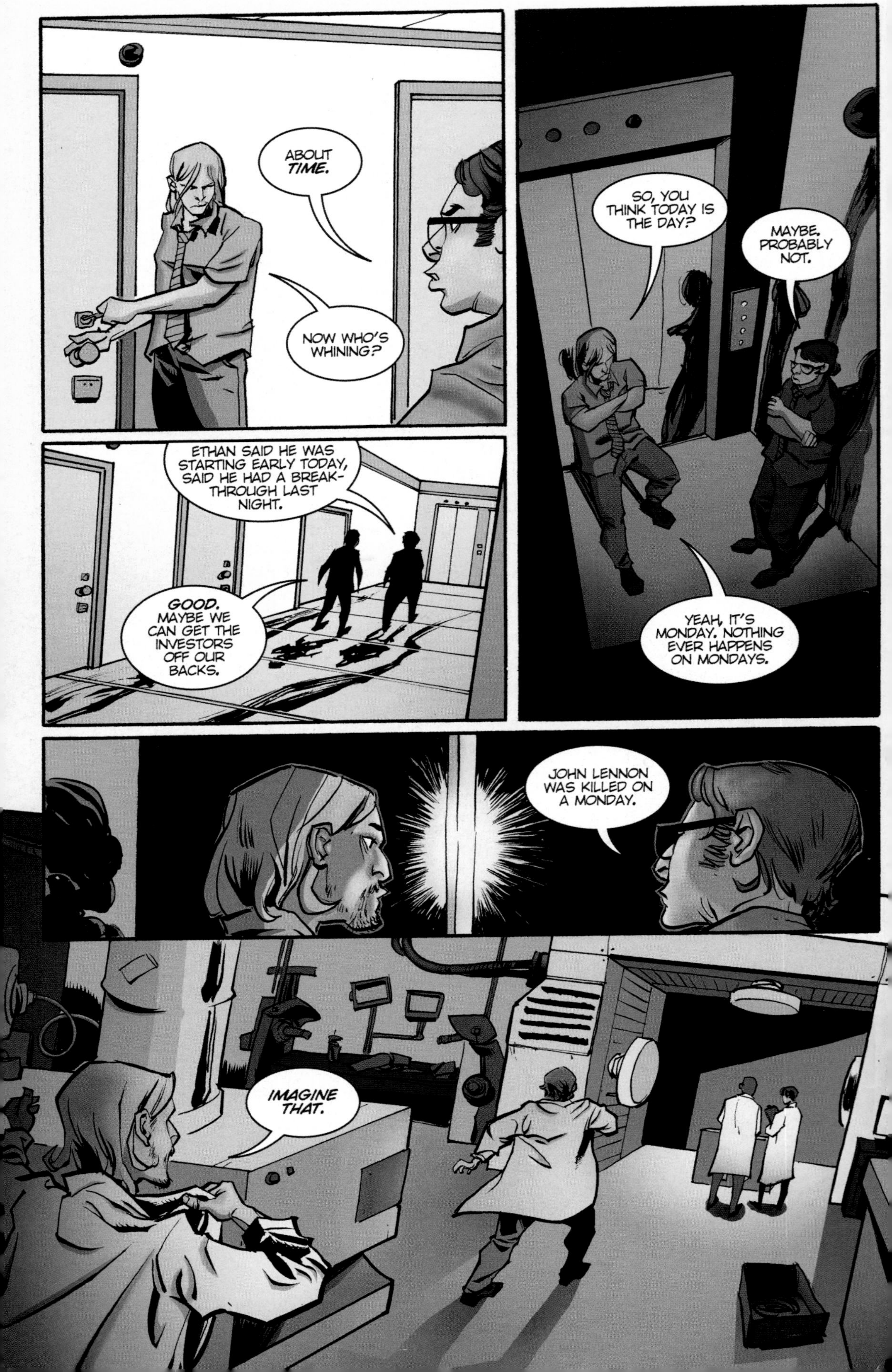
ABOUT *TIME.*
NOW WHO'S WHINING?
SO, YOU THINK TODAY IS THE DAY?
MAYBE. PROBABLY NOT.
ETHAN SAID HE WAS STARTING EARLY TODAY, SAID HE HAD A BREAK-THROUGH LAST NIGHT.
GOOD. MAYBE WE CAN GET THE INVESTORS OFF OUR BACKS.
YEAH, IT'S MONDAY. NOTHING EVER HAPPENS ON MONDAYS.
JOHN LENNON WAS KILLED ON A MONDAY.
IMAGINE THAT.

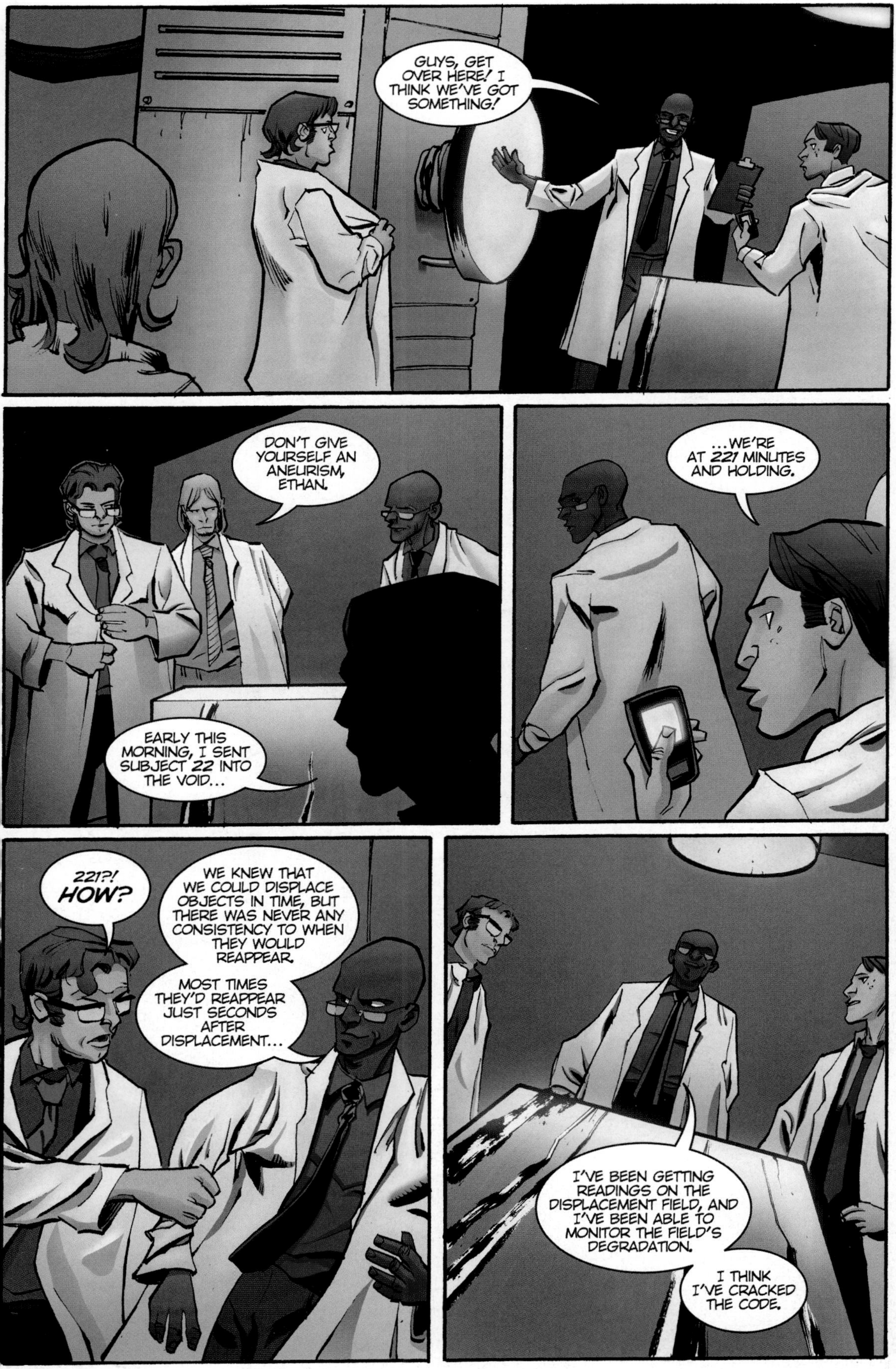
GUYS, GET OVER HERE! I THINK WE'VE GOT SOMETHING!
DON'T GIVE YOURSELF AN ANEURISM, ETHAN.
EARLY THIS MORNING, I SENT SUBJECT 22 INTO THE VOID...
...WE'RE AT 221 MINUTES AND HOLDING.
221?! HOW?
WE KNEW THAT WE COULD DISPLACE OBJECTS IN TIME, BUT THERE WAS NEVER ANY CONSISTENCY TO WHEN THEY WOULD REAPPEAR.
MOST TIMES THEY'D REAPPEAR JUST SECONDS AFTER DISPLACEMENT...
I'VE BEEN GETTING READINGS ON THE DISPLACEMENT FIELD, AND I'VE BEEN ABLE TO MONITOR THE FIELD'S DEGRADATION.
I THINK I'VE CRACKED THE CODE.

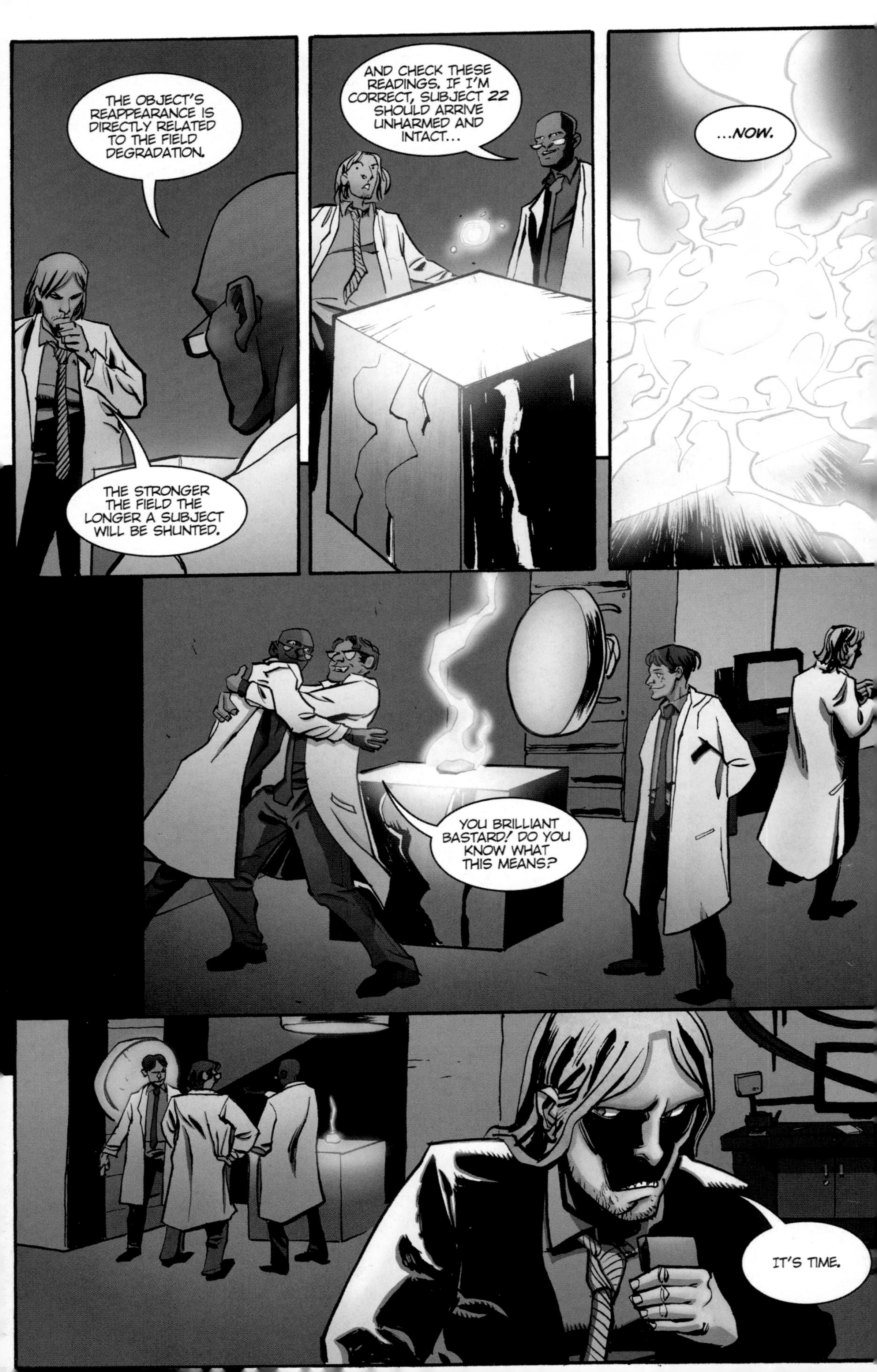
THE OBJECT'S REAPPEARANCE IS DIRECTLY RELATED TO THE FIELD DEGRADATION.
THE STRONGER THE FIELD THE LONGER A SUBJECT WILL BE SHUNTED.
AND CHECK THESE READINGS. IF I'M CORRECT, SUBJECT 22 SHOULD ARRIVE UNHARMED AND INTACT...
...NOW.
YOU BRILLIANT BASTARD! DO YOU KNOW WHAT THIS MEANS?
IT'S TIME.

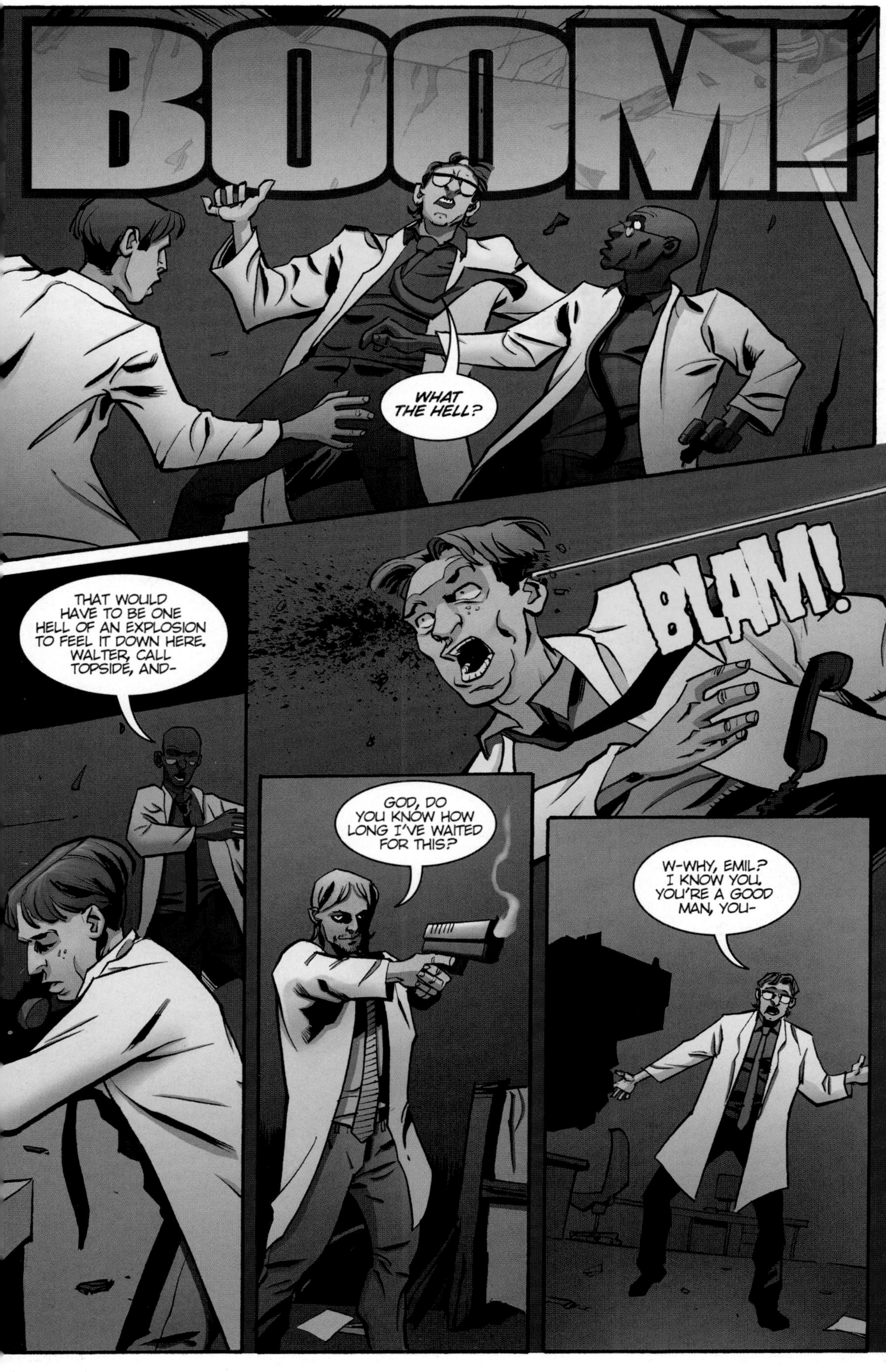
BOOM!
WHAT THE HELL?
THAT WOULD HAVE TO BE ONE HELL OF AN EXPLOSION TO FEEL IT DOWN HERE. WALTER, CALL TOPSIDE, AND-
BLAM!
GOD, DO YOU KNOW HOW LONG I'VE WAITED FOR THIS?
W-WHY, EMIL? I KNOW YOU. YOU'RE A GOOD MAN, YOU-

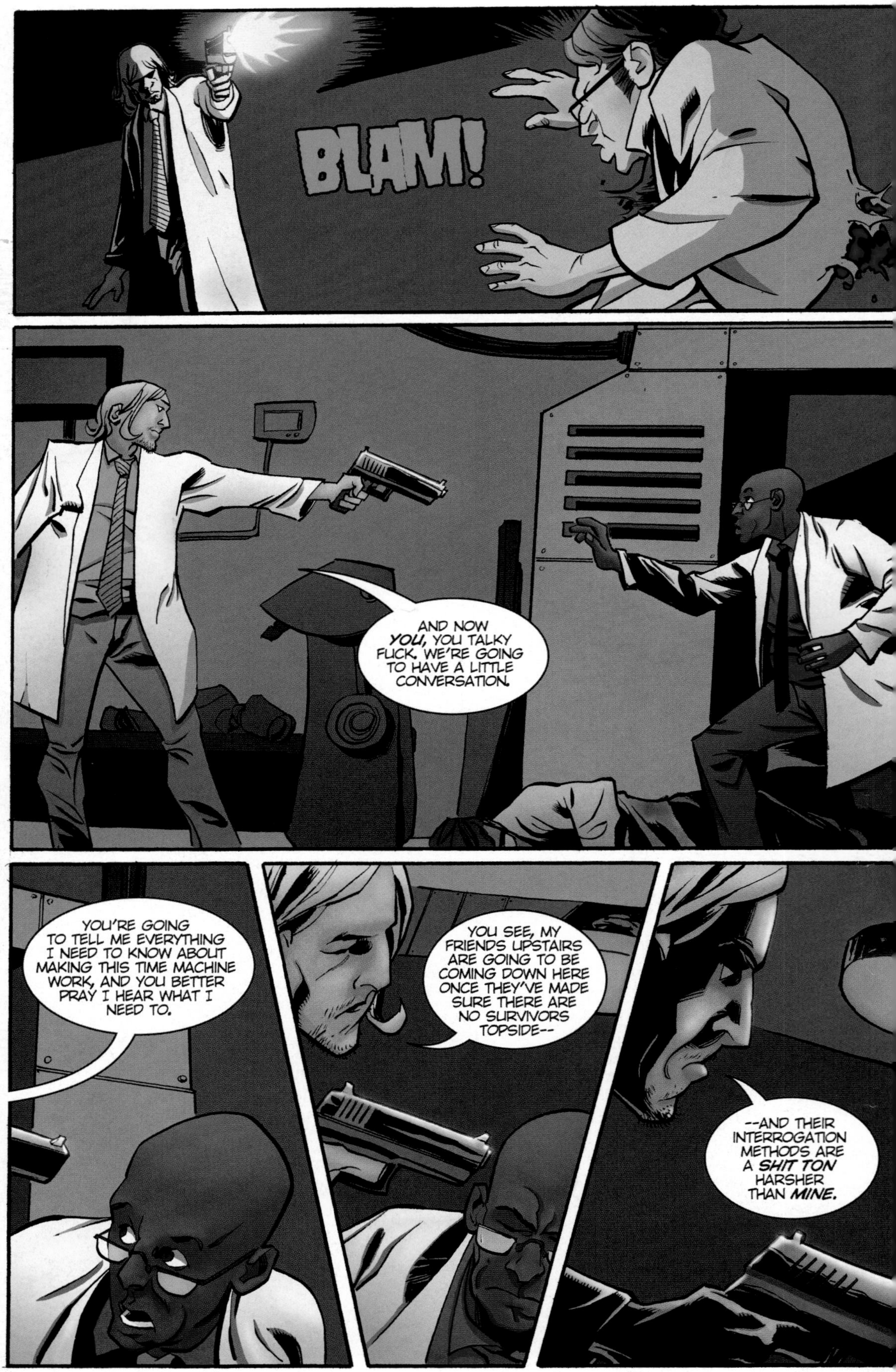
BLAM!
AND NOW YOU, YOU TALKY FUCK. WE'RE GOING TO HAVE A LITTLE CONVERSATION.
YOU'RE GOING TO TELL ME EVERYTHING I NEED TO KNOW ABOUT MAKING THIS TIME MACHINE WORK, AND YOU BETTER PRAY I HEAR WHAT I NEED TO.
YOU SEE, MY FRIENDS UPSTAIRS ARE GOING TO BE COMING DOWN HERE ONCE THEY'VE MADE SURE THERE ARE NO SURVIVORS TOPSIDE--
--AND THEIR INTERROGATION METHODS ARE A SHIT TON HARSHER THAN MINE.

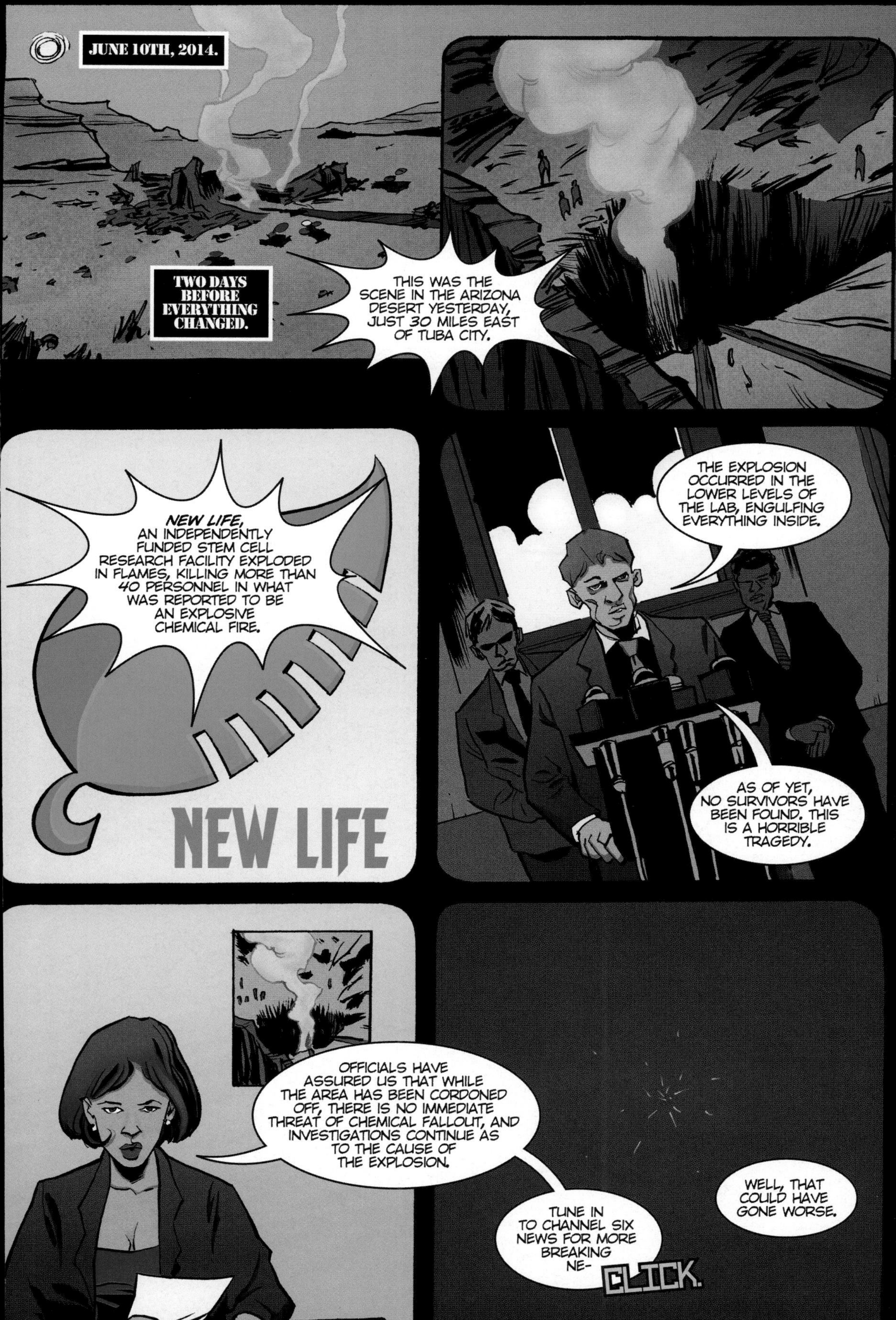
JUNE 10TH, 2014.
TWO DAYS BEFORE EVERYTHING CHANGED.
THIS WAS THE SCENE IN THE ARIZONA DESERT YESTERDAY, JUST 30 MILES EAST OF TUBA CITY.
NEW LIFE, AN INDEPENDENTLY FUNDED STEM CELL RESEARCH FACILITY EXPLODED IN FLAMES, KILLING MORE THAN 40 PERSONNEL IN WHAT WAS REPORTED TO BE AN EXPLOSIVE CHEMICAL FIRE.
NEW LIFE
THE EXPLOSION OCCURRED IN THE LOWER LEVELS OF THE LAB, ENGULFING EVERYTHING INSIDE.
AS OF YET, NO SURVIVORS HAVE BEEN FOUND. THIS IS A HORRIBLE TRAGEDY.
OFFICIALS HAVE ASSURED US THAT WHILE THE AREA HAS BEEN CORDONED OFF, THERE IS NO IMMEDIATE THREAT OF CHEMICAL FALLOUT, AND INVESTIGATIONS CONTINUE AS TO THE CAUSE OF THE EXPLOSION.
TUNE IN TO CHANNEL SIX NEWS FOR MORE BREAKING NE-
CLICK.
WELL, THAT COULD HAVE GONE WORSE.

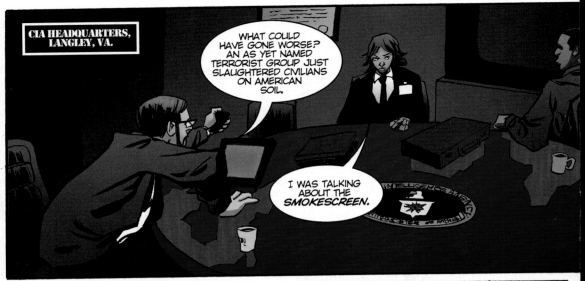

CIA HEADQUARTERS, LANGLEY, VA.
WHAT COULD HAVE GONE WORSE? AN AS YET NAMED TERRORIST GROUP JUST SLAUGHTERED CIVILIANS ON AMERICAN SOIL.
I WAS TALKING ABOUT THE SMOKESCREEN.
WELL, I'M GLAD ONE OF US CAN BE GLIB. OKAY, HERE'S WHAT WE KNOW.
ON JUNE 9TH AT OH-EIGHT-TWENTY, AN ASSAULT TEAM STORMED THE NEW LIFE BUILDING, LAYING SIEGE TO EVERYONE INSIDE.
WHILE ALL THIS IS BEING KEPT OUT OF THE PRESS, AN ESTIMATED 200 EMPLOYEES WERE CAUGHT IN THE CROSSFIRE. WHILE INITIAL REPORTS INDICATED THAT THERE WERE NO SURVIVORS, ONE DID MAKE IT OUT ALIVE.
THIS MAN. JONATHAN O'HARE. HE WAS SEVERELY INJURED-- BULLET IN THE CHEST-- AND IS IN CRITICAL.
SATELLITES PINPOINT A CELL CALL COMING OUT OF THE NEW LIFE BUILDING MINUTES BEFORE THE ATTACK. THE CALL WAS MADE BY THIS MAN--
EMIL HARRISON.
EMIL... THAT'S RUSSIAN, RIGHT?
VERY ASTUTE, BRONSON, BUT THIS ONE IS HOMEGROWN.
GREW UP IN GRAND RAPIDS WITH A QUICK STINT AT MIT BEFORE THE NEW LIFE CORP. PICKED HIM UP. REAL WUNDERKIND. WE THINK HE WAS THE POINT MAN FOR WHOEVER IS BEHIND THIS.

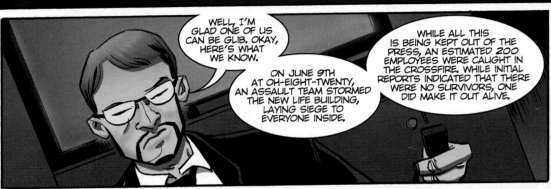

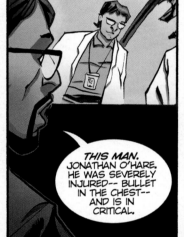

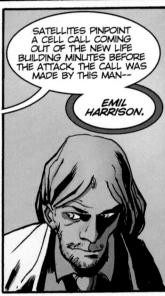

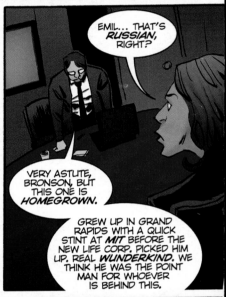

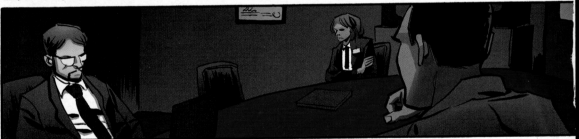

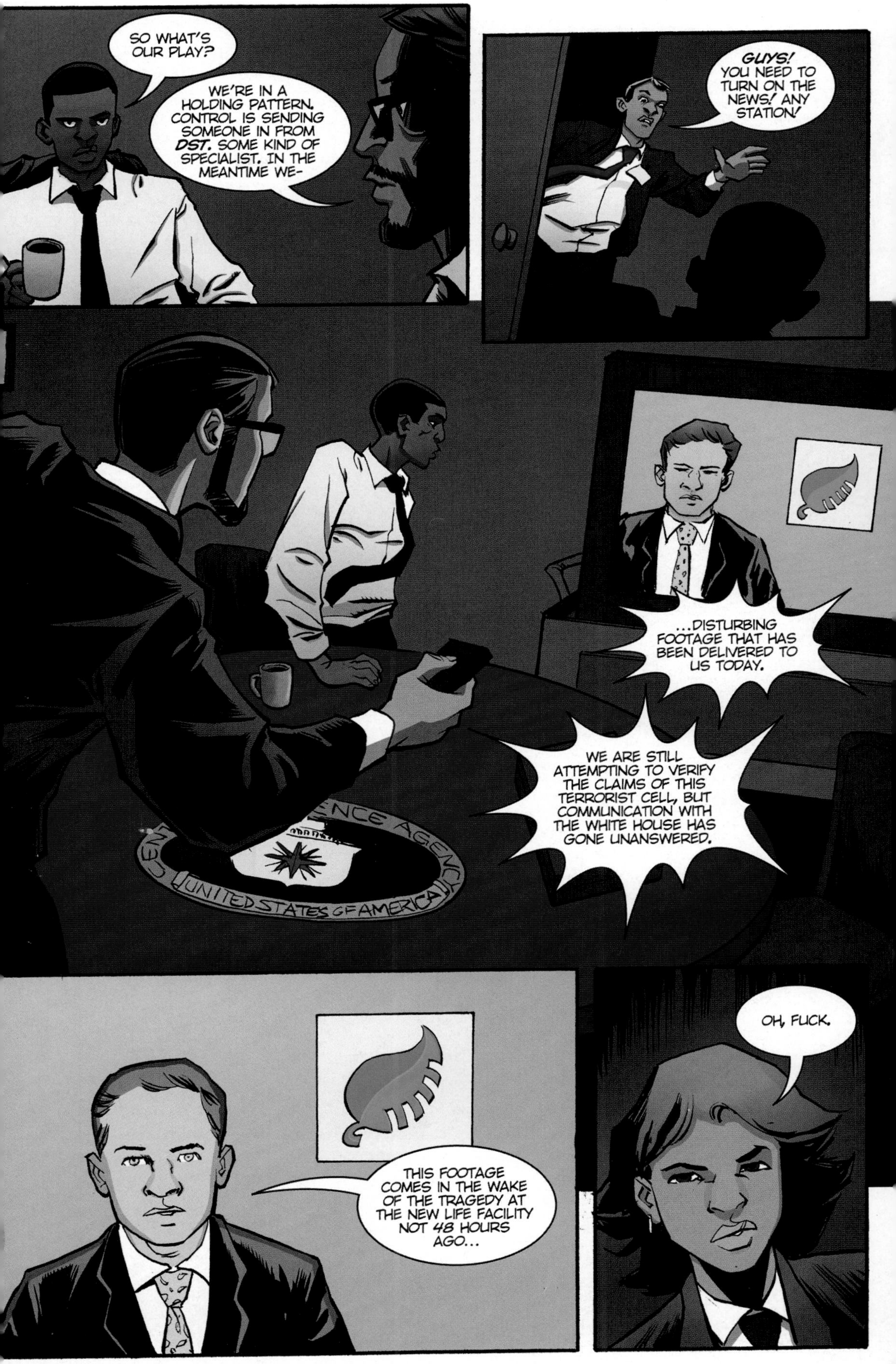
SO WHAT'S OUR PLAY?
WE'RE IN A HOLDING PATTERN. CONTROL IS SENDING SOMEONE IN FROM DST. SOME KIND OF SPECIALIST. IN THE MEANTIME WE-
GUYS! YOU NEED TO TURN ON THE NEWS! ANY STATION!
...DISTURBING FOOTAGE THAT HAS BEEN DELIVERED TO US TODAY.
WE ARE STILL ATTEMPTING TO VERIFY THE CLAIMS OF THIS TERRORIST CELL, BUT COMMUNICATION WITH THE WHITE HOUSE HAS GONE UNANSWERED.
UNITED STATES OF AMERICA
THIS FOOTAGE COMES IN THE WAKE OF THE TRAGEDY AT THE NEW LIFE FACILITY NOT 48 HOURS AGO...
OH, FUCK.

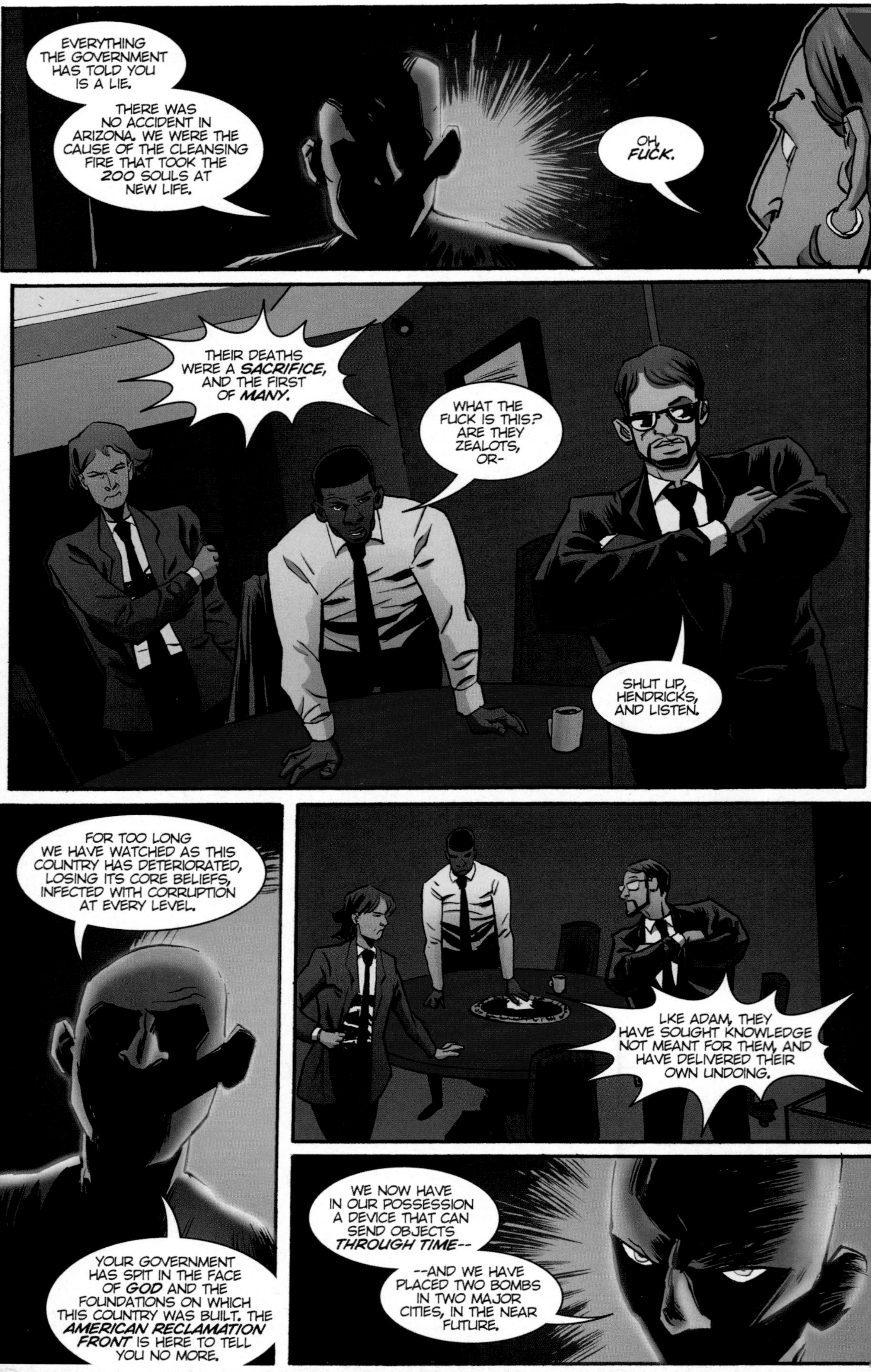
EVERYTHING THE GOVERNMENT HAS TOLD YOU IS A LIE.
THERE WAS NO ACCIDENT IN ARIZONA. WE WERE THE CAUSE OF THE CLEANSING FIRE THAT TOOK THE 200 SOULS AT NEW LIFE.
OH, FUCK.
THEIR DEATHS WERE A SACRIFICE, AND THE FIRST OF MANY.
WHAT THE FUCK IS THIS? ARE THEY ZEALOTS, OR-
SHUT UP, HENDRICKS, AND LISTEN.
FOR TOO LONG WE HAVE WATCHED AS THIS COUNTRY HAS DETERIORATED, LOSING ITS CORE BELIEFS, INFECTED WITH CORRUPTION AT EVERY LEVEL.
YOUR GOVERNMENT HAS SPIT IN THE FACE OF GOD AND THE FOUNDATIONS ON WHICH THIS COUNTRY WAS BUILT. THE AMERICAN RECLAMATION FRONT IS HERE TO TELL YOU NO MORE.
LKE ADAM, THEY HAVE SOUGHT KNOWLEDGE NOT MEANT FOR THEM, AND HAVE DELIVERED THEIR OWN UNDOING.
WE NOW HAVE IN OUR POSSESSION A DEVICE THAT CAN SEND OBJECTS THROUGH TIME--
--AND WE HAVE PLACED TWO BOMBS IN TWO MAJOR CITIES, IN THE NEAR FUTURE.

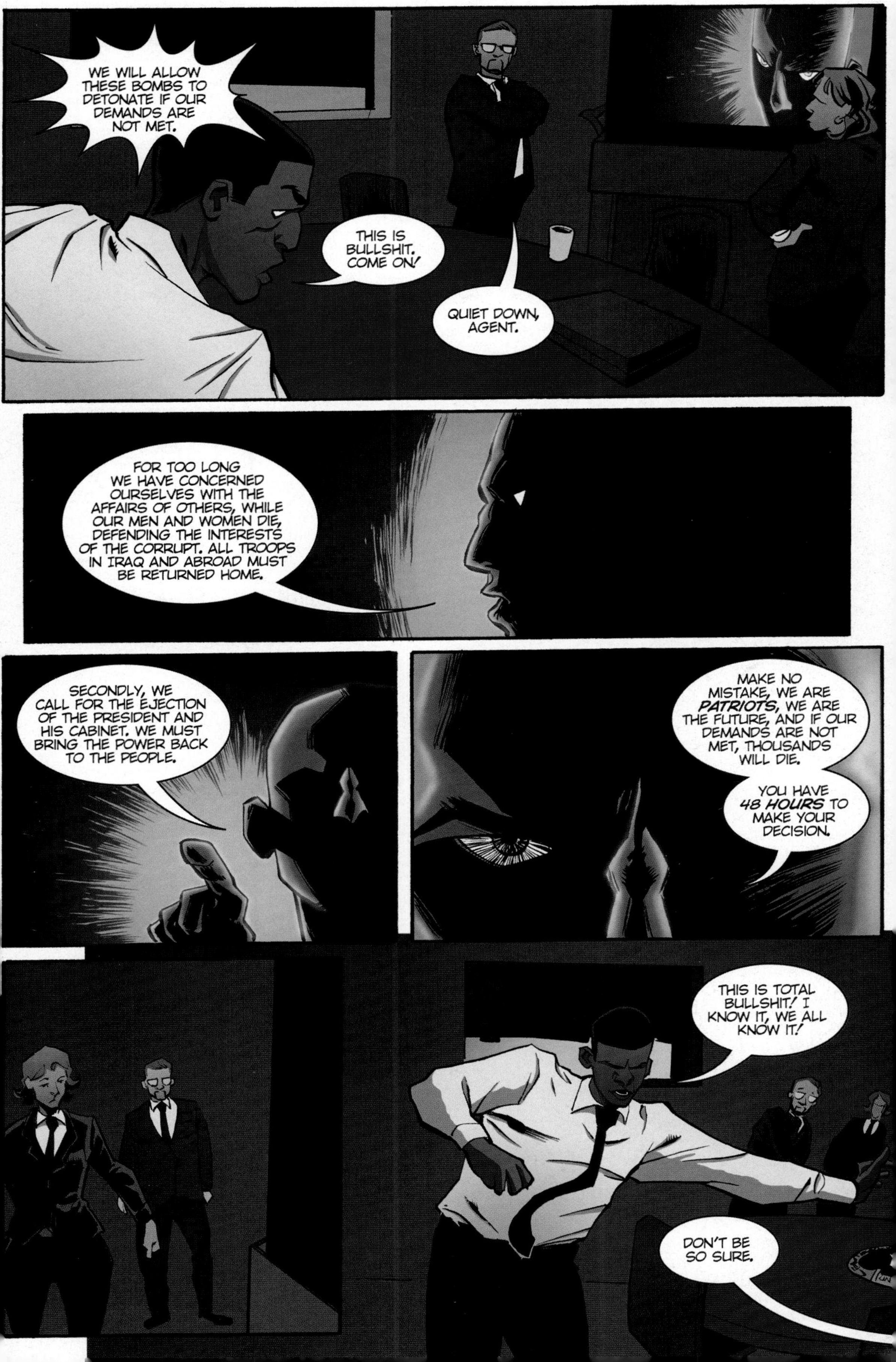
WE WILL ALLOW THESE BOMBS TO DETONATE IF OUR DEMANDS ARE NOT MET.
THIS IS BULLSHIT. COME ON!
QUIET DOWN, AGENT.
FOR TOO LONG WE HAVE CONCERNED OURSELVES WITH THE AFFAIRS OF OTHERS, WHILE OUR MEN AND WOMEN DIE, DEFENDING THE INTERESTS OF THE CORRUPT. ALL TROOPS IN IRAQ AND ABROAD MUST BE RETURNED HOME.
SECONDLY, WE CALL FOR THE EJECTION OF THE PRESIDENT AND HIS CABINET. WE MUST BRING THE POWER BACK TO THE PEOPLE.
MAKE NO MISTAKE, WE ARE PATRIOTS, WE ARE THE FUTURE, AND IF OUR DEMANDS ARE NOT MET, THOUSANDS WILL DIE.
YOU HAVE 48 HOURS TO MAKE YOUR DECISION.
THIS IS TOTAL BULLSHIT! I KNOW IT, WE ALL KNOW IT!
DON'T BE SO SURE.

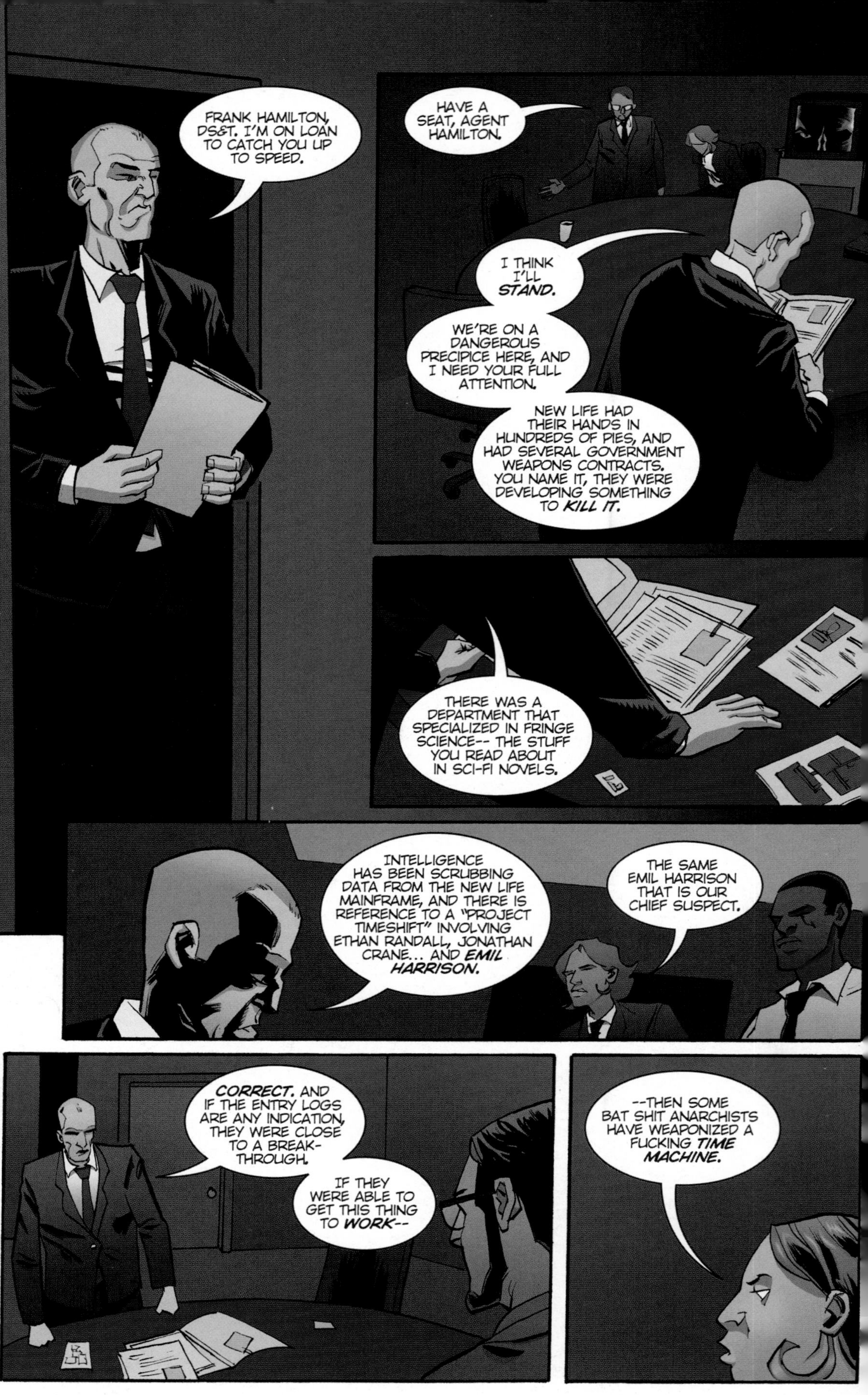

FRANK HAMILTON, DS&T. I'M ON LOAN TO CATCH YOU UP TO SPEED.
HAVE A SEAT, AGENT HAMILTON.
I THINK I'LL *STAND.*
WE'RE ON A DANGEROUS PRECIPICE HERE, AND I NEED YOUR FULL ATTENTION.
NEW LIFE HAD THEIR HANDS IN HUNDREDS OF PIES, AND HAD SEVERAL GOVERNMENT WEAPONS CONTRACTS. YOU NAME IT, THEY WERE DEVELOPING SOMETHING TO *KILL IT.*
THERE WAS A DEPARTMENT THAT SPECIALIZED IN FRINGE SCIENCE-- THE STUFF YOU READ ABOUT IN SCI-FI NOVELS.
INTELLIGENCE HAS BEEN SCRUBBING DATA FROM THE NEW LIFE MAINFRAME, AND THERE IS REFERENCE TO A "PROJECT TIMESHIFT" INVOLVING ETHAN RANDALL, JONATHAN CRANE... AND *EMIL HARRISON.*
THE SAME EMIL HARRISON THAT IS OUR CHIEF SUSPECT.
CORRECT. AND IF THE ENTRY LOGS ARE ANY INDICATION, THEY WERE CLOSE TO A BREAK-THROUGH.
IF THEY WERE ABLE TO GET THIS THING TO *WORK--*
--THEN SOME BAT SHIT ANARCHISTS HAVE WEAPONIZED A FUCKING *TIME MACHINE.*

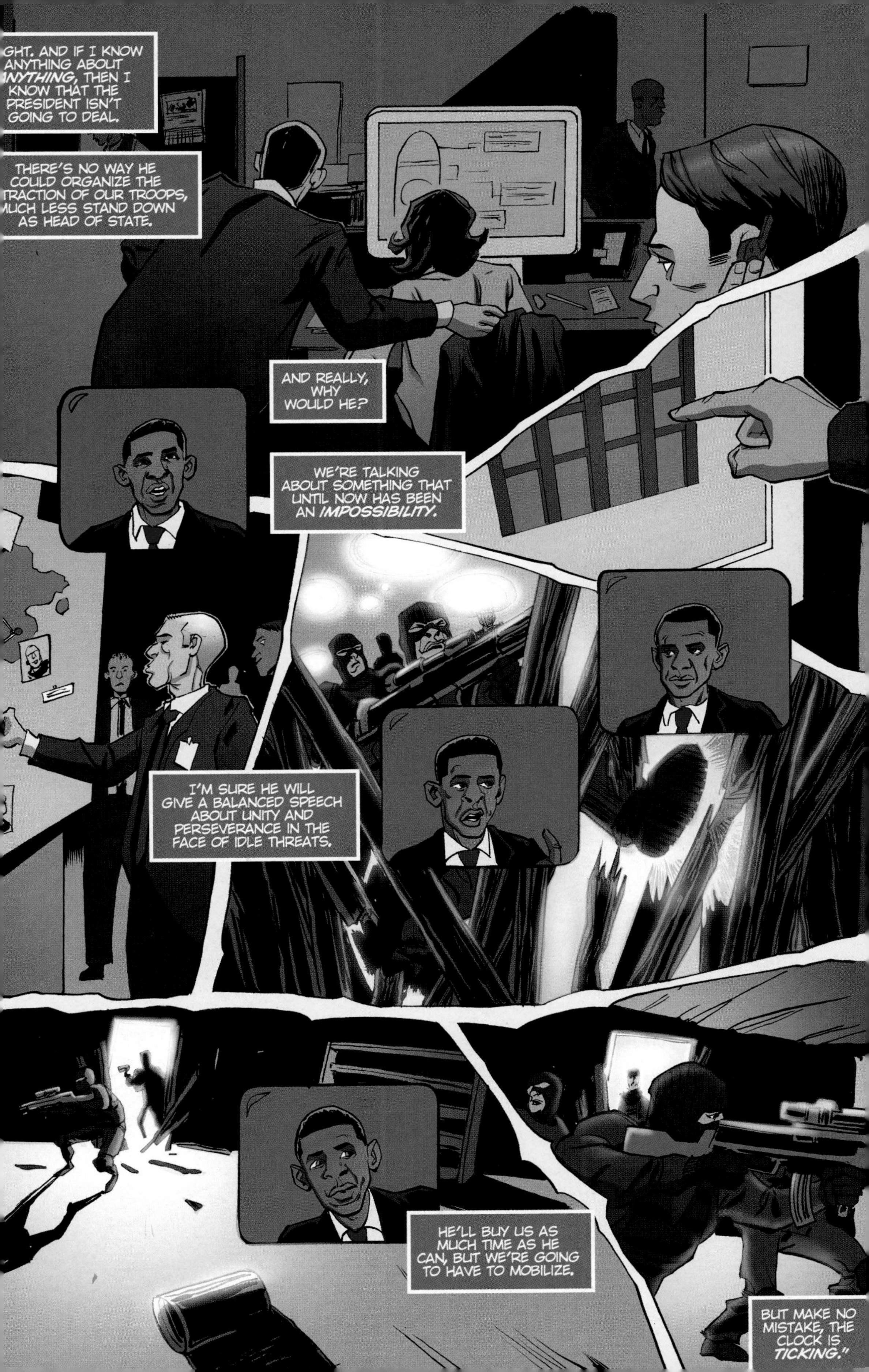
GHT. AND IF I KNOW ANYTHING ABOUT ANYTHING, THEN I KNOW THAT THE PRESIDENT ISN'T GOING TO DEAL.
THERE'S NO WAY HE COULD ORGANIZE THE TRACTION OF OUR TROOPS, MUCH LESS STAND DOWN AS HEAD OF STATE.
AND REALLY, WHY WOULD HE?
WE'RE TALKING ABOUT SOMETHING THAT UNTIL NOW HAS BEEN AN IMPOSSIBILITY.
I'M SURE HE WILL GIVE A BALANCED SPEECH ABOUT UNITY AND PERSEVERANCE IN THE FACE OF IDLE THREATS.
HE'LL BUY US AS MUCH TIME AS HE CAN, BUT WE'RE GOING TO HAVE TO MOBILIZE.
BUT MAKE NO MISTAKE, THE CLOCK IS TICKING."

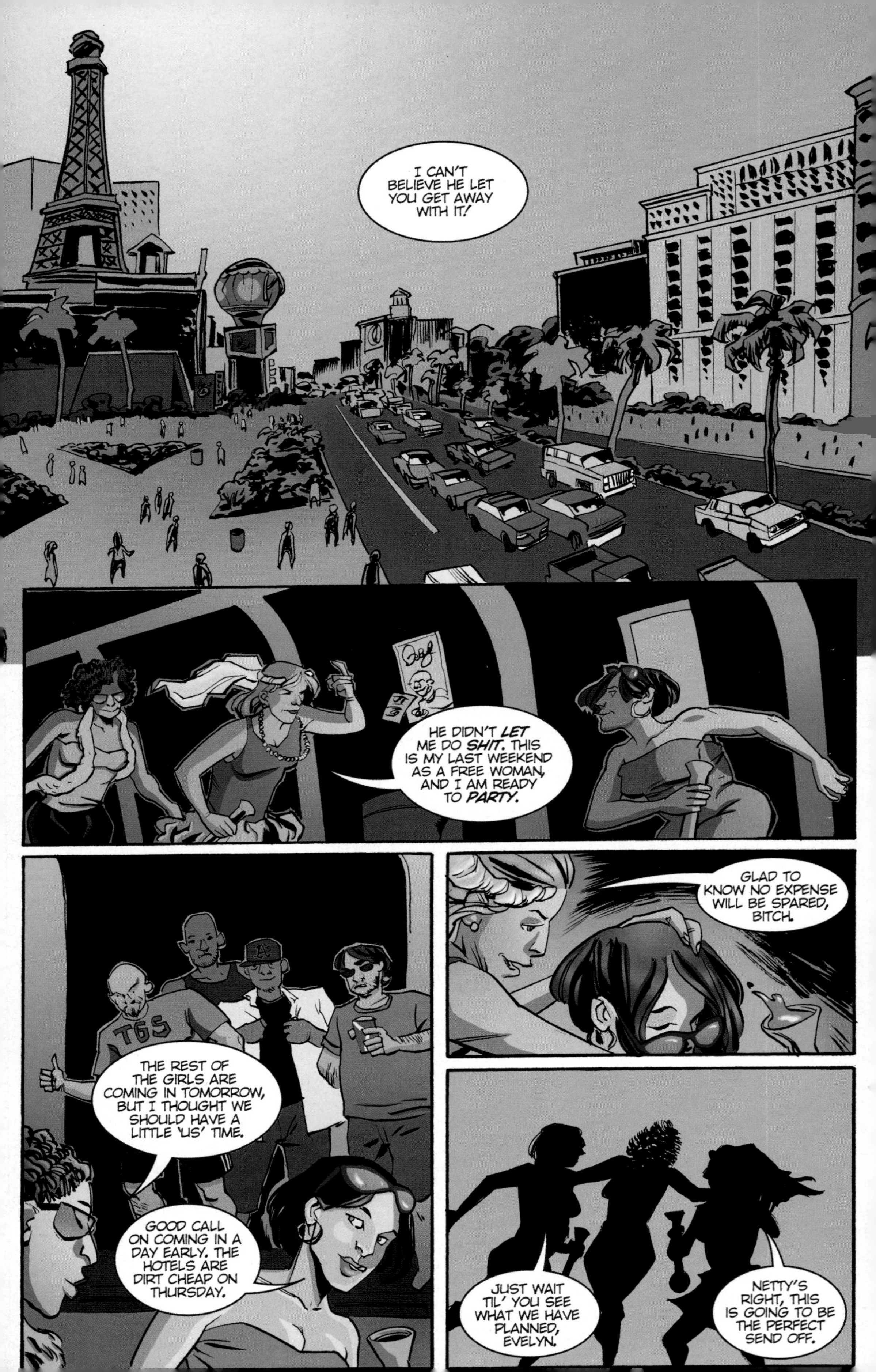
I CAN'T BELIEVE HE LET YOU GET AWAY WITH IT!
HE DIDN'T LET ME DO SHIT. THIS IS MY LAST WEEKEND AS A FREE WOMAN, AND I AM READY TO PARTY.
TGS
THE REST OF THE GIRLS ARE COMING IN TOMORROW, BUT I THOUGHT WE SHOULD HAVE A LITTLE 'US' TIME.
GOOD CALL ON COMING IN A DAY EARLY. THE HOTELS ARE DIRT CHEAP ON THURSDAY.
GLAD TO KNOW NO EXPENSE WILL BE SPARED, BITCH.
JUST WAIT TIL' YOU SEE WHAT WE HAVE PLANNED, EVELYN.
NETTY'S RIGHT, THIS IS GOING TO BE THE PERFECT SEND OFF.

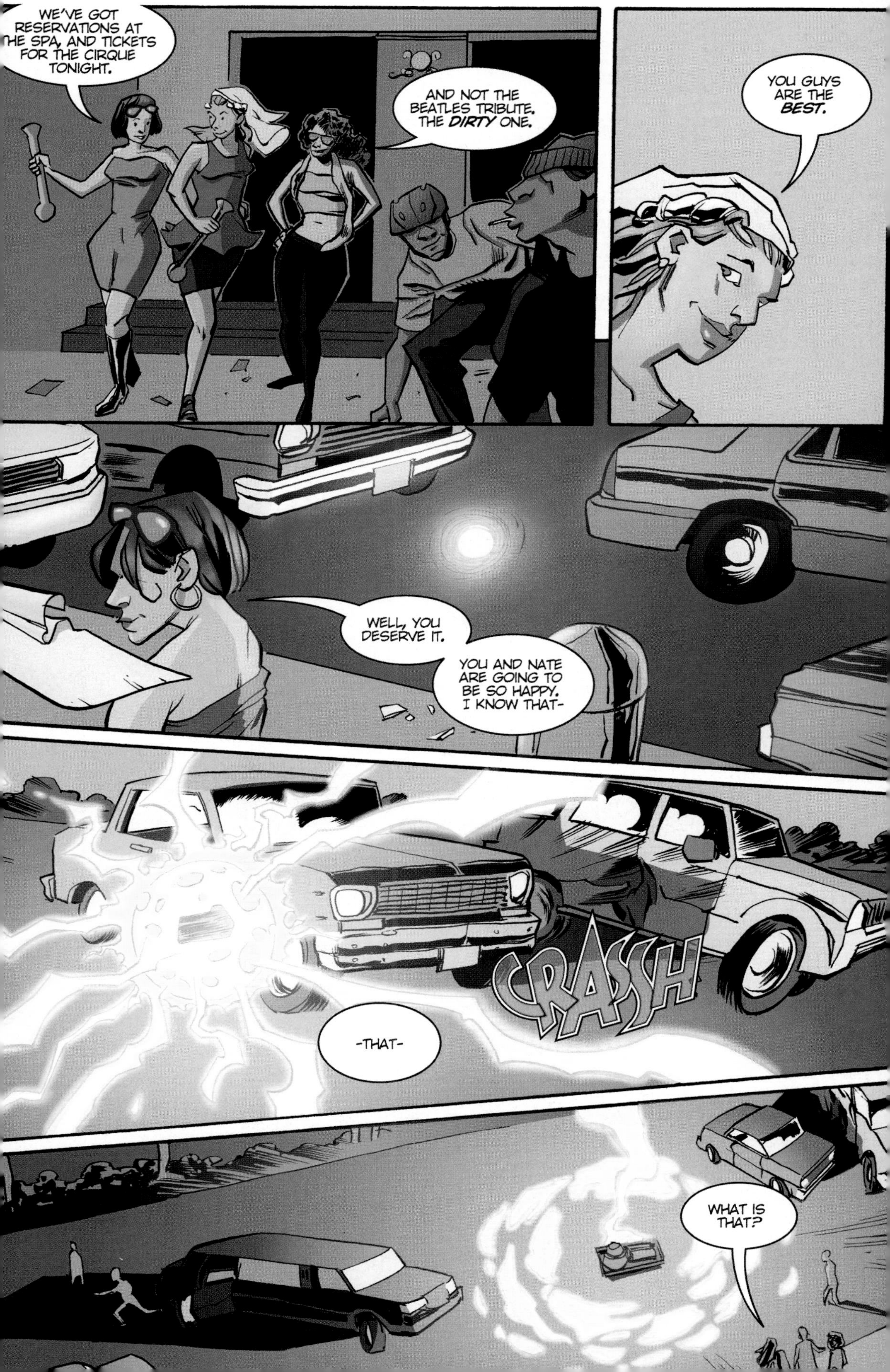
WE'VE GOT RESERVATIONS AT THE SPA, AND TICKETS FOR THE CIRQUE TONIGHT.
AND NOT THE BEATLES TRIBUTE. THE DIRTY ONE.
YOU GUYS ARE THE BEST.
WELL, YOU DESERVE IT.
YOU AND NATE ARE GOING TO BE SO HAPPY. I KNOW THAT-
CRASH
-THAT-
WHAT IS THAT?

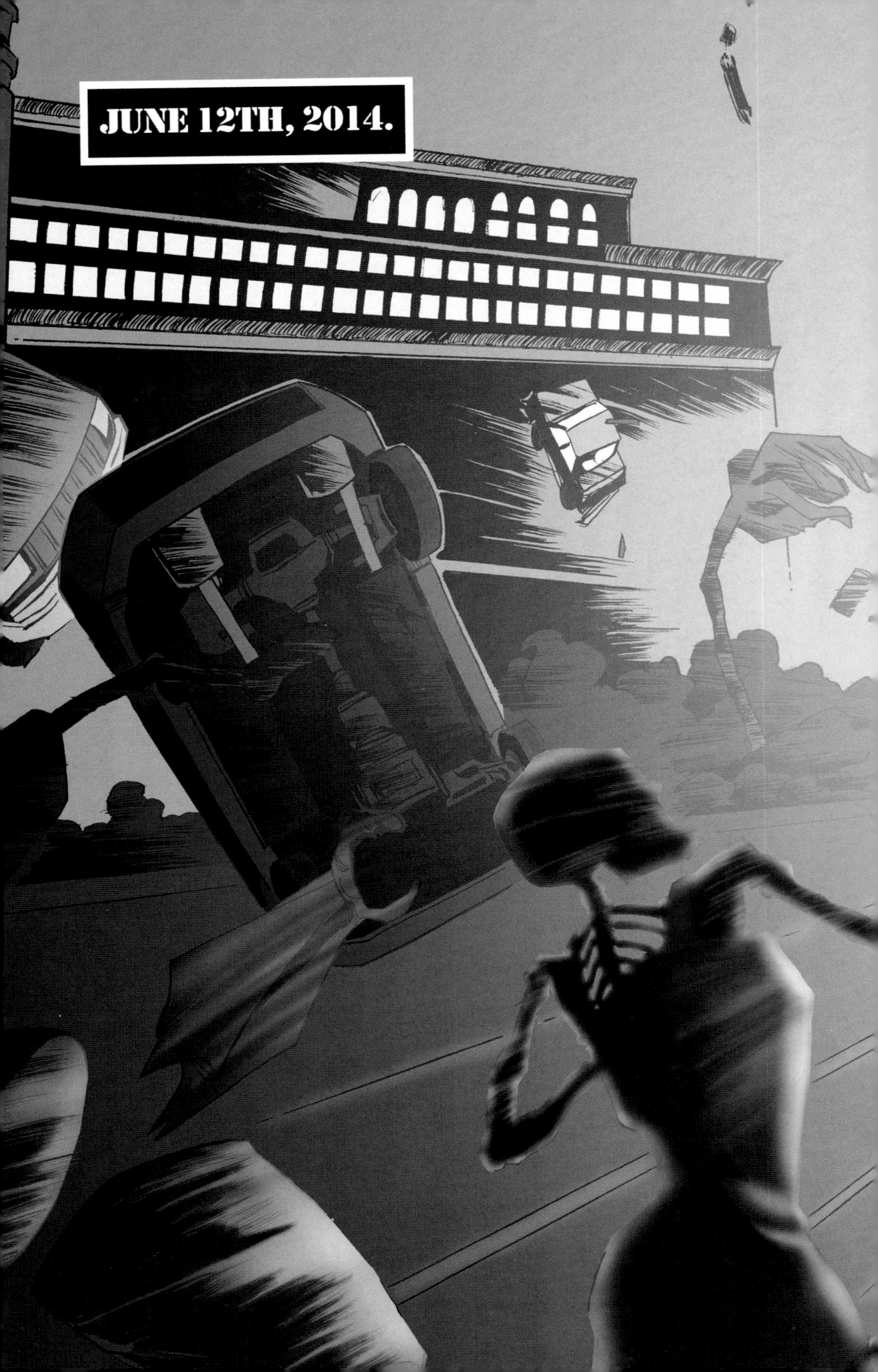
JUNE 12TH, 2014.

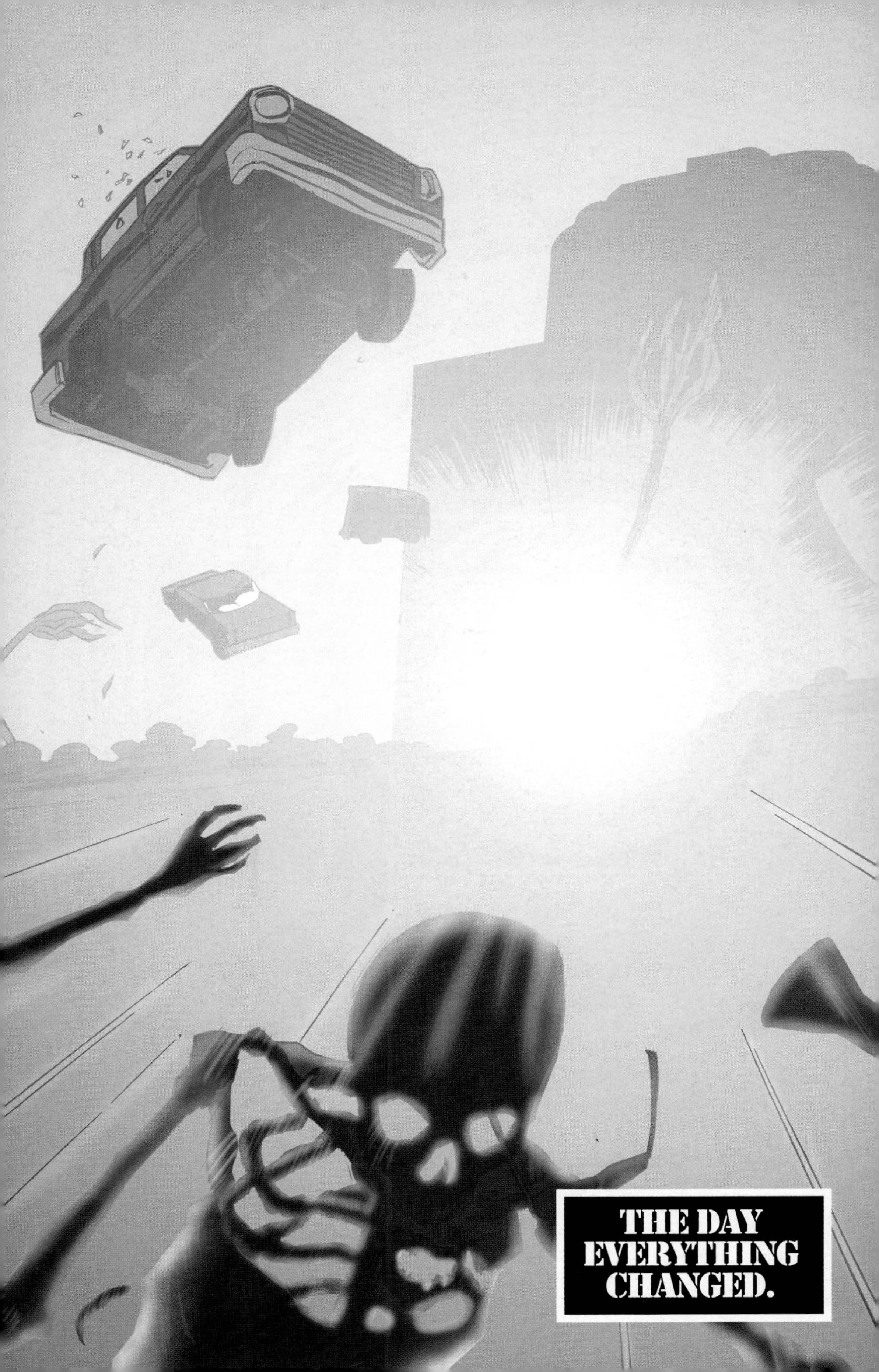
THE DAY EVERYTHING CHANGED.

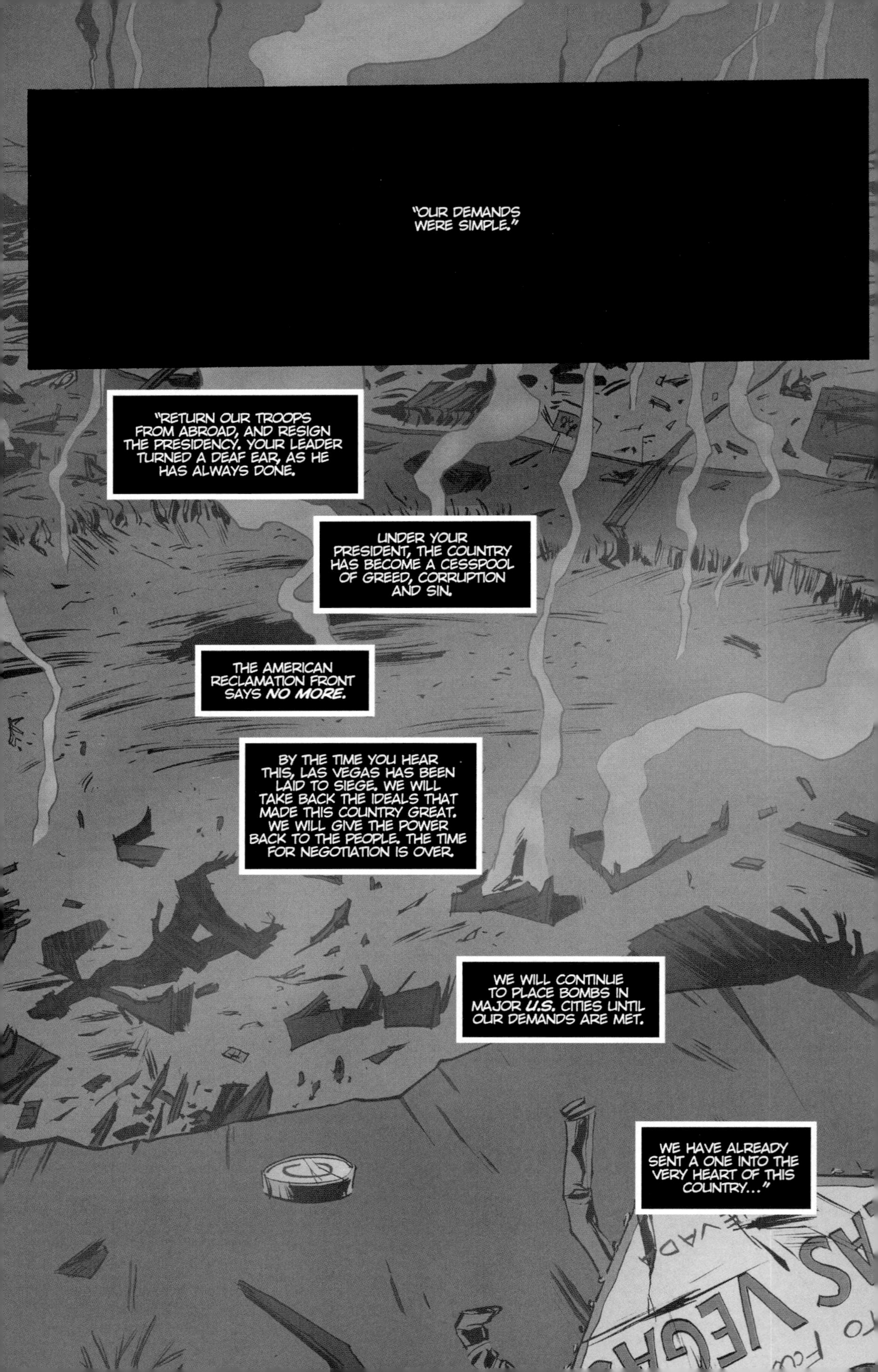
"OUR DEMANDS WERE SIMPLE."
"RETURN OUR TROOPS FROM ABROAD, AND RESIGN THE PRESIDENCY. YOUR LEADER TURNED A DEAF EAR, AS HE HAS ALWAYS DONE.
UNDER YOUR PRESIDENT, THE COUNTRY HAS BECOME A CESSPOOL OF GREED, CORRUPTION AND SIN.
THE AMERICAN RECLAMATION FRONT SAYS *NO MORE.*
BY THE TIME YOU HEAR THIS, LAS VEGAS HAS BEEN LAID TO SIEGE. WE WILL TAKE BACK THE IDEALS THAT MADE THIS COUNTRY GREAT. WE WILL GIVE THE POWER BACK TO THE PEOPLE. THE TIME FOR NEGOTIATION IS OVER.
WE WILL CONTINUE TO PLACE BOMBS IN MAJOR *U.S.* CITIES UNTIL OUR DEMANDS ARE MET.
WE HAVE ALREADY SENT A ONE INTO THE VERY HEART OF THIS COUNTRY..."

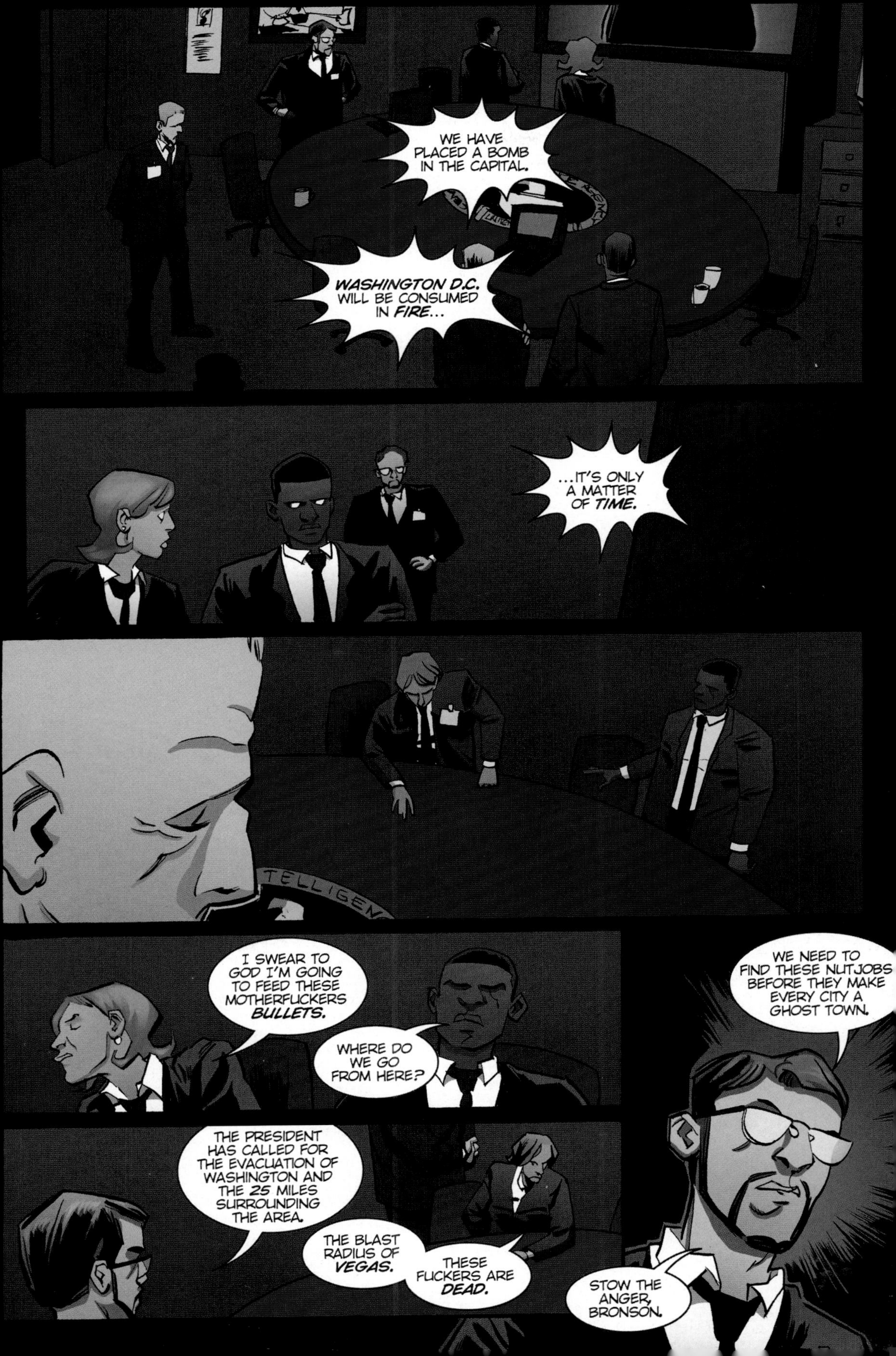
WE HAVE PLACED A BOMB IN THE CAPITAL.
WASHINGTON D.C. WILL BE CONSUMED IN FIRE...
...IT'S ONLY A MATTER OF TIME.
TELLIGEN
I SWEAR TO GOD I'M GOING TO FEED THESE MOTHERFUCKERS BULLETS.
WHERE DO WE GO FROM HERE?
WE NEED TO FIND THESE NUTJOBS BEFORE THEY MAKE EVERY CITY A GHOST TOWN.
THE PRESIDENT HAS CALLED FOR THE EVACUATION OF WASHINGTON AND THE 25 MILES SURROUNDING THE AREA.
THE BLAST RADIUS OF VEGAS.
THESE FUCKERS ARE DEAD.
STOW THE ANGER, BRONSON.

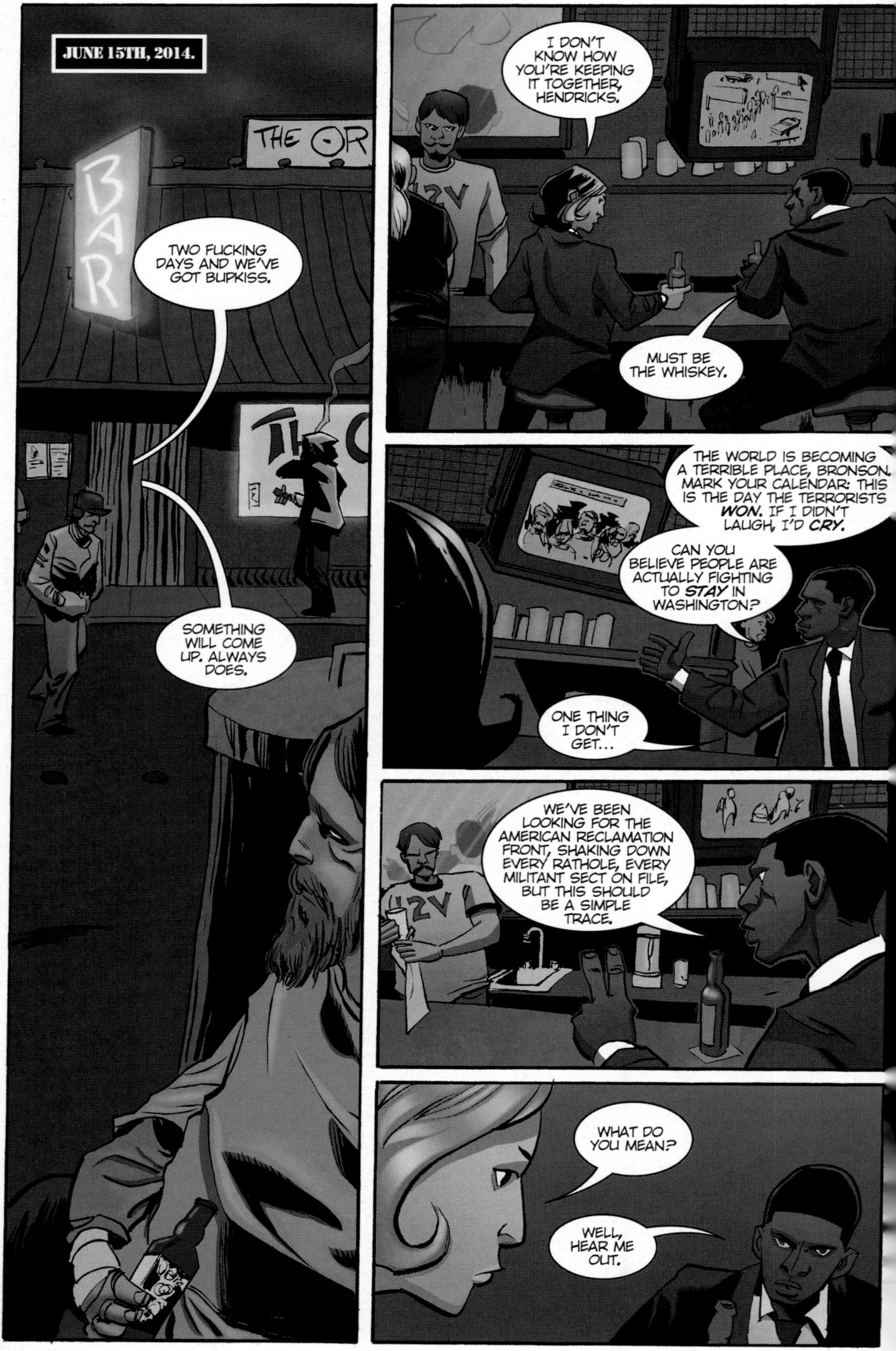
JUNE 15TH, 2014.
THE OR
BAR
TWO FUCKING DAYS AND WE'VE GOT BUPKISS.
SOMETHING WILL COME UP. ALWAYS DOES.
I DON'T KNOW HOW YOU'RE KEEPING IT TOGETHER, HENDRICKS.
MUST BE THE WHISKEY.
THE WORLD IS BECOMING A TERRIBLE PLACE, BRONSON. MARK YOUR CALENDAR: THIS IS THE DAY THE TERRORISTS WON. IF I DIDN'T LAUGH, I'D CRY.
CAN YOU BELIEVE PEOPLE ARE ACTUALLY FIGHTING TO STAY IN WASHINGTON?
ONE THING I DON'T GET...
WE'VE BEEN LOOKING FOR THE AMERICAN RECLAMATION FRONT, SHAKING DOWN EVERY RATHOLE, EVERY MILITANT SECT ON FILE, BUT THIS SHOULD BE A SIMPLE TRACE.
WHAT DO YOU MEAN?
WELL, HEAR ME OUT.

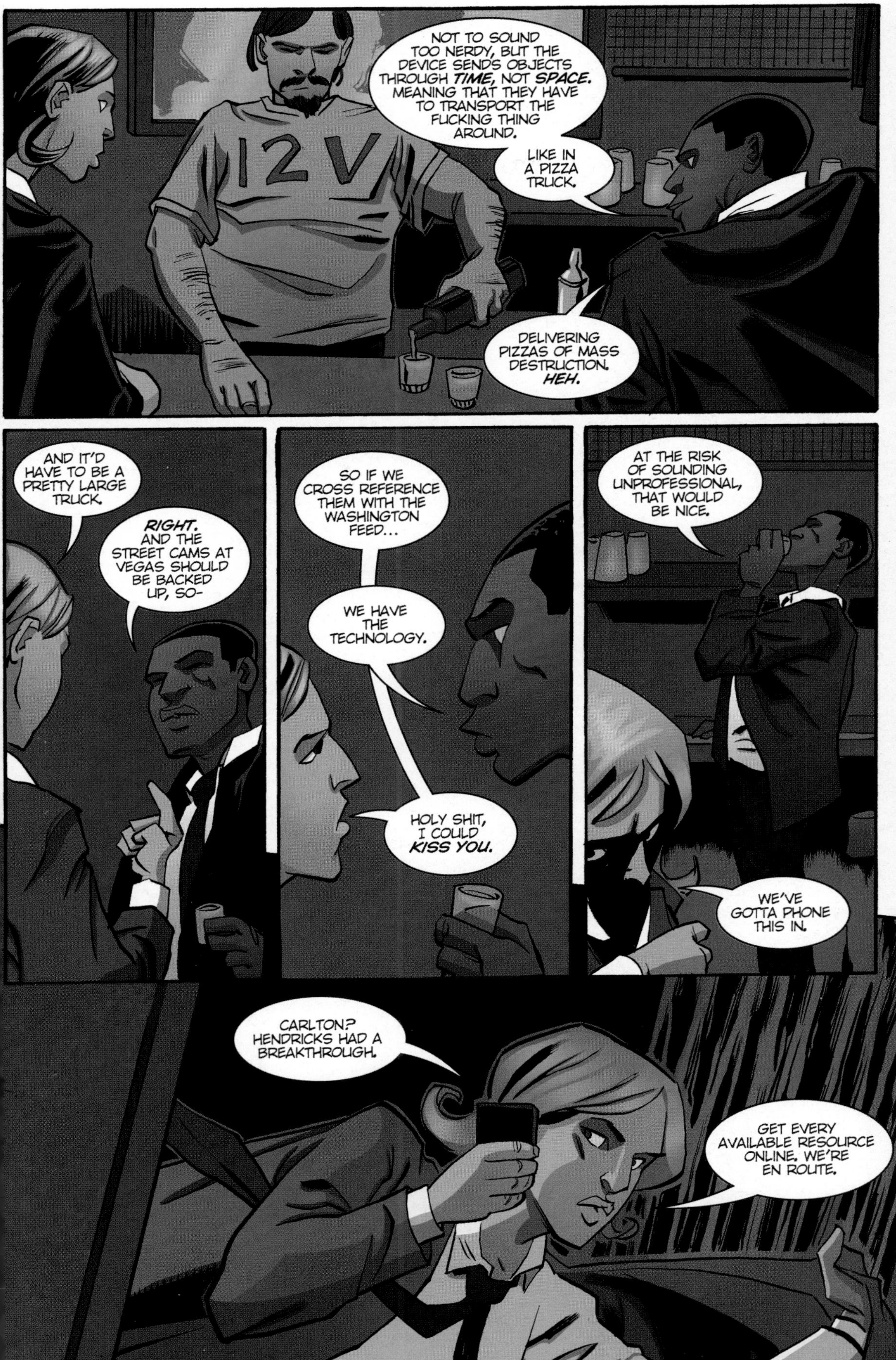
NOT TO SOUND TOO NERDY, BUT THE DEVICE SENDS OBJECTS THROUGH *TIME,* NOT *SPACE.* MEANING THAT THEY HAVE TO TRANSPORT THE FUCKING THING AROUND.
LIKE IN A PIZZA TRUCK.
DELIVERING PIZZAS OF MASS DESTRUCTION. *HEH.*
AND IT'D HAVE TO BE A PRETTY LARGE TRUCK.
RIGHT. AND THE STREET CAMS AT VEGAS SHOULD BE BACKED UP, SO-
SO IF WE CROSS REFERENCE THEM WITH THE WASHINGTON FEED...
WE HAVE THE TECHNOLOGY.
HOLY SHIT, I COULD *KISS YOU.*
AT THE RISK OF SOUNDING UNPROFESSIONAL, THAT WOULD BE NICE.
WE'VE GOTTA PHONE THIS IN.
CARLTON? HENDRICKS HAD A BREAKTHROUGH.
GET EVERY AVAILABLE RESOURCE ONLINE. WE'RE EN ROUTE.

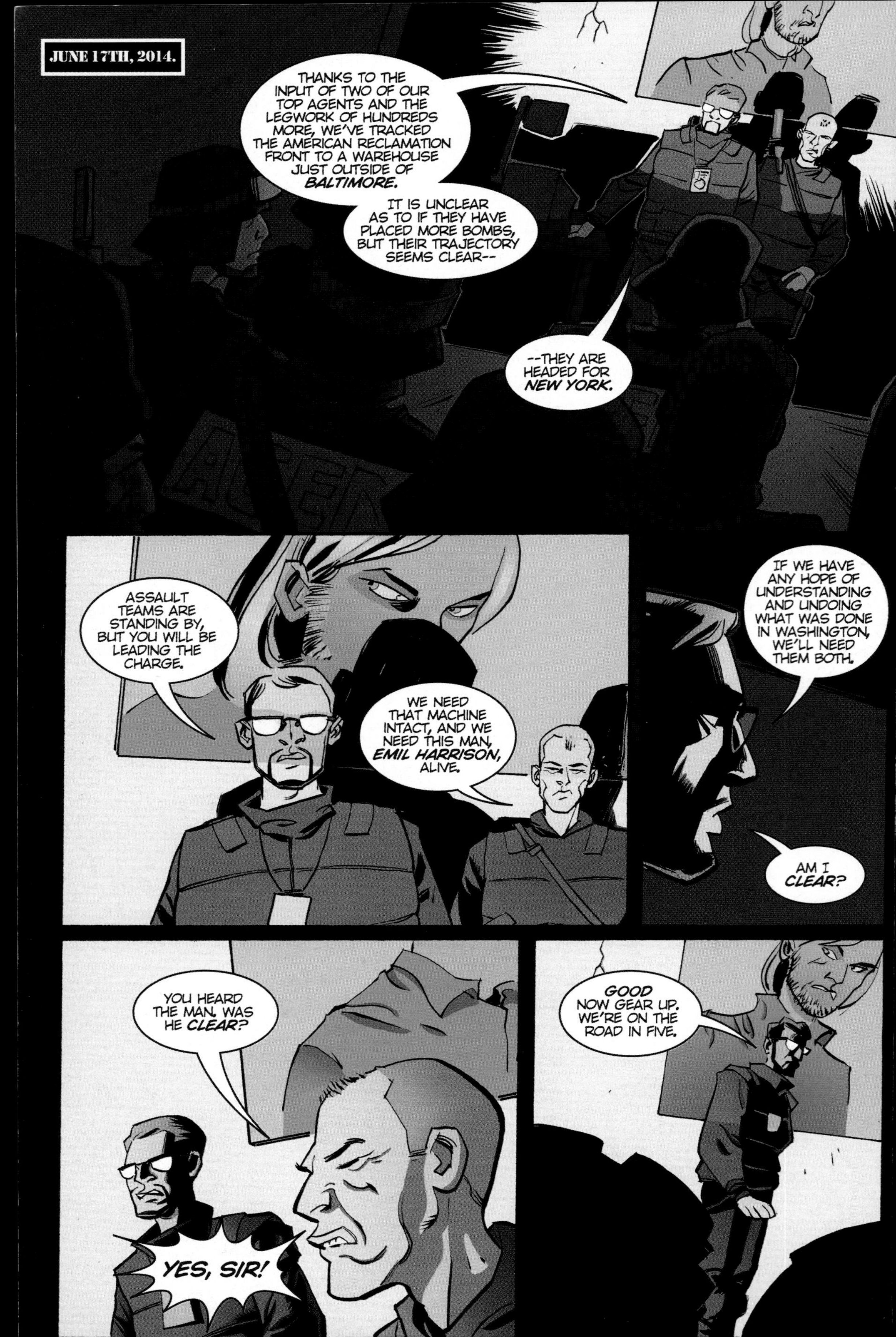
JUNE 17TH, 2014.
THANKS TO THE INPUT OF TWO OF OUR TOP AGENTS AND THE LEGWORK OF HUNDREDS MORE, WE'VE TRACKED THE AMERICAN RECLAMATION FRONT TO A WAREHOUSE JUST OUTSIDE OF BALTIMORE.
IT IS UNCLEAR AS TO IF THEY HAVE PLACED MORE BOMBS, BUT THEIR TRAJECTORY SEEMS CLEAR--
--THEY ARE HEADED FOR NEW YORK.
ASSAULT TEAMS ARE STANDING BY, BUT YOU WILL BE LEADING THE CHARGE.
WE NEED THAT MACHINE INTACT, AND WE NEED THIS MAN, EMIL HARRISON, ALIVE.
IF WE HAVE ANY HOPE OF UNDERSTANDING AND UNDOING WHAT WAS DONE IN WASHINGTON, WE'LL NEED THEM BOTH.
AM I CLEAR?
YOU HEARD THE MAN. WAS HE CLEAR?
YES, SIR!
GOOD NOW GEAR UP. WE'RE ON THE ROAD IN FIVE.

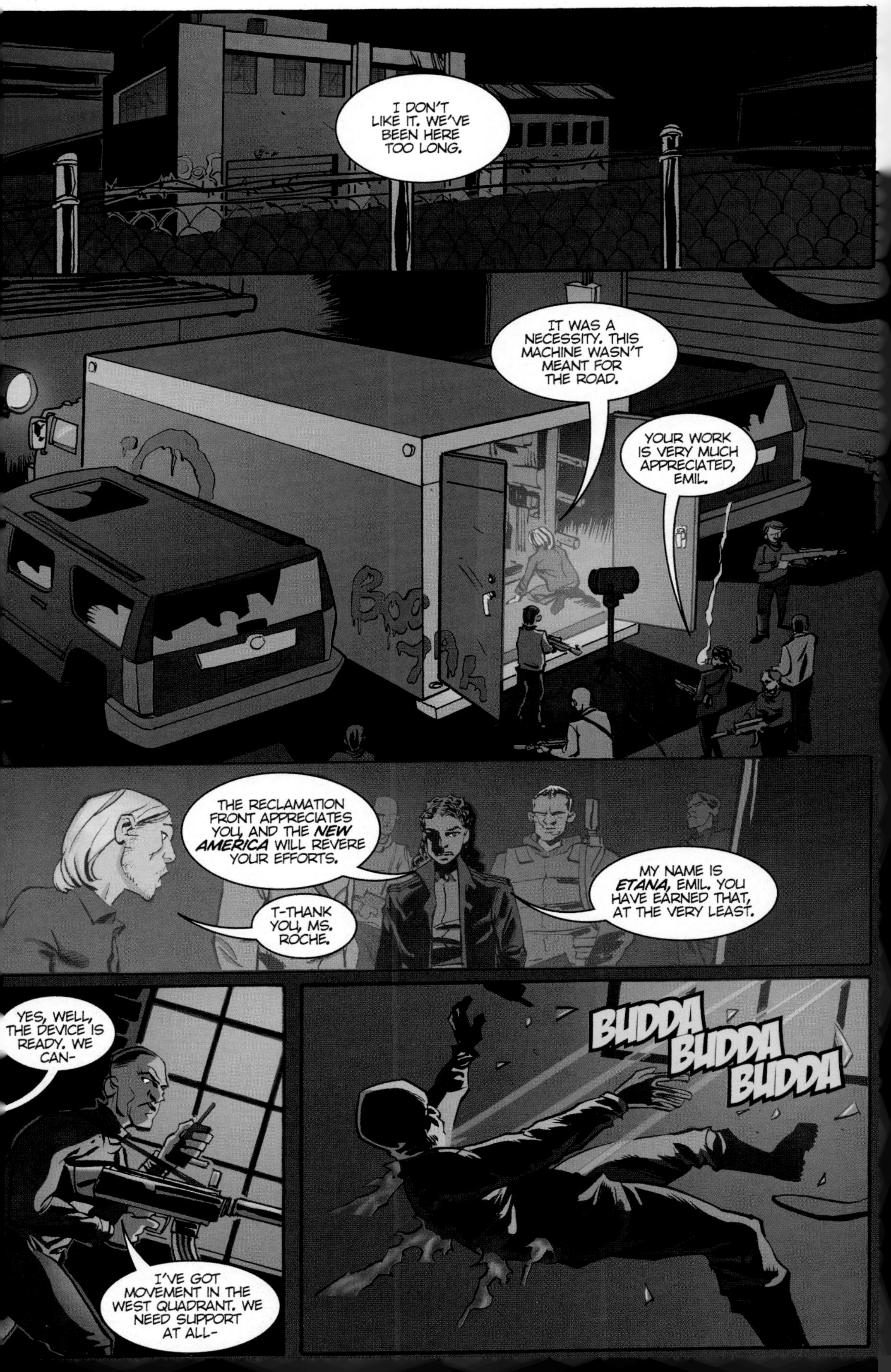
I DON'T LIKE IT. WE'VE BEEN HERE TOO LONG.
IT WAS A NECESSITY. THIS MACHINE WASN'T MEANT FOR THE ROAD.
YOUR WORK IS VERY MUCH APPRECIATED, EMIL.
THE RECLAMATION FRONT APPRECIATES YOU, AND THE NEW AMERICA WILL REVERE YOUR EFFORTS.
T-THANK YOU, MS. ROCHE.
MY NAME IS ETANA, EMIL. YOU HAVE EARNED THAT, AT THE VERY LEAST.
YES, WELL, THE DEVICE IS READY. WE CAN-
I'VE GOT MOVEMENT IN THE WEST QUADRANT. WE NEED SUPPORT AT ALL-
BUDDA BUDDA BUDDA

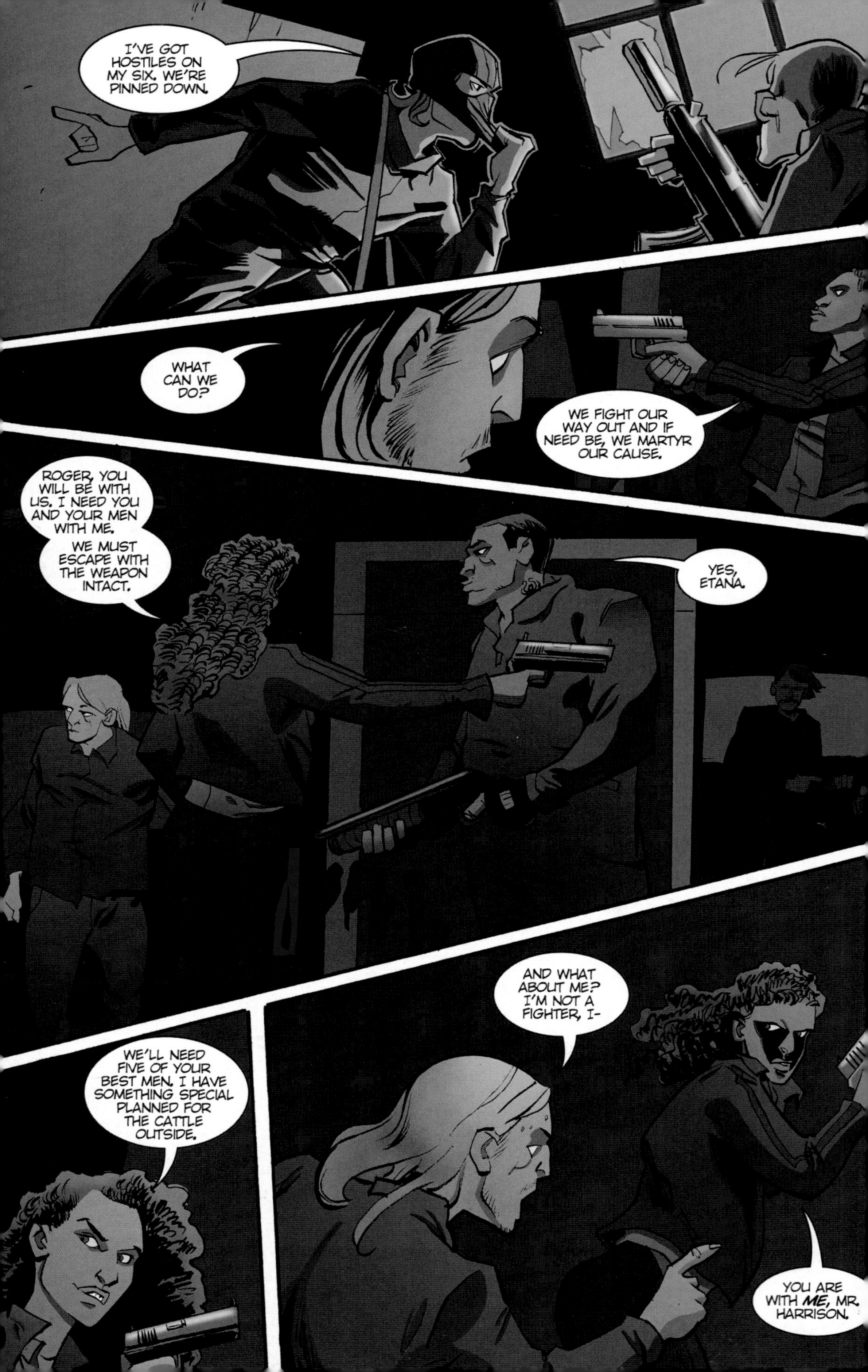
I'VE GOT HOSTILES ON MY SIX. WE'RE PINNED DOWN.
WHAT CAN WE DO?
WE FIGHT OUR WAY OUT AND IF NEED BE, WE MARTYR OUR CAUSE.
ROGER, YOU WILL BE WITH US. I NEED YOU AND YOUR MEN WITH ME.
WE MUST ESCAPE WITH THE WEAPON INTACT.
YES, ETANA.
WE'LL NEED FIVE OF YOUR BEST MEN. I HAVE SOMETHING SPECIAL PLANNED FOR THE CATTLE OUTSIDE.
AND WHAT ABOUT ME? I'M NOT A FIGHTER, I-
YOU ARE WITH *ME*, MR. HARRISON.

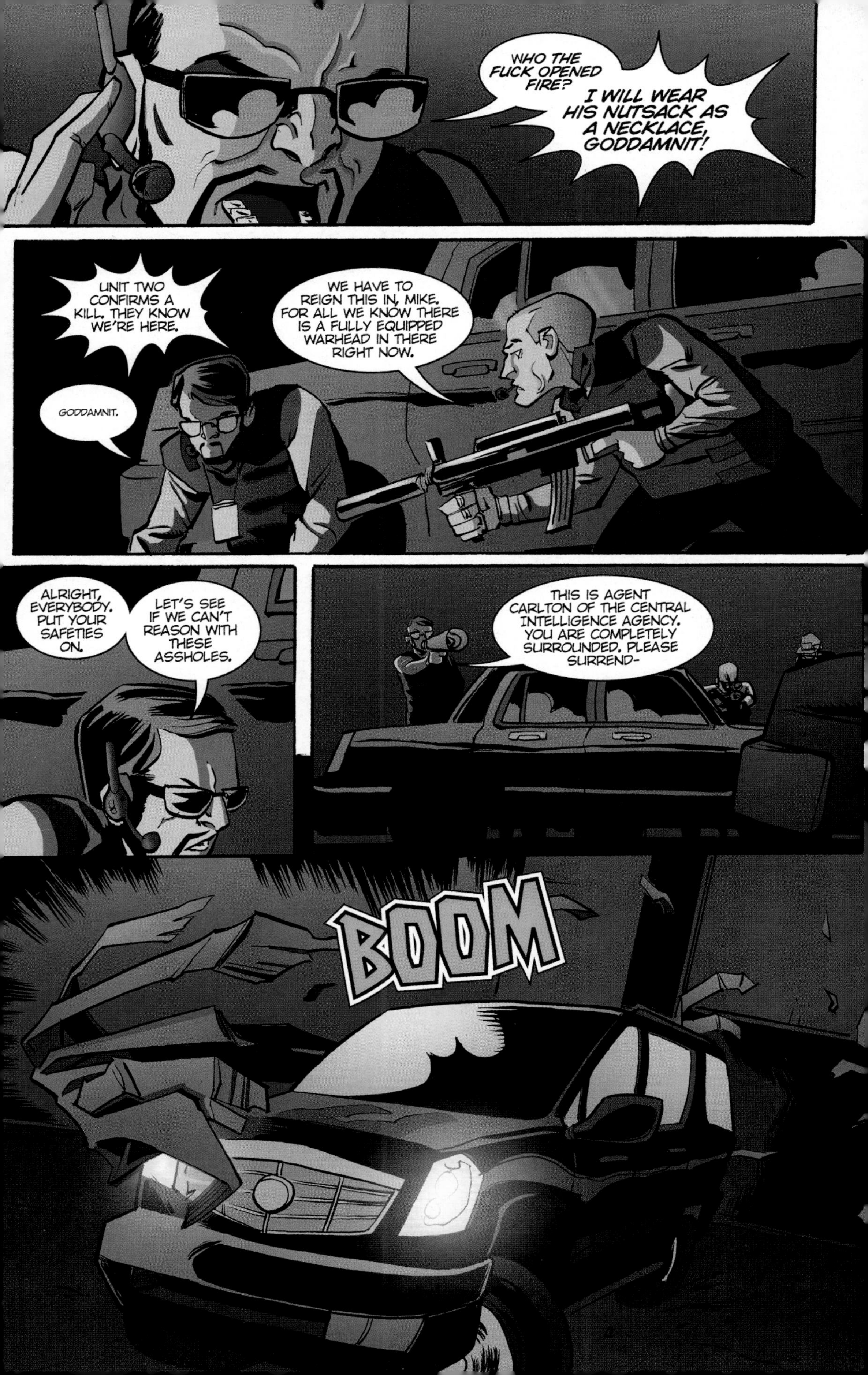
WHO THE FUCK OPENED FIRE?
I WILL WEAR HIS NUTSACK AS A NECKLACE, GODDAMNIT!
UNIT TWO CONFIRMS A KILL. THEY KNOW WE'RE HERE.
GODDAMNIT.
WE HAVE TO REIGN THIS IN, MIKE. FOR ALL WE KNOW THERE IS A FULLY EQUIPPED WARHEAD IN THERE RIGHT NOW.
ALRIGHT, EVERYBODY. PUT YOUR SAFETIES ON.
LET'S SEE IF WE CAN'T REASON WITH THESE ASSHOLES.
THIS IS AGENT CARLTON OF THE CENTRAL INTELLIGENCE AGENCY. YOU ARE COMPLETELY SURROUNDED. PLEASE SURREND-
BOOM

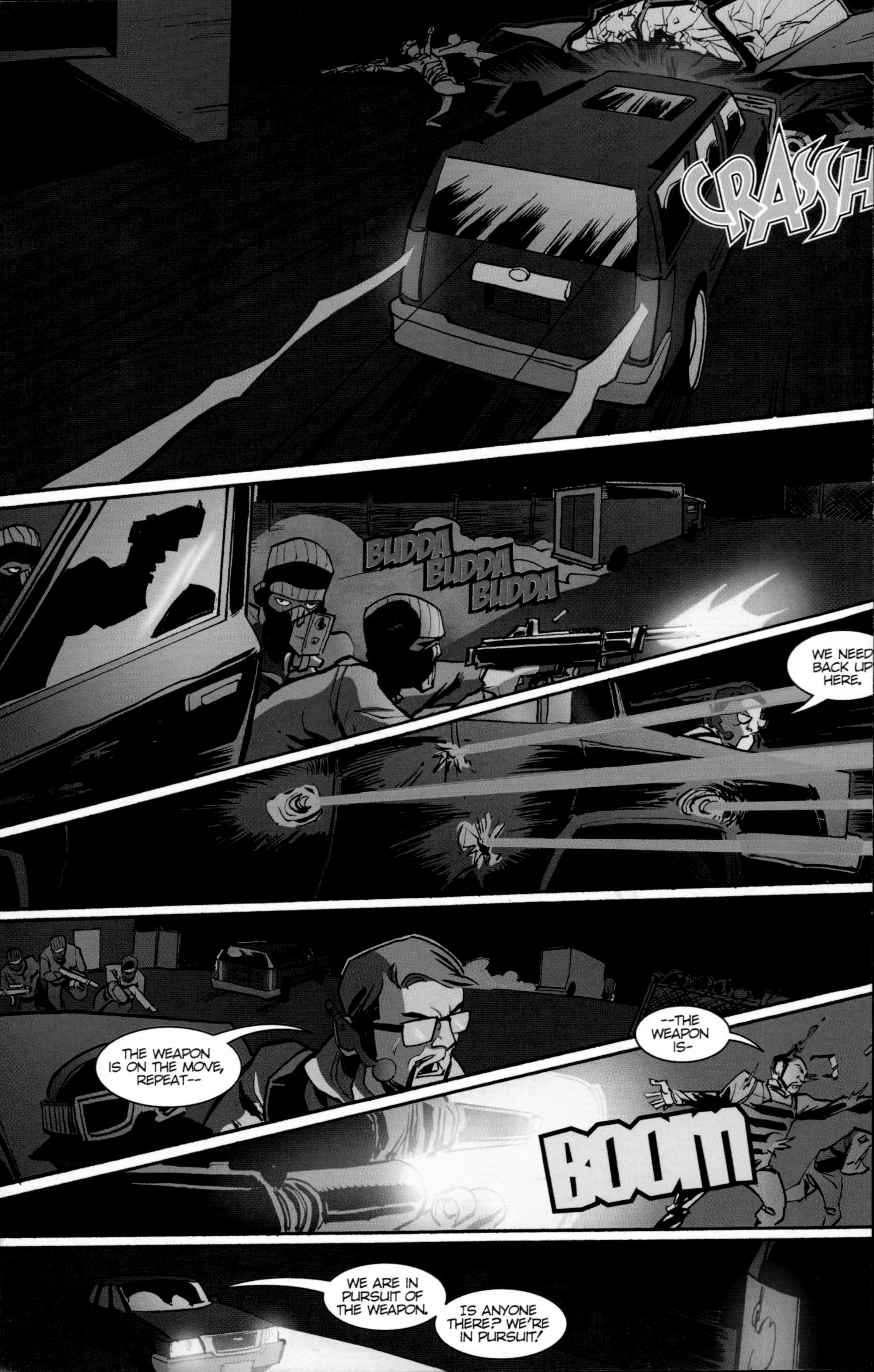
CRASSH
BUDDA BUDDA BUDDA
WE NEED BACK UP HERE.
THE WEAPON IS ON THE MOVE, REPEAT--
--THE WEAPON IS-
BOOM
WE ARE IN PURSUIT OF THE WEAPON.
IS ANYONE THERE? WE'RE IN PURSUIT!

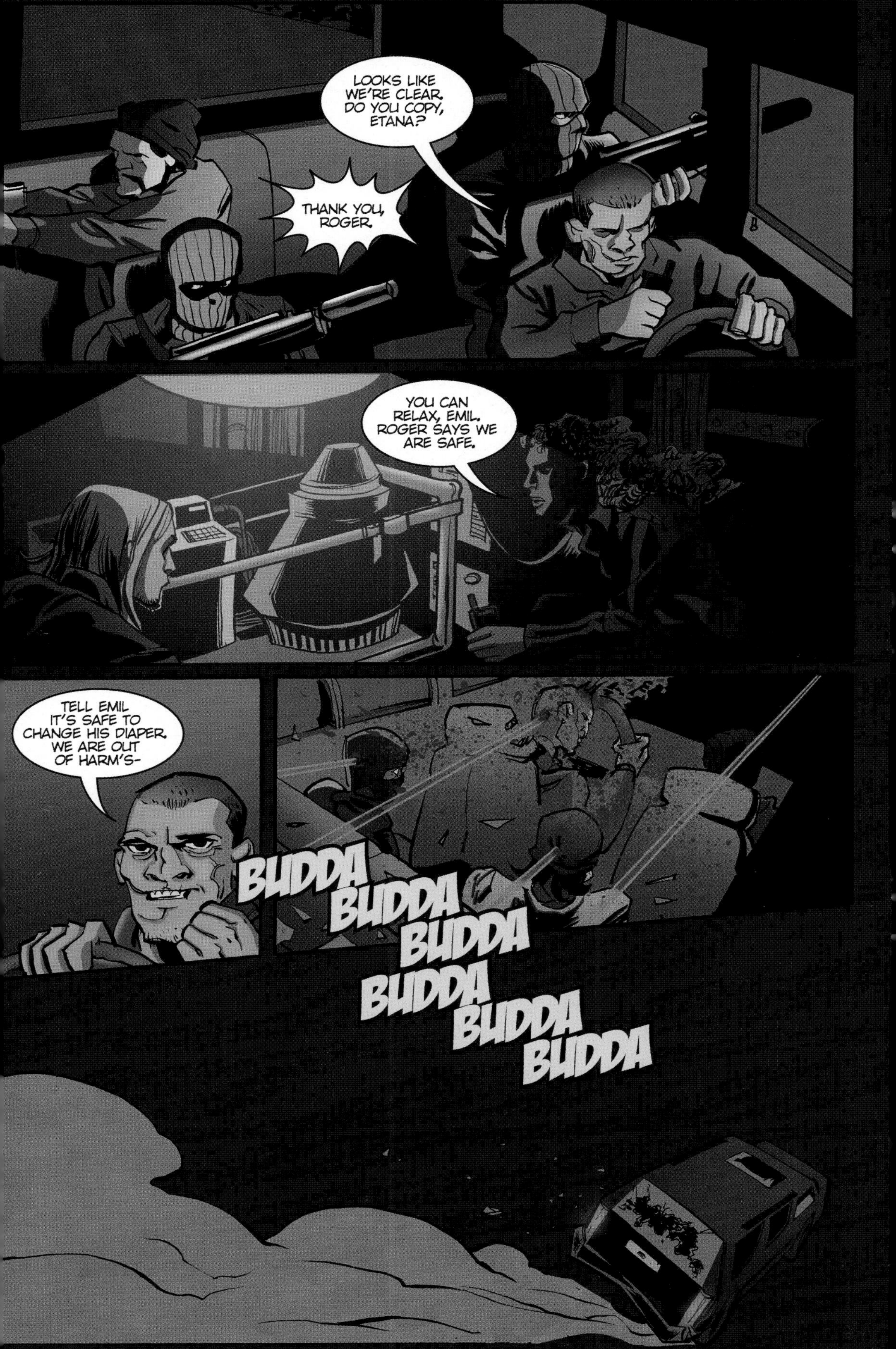
LOOKS LIKE WE'RE CLEAR. DO YOU COPY, ETANA?
THANK YOU, ROGER.
YOU CAN RELAX, EMIL. ROGER SAYS WE ARE SAFE.
TELL EMIL IT'S SAFE TO CHANGE HIS DIAPER. WE ARE OUT OF HARM'S-
BUDDA BUDDA BUDDA BUDDA BUDDA BUDDA

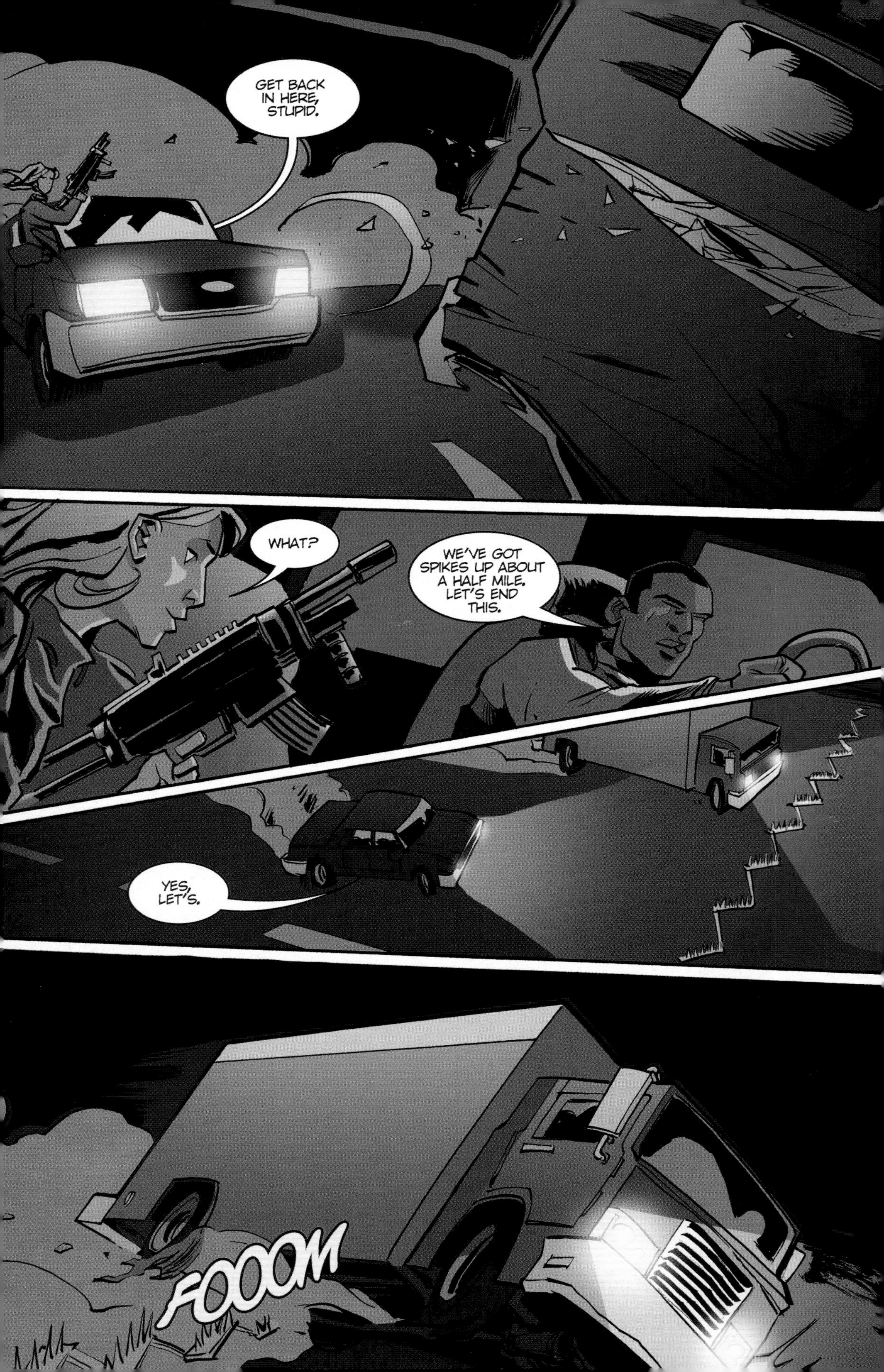
GET BACK IN HERE, STUPID.
WHAT?
WE'VE GOT SPIKES UP ABOUT A HALF MILE. LET'S END THIS.
YES, LET'S.
FOOOM

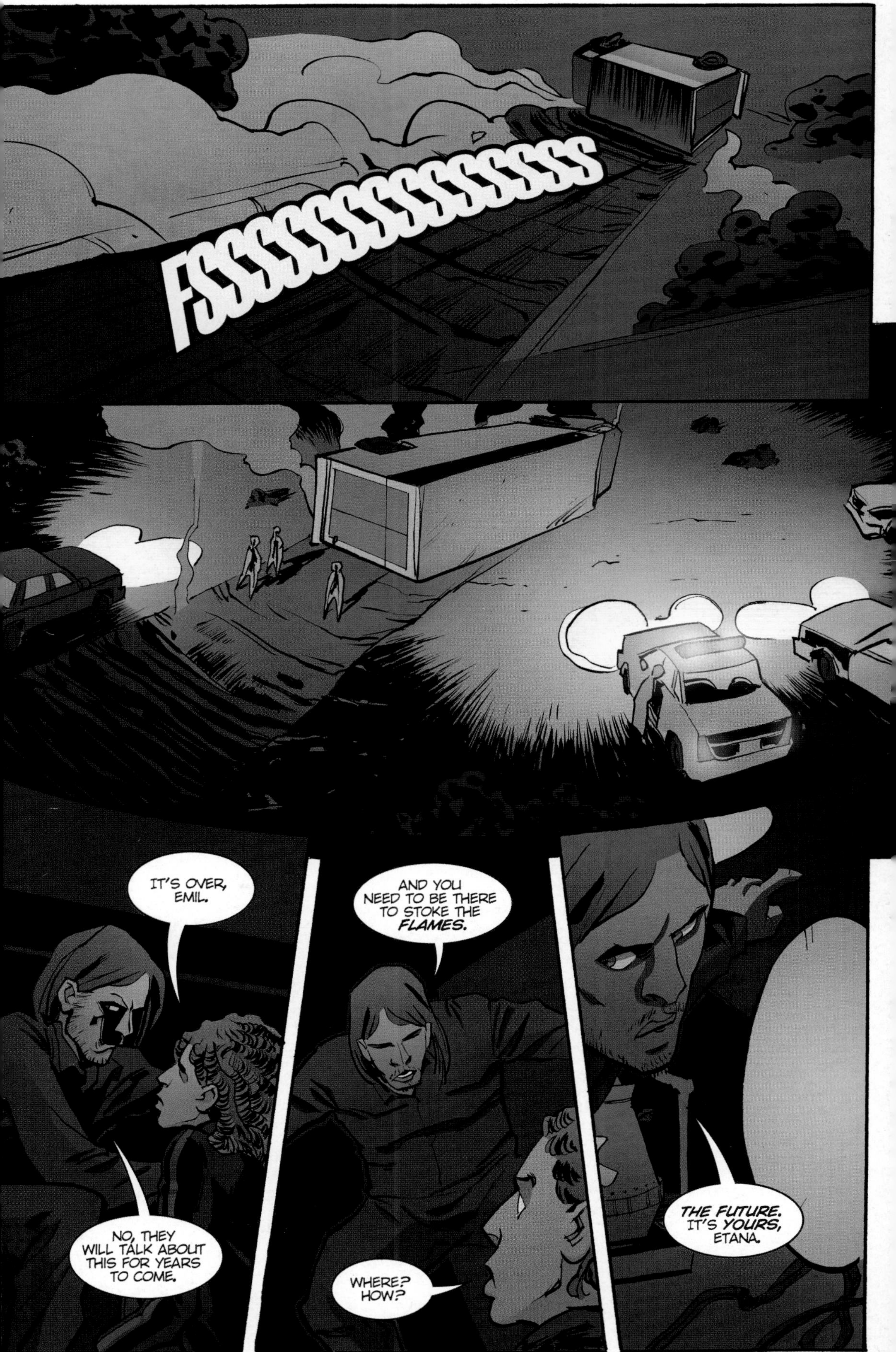
FSSSSSSSSSSSSSSS
IT'S OVER, EMIL.
NO, THEY WILL TALK ABOUT THIS FOR YEARS TO COME.
AND YOU NEED TO BE THERE TO STOKE THE FLAMES.
WHERE? HOW?
THE FUTURE. IT'S YOURS, ETANA.

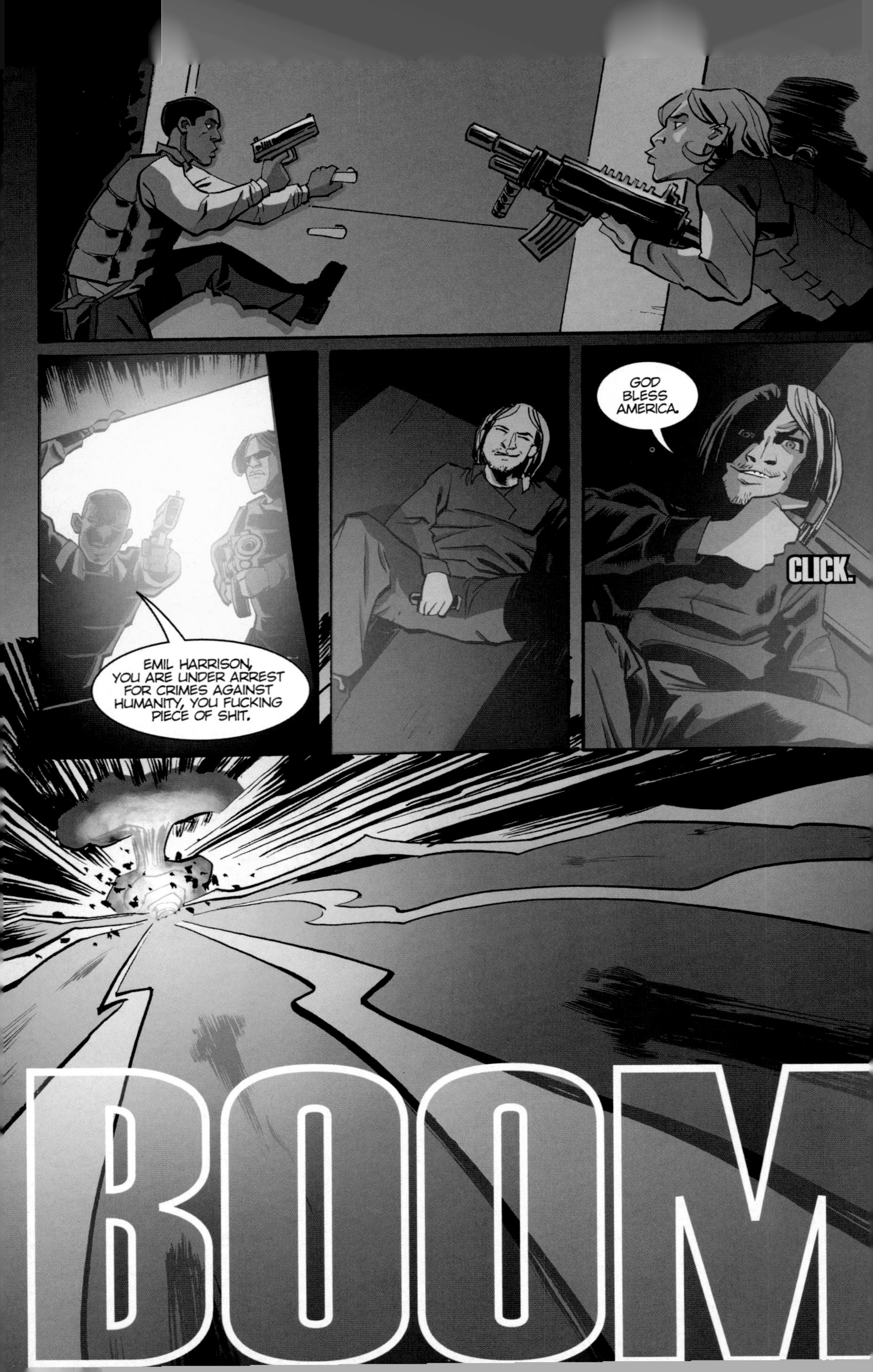
EMIL HARRISON, YOU ARE UNDER ARREST FOR CRIMES AGAINST HUMANITY, YOU FUCKING PIECE OF SHIT.
GOD BLESS AMERICA.
CLICK.
BOOM

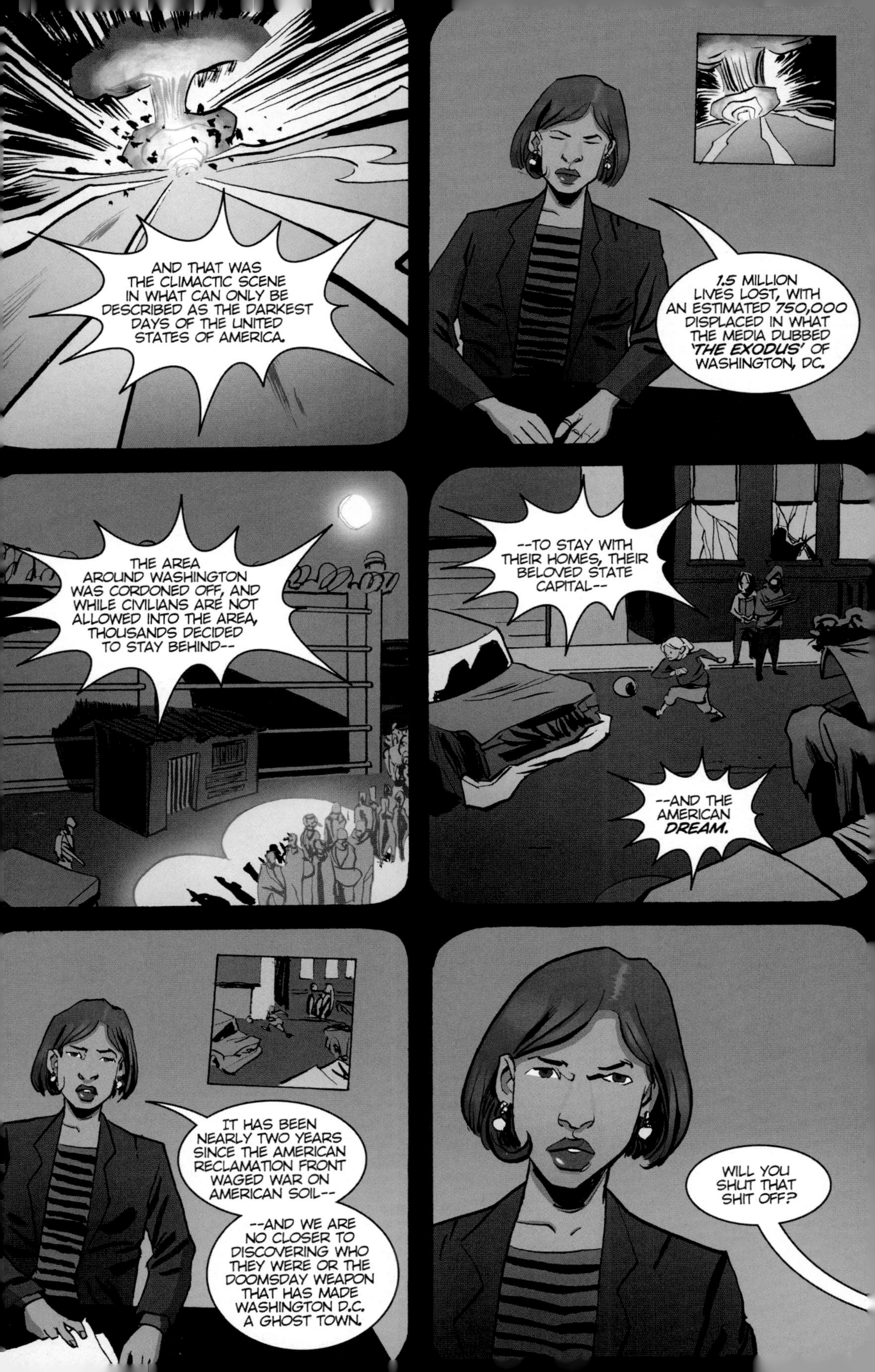
AND THAT WAS THE CLIMACTIC SCENE IN WHAT CAN ONLY BE DESCRIBED AS THE DARKEST DAYS OF THE UNITED STATES OF AMERICA.
1.5 MILLION LIVES LOST, WITH AN ESTIMATED 750,000 DISPLACED IN WHAT THE MEDIA DUBBED 'THE EXODUS' OF WASHINGTON, DC.
THE AREA AROUND WASHINGTON WAS CORDONED OFF, AND WHILE CIVILIANS ARE NOT ALLOWED INTO THE AREA, THOUSANDS DECIDED TO STAY BEHIND--
--TO STAY WITH THEIR HOMES, THEIR BELOVED STATE CAPITAL--
--AND THE AMERICAN DREAM.
IT HAS BEEN NEARLY TWO YEARS SINCE THE AMERICAN RECLAMATION FRONT WAGED WAR ON AMERICAN SOIL--
--AND WE ARE NO CLOSER TO DISCOVERING WHO THEY WERE OR THE DOOMSDAY WEAPON THAT HAS MADE WASHINGTON D.C. A GHOST TOWN.
WILL YOU SHUT THAT SHIT OFF?

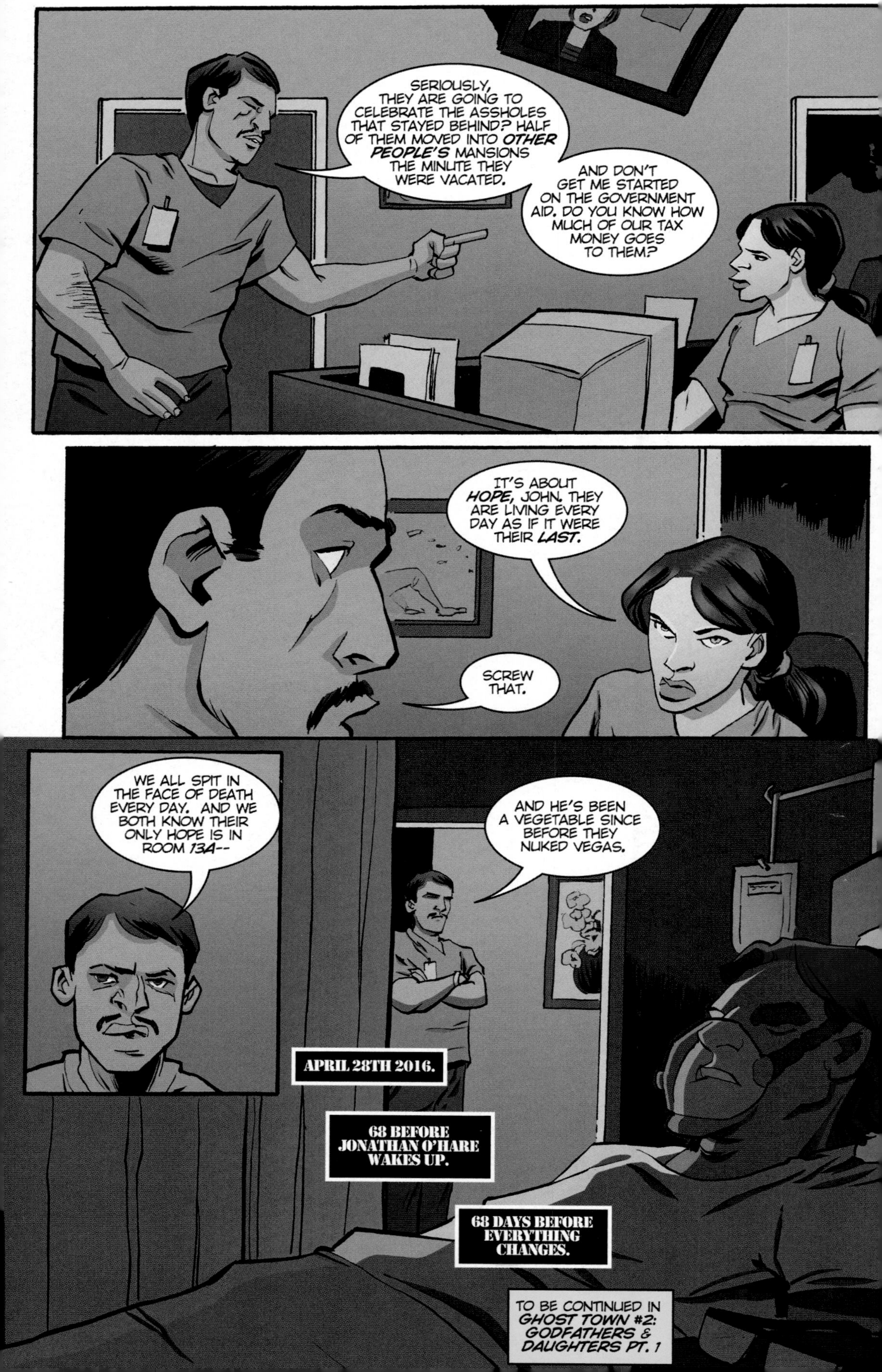
SERIOUSLY, THEY ARE GOING TO CELEBRATE THE ASSHOLES THAT STAYED BEHIND? HALF OF THEM MOVED INTO OTHER PEOPLE'S MANSIONS THE MINUTE THEY WERE VACATED.
AND DON'T GET ME STARTED ON THE GOVERNMENT AID. DO YOU KNOW HOW MUCH OF OUR TAX MONEY GOES TO THEM?
IT'S ABOUT HOPE, JOHN. THEY ARE LIVING EVERY DAY AS IF IT WERE THEIR LAST.
SCREW THAT.
WE ALL SPIT IN THE FACE OF DEATH EVERY DAY. AND WE BOTH KNOW THEIR ONLY HOPE IS IN ROOM 13A--
AND HE'S BEEN A VEGETABLE SINCE BEFORE THEY NUKED VEGAS.
APRIL 28TH 2016.
68 BEFORE JONATHAN O'HARE WAKES UP.
68 DAYS BEFORE EVERYTHING CHANGES.
TO BE CONTINUED IN GHOST TOWN #2: GODFATHERS & DAUGHTERS PT. 1

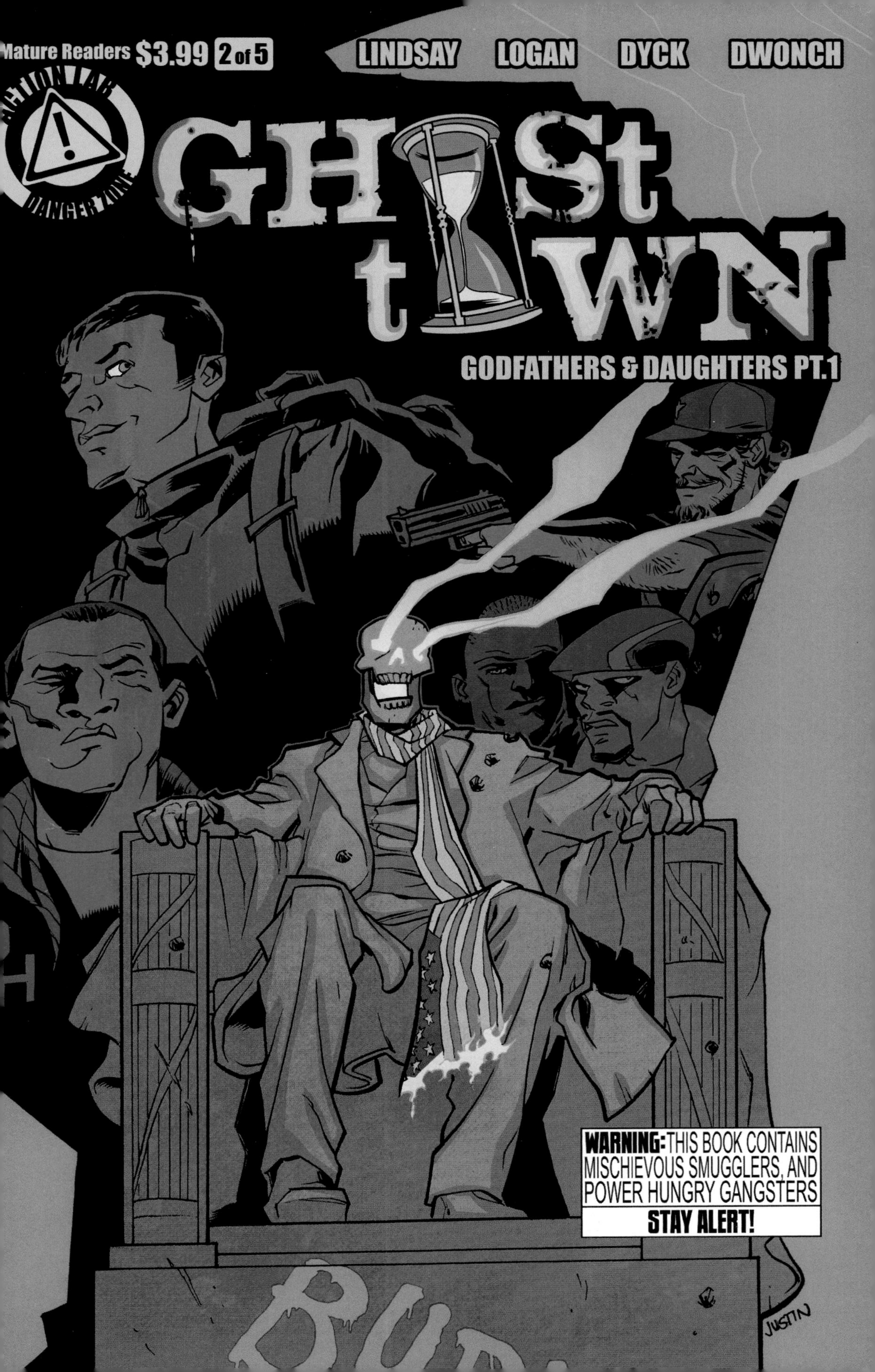

Mature Readers $3.99 2 of 5
LINDSAY LOGAN DYCK DWONCH
ACTION LAB DANGER ZONE
GHOSt tOWN
GODFATHERS & DAUGHTERS PT.1
WARNING: THIS BOOK CONTAINS MISCHIEVOUS SMUGGLERS, AND POWER HUNGRY GANGSTERS
STAY ALERT!
JUSTIN

GODFATHERS & DAUGHTERS
PART 1

GHOST TOWN CREATED BY ROB RUDDELL & DAVE DWONCH
EDITED BY SHAWN GABBORIN
COVER BY JUSTIN GREENWOOD & JORDIE BELLAIRE

RYAN K LINDSAY
WORDS
DANIEL LOGAN
PICTURES
BRIAN DYCK
COLORS
DAVE DWONCH
LETTERS

JASON MARTIN - PUBLISHER
KEVIN FREEMAN - PRESIDENT
SHAWN PRYOR - VP DIGITAL MEDIA
DAVE DWONCH - CREATIVE DIRECTOR
SHAWN GABBORIN - EDITOR IN CHIEF
JEREMY WHITLEY - MARKETING DIRECTOR
CHAD CICCONI - ASSOCIATE EDITOR
COLLEEN BOYD - ASSOCIATE EDITOR

GHOST TOWN #2, July 2013.

Printed in Canada.
First printing.
ACTIONLABCOMICS.COM/DANGER-ZONE

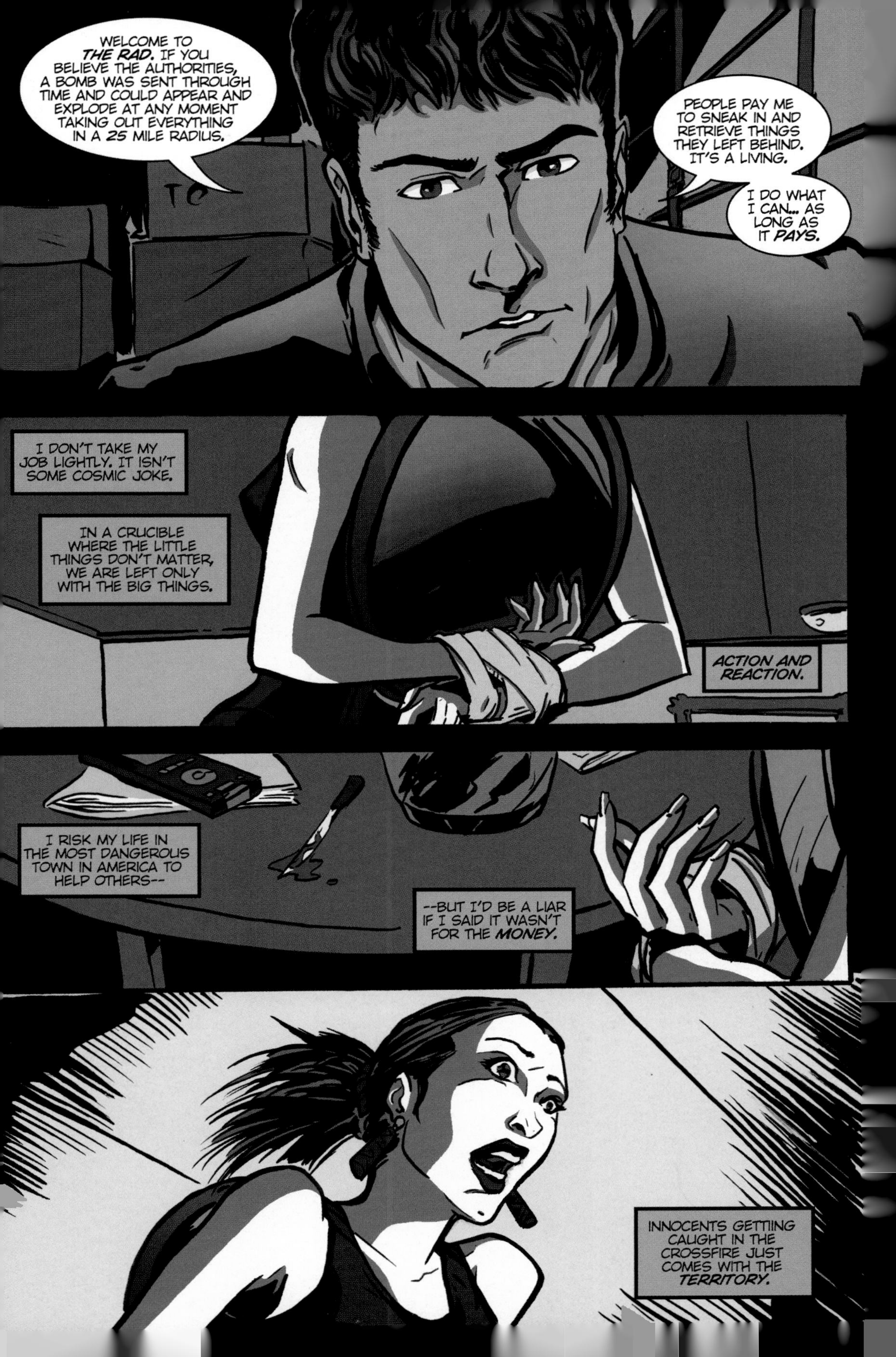
WELCOME TO THE RAD. IF YOU BELIEVE THE AUTHORITIES, A BOMB WAS SENT THROUGH TIME AND COULD APPEAR AND EXPLODE AT ANY MOMENT TAKING OUT EVERYTHING IN A 25 MILE RADIUS.
PEOPLE PAY ME TO SNEAK IN AND RETRIEVE THINGS THEY LEFT BEHIND. IT'S A LIVING.
I DO WHAT I CAN... AS LONG AS IT PAYS.
I DON'T TAKE MY JOB LIGHTLY. IT ISN'T SOME COSMIC JOKE.
IN A CRUCIBLE WHERE THE LITTLE THINGS DON'T MATTER, WE ARE LEFT ONLY WITH THE BIG THINGS.
ACTION AND REACTION.
I RISK MY LIFE IN THE MOST DANGEROUS TOWN IN AMERICA TO HELP OTHERS--
--BUT I'D BE A LIAR IF I SAID IT WASN'T FOR THE MONEY.
INNOCENTS GETTING CAUGHT IN THE CROSSFIRE JUST COMES WITH THE TERRITORY.

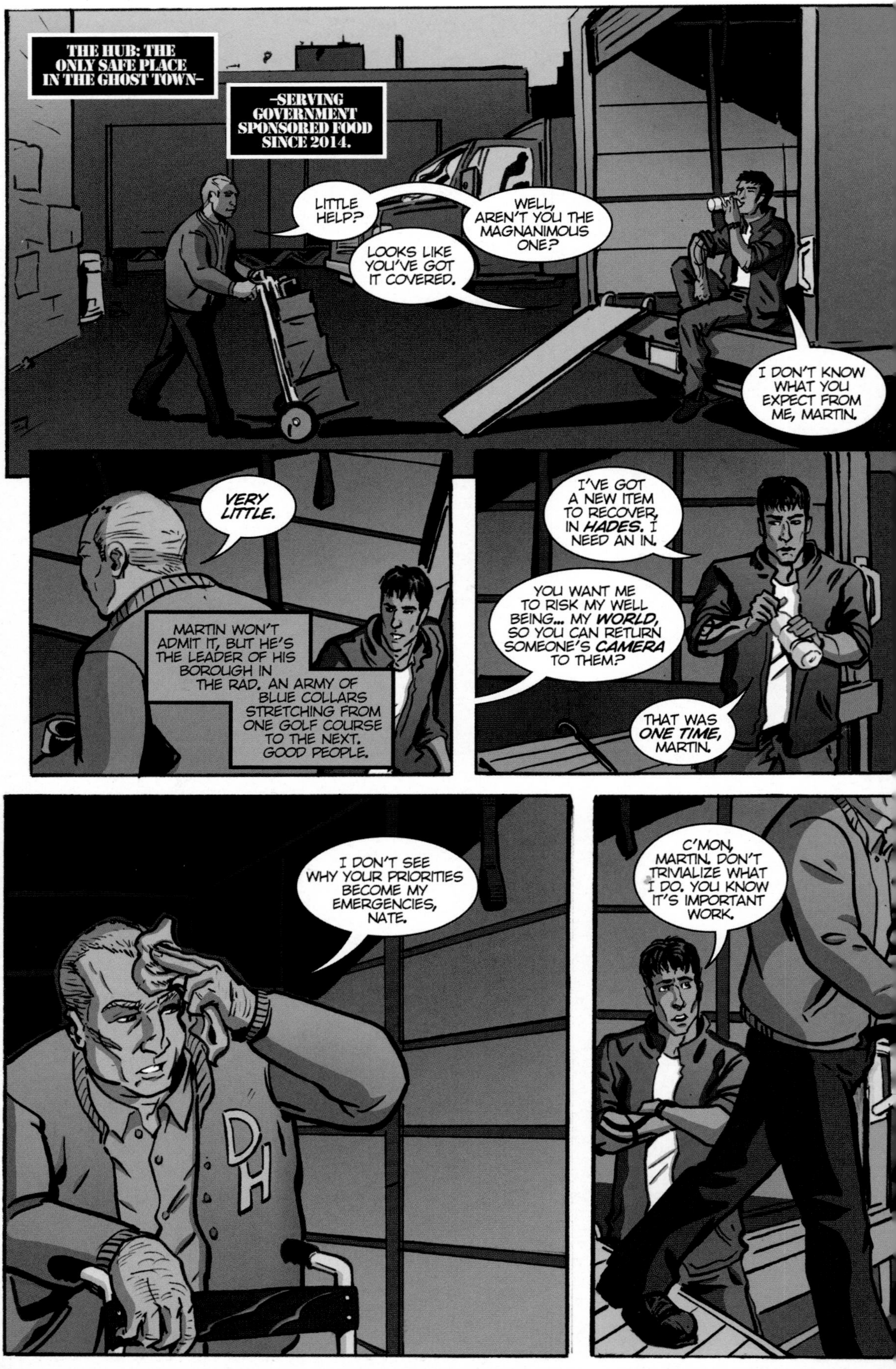
THE HUB: THE ONLY SAFE PLACE IN THE GHOST TOWN–
–SERVING GOVERNMENT SPONSORED FOOD SINCE 2014.
LITTLE HELP?
WELL, AREN'T YOU THE MAGNANIMOUS ONE?
LOOKS LIKE YOU'VE GOT IT COVERED.
I DON'T KNOW WHAT YOU EXPECT FROM ME, MARTIN.
VERY LITTLE.
MARTIN WON'T ADMIT IT, BUT HE'S THE LEADER OF HIS BOROUGH IN THE RAD. AN ARMY OF BLUE COLLARS STRETCHING FROM ONE GOLF COURSE TO THE NEXT. GOOD PEOPLE.
I'VE GOT A NEW ITEM TO RECOVER, IN HADES. I NEED AN IN.
YOU WANT ME TO RISK MY WELL BEING... MY WORLD, SO YOU CAN RETURN SOMEONE'S CAMERA TO THEM?
THAT WAS ONE TIME, MARTIN.
I DON'T SEE WHY YOUR PRIORITIES BECOME MY EMERGENCIES, NATE.
C'MON, MARTIN. DON'T TRIVIALIZE WHAT I DO. YOU KNOW IT'S IMPORTANT WORK.

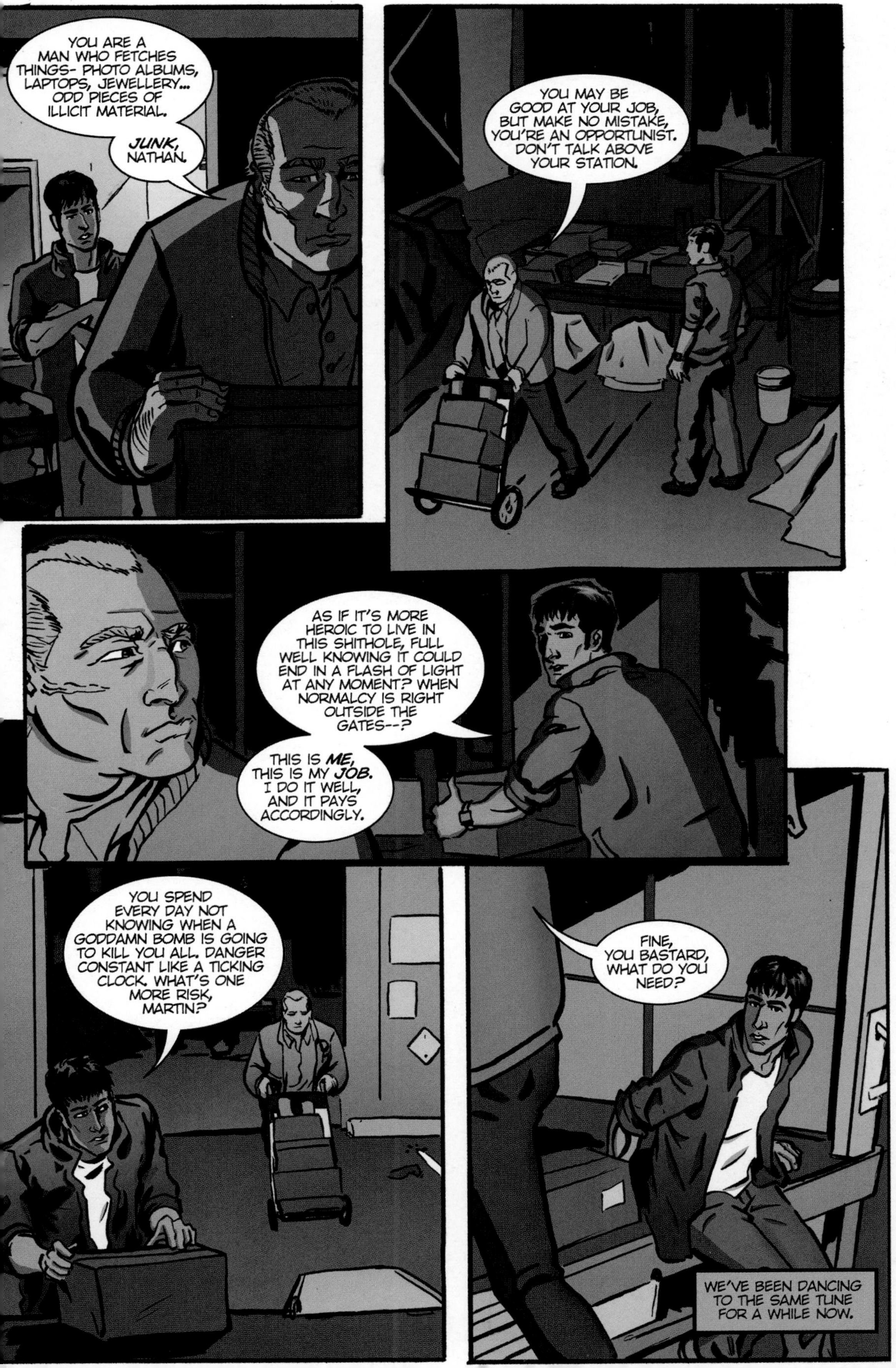
YOU ARE A MAN WHO FETCHES THINGS- PHOTO ALBUMS, LAPTOPS, JEWELLERY... ODD PIECES OF ILLICIT MATERIAL.
JUNK, NATHAN.
YOU MAY BE GOOD AT YOUR JOB, BUT MAKE NO MISTAKE, YOU'RE AN OPPORTUNIST. DON'T TALK ABOVE YOUR STATION.
AS IF IT'S MORE HEROIC TO LIVE IN THIS SHITHOLE, FULL WELL KNOWING IT COULD END IN A FLASH OF LIGHT AT ANY MOMENT? WHEN NORMALCY IS RIGHT OUTSIDE THE GATES--?
THIS IS ME, THIS IS MY JOB. I DO IT WELL, AND IT PAYS ACCORDINGLY.
YOU SPEND EVERY DAY NOT KNOWING WHEN A GODDAMN BOMB IS GOING TO KILL YOU ALL. DANGER CONSTANT LIKE A TICKING CLOCK. WHAT'S ONE MORE RISK, MARTIN?
FINE, YOU BASTARD, WHAT DO YOU NEED?
WE'VE BEEN DANCING TO THE SAME TUNE FOR A WHILE NOW.

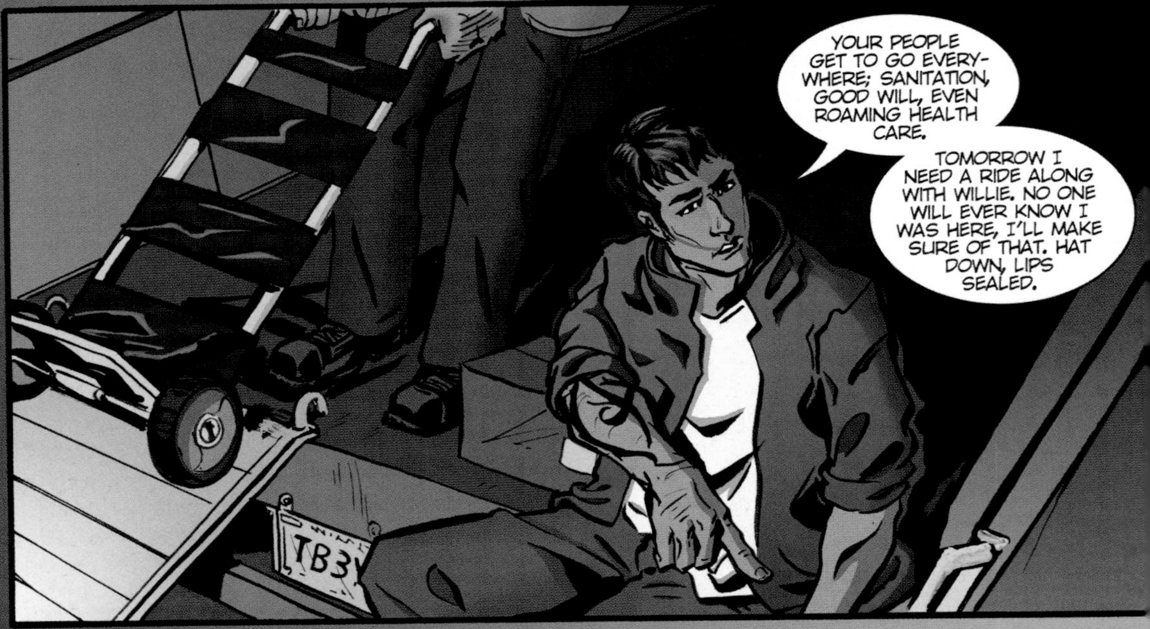
YOUR PEOPLE GET TO GO EVERY-WHERE; SANITATION, GOOD WILL, EVEN ROAMING HEALTH CARE.
TOMORROW I NEED A RIDE ALONG WITH WILLIE. NO ONE WILL EVER KNOW I WAS HERE, I'LL MAKE SURE OF THAT. HAT DOWN, LIPS SEALED.
TB3

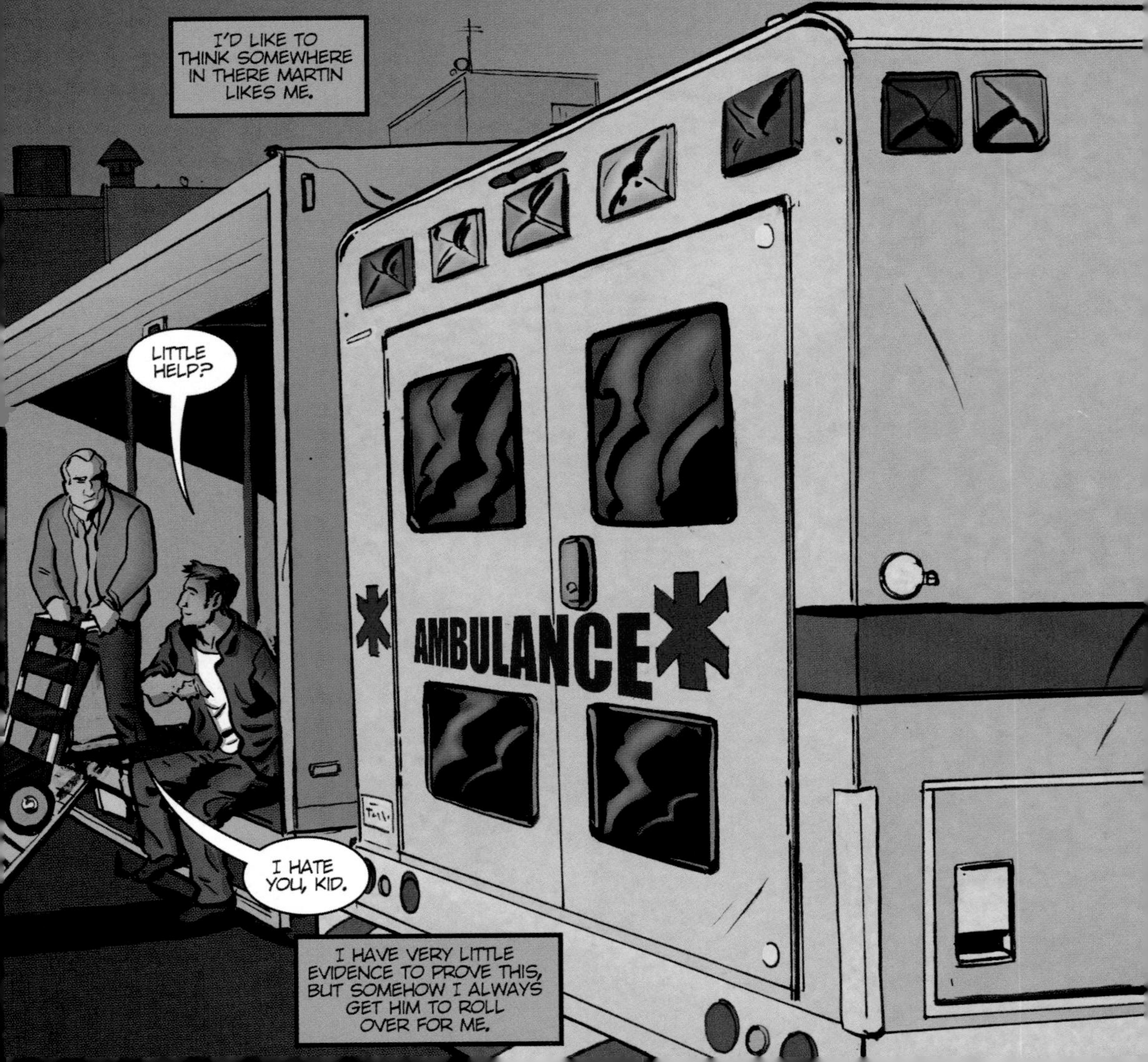
I'D LIKE TO THINK SOMEWHERE IN THERE MARTIN LIKES ME.
LITTLE HELP?
AMBULANCE
I HATE YOU, KID.
I HAVE VERY LITTLE EVIDENCE TO PROVE THIS, BUT SOMEHOW I ALWAYS GET HIM TO ROLL OVER FOR ME.

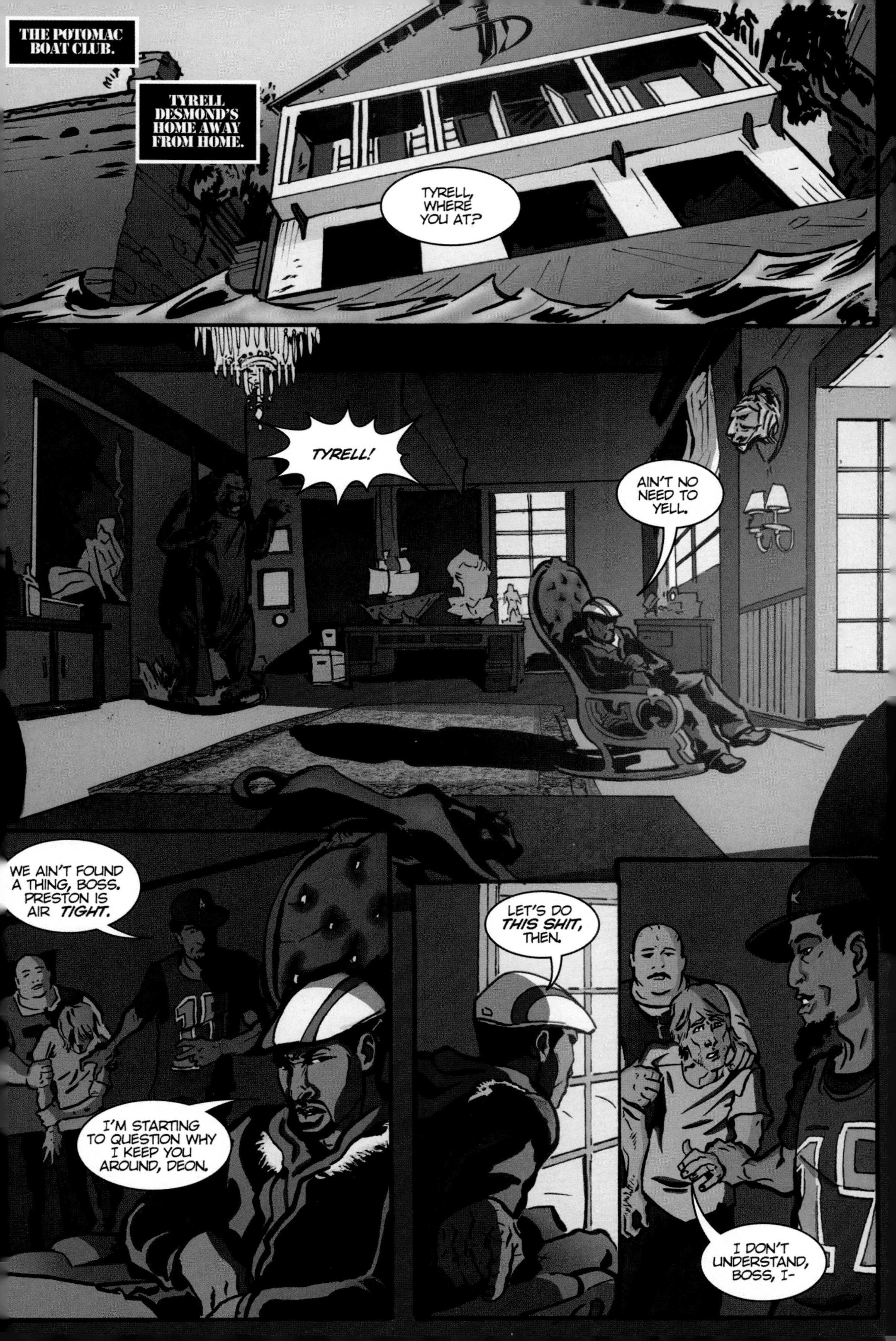
THE POTOMAC BOAT CLUB.
TYRELL DESMOND'S HOME AWAY FROM HOME.
TYRELL, WHERE YOU AT?
TYRELL!
AIN'T NO NEED TO YELL.
WE AIN'T FOUND A THING, BOSS. PRESTON IS AIR TIGHT.
I'M STARTING TO QUESTION WHY I KEEP YOU AROUND, DEON.
LET'S DO THIS SHIT, THEN.
I DON'T UNDERSTAND, BOSS, I-

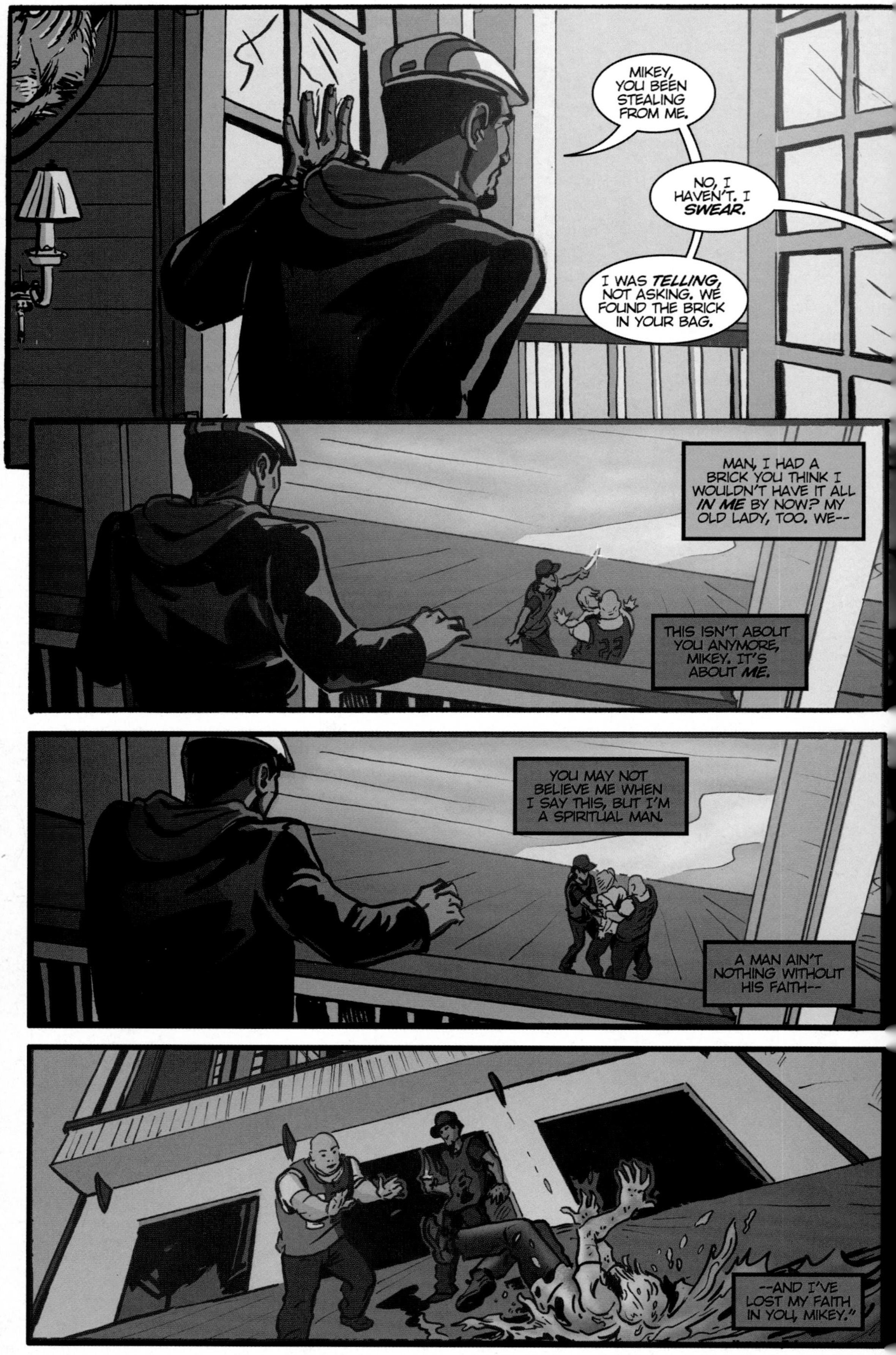
MIKEY, YOU BEEN STEALING FROM ME.
NO, I HAVEN'T. I SWEAR.
I WAS TELLING, NOT ASKING. WE FOUND THE BRICK IN YOUR BAG.
MAN, I HAD A BRICK YOU THINK I WOULDN'T HAVE IT ALL IN ME BY NOW? MY OLD LADY, TOO. WE--
THIS ISN'T ABOUT YOU ANYMORE, MIKEY. IT'S ABOUT ME.
YOU MAY NOT BELIEVE ME WHEN I SAY THIS, BUT I'M A SPIRITUAL MAN.
A MAN AIN'T NOTHING WITHOUT HIS FAITH--
--AND I'VE LOST MY FAITH IN YOU, MIKEY."

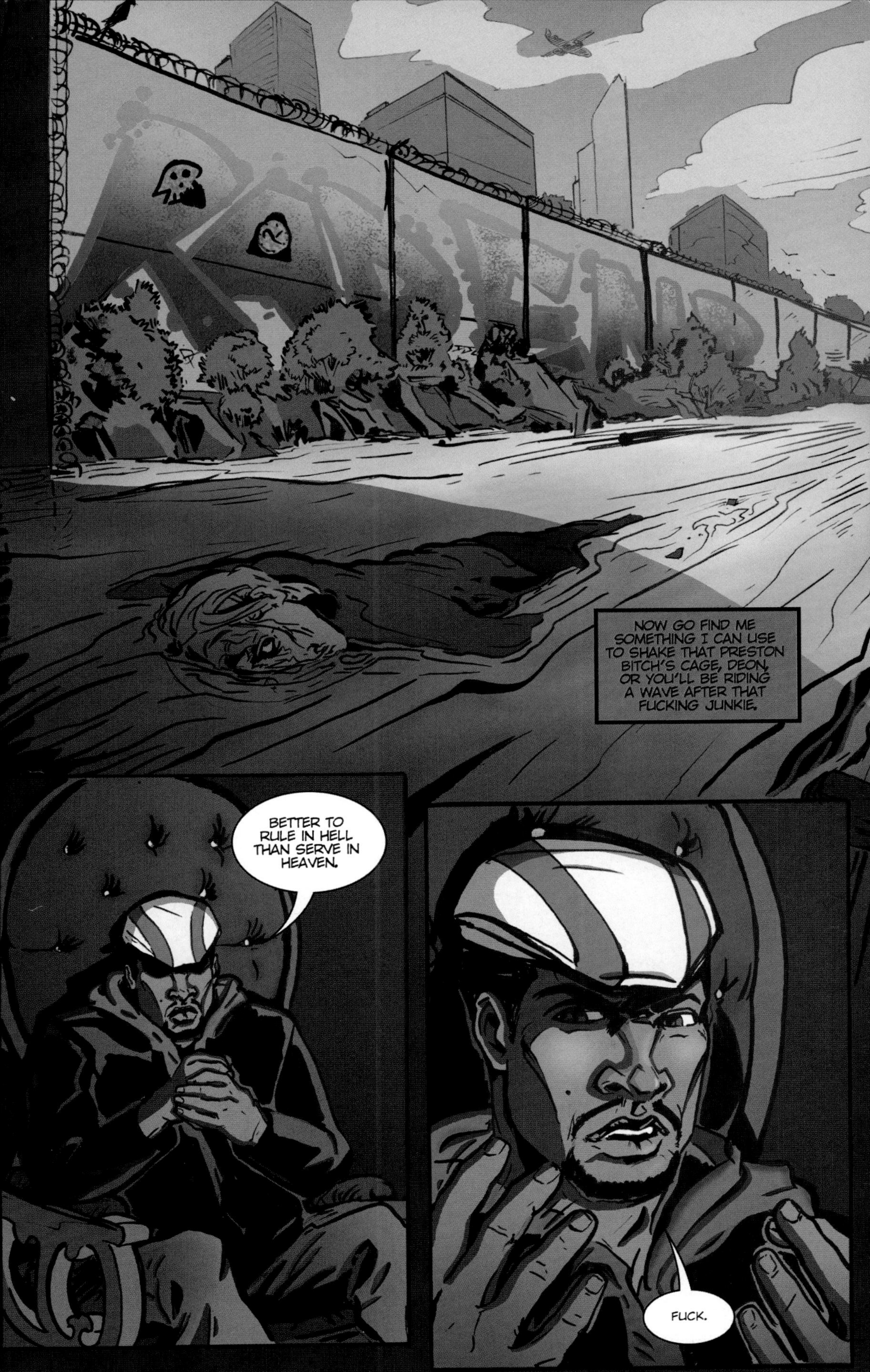
NOW GO FIND ME SOMETHING I CAN USE TO SHAKE THAT PRESTON BITCH'S CAGE, DEON, OR YOU'LL BE RIDING A WAVE AFTER THAT FUCKING JUNKIE.
BETTER TO RULE IN HELL THAN SERVE IN HEAVEN.
FUCK.

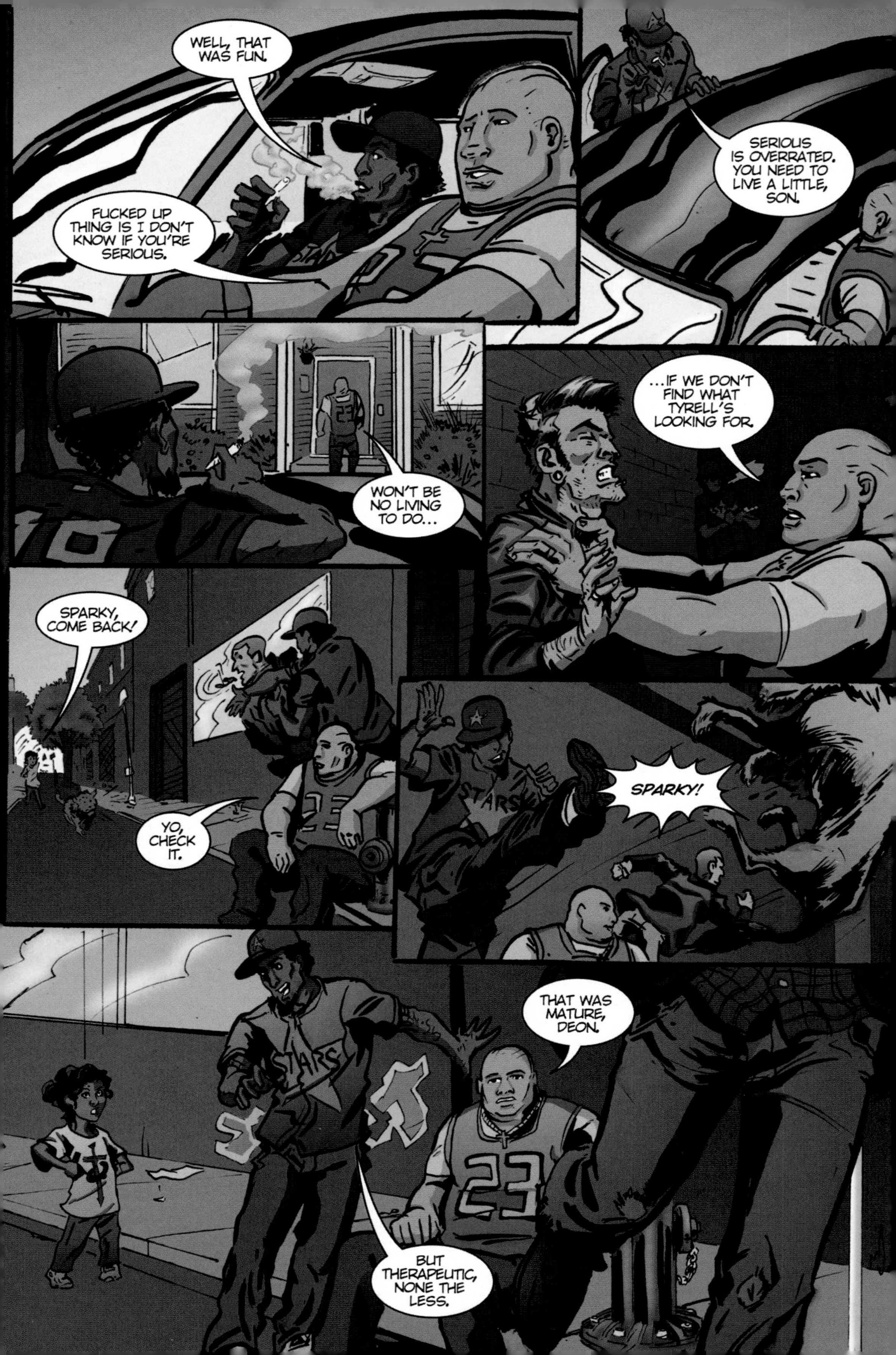
WELL, THAT WAS FUN.
FUCKED UP THING IS I DON'T KNOW IF YOU'RE SERIOUS.
SERIOUS IS OVERRATED. YOU NEED TO LIVE A LITTLE, SON.
WON'T BE NO LIVING TO DO...
...IF WE DON'T FIND WHAT TYRELL'S LOOKING FOR.
SPARKY, COME BACK!
YO, CHECK IT.
SPARKY!
THAT WAS MATURE, DEON.
BUT THERAPEUTIC, NONE THE LESS.

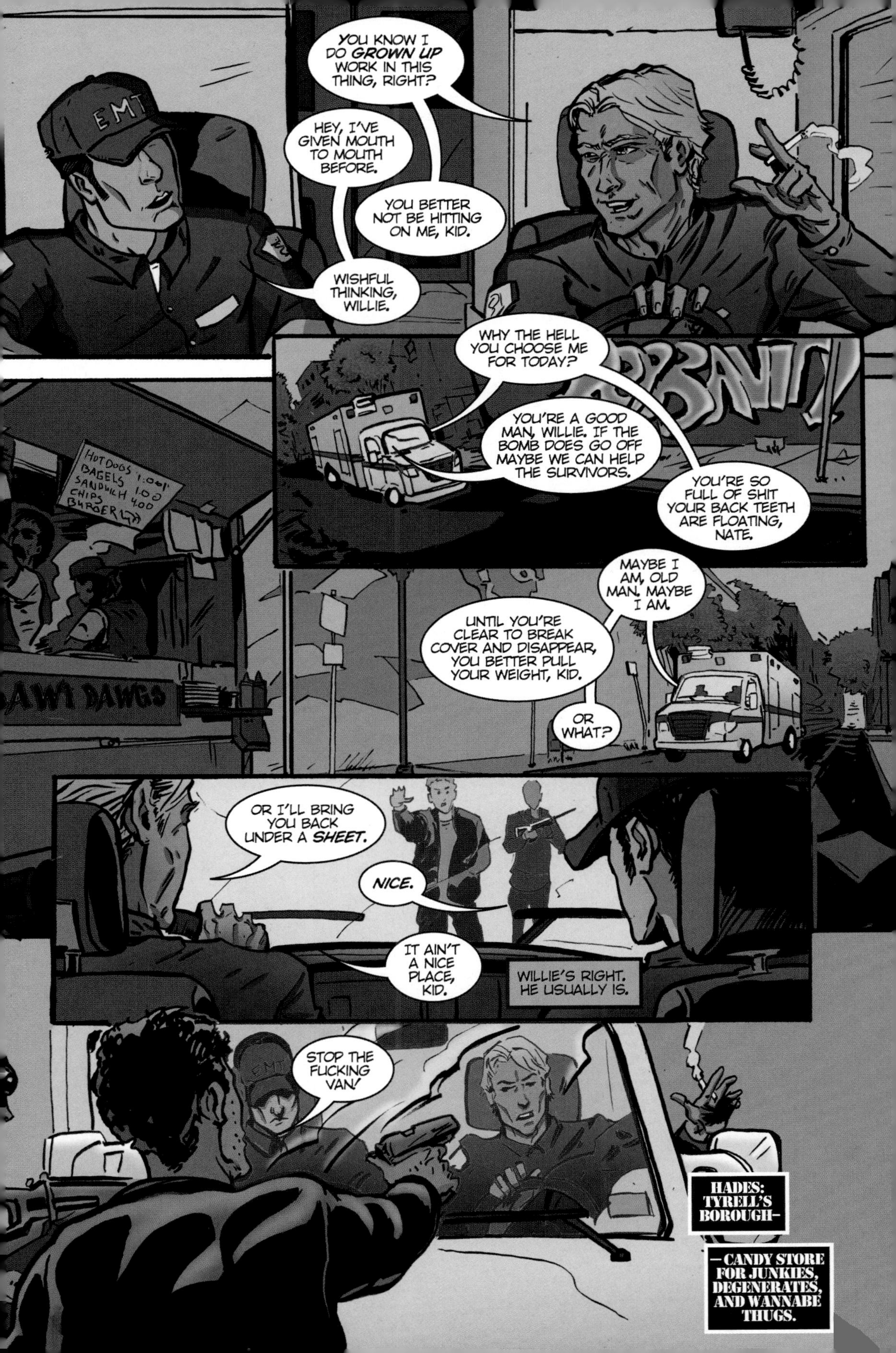
YOU KNOW I DO GROWN UP WORK IN THIS THING, RIGHT?
HEY, I'VE GIVEN MOUTH TO MOUTH BEFORE.
YOU BETTER NOT BE HITTING ON ME, KID.
WISHFUL THINKING, WILLIE.
WHY THE HELL YOU CHOOSE ME FOR TODAY?
YOU'RE A GOOD MAN, WILLIE. IF THE BOMB DOES GO OFF MAYBE WE CAN HELP THE SURVIVORS.
YOU'RE SO FULL OF SHIT YOUR BACK TEETH ARE FLOATING, NATE.
UNTIL YOU'RE CLEAR TO BREAK COVER AND DISAPPEAR, YOU BETTER PULL YOUR WEIGHT, KID.
MAYBE I AM, OLD MAN. MAYBE I AM.
OR WHAT?
OR I'LL BRING YOU BACK UNDER A SHEET.
NICE.
IT AIN'T A NICE PLACE, KID.
WILLIE'S RIGHT. HE USUALLY IS.
HOT DOGS 1.00
BAGELS 1.00
SANDWICH 1.00
CHIPS 4.00
STOP THE FUCKING VAN!
HADES: TYRELL'S BOROUGH—
—CANDY STORE FOR JUNKIES, DEGENERATES, AND WANNABE THUGS.

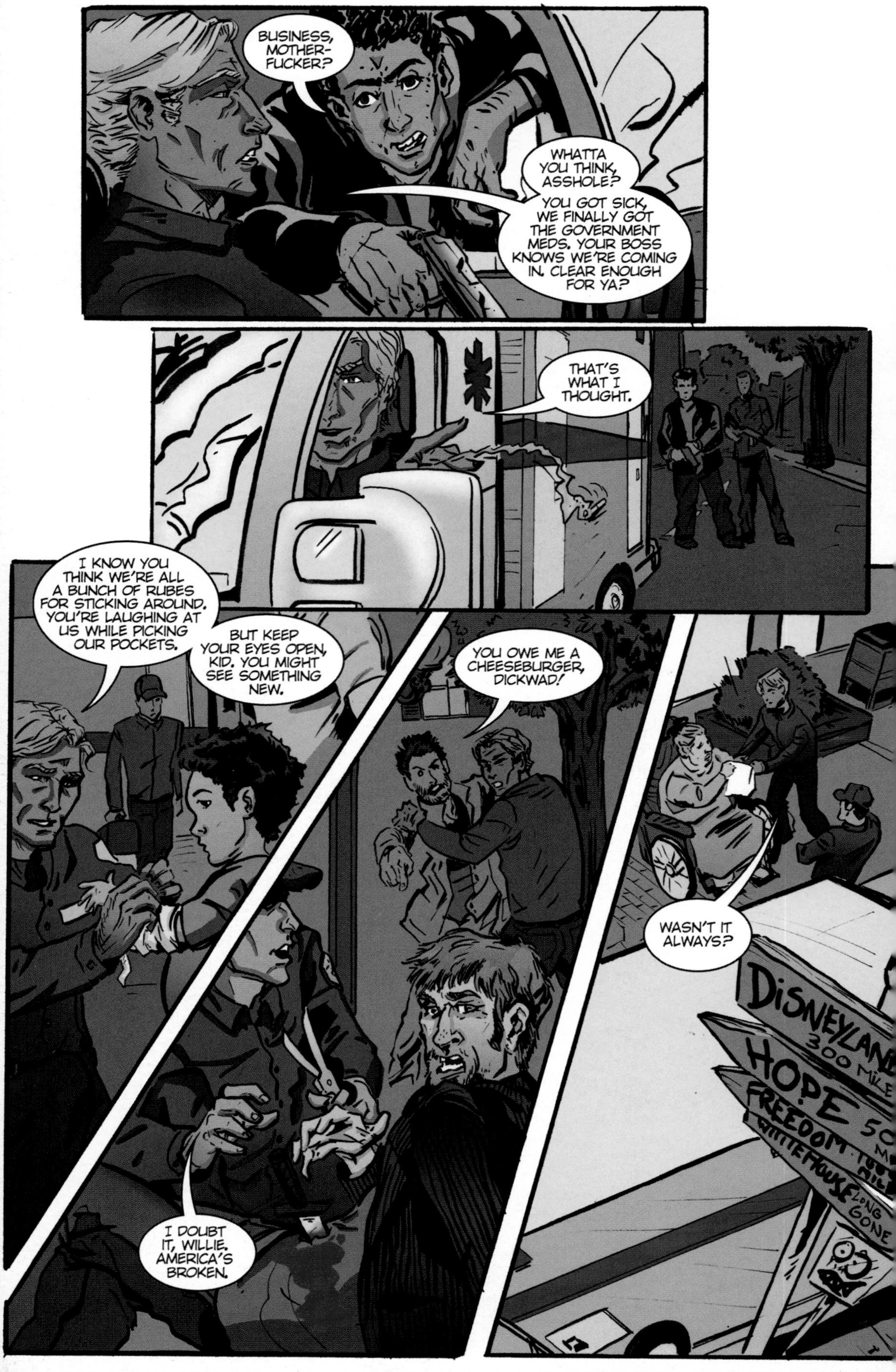
BUSINESS, MOTHER-FUCKER?
WHATTA YOU THINK, ASSHOLE?
YOU GOT SICK, WE FINALLY GOT THE GOVERNMENT MEDS. YOUR BOSS KNOWS WE'RE COMING IN. CLEAR ENOUGH FOR YA?
THAT'S WHAT I THOUGHT.
I KNOW YOU THINK WE'RE ALL A BUNCH OF RUBES FOR STICKING AROUND. YOU'RE LAUGHING AT US WHILE PICKING OUR POCKETS.
BUT KEEP YOUR EYES OPEN, KID. YOU MIGHT SEE SOMETHING NEW.
I DOUBT IT, WILLIE. AMERICA'S BROKEN.
YOU OWE ME A CHEESEBURGER, DICKWAD!
WASN'T IT ALWAYS?
DISNEYLAND
HOPE
FREEDOM
WHITEHOUSE
LONG GONE

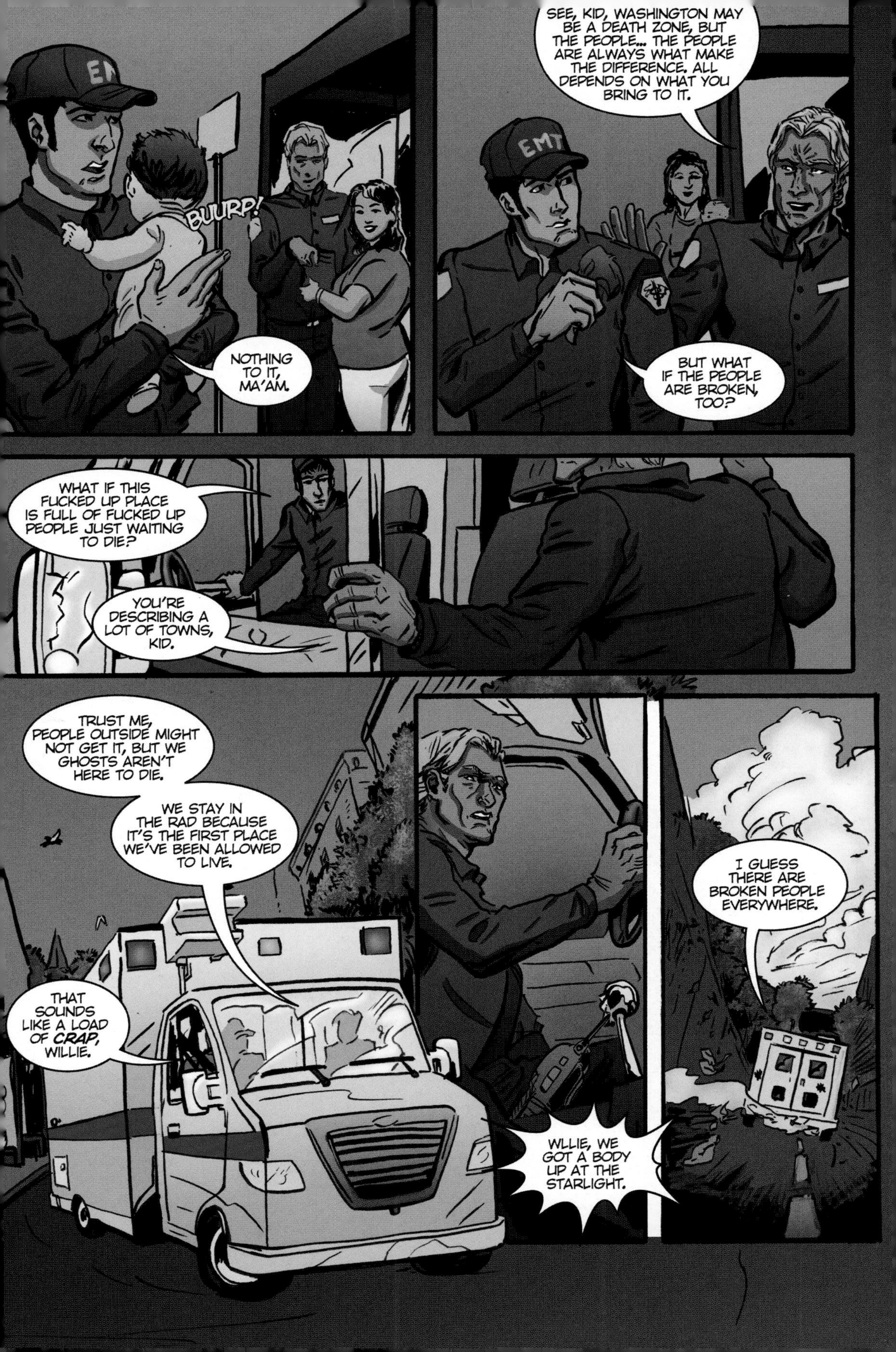
BUURP!
NOTHING TO IT, MA'AM.
SEE, KID, WASHINGTON MAY BE A DEATH ZONE, BUT THE PEOPLE... THE PEOPLE ARE ALWAYS WHAT MAKE THE DIFFERENCE. ALL DEPENDS ON WHAT YOU BRING TO IT.
BUT WHAT IF THE PEOPLE ARE BROKEN, TOO?
WHAT IF THIS FUCKED UP PLACE IS FULL OF FUCKED UP PEOPLE JUST WAITING TO DIE?
YOU'RE DESCRIBING A LOT OF TOWNS, KID.
TRUST ME, PEOPLE OUTSIDE MIGHT NOT GET IT, BUT WE GHOSTS AREN'T HERE TO DIE.
WE STAY IN THE RAD BECAUSE IT'S THE FIRST PLACE WE'VE BEEN ALLOWED TO LIVE.
THAT SOUNDS LIKE A LOAD OF ***CRAP***, WILLIE.
WLLIE, WE GOT A BODY UP AT THE STARLIGHT.
I GUESS THERE ARE BROKEN PEOPLE EVERYWHERE.

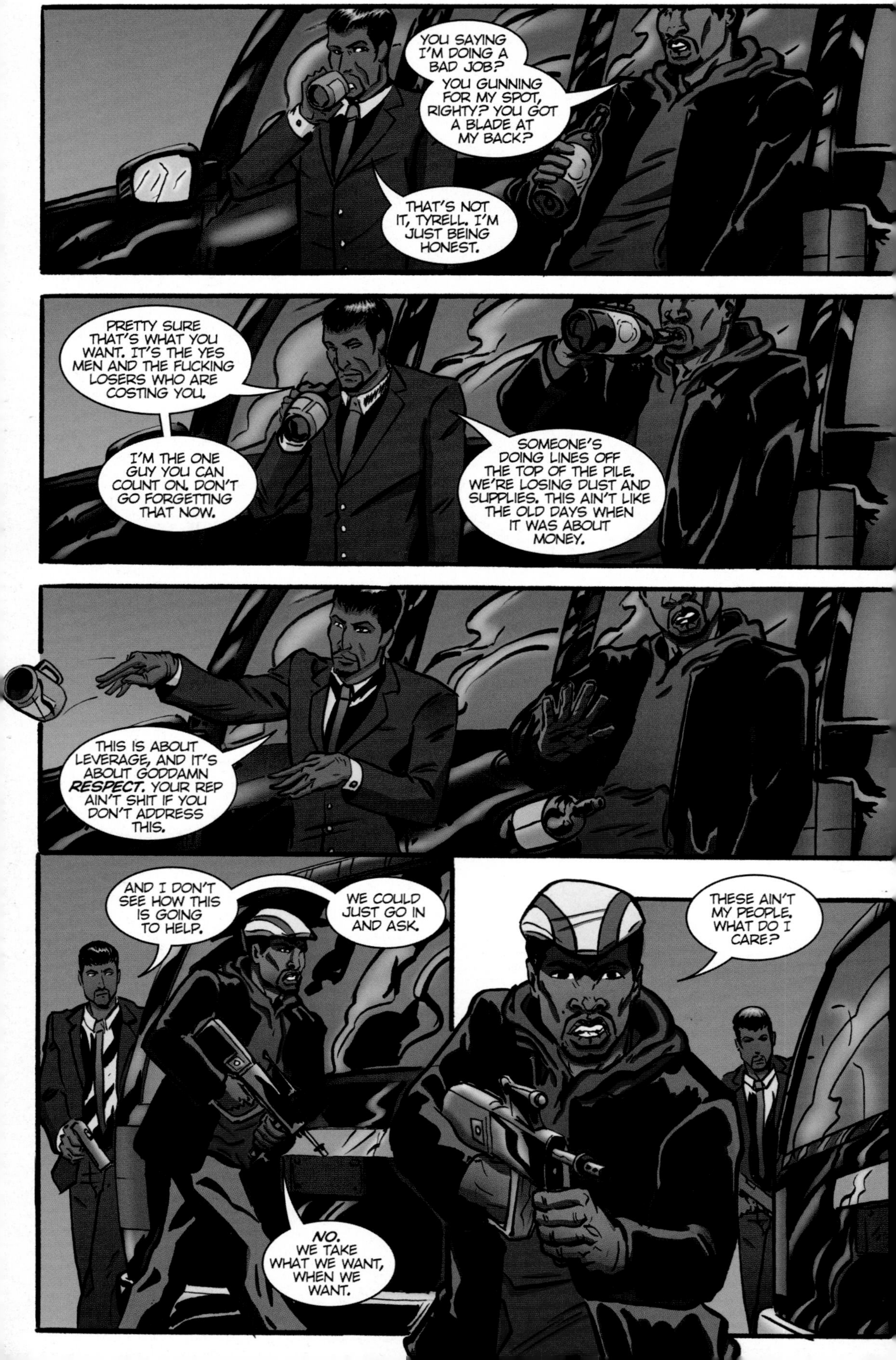

YOU SAYING I'M DOING A BAD JOB?
YOU GUNNING FOR MY SPOT, RIGHTY? YOU GOT A BLADE AT MY BACK?
THAT'S NOT IT, TYRELL. I'M JUST BEING HONEST.
PRETTY SURE THAT'S WHAT YOU WANT. IT'S THE YES MEN AND THE FUCKING LOSERS WHO ARE COSTING YOU.
I'M THE ONE GUY YOU CAN COUNT ON. DON'T GO FORGETTING THAT NOW.
SOMEONE'S DOING LINES OFF THE TOP OF THE PILE. WE'RE LOSING DUST AND SUPPLIES. THIS AIN'T LIKE THE OLD DAYS WHEN IT WAS ABOUT MONEY.
THIS IS ABOUT LEVERAGE, AND IT'S ABOUT GODDAMN *RESPECT*. YOUR REP AIN'T SHIT IF YOU DON'T ADDRESS THIS.
AND I DON'T SEE HOW THIS IS GOING TO HELP.
WE COULD JUST GO IN AND ASK.
NO. WE TAKE WHAT WE WANT, WHEN WE WANT.
THESE AIN'T MY PEOPLE. WHAT DO I CARE?

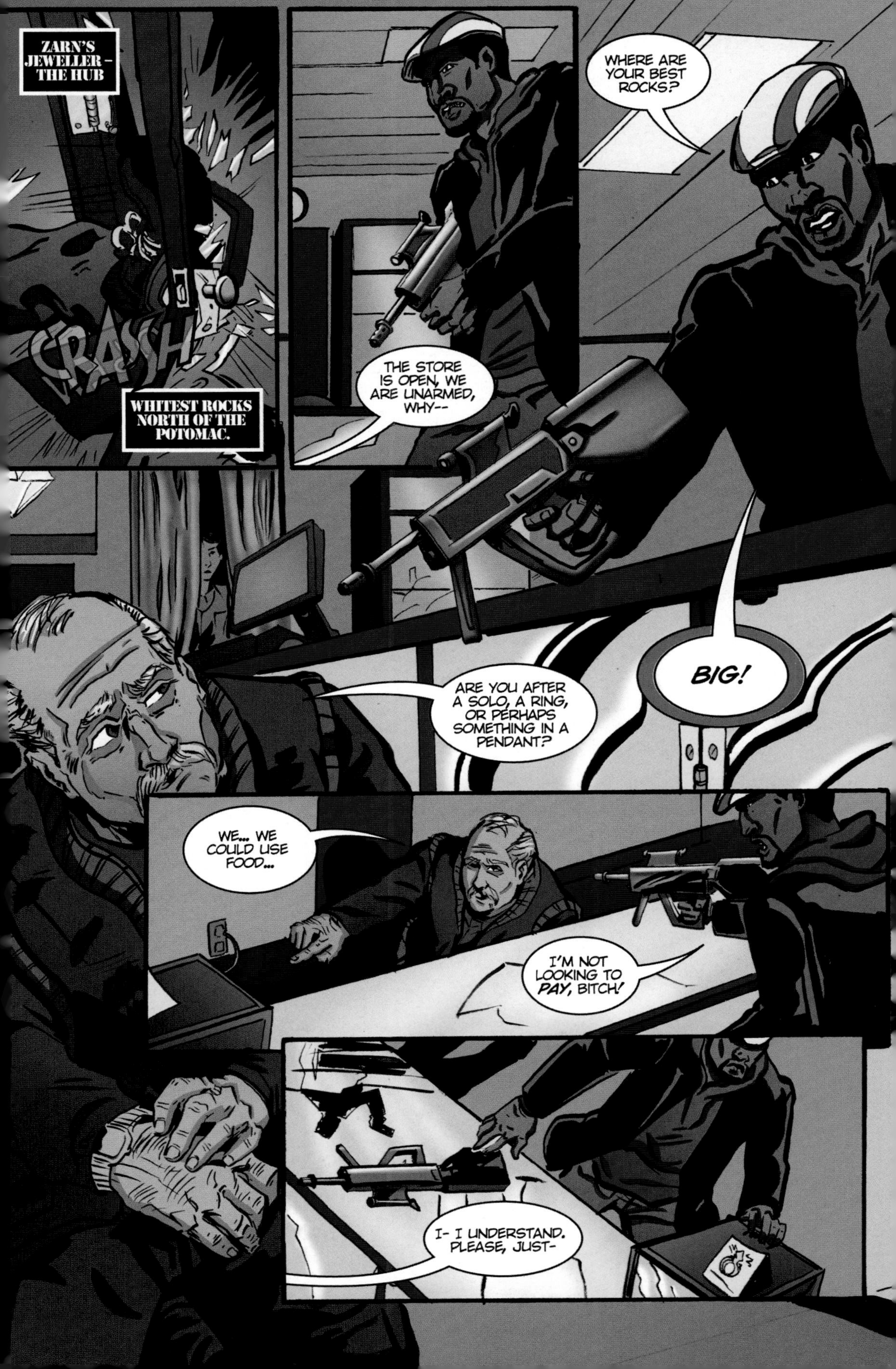
ZARN'S JEWELLER – THE HUB
CRASH
WHITEST ROCKS NORTH OF THE POTOMAC.
WHERE ARE YOUR BEST ROCKS?
THE STORE IS OPEN, WE ARE UNARMED, WHY--
ARE YOU AFTER A SOLO, A RING, OR PERHAPS SOMETHING IN A PENDANT?
BIG!
WE... WE COULD USE FOOD...
I'M NOT LOOKING TO PAY, BITCH!
I- I UNDERSTAND. PLEASE, JUST-

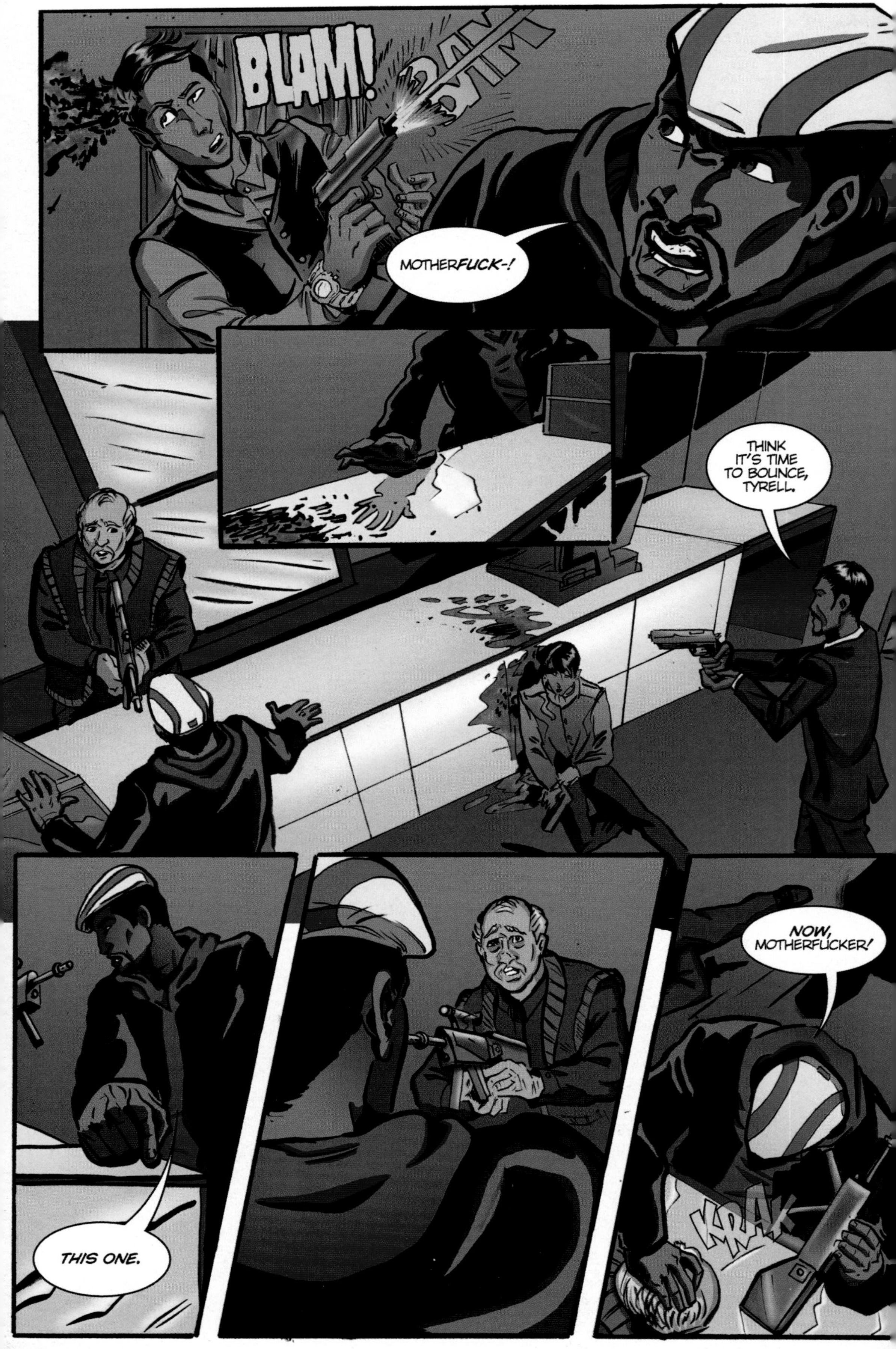
BLAM!
MOTHERFUCK-!
THINK IT'S TIME TO BOUNCE, TYRELL.
THIS ONE.
NOW, MOTHERFUCKER!
KRAK

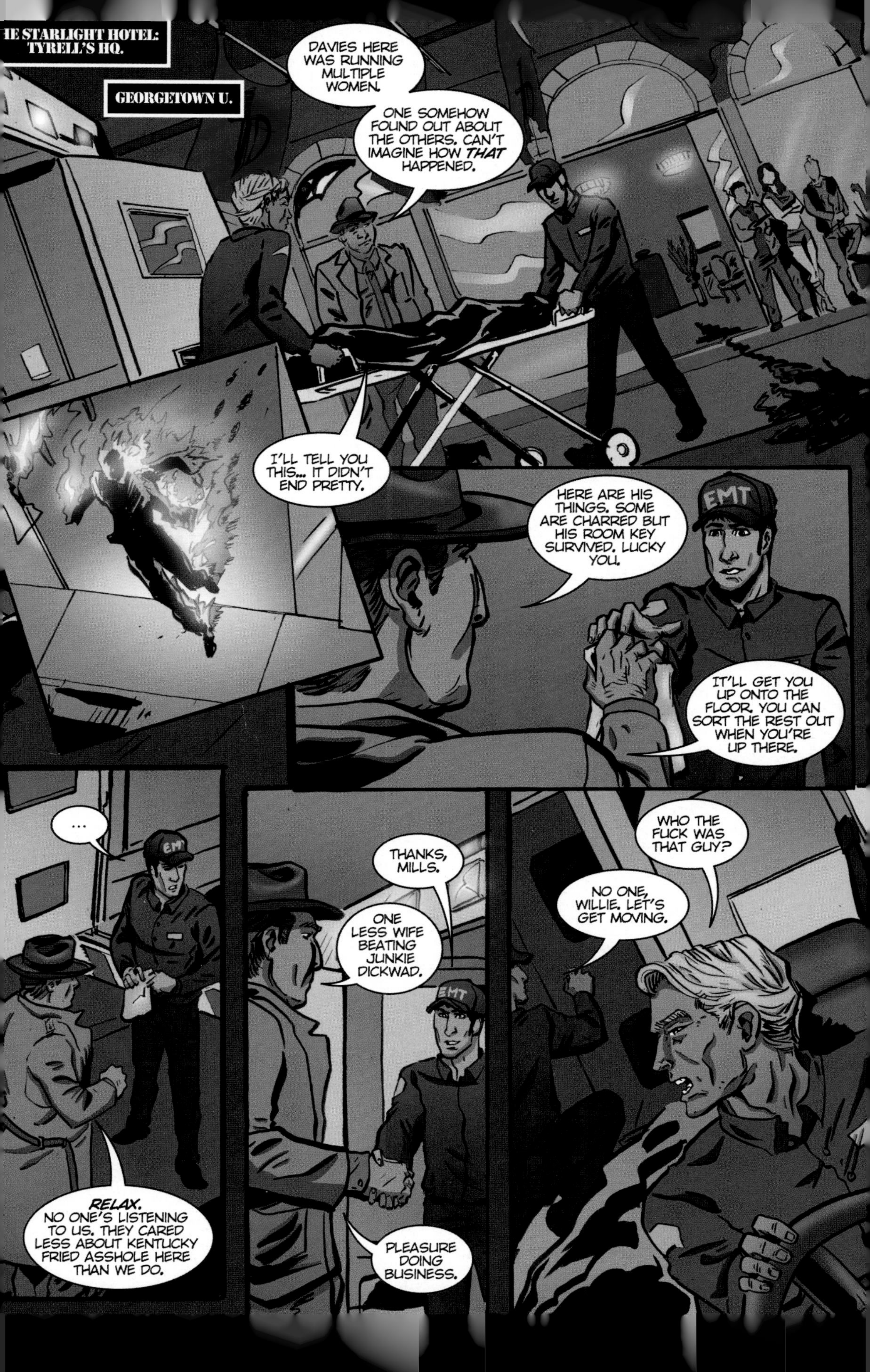

HE STARLIGHT HOTEL: TYRELL'S HQ.
GEORGETOWN U.
DAVIES HERE WAS RUNNING MULTIPLE WOMEN.
ONE SOMEHOW FOUND OUT ABOUT THE OTHERS. CAN'T IMAGINE HOW THAT HAPPENED.
I'LL TELL YOU THIS... IT DIDN'T END PRETTY.
HERE ARE HIS THINGS. SOME ARE CHARRED BUT HIS ROOM KEY SURVIVED. LUCKY YOU.
IT'LL GET YOU UP ONTO THE FLOOR. YOU CAN SORT THE REST OUT WHEN YOU'RE UP THERE.
...
RELAX. NO ONE'S LISTENING TO US. THEY CARED LESS ABOUT KENTUCKY FRIED ASSHOLE HERE THAN WE DO.
THANKS, MILLS.
ONE LESS WIFE BEATING JUNKIE DICKWAD.
PLEASURE DOING BUSINESS.
WHO THE FUCK WAS THAT GUY?
NO ONE, WILLIE. LET'S GET MOVING.

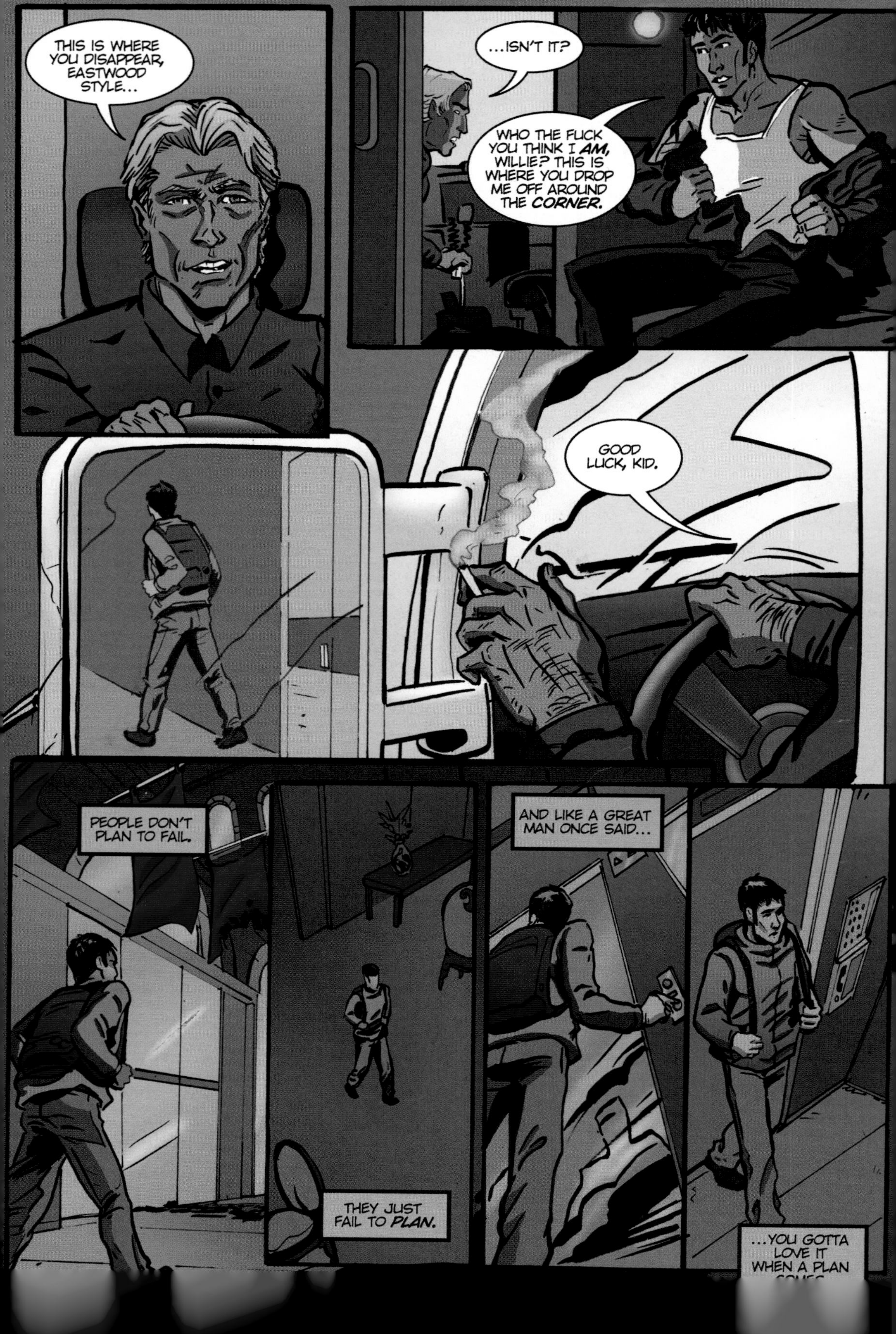
THIS IS WHERE YOU DISAPPEAR, EASTWOOD STYLE...
...ISN'T IT?
WHO THE FUCK YOU THINK I **AM**, WILLIE? THIS IS WHERE YOU DROP ME OFF AROUND THE **CORNER.**
GOOD LUCK, KID.
PEOPLE DON'T PLAN TO FAIL.
THEY JUST FAIL TO **PLAN.**
AND LIKE A GREAT MAN ONCE SAID...
...YOU GOTTA LOVE IT WHEN A PLAN

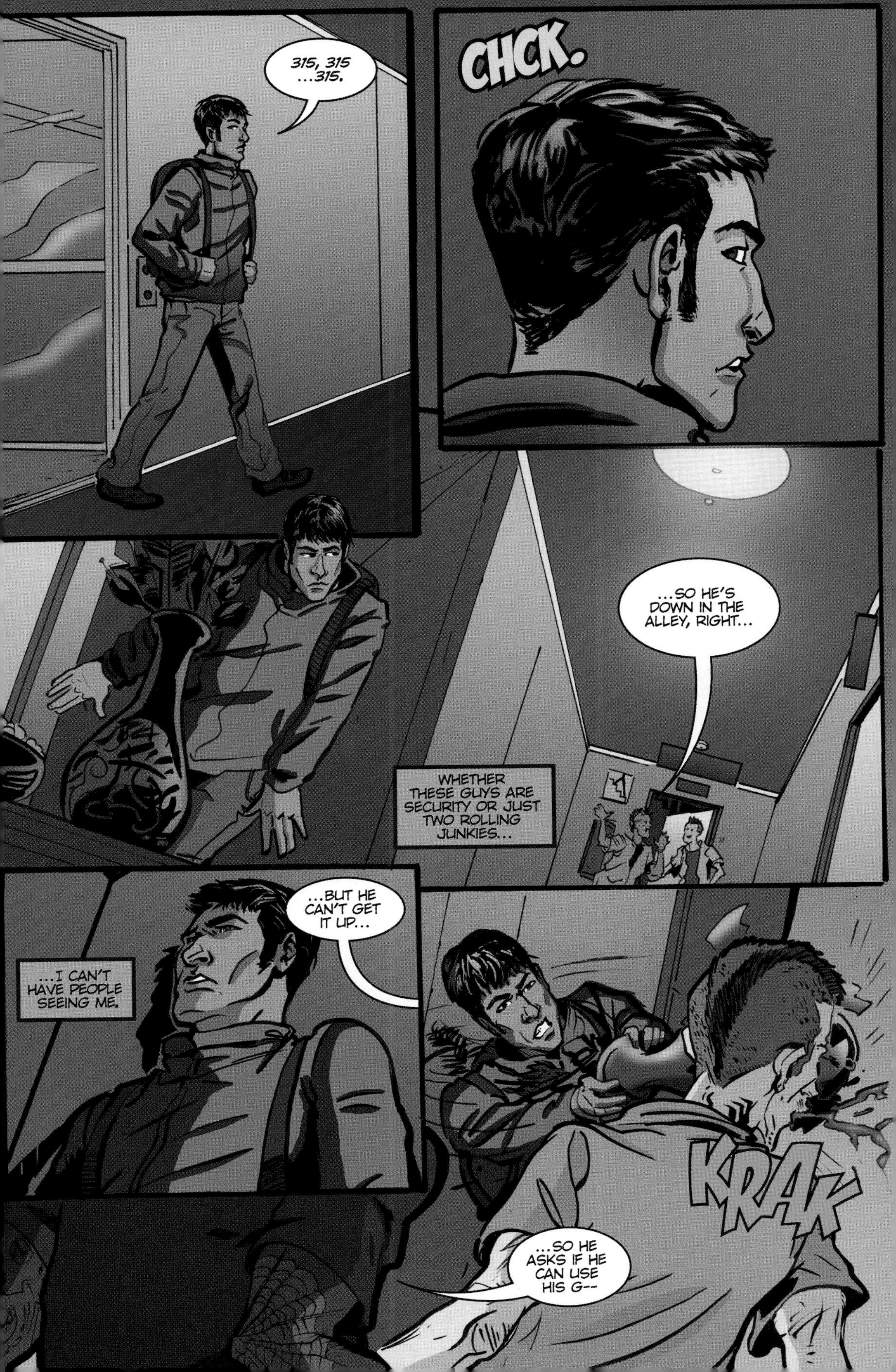

315, 315
...315.
CHCK.
...SO HE'S DOWN IN THE ALLEY, RIGHT...
WHETHER THESE GUYS ARE SECURITY OR JUST TWO ROLLING JUNKIES...
...BUT HE CAN'T GET IT UP...
...I CAN'T HAVE PEOPLE SEEING ME.
KRAK
...SO HE ASKS IF HE CAN USE HIS G--

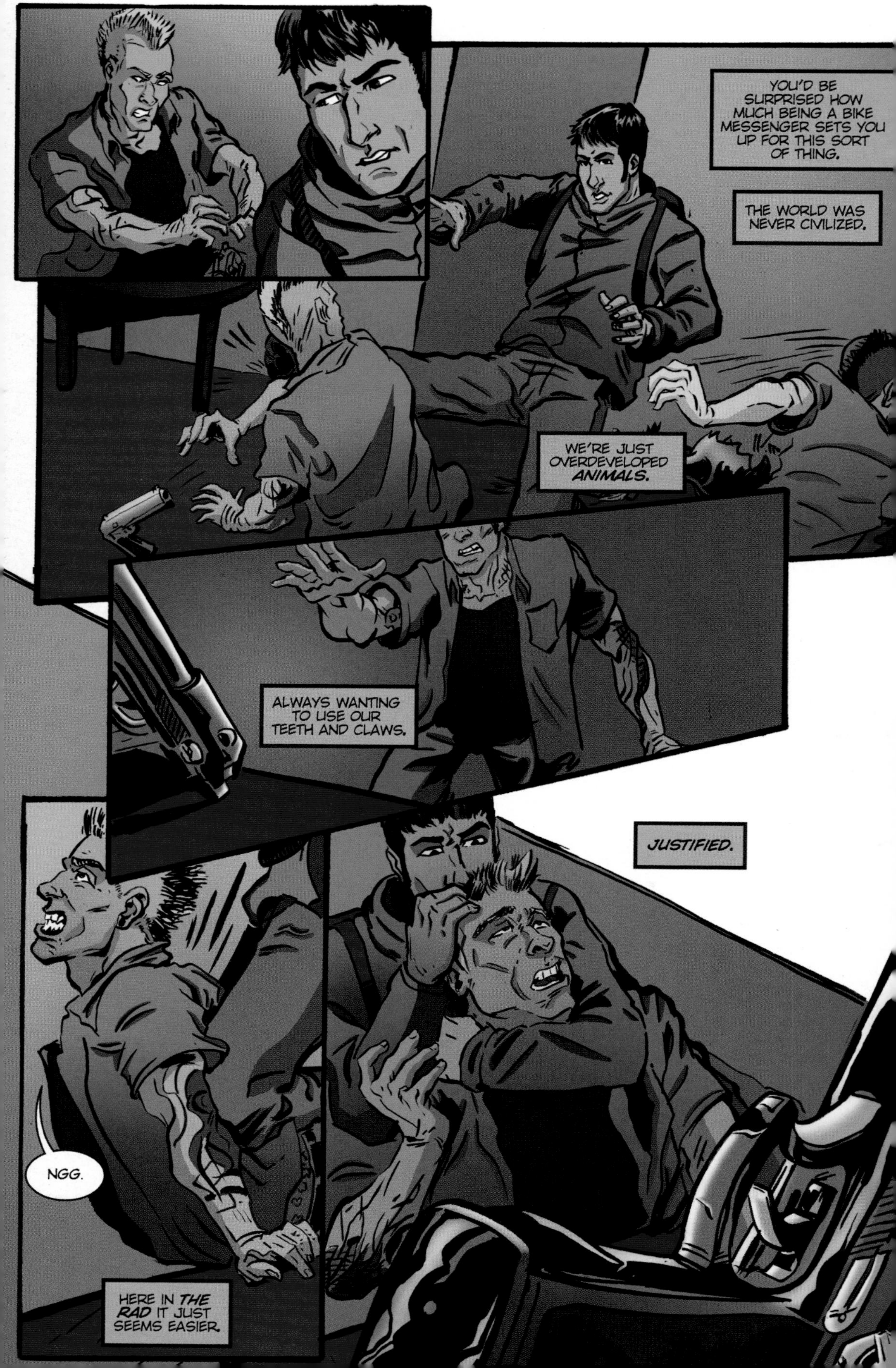
YOU'D BE SURPRISED HOW MUCH BEING A BIKE MESSENGER SETS YOU UP FOR THIS SORT OF THING.
THE WORLD WAS NEVER CIVILIZED.
WE'RE JUST OVERDEVELOPED ANIMALS.
ALWAYS WANTING TO USE OUR TEETH AND CLAWS.
JUSTIFIED.
NGG.
HERE IN THE RAD IT JUST SEEMS EASIER.

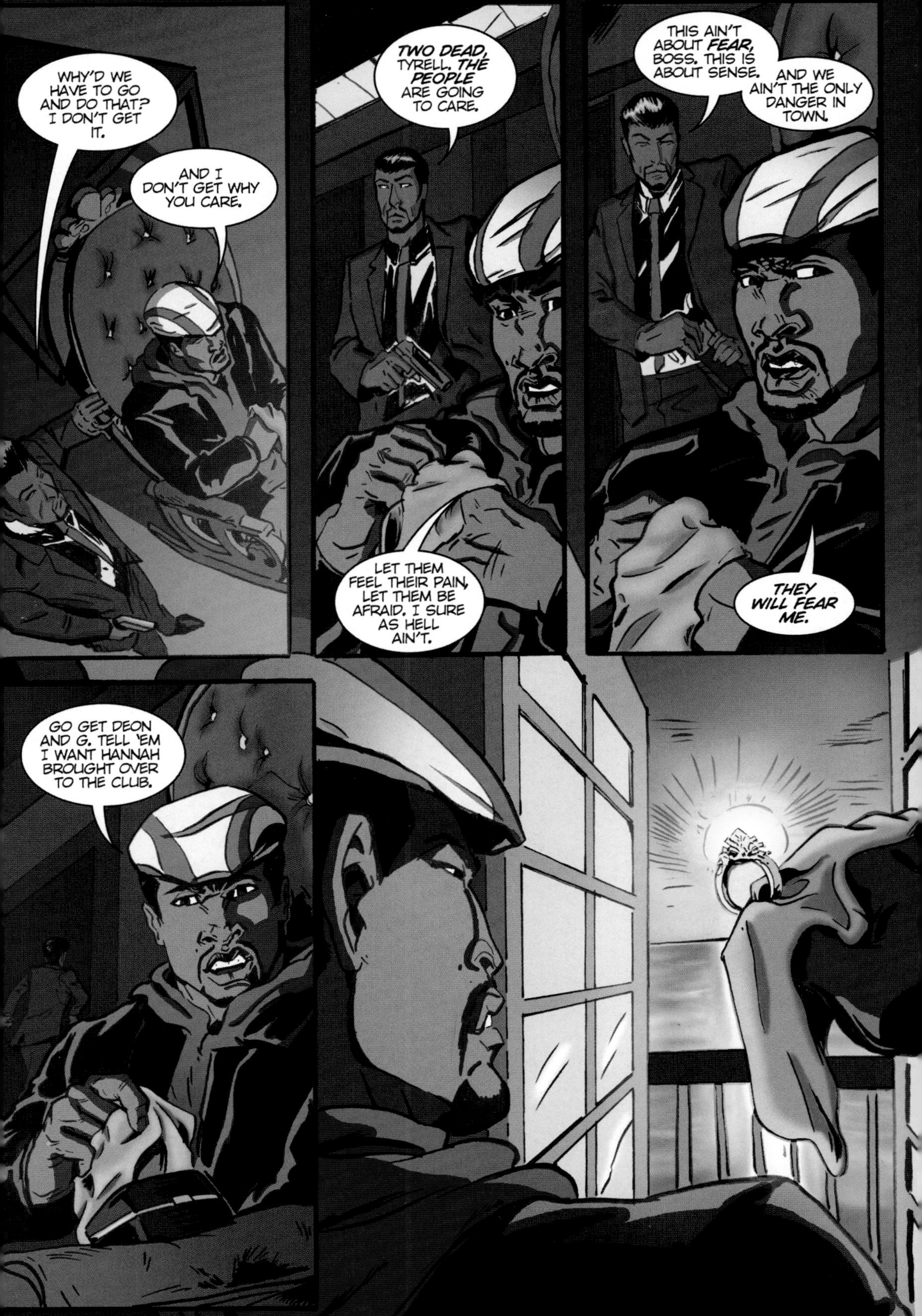
WHY'D WE HAVE TO GO AND DO THAT? I DON'T GET IT.
AND I DON'T GET WHY YOU CARE.
TWO DEAD, TYRELL. *THE PEOPLE* ARE GOING TO CARE.
LET THEM FEEL THEIR PAIN, LET THEM BE AFRAID. I SURE AS HELL AIN'T.
THIS AIN'T ABOUT *FEAR,* BOSS. THIS IS ABOUT SENSE.
AND WE AIN'T THE ONLY DANGER IN TOWN.
THEY WILL FEAR ME.
GO GET DEON AND G. TELL 'EM I WANT HANNAH BROUGHT OVER TO THE CLUB.

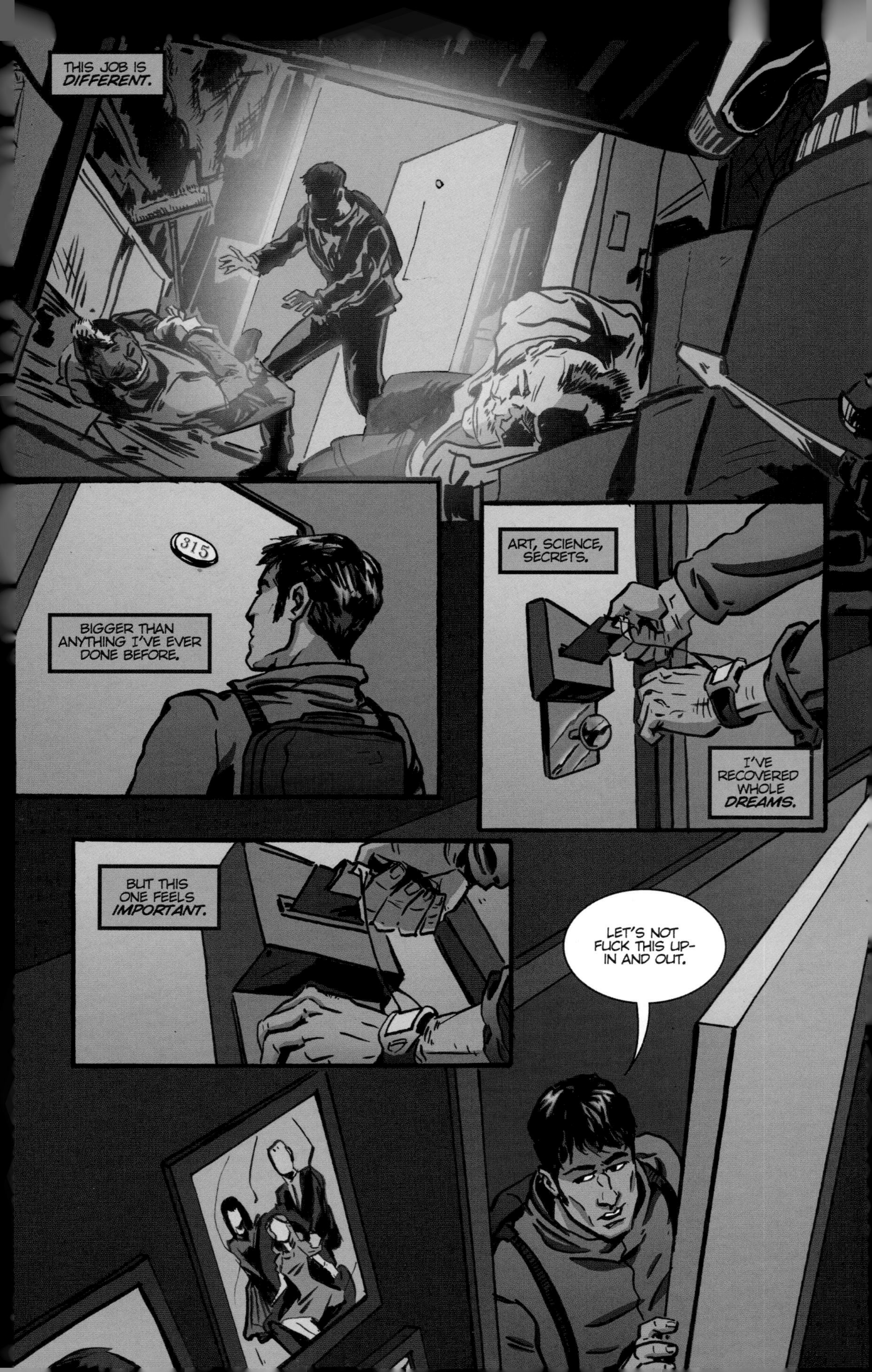
THIS JOB IS DIFFERENT.
BIGGER THAN ANYTHING I'VE EVER DONE BEFORE.
315
ART, SCIENCE, SECRETS.
I'VE RECOVERED WHOLE DREAMS.
BUT THIS ONE FEELS IMPORTANT.
LET'S NOT FUCK THIS UP- IN AND OUT.

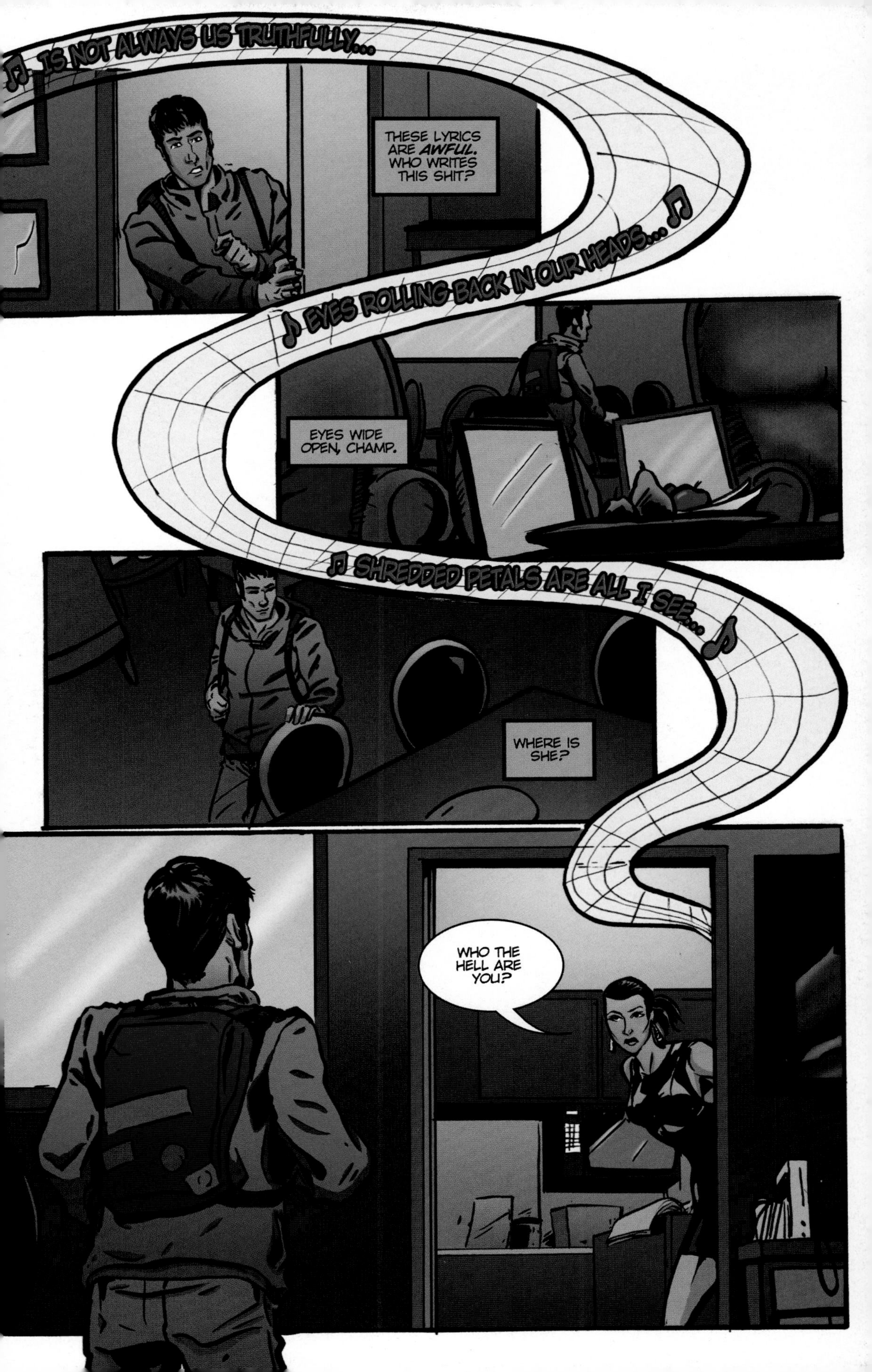
♫ IS NOT ALWAYS US TRUTHFULLY...
THESE LYRICS ARE *AWFUL.* WHO WRITES THIS SHIT?
EYES ROLLING BACK IN OUR HEADS... ♫
♫ EYES ROLLING BACK IN OUR HEADS... ♫
EYES WIDE OPEN, CHAMP.
♫ SHREDDED PETALS ARE ALL I SEE... ♫
WHERE IS SHE?
WHO THE HELL ARE YOU?

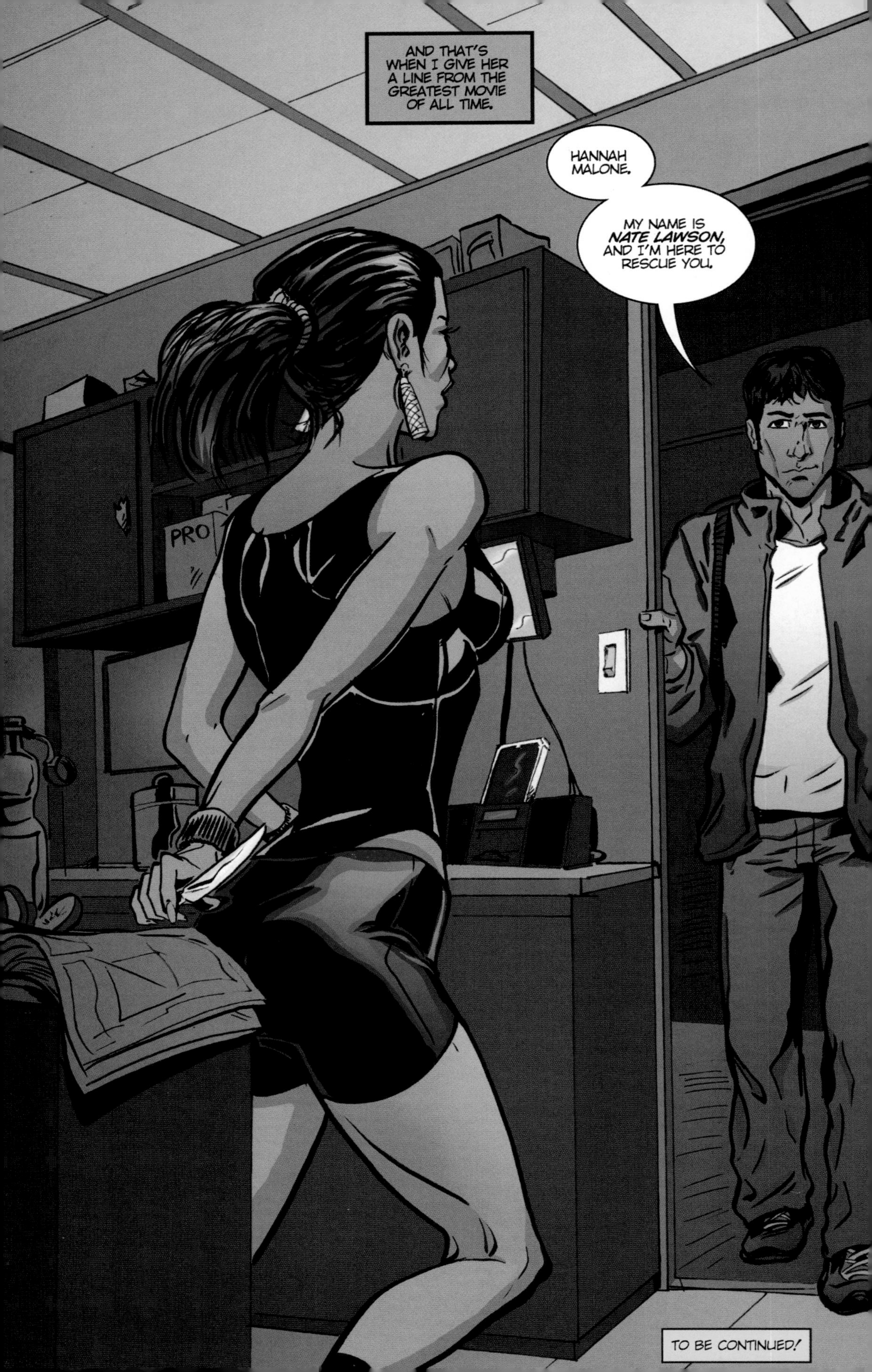
AND THAT'S WHEN I GIVE HER A LINE FROM THE GREATEST MOVIE OF ALL TIME.
HANNAH MALONE.
MY NAME IS *NATE LAWSON,* AND I'M HERE TO RESCUE YOU.
PRO
TO BE CONTINUED!

GHOSTWRITTEN

Hey there Townies (yep, you awesome fans have a collective noun already), it's nice to have you back here. Back matter is my favourite so stick around, have a chat, this is going to be fun. This is my first issue on GHOST TOWN and I have to thank Dave Dwonch and Rob Ruddell for giving me enough rope on this gig. We've had a hell of a time world building on this one and I'm really proud of this intro arc I've built with my brother in arms Daniel J Logan. He and I have done a few shorts before (top marks to whoever can track all three of them down) and it's always a serious pleasure to work with him.

In this issue you just met many people but I hope you really paid attention to Nate Lawson. He's going to be your eyes and ears in the Rad, and I really like the tone he sets as the protagonist in my take on this world. You can see we've jumped far and ahead from what Dave and Justin Greenwood did in #1. Those fine gents set up some serious game and now I get to play with it and we tweak the genre a little and really ground ourselves in this desolate area that once was the thriving capital. I think of the Rad as being a mash up of THE WIRE and ESCAPE FROM NEW YORK.

Next issue has a shoot out and one of my favourite pages from Daniel ever, not to mention some more superb colours from Brian V Dyck. It is not to be missed.

This is my first ongoing series so I wanted to share some of myself with you fine people. Think of it as the writer stripped bare.

I try to read a comic a day, at least. Lately I find myself gravitating to books I can learn a little something from. LOCKE & KEY from Joe Hill and Gabriel Rodriguez is about to end and that makes me pretty sad. It's one of the few classic horror comics of the modern age. Scope the first trade and blame me for the next few hundred dollars you spend. I'm also massively immersing myself in the first volume of the FEAR AGENT Library Edition HCs. Tony Moore's art at that size is superb and I always dig Rick Remender at his pulpiest.

I'm digging some shows lately - and having a baby girl to sometimes pace around with gives me time to dive into things - so it's nice to have quality small screen literature to lose myself in. I find I'm really enjoying THE AMERICANS for all its period tics and just flat out high quality spy hijinks (spy-jinks, yeah?) - and it's not getting raving press but it continually impresses me with how solid it is. I'm also madly in love with OFFSPRING (the greatest Australian show of all time) and it's rad to have a season in full swing over here right now. Some of the best relationship writing on screen you'll find anywhere.

I recently caught two docos that completely captured my attention - PAGE ONE was all about the New York Times and chronicles its melding with the digital age, and ROMAN POLANSKI: WANTED AND DESIRED was a fascinating insight into a filmmaker whose output constantly inspires me. Both flicks were superbly well made and just gave me tonnes of things to think about.

I finally got on the Spotify bandwagon. It is sharpening my focus and inspiration. And man, any place that gives me the THEY LIVE OST for free is alright in my book.

By the time you are reading this, you should also be able to pick up THE DEVIL IS IN THE DETAILS: EXAMINING MATT MURDOCK AND DAREDEVIL. This book from Sequart is a collection of essays about Marvel's Daredevil that I edited and wrote a few pieces for. It's a dream project for me and if you have some interest in the character I know you'll need to be all over this book. It's a lot of fun and really gets into some interesting Daredevil topics.

We here at Ghost Town HQ hope you are digging where we are taking this book. We've got a big tale to tell, and some very cool characters to deliver to you, and a plethora of the most amazing moments you could hope to read in a book dealing with time travel and terrorists. We are sure you'll stick with us but we also hope you might support us to ensure this indie book gets a strong shelf life. If you like this book please tell a friend, talk about it at the water cooler, tweet/link/blog/share it. Books like this get a voracious fan base but we also need the sales numbers to stay alive. Be open with your praise and you can always find me on Twitter as @ryanklindsay - I'd love to hear from you.

RKL

BEAUCOUP POP

EHMM THEORY

"THE PERFECT BALANCE OF ABSURDITY AND GORE"
FANGORIA

"INCREDIBLY INVENTIVE, ORIGINAL AND HIGHLY ENTERTAINING"
FLIGHT RING

"FUN, FUNNY, AND ENTIRELY ABSORBING."
FANBOY COMICS

"THIS COMIC IS SERIOUSLY EPIC."
10 OUT OF 10 - SEQUENTIAL TART

WARNING: THIS BOOK CONTAINS BLOODTHIRSTY CYBERNETIC CRABS, SUPERPOWERED ASSHOLES, AND CUTE THINGS CURSING
STAY ALERT!

ACTIONLABCOMICS.COM/DANGER-ZONE

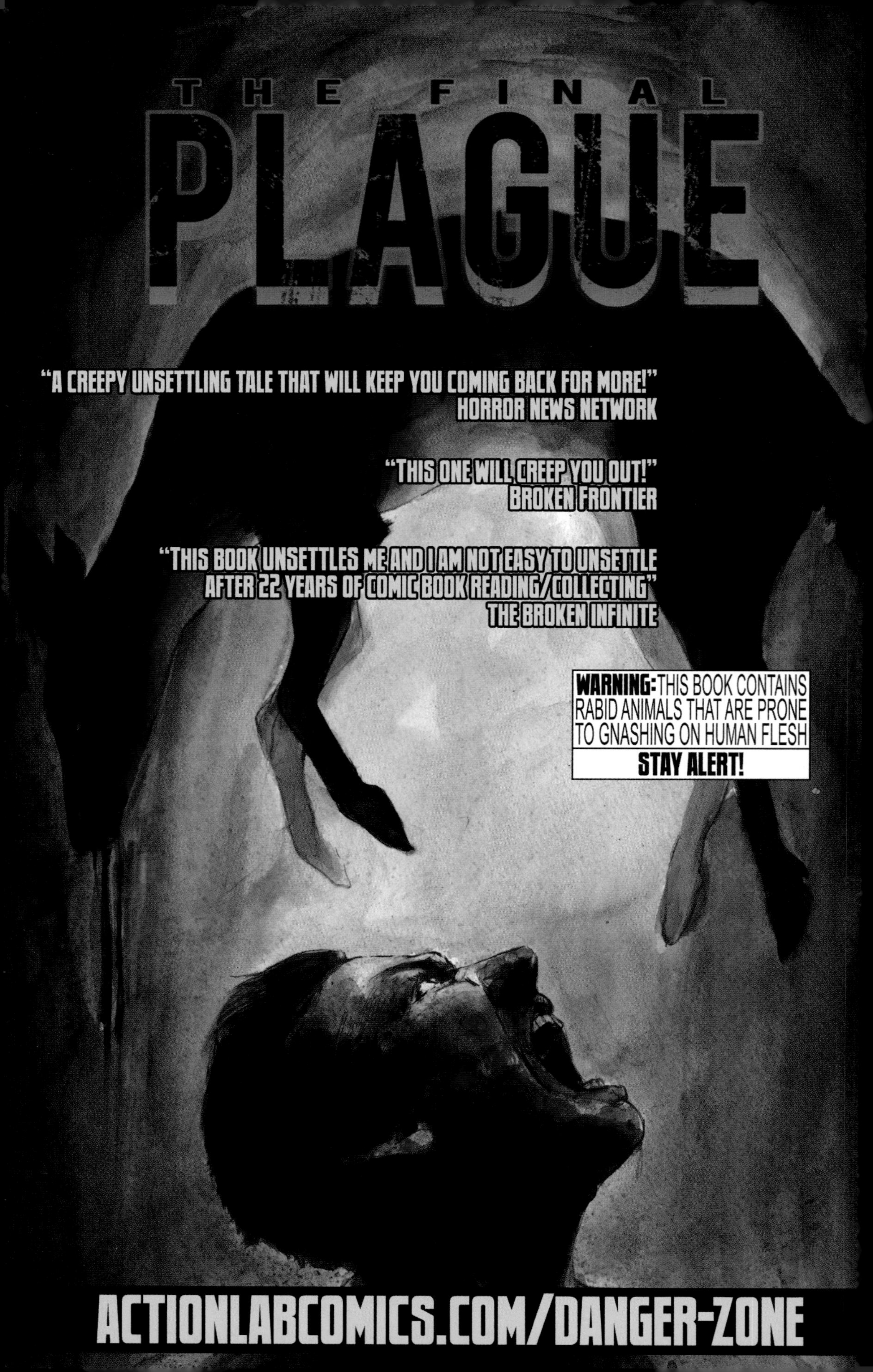
THE FINAL
PLAGUE
"A CREEPY UNSETTLING TALE THAT WILL KEEP YOU COMING BACK FOR MORE!"
HORROR NEWS NETWORK
"THIS ONE WILL CREEP YOU OUT!"
BROKEN FRONTIER
"THIS BOOK UNSETTLES ME AND I AM NOT EASY TO UNSETTLE AFTER 22 YEARS OF COMIC BOOK READING/COLLECTING"
THE BROKEN INFINITE
WARNING: THIS BOOK CONTAINS RABID ANIMALS THAT ARE PRONE TO GNASHING ON HUMAN FLESH
STAY ALERT!
ACTIONLABCOMICS.COM/DANGER-ZONE

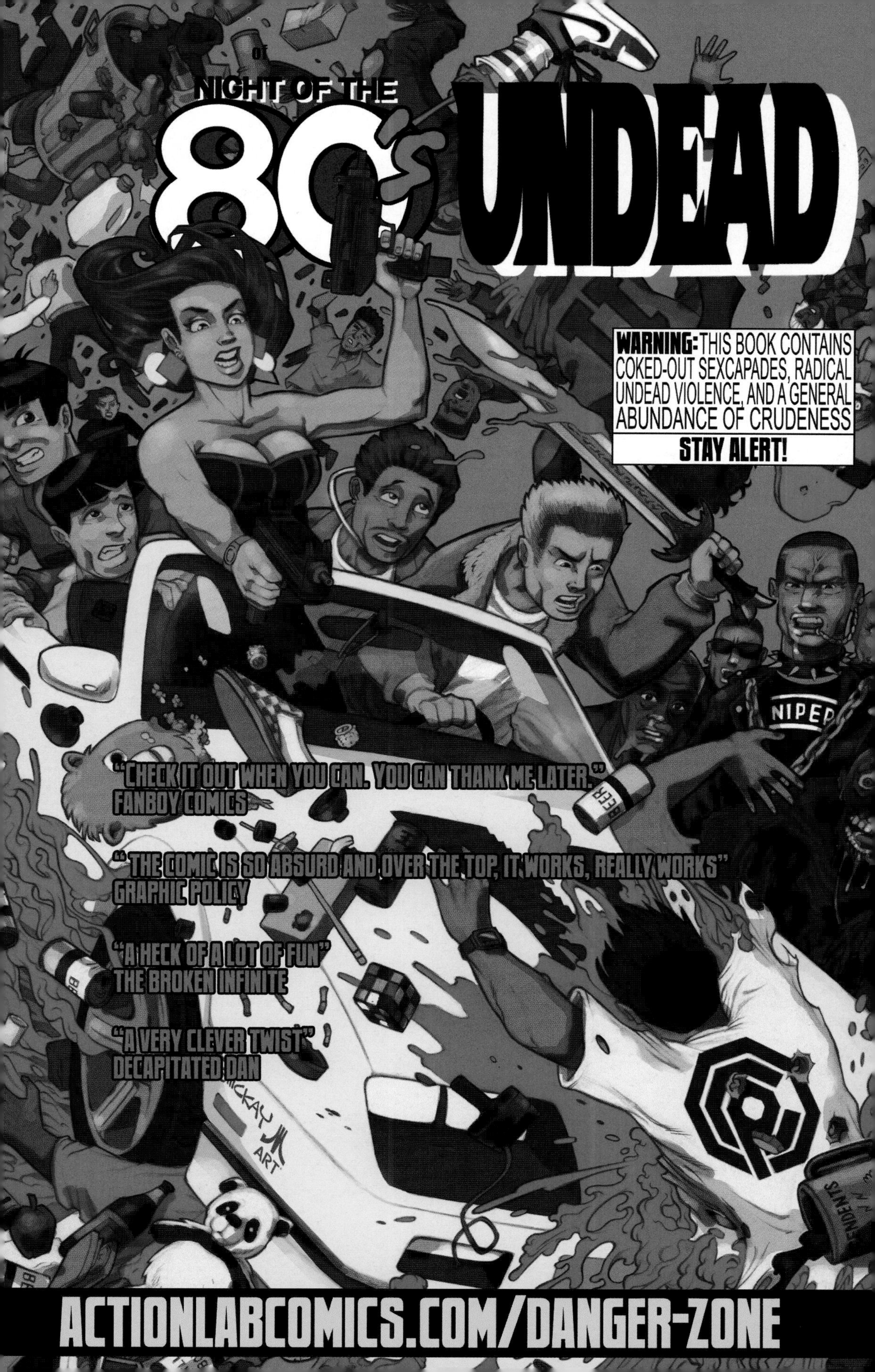
NIGHT OF THE
80's UNDEAD
WARNING: THIS BOOK CONTAINS COKED-OUT SEXCAPADES, RADICAL UNDEAD VIOLENCE, AND A GENERAL ABUNDANCE OF CRUDENESS
STAY ALERT!
"CHECK IT OUT WHEN YOU CAN. YOU CAN THANK ME LATER."
FANBOY COMICS
" THE COMIC IS SO ABSURD AND OVER THE TOP, IT WORKS, REALLY WORKS"
GRAPHIC POLICY
"A HECK OF A LOT OF FUN"
THE BROKEN INFINITE
"A VERY CLEVER TWIST"
DECAPITATED DAN
ACTIONLABCOMICS.COM/DANGER-ZONE

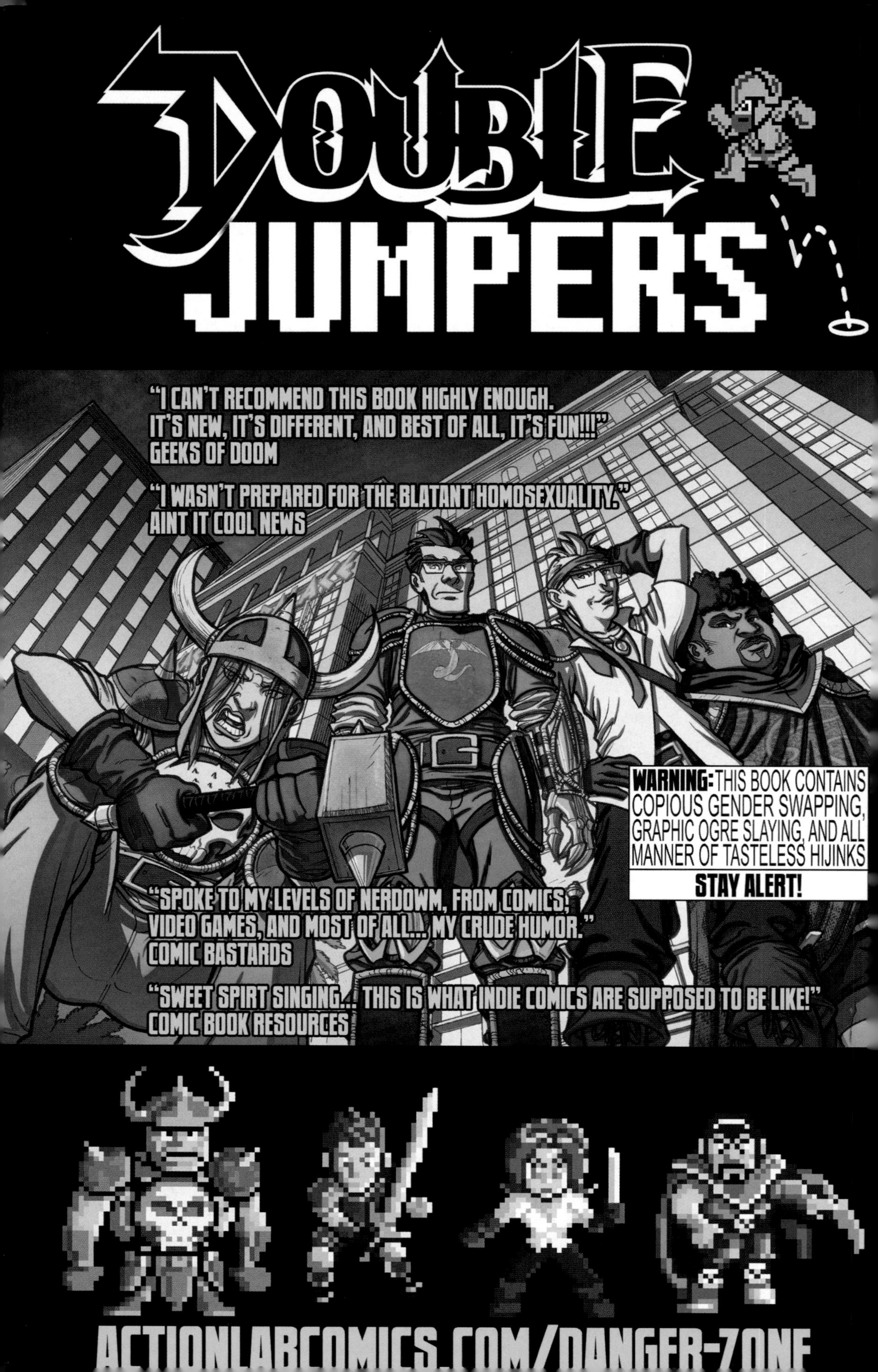
DOUBLE JUMPERS
"I CAN'T RECOMMEND THIS BOOK HIGHLY ENOUGH. IT'S NEW, IT'S DIFFERENT, AND BEST OF ALL, IT'S FUN!!!"
GEEKS OF DOOM
"I WASN'T PREPARED FOR THE BLATANT HOMOSEXUALITY."
AINT IT COOL NEWS
WARNING: THIS BOOK CONTAINS COPIOUS GENDER SWAPPING, GRAPHIC OGRE SLAYING, AND ALL MANNER OF TASTELESS HIJINKS
STAY ALERT!
"SPOKE TO MY LEVELS OF NERDOWM, FROM COMICS, VIDEO GAMES, AND MOST OF ALL... MY CRUDE HUMOR."
COMIC BASTARDS
"SWEET SPIRT SINGING... THIS IS WHAT INDIE COMICS ARE SUPPOSED TO BE LIKE!"
COMIC BOOK RESOURCES
ACTIONLABCOMICS.COM/DANGER-ZONE

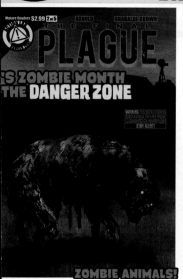

STAY ALERT!

SHIPPING NEXT MONTH

WARNING: THESE BOOKS MAY CONTAIN SUPER-COOL CONTENT THAT COULD BLOW YOUR MIND!

Mature Readers $2.99 2 of 5
ARNOLD
GUARALDI-BROWN
THE FINAL
PLAGUE
'S ZOMBIE MONTH
THE DANGER ZONE
STAY ALERT!
ZOMBIE ANIMALS!

HE FINAL PLAGUE
2 (OF 5) $2.99

RITER: **JD ARNOLD**
RTIST: **TONY GUARALDI-BROWN**

mutated rabies virus continues to read across the planet, infecting, ling, and reanimating animals, both eat and small.
n mankind survive?

THIS BOOK CONTAINS: COKED-OUT SEXCAPADES, RADICAL VIOLENCE, & TOTALLY EPIC CRUDENESS!
2 of 3
$2.99
Aug 13
APPROVED FOR MATURE READERS
NIGHT OF THE
80'S UNDEAD
STORY BY JASON MARTIN
ART BY BILL MCKAY
ZOMBIE COKE-HEADS!

NIGHT OF THE 80'S UNDEAD
#2 (OF 3) $2.99

WRITER: **JASON MARTIN**
ARTIST: **BILL McKAY**

Having broken into the biggest Holly-wood party of 1986, our gang of teens must now survive what's become a commie coke zombie bash of epic proportions!

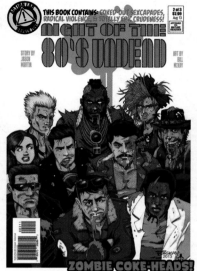

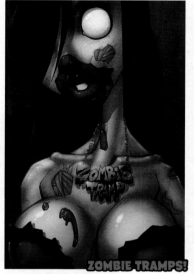

ZOMBIE TRAMPS!

ZOMBIE TRAMP
Vol.1 TPB $14.99

WRITER/ARTIST: **DAN MENDOZA**

The out of print cult hit gets the deluxe remastered treatment!
A high priced call girl gets bitten by a zombie, and then seeks out vengeance on those who wronged her.
Cartoon grindhouse action ensues!!

ROM THE ZONE

ly means one thing when you publish comic books, *San Diego Comic-on*!! Not only is it the single biggest stage to exhibit in the U.S.industry, t it's also, to me, the marker by which everything is measured against. e publishing year starts and ends during this one magical week in July.

you haven't been, *SDCC* is unlike any other experience you'll have as a mic book fan... something akin to Christmas by way of Disneyland is e best that I can describe it. New York Comic-Con is getting close in ale, but the perpetual 78 degree sunshine of San Diego in July, coupled th the take-over of the relatively small downtown, makes for a truly ique world of comics and pop culture. There's a buzz around the show, d the town, that feels as if these books that we work so hard on all ar, really can become everything we dreamed!

tion Lab will of course be there this year, and if you haven't seen us at show yet, be sure to visit us if you make the con. We've had limited ition early versions of the Danger Zone titles all year (some of which e still available on our website), and we'll have a new special edition of exciting upcoming title debuting at the show, in addition to all of the oks we've released so far! Some "Christmas presents" if you will, for ose who "take the ride".

usual, the next two months will see many new books from our owing imprint releasing in stores and online as well, including a book at I previously published, *Zombie Tramp*! Zombie Tramp is not only ldly popular, it's a deceptively good read - especially if you like indhouse with a side of anime!! Don't let the title fool you, she really is ombie, and a tramp, but despite being an undead call-girl, she'll still e you a good time! So be sure to check out the new expanded Danger ne TPB edition of her first comic series this August (followed up with e debut of her sequel series, starting in October). Plus we've got issue of all of our launch titles too!

AY ALERT!

son Martin - President, Action Lab: Danger Zone

OUT NOW!

Mature Readers $3.99 2 of 4
McKINNEY
FORD
STRUTZ
EHMM
THEORY
WARNING: THIS BOOK CONTAINS BLOODTHIRSTY CYBERNETIC CRABS, SUPERPOWERED ASSHOLES, AND CUTE THINGS CURSING
STAY ALERT!

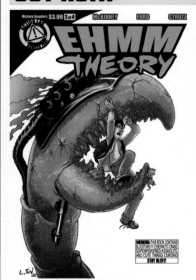

EHMM THEORY
#2 (OF 4) $3.99

WRITER: **BROCKTON McKINNEY**
ARTIST: **LARKIN FORD**
COLORIST: **JASON STRUTZ**

What started out as a horror comedy begins to shift into more genres, as Gabe & Mr Whispers try to solve the mystery of what's happening to them!

Get free previews of all the books at our website!
TIONLABCOMICS.COM/DANGER-ZONE

FOLLOW US ONLINE:
Facebook.com/ActionLabDangerZone
Twitter.com/ActionLabDanger
ActionLabDangerZone.tumblr.com

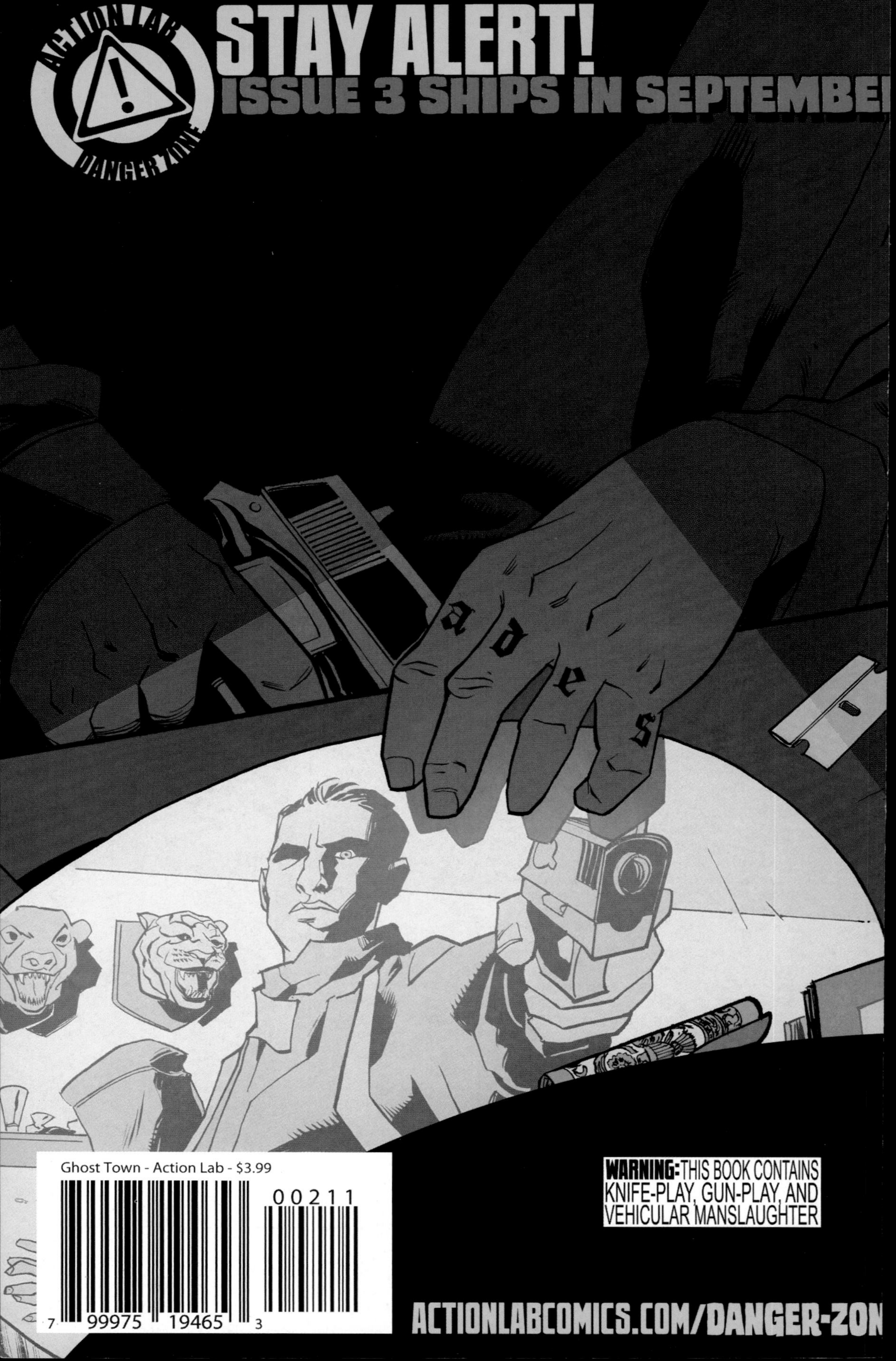
ACTION LAB
DANGER ZONE
STAY ALERT!
ISSUE 3 SHIPS IN SEPTEMBE
Ghost Town - Action Lab - $3.99
00211
7 99975 19465 3
WARNING: THIS BOOK CONTAINS KNIFE-PLAY, GUN-PLAY, AND VEHICULAR MANSLAUGHTER
ACTIONLABCOMICS.COM/DANGER-ZON

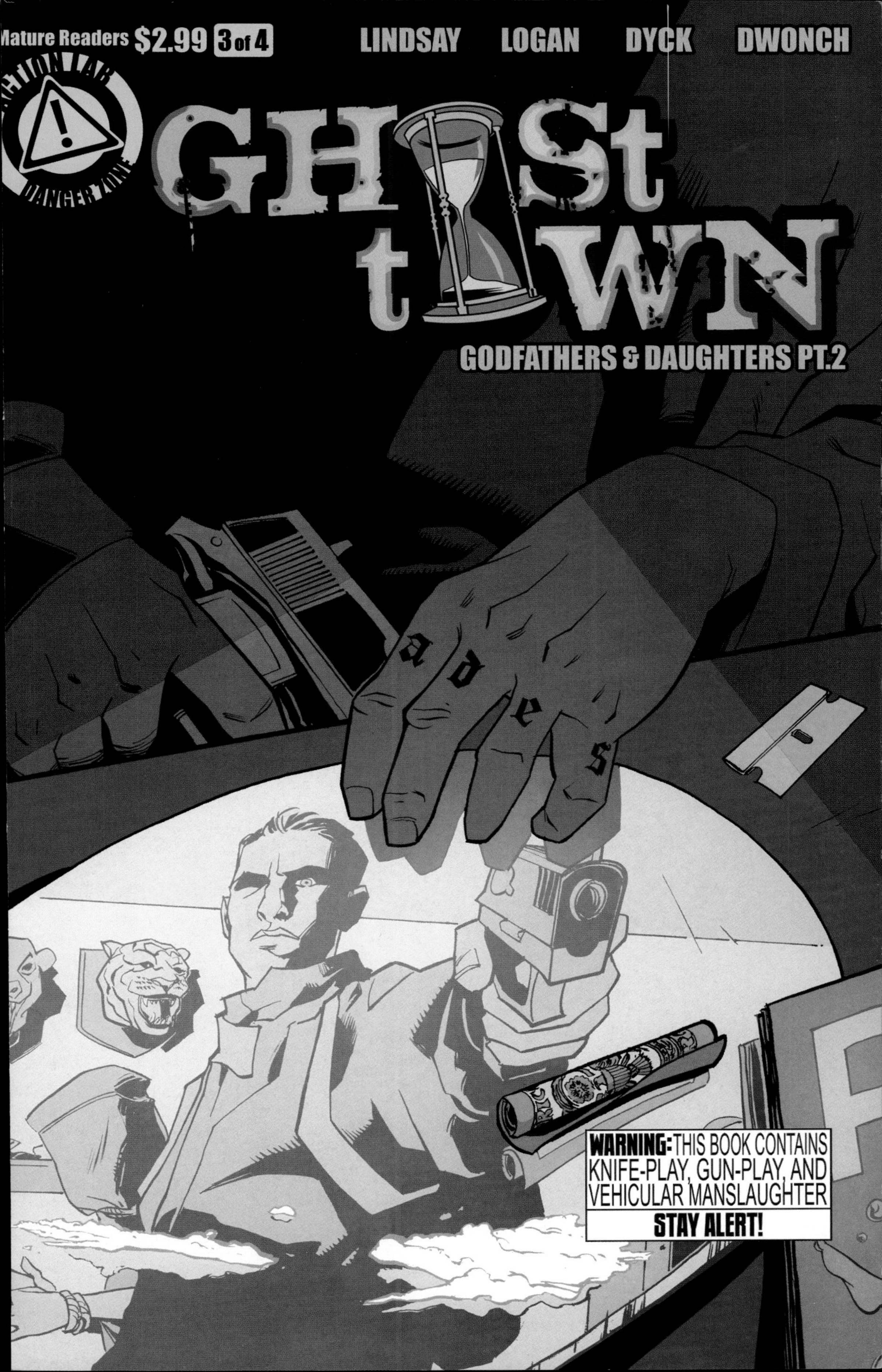

Mature Readers $2.99 3 of 4
LINDSAY LOGAN DYCK DWONCH
ACTION LAB DANGER ZONE
GHOSt tOWN
GODFATHERS & DAUGHTERS PT.2
a d e s
WARNING: THIS BOOK CONTAINS KNIFE-PLAY, GUN-PLAY, AND VEHICULAR MANSLAUGHTER
STAY ALERT!

GODFATHERS & DAUGHTERS
PART 2

GHOST TOWN CREATED BY ROB RUDDELL & DAVE DWONCH
EDITED BY SHAWN GABBORIN
COVER BY JUSTIN GREENWOOD & JORDIE BELLAIRE

RYAN K LINDSAY
WORDS
DANIEL LOGAN
PICTURES
BRIAN DYCK
COLORS
DAVE DWONCH
LETTERS

ACTION LAB DANGER ZONE

JASON MARTIN - PUBLISHER
KEVIN FREEMAN - PRESIDENT
SHAWN PRYOR - VP DIGITAL MEDIA
DAVE DWONCH - CREATIVE DIRECTOR
SHAWN GABBORIN - EDITOR IN CHIEF
JEREMY WHITLEY - MARKETING DIRECTOR
CHAD CICCONI - ASSOCIATE EDITOR
COLLEEN BOYD - ASSOCIATE EDITOR

GHOST TOWN #3, September 2013.

Printed in Canada.
First printing.
ACTIONLABCOMICS.COM/DANGER-ZONE

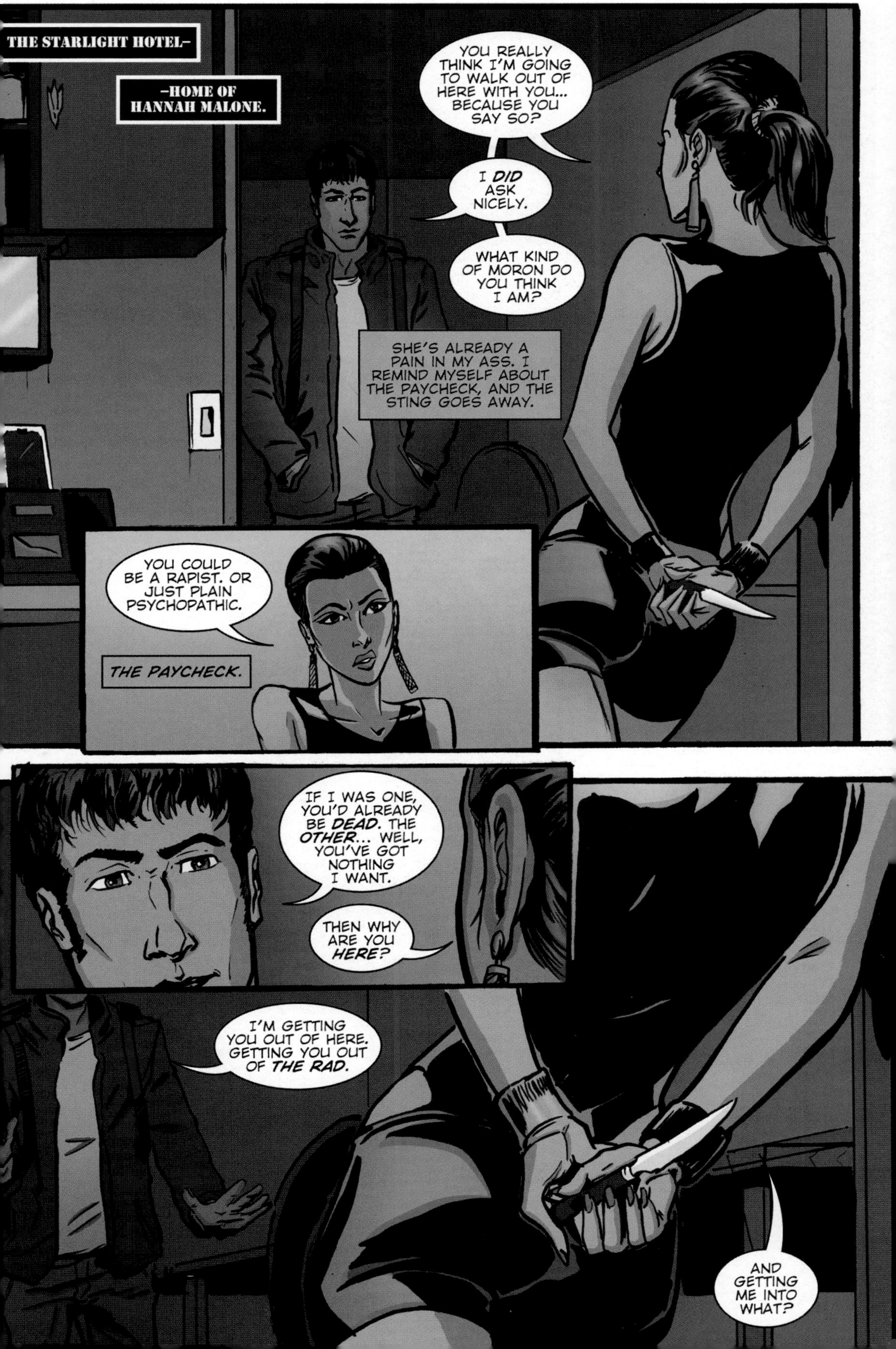

THE STARLIGHT HOTEL–
–HOME OF HANNAH MALONE.
YOU REALLY THINK I'M GOING TO WALK OUT OF HERE WITH YOU... BECAUSE YOU SAY SO?
I *DID* ASK NICELY.
WHAT KIND OF MORON DO YOU THINK I AM?
SHE'S ALREADY A PAIN IN MY ASS. I REMIND MYSELF ABOUT THE PAYCHECK, AND THE STING GOES AWAY.
YOU COULD BE A RAPIST. OR JUST PLAIN PSYCHOPATHIC.
THE PAYCHECK.
IF I WAS ONE, YOU'D ALREADY BE *DEAD*. THE *OTHER*... WELL, YOU'VE GOT NOTHING I WANT.
THEN WHY ARE YOU *HERE?*
I'M GETTING YOU OUT OF HERE. GETTING YOU OUT OF *THE RAD.*
AND GETTING ME INTO WHAT?

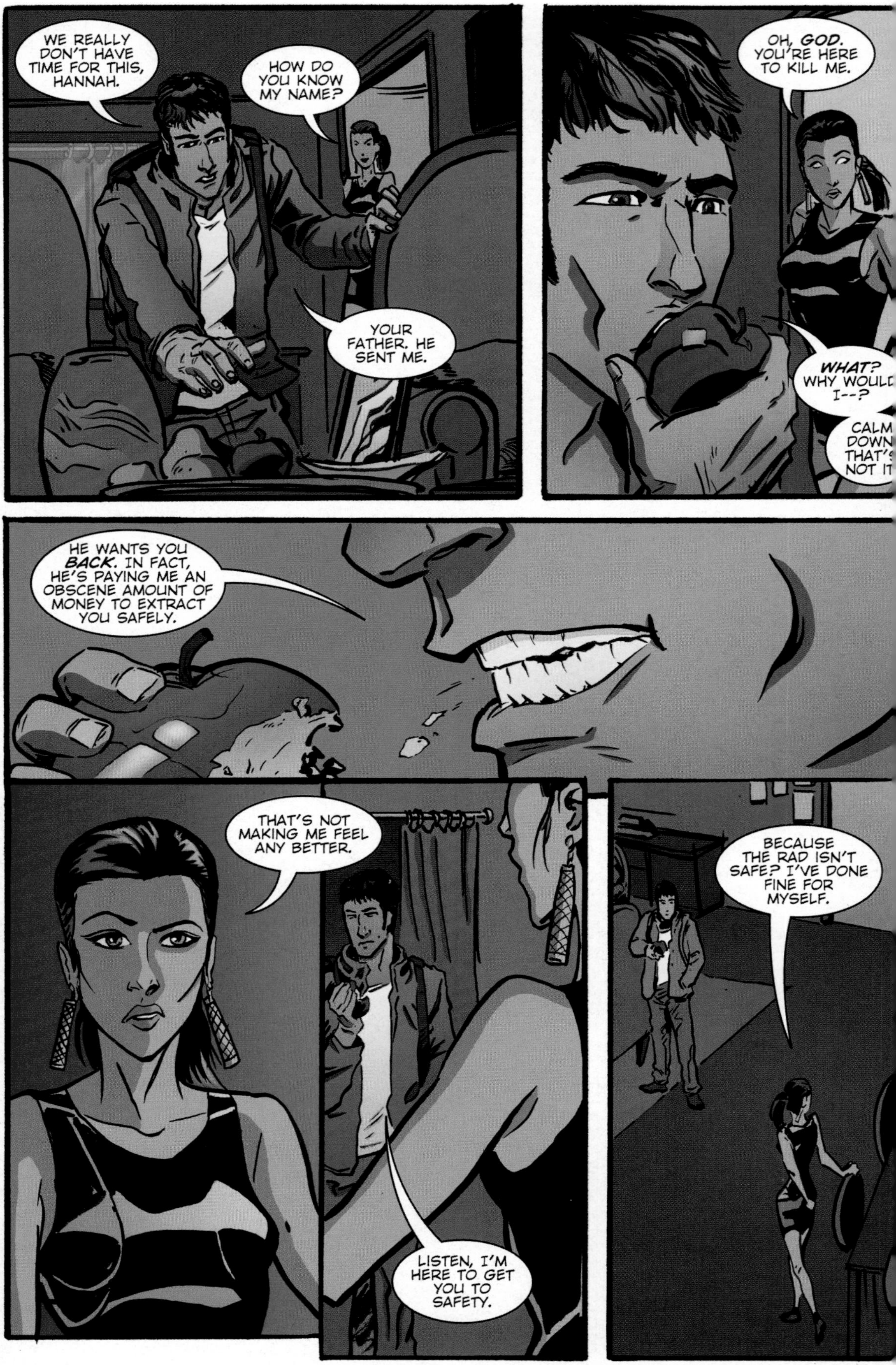
WE REALLY DON'T HAVE TIME FOR THIS, HANNAH.
HOW DO YOU KNOW MY NAME?
YOUR FATHER. HE SENT ME.
OH, **GOD**. YOU'RE HERE TO KILL ME.
WHAT? WHY WOULD I--?
CALM DOWN THAT'S NOT IT
HE WANTS YOU **BACK**. IN FACT, HE'S PAYING ME AN OBSCENE AMOUNT OF MONEY TO EXTRACT YOU SAFELY.
THAT'S NOT MAKING ME FEEL ANY BETTER.
LISTEN, I'M HERE TO GET YOU TO SAFETY.
BECAUSE THE RAD ISN'T SAFE? I'VE DONE FINE FOR MYSELF.

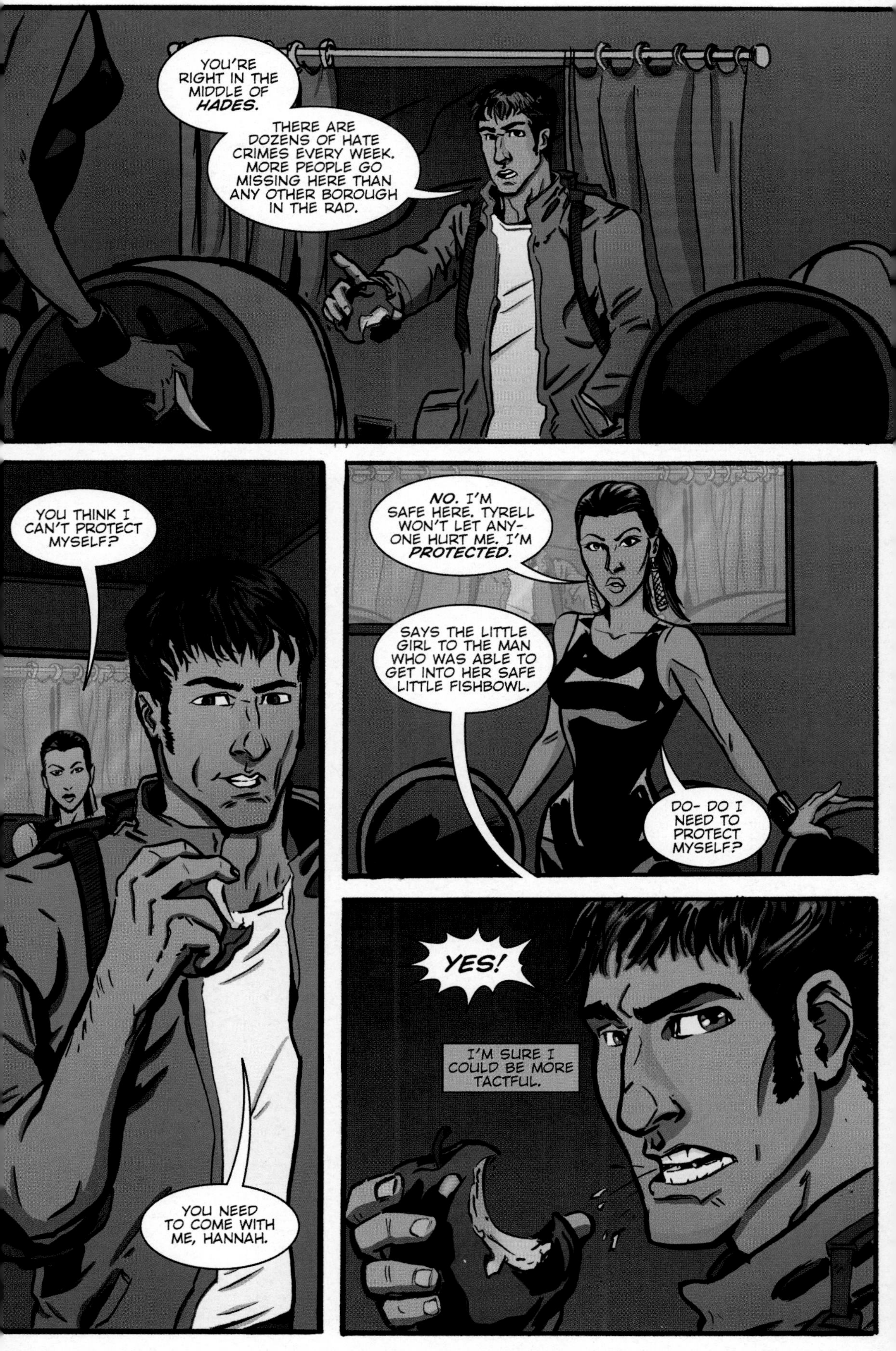
YOU'RE RIGHT IN THE MIDDLE OF HADES.
THERE ARE DOZENS OF HATE CRIMES EVERY WEEK. MORE PEOPLE GO MISSING HERE THAN ANY OTHER BOROUGH IN THE RAD.
YOU THINK I CAN'T PROTECT MYSELF?
YOU NEED TO COME WITH ME, HANNAH.
NO. I'M SAFE HERE. TYRELL WON'T LET ANY-ONE HURT ME. I'M PROTECTED.
SAYS THE LITTLE GIRL TO THE MAN WHO WAS ABLE TO GET INTO HER SAFE LITTLE FISHBOWL.
DO- DO I NEED TO PROTECT MYSELF?
YES!
I'M SURE I COULD BE MORE TACTFUL.

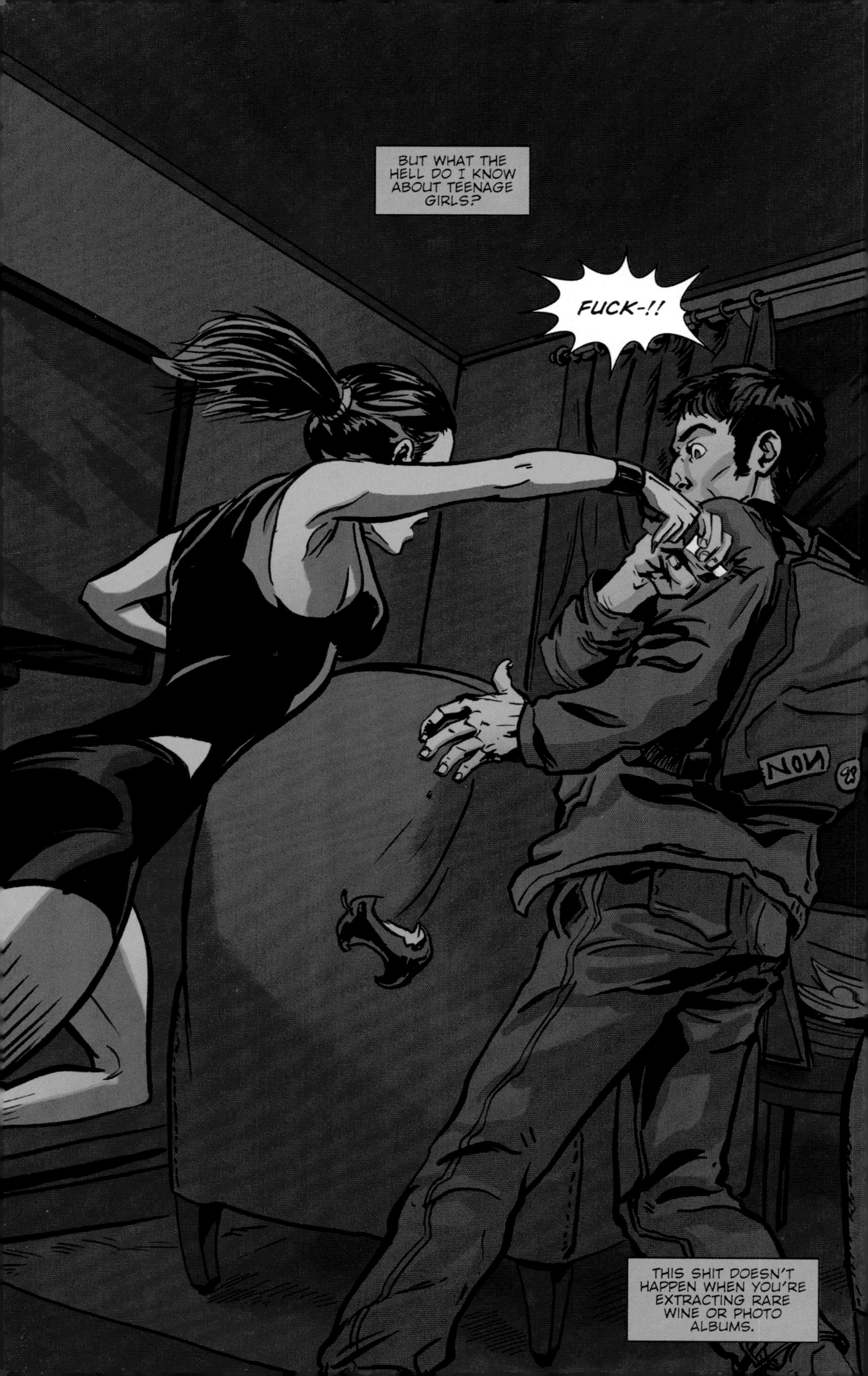
BUT WHAT THE HELL DO I KNOW ABOUT TEENAGE GIRLS?
FUCK-!!
NOV
THIS SHIT DOESN'T HAPPEN WHEN YOU'RE EXTRACTING RARE WINE OR PHOTO ALBUMS.

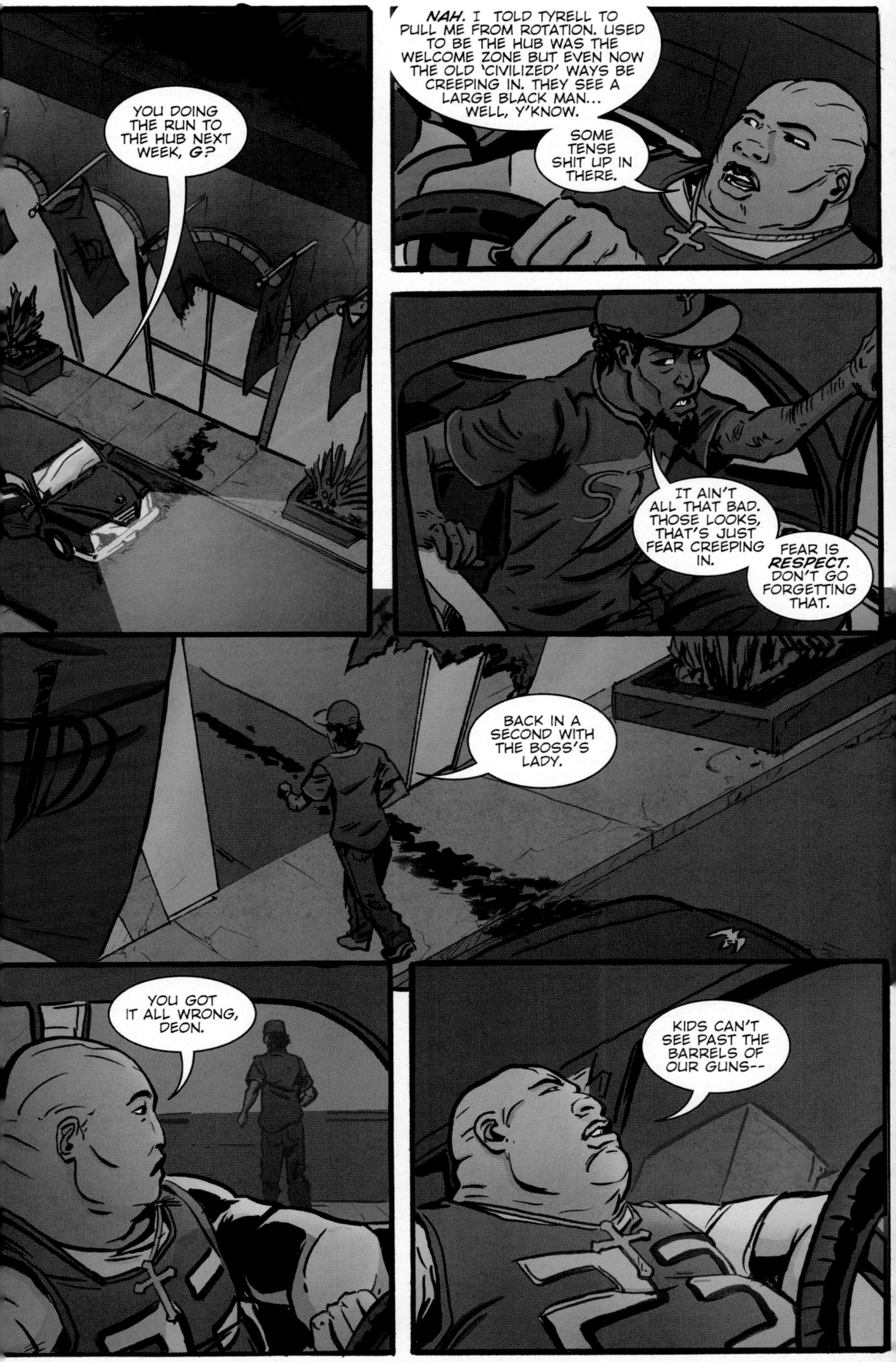
YOU DOING THE RUN TO THE HUB NEXT WEEK, G?
NAH. I TOLD TYRELL TO PULL ME FROM ROTATION. USED TO BE THE HUB WAS THE WELCOME ZONE BUT EVEN NOW THE OLD 'CIVILIZED' WAYS BE CREEPING IN. THEY SEE A LARGE BLACK MAN... WELL, Y'KNOW.
SOME TENSE SHIT UP IN THERE.
IT AIN'T ALL THAT BAD. THOSE LOOKS, THAT'S JUST FEAR CREEPING IN.
FEAR IS RESPECT. DON'T GO FORGETTING THAT.
BACK IN A SECOND WITH THE BOSS'S LADY.
YOU GOT IT ALL WRONG, DEON.
KIDS CAN'T SEE PAST THE BARRELS OF OUR GUNS--

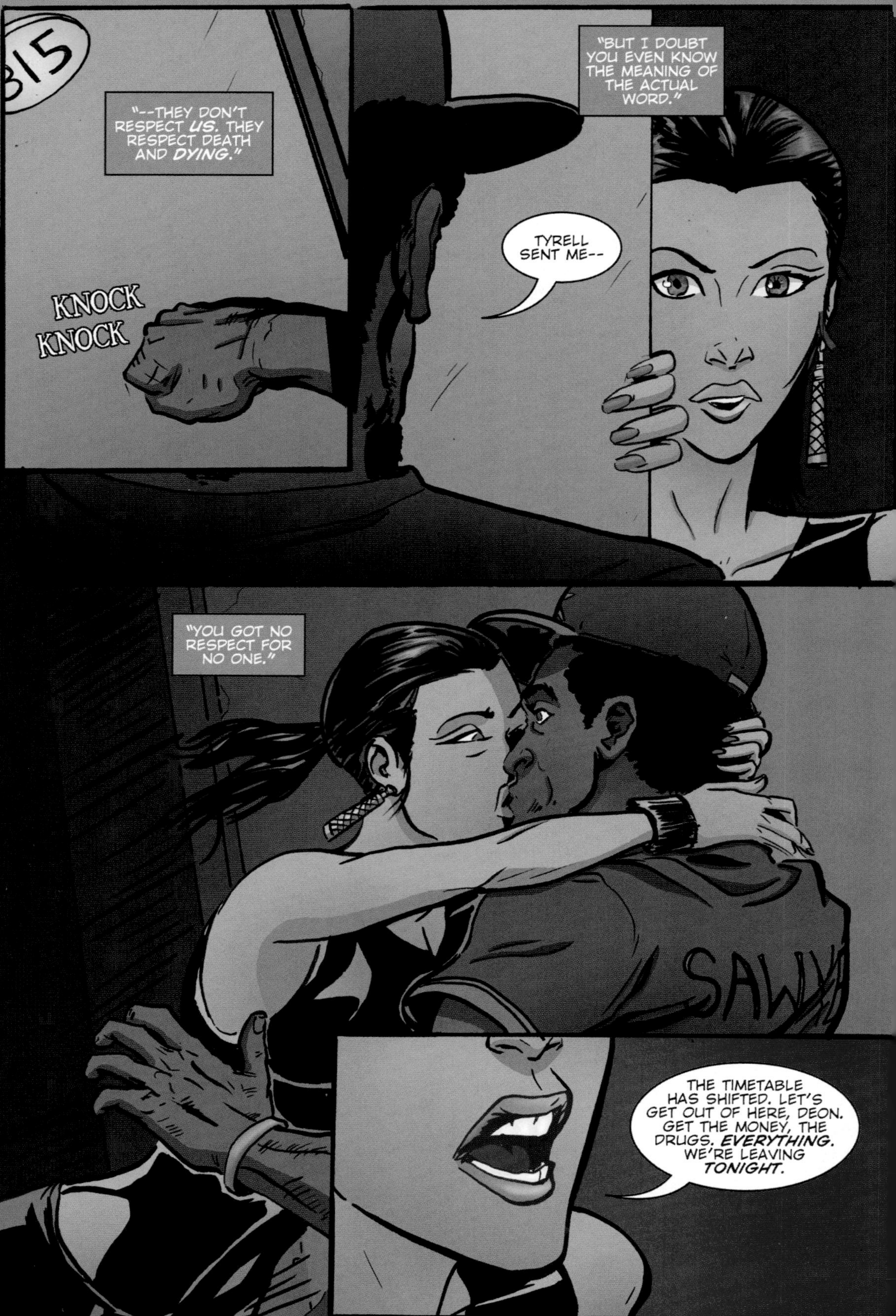
315
"--THEY DON'T RESPECT *US.* THEY RESPECT DEATH AND *DYING.*"
KNOCK KNOCK
"BUT I DOUBT YOU EVEN KNOW THE MEANING OF THE ACTUAL WORD."
TYRELL SENT ME--
"YOU GOT NO RESPECT FOR NO ONE."
SAWY
THE TIMETABLE HAS SHIFTED. LET'S GET OUT OF HERE, DEON. GET THE MONEY, THE DRUGS. *EVERYTHING.* WE'RE LEAVING *TONIGHT.*

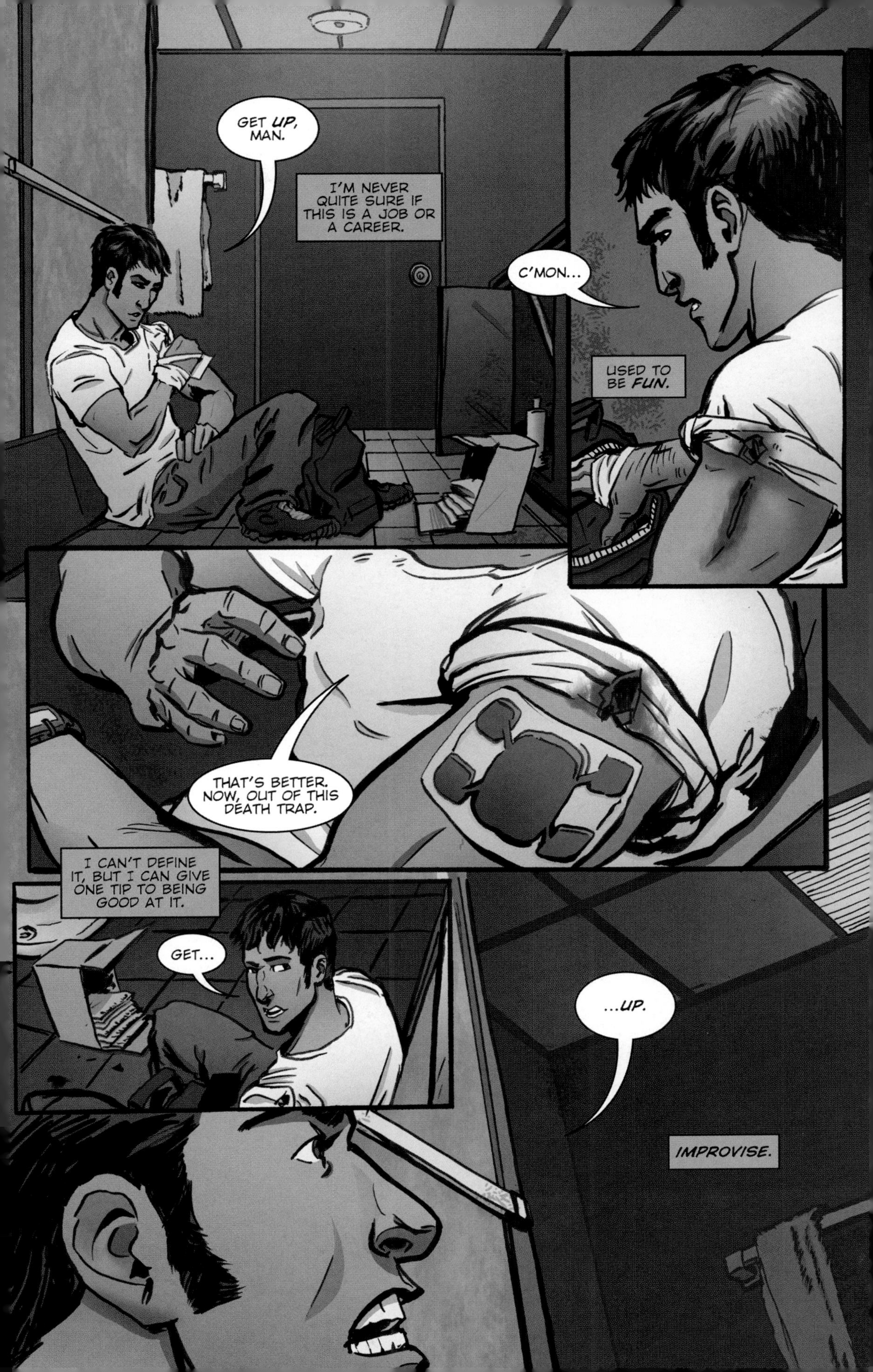
GET UP, MAN.
I'M NEVER QUITE SURE IF THIS IS A JOB OR A CAREER.
C'MON...
USED TO BE FUN.
THAT'S BETTER. NOW, OUT OF THIS DEATH TRAP.
I CAN'T DEFINE IT, BUT I CAN GIVE ONE TIP TO BEING GOOD AT IT.
GET...
...UP.
IMPROVISE.

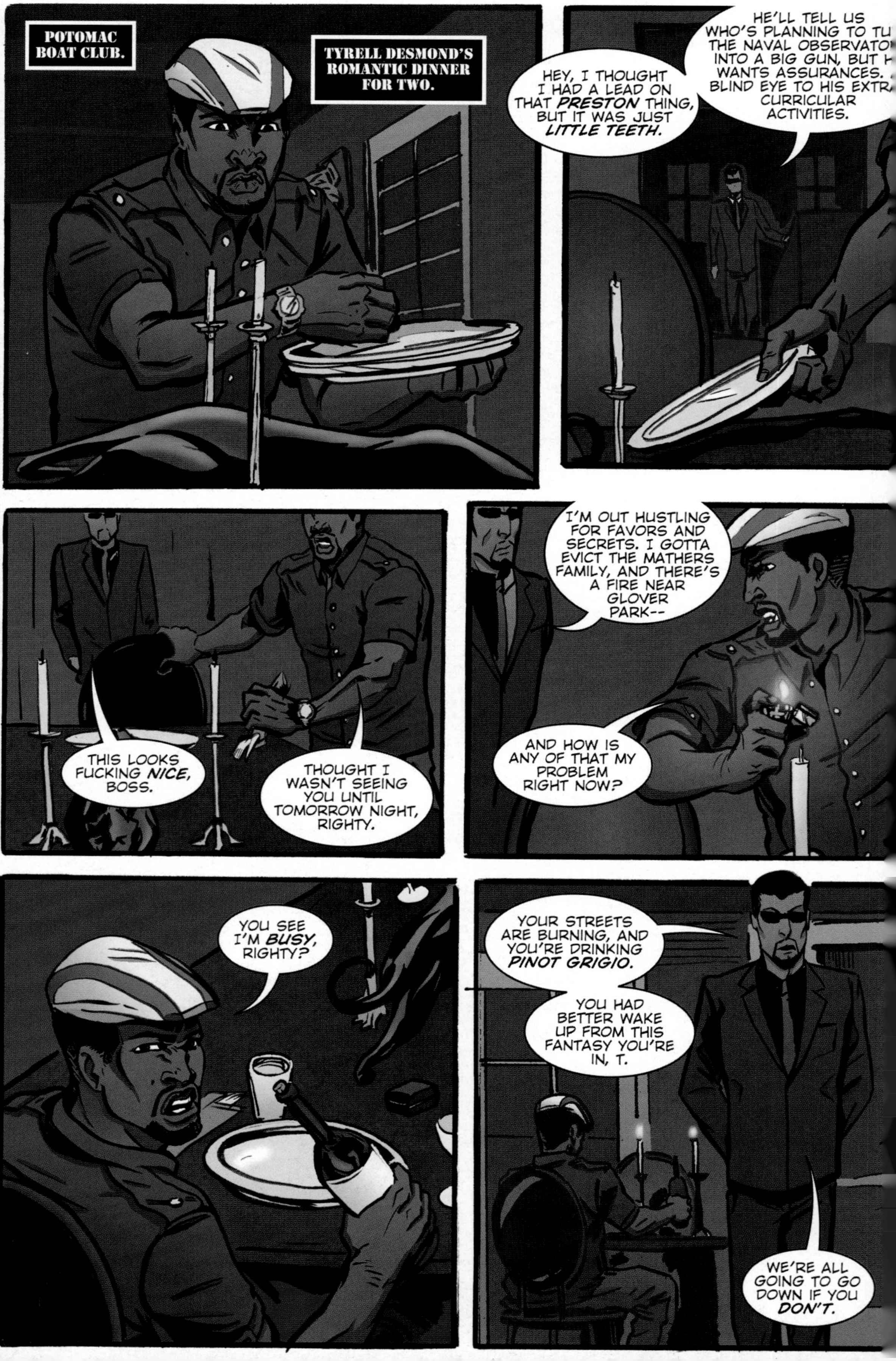
POTOMAC BOAT CLUB.
TYRELL DESMOND'S ROMANTIC DINNER FOR TWO.
HEY, I THOUGHT I HAD A LEAD ON THAT PRESTON THING, BUT IT WAS JUST LITTLE TEETH.
HE'LL TELL US WHO'S PLANNING TO TU THE NAVAL OBSERVATO INTO A BIG GUN, BUT H WANTS ASSURANCES. BLIND EYE TO HIS EXTR CURRICULAR ACTIVITIES.
THIS LOOKS FUCKING NICE, BOSS.
THOUGHT I WASN'T SEEING YOU UNTIL TOMORROW NIGHT, RIGHTY.
I'M OUT HUSTLING FOR FAVORS AND SECRETS. I GOTTA EVICT THE MATHERS FAMILY, AND THERE'S A FIRE NEAR GLOVER PARK--
AND HOW IS ANY OF THAT MY PROBLEM RIGHT NOW?
YOU SEE I'M BUSY, RIGHTY?
YOUR STREETS ARE BURNING, AND YOU'RE DRINKING PINOT GRIGIO.
YOU HAD BETTER WAKE UP FROM THIS FANTASY YOU'RE IN, T.
WE'RE ALL GOING TO GO DOWN IF YOU DON'T.

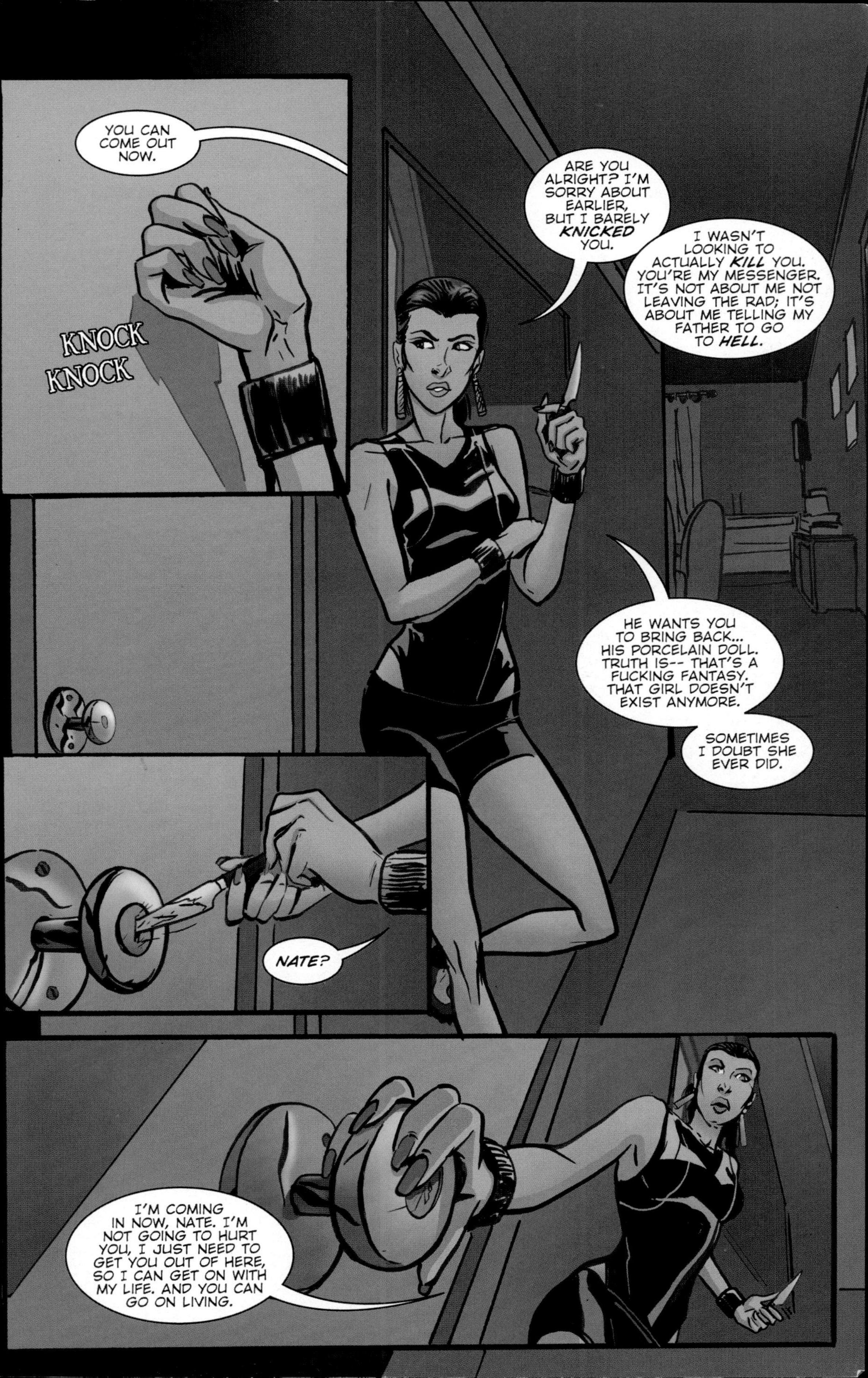
YOU CAN COME OUT NOW.
KNOCK KNOCK
ARE YOU ALRIGHT? I'M SORRY ABOUT EARLIER, BUT I BARELY KNICKED YOU.
I WASN'T LOOKING TO ACTUALLY KILL YOU. YOU'RE MY MESSENGER. IT'S NOT ABOUT ME NOT LEAVING THE RAD; IT'S ABOUT ME TELLING MY FATHER TO GO TO HELL.
HE WANTS YOU TO BRING BACK... HIS PORCELAIN DOLL. TRUTH IS-- THAT'S A FUCKING FANTASY. THAT GIRL DOESN'T EXIST ANYMORE.
SOMETIMES I DOUBT SHE EVER DID.
NATE?
I'M COMING IN NOW, NATE. I'M NOT GOING TO HURT YOU, I JUST NEED TO GET YOU OUT OF HERE, SO I CAN GET ON WITH MY LIFE. AND YOU CAN GO ON LIVING.

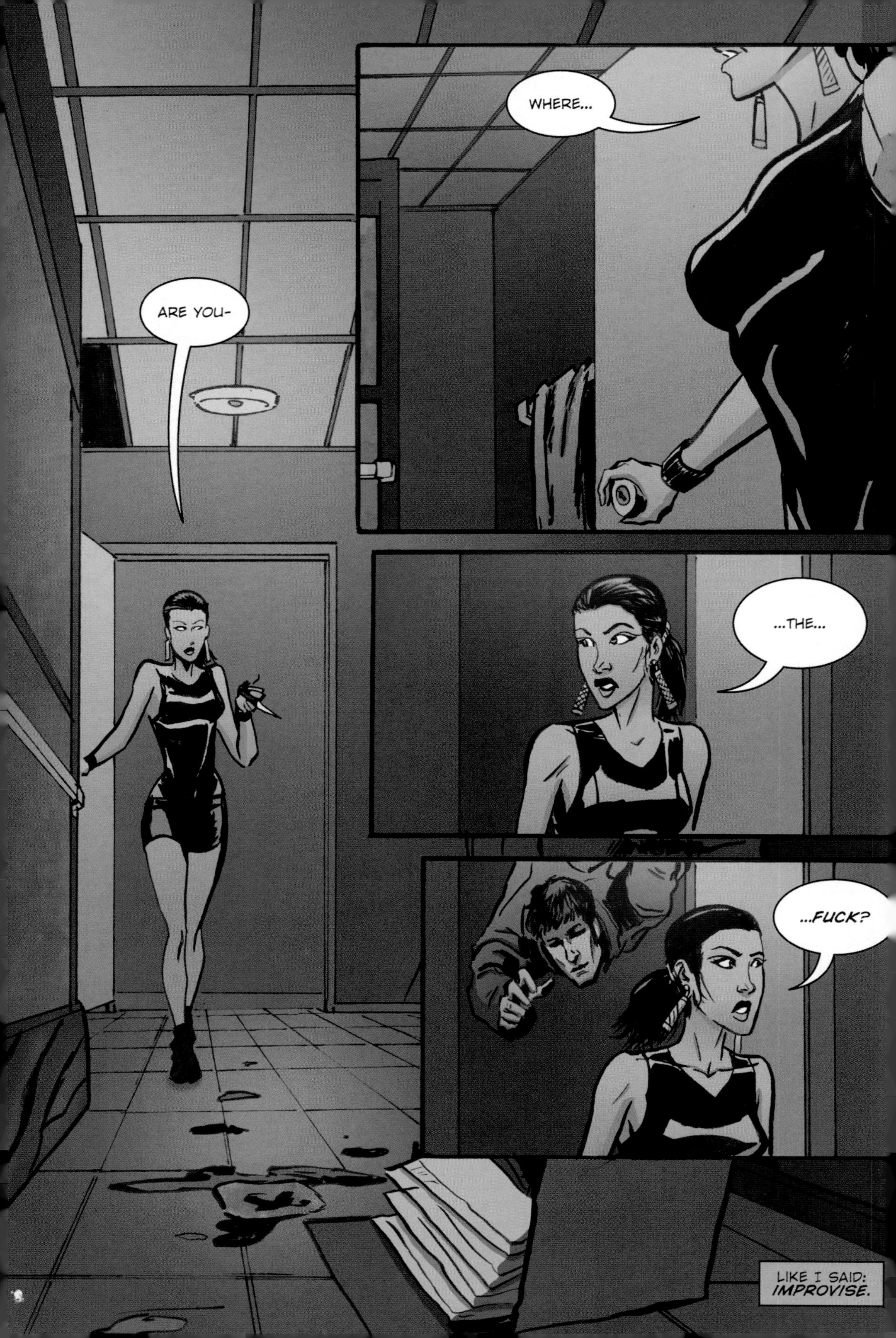
ARE YOU-
WHERE...
...THE...
...FUCK?
LIKE I SAID: IMPROVISE.

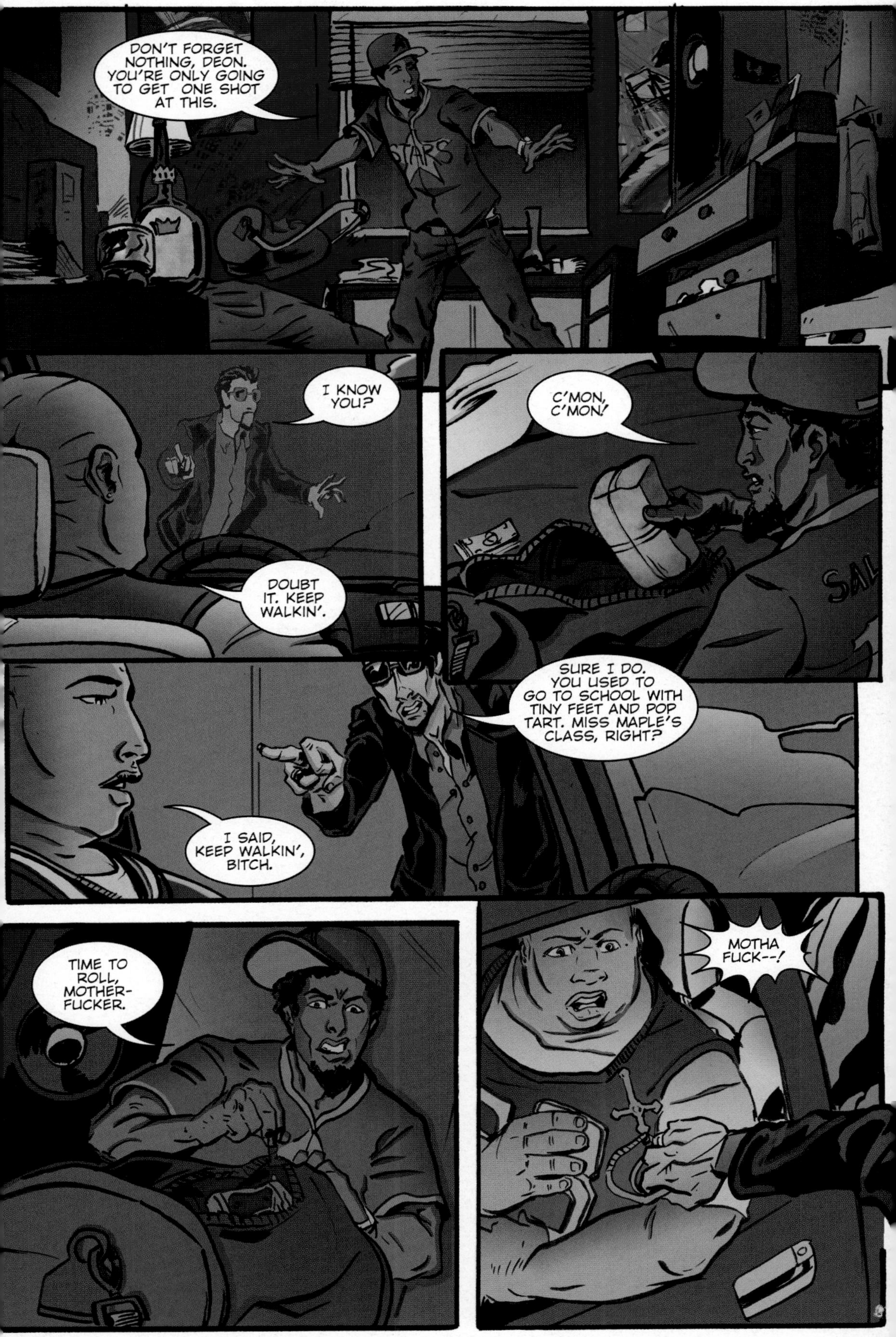
DON'T FORGET NOTHING, DEON. YOU'RE ONLY GOING TO GET ONE SHOT AT THIS.
I KNOW YOU?
DOUBT IT. KEEP WALKIN'.
C'MON, C'MON!
SURE I DO. YOU USED TO GO TO SCHOOL WITH TINY FEET AND POP TART. MISS MAPLE'S CLASS, RIGHT?
I SAID, KEEP WALKIN', BITCH.
TIME TO ROLL, MOTHER-FUCKER.
MOTHA FUCK--!

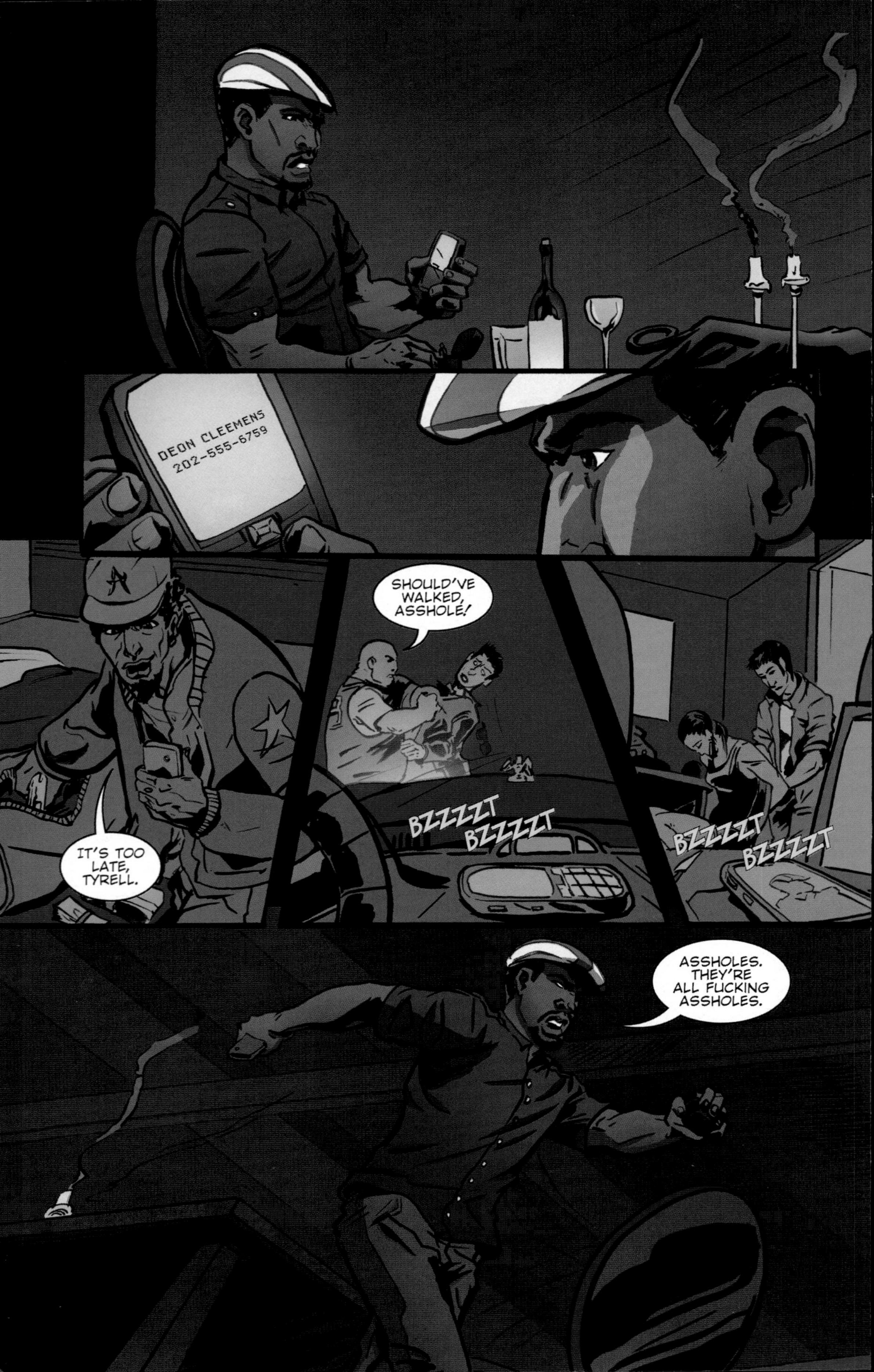
DEON CLEEMENS
202-555-6759
IT'S TOO LATE, TYRELL.
SHOULD'VE WALKED, ASSHOLE!
BZZZZZT BZZZZZT
BZZZZZT BZZZZZT
ASSHOLES. THEY'RE ALL FUCKING ASSHOLES.

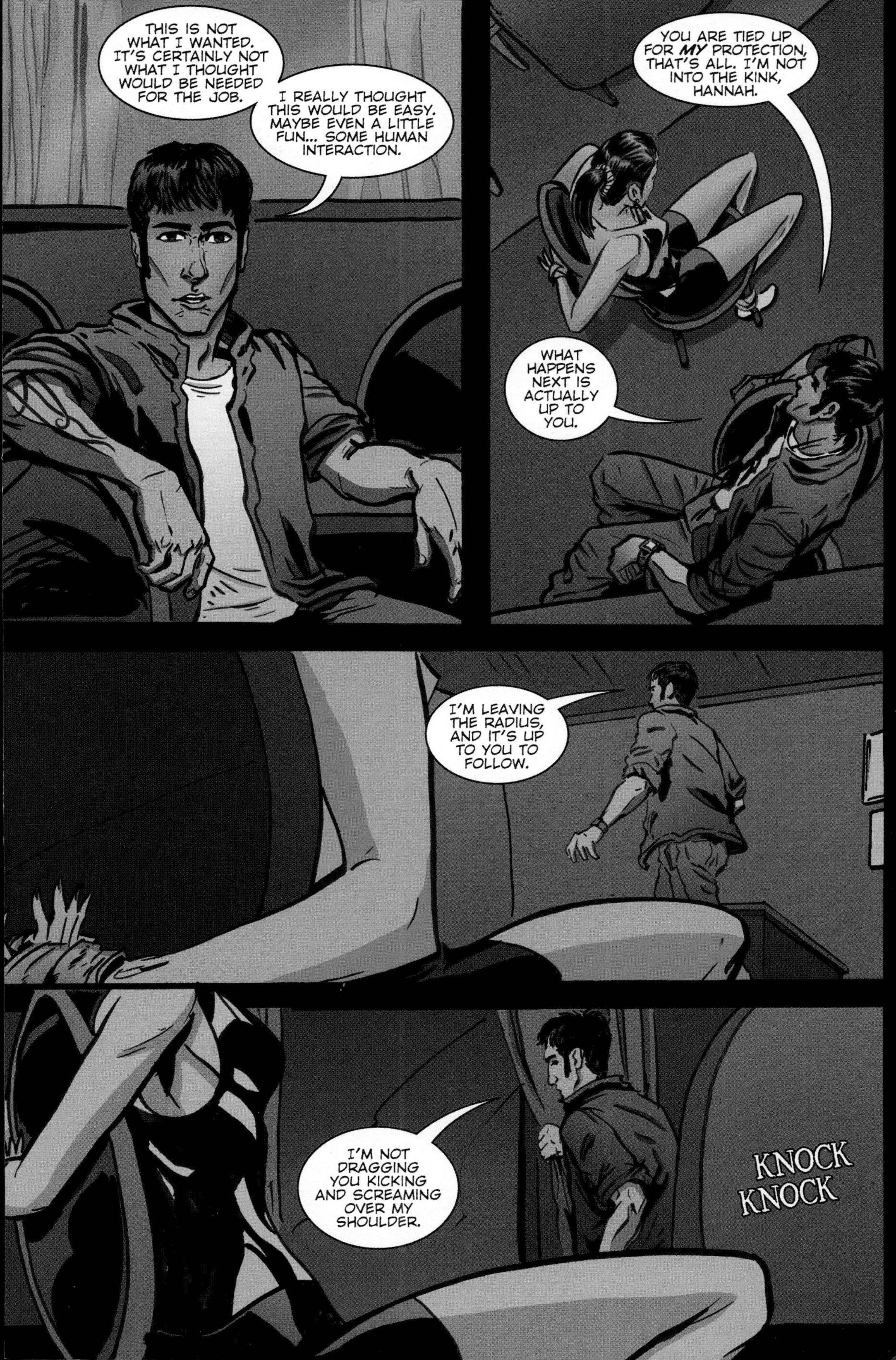
THIS IS NOT WHAT I WANTED. IT'S CERTAINLY NOT WHAT I THOUGHT WOULD BE NEEDED FOR THE JOB.
I REALLY THOUGHT THIS WOULD BE EASY. MAYBE EVEN A LITTLE FUN... SOME HUMAN INTERACTION.
YOU ARE TIED UP FOR *MY* PROTECTION, THAT'S ALL. I'M NOT INTO THE KINK, HANNAH.
WHAT HAPPENS NEXT IS ACTUALLY UP TO YOU.
I'M LEAVING THE RADIUS, AND IT'S UP TO YOU TO FOLLOW.
I'M NOT DRAGGING YOU KICKING AND SCREAMING OVER MY SHOULDER.
KNOCK KNOCK

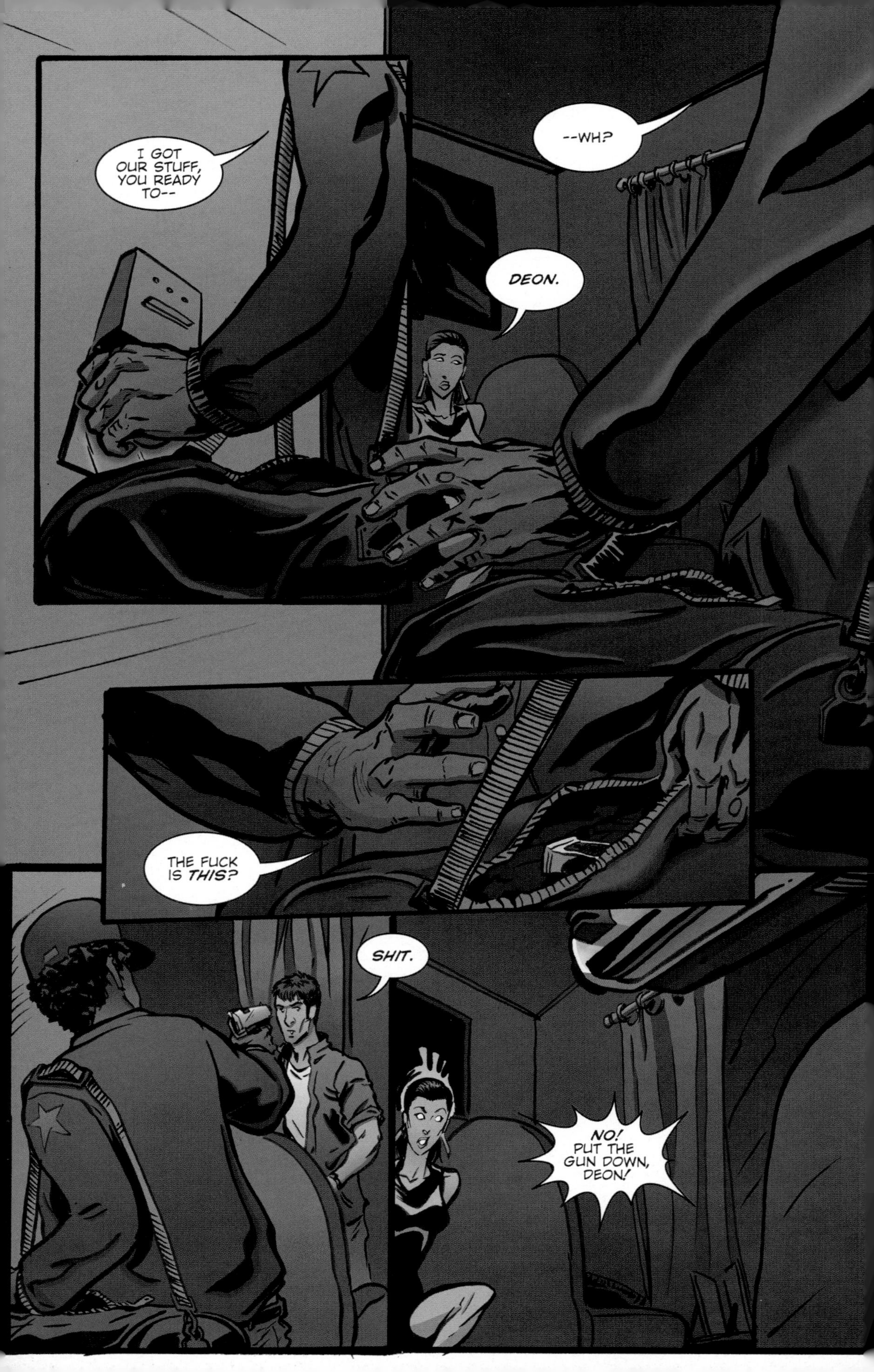
I GOT OUR STUFF, YOU READY TO--
--WH?
DEON.
THE FUCK IS *THIS?*
SHIT.
NO! PUT THE GUN DOWN, DEON!

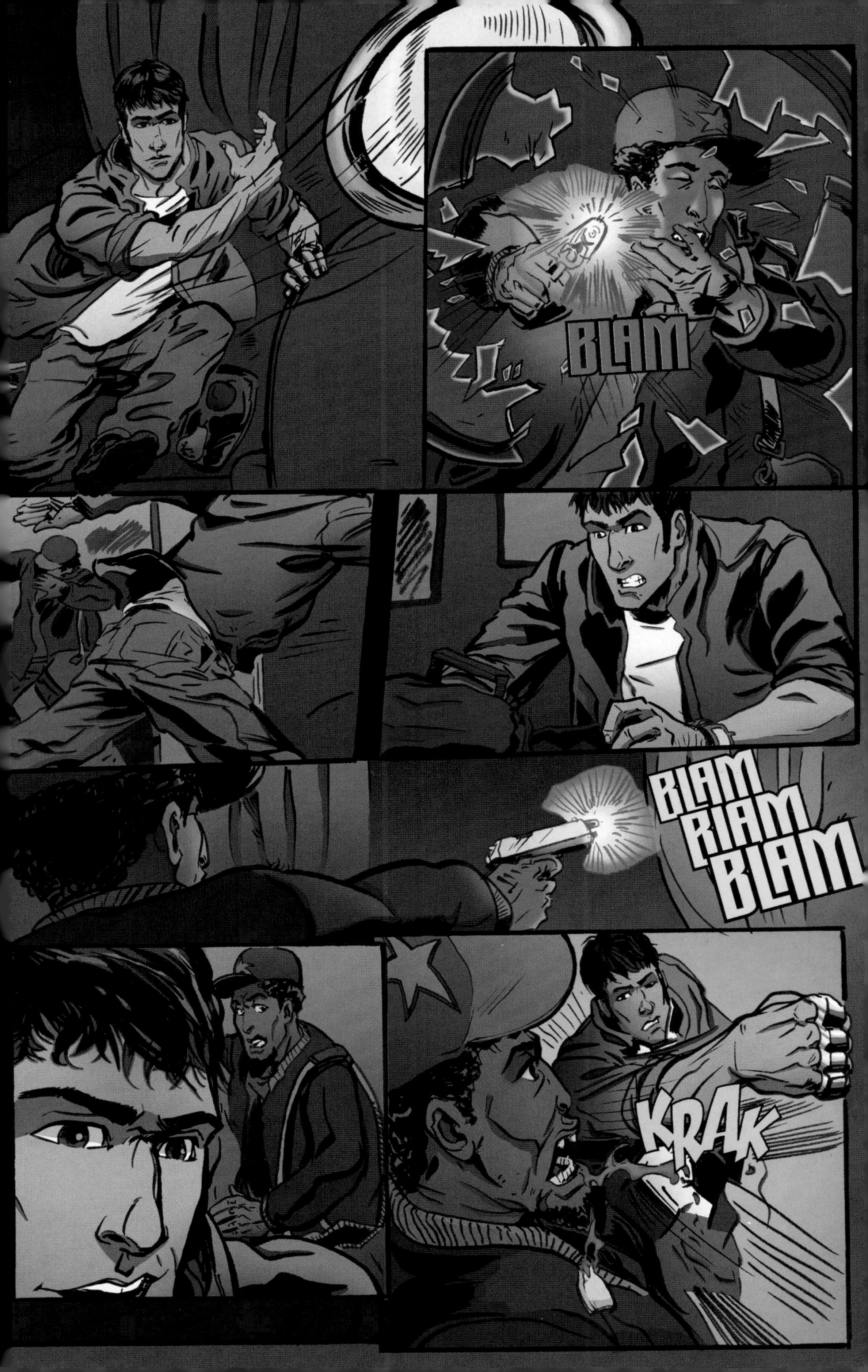
BLAM
BLAM
BLAM
BLAM
KRAK

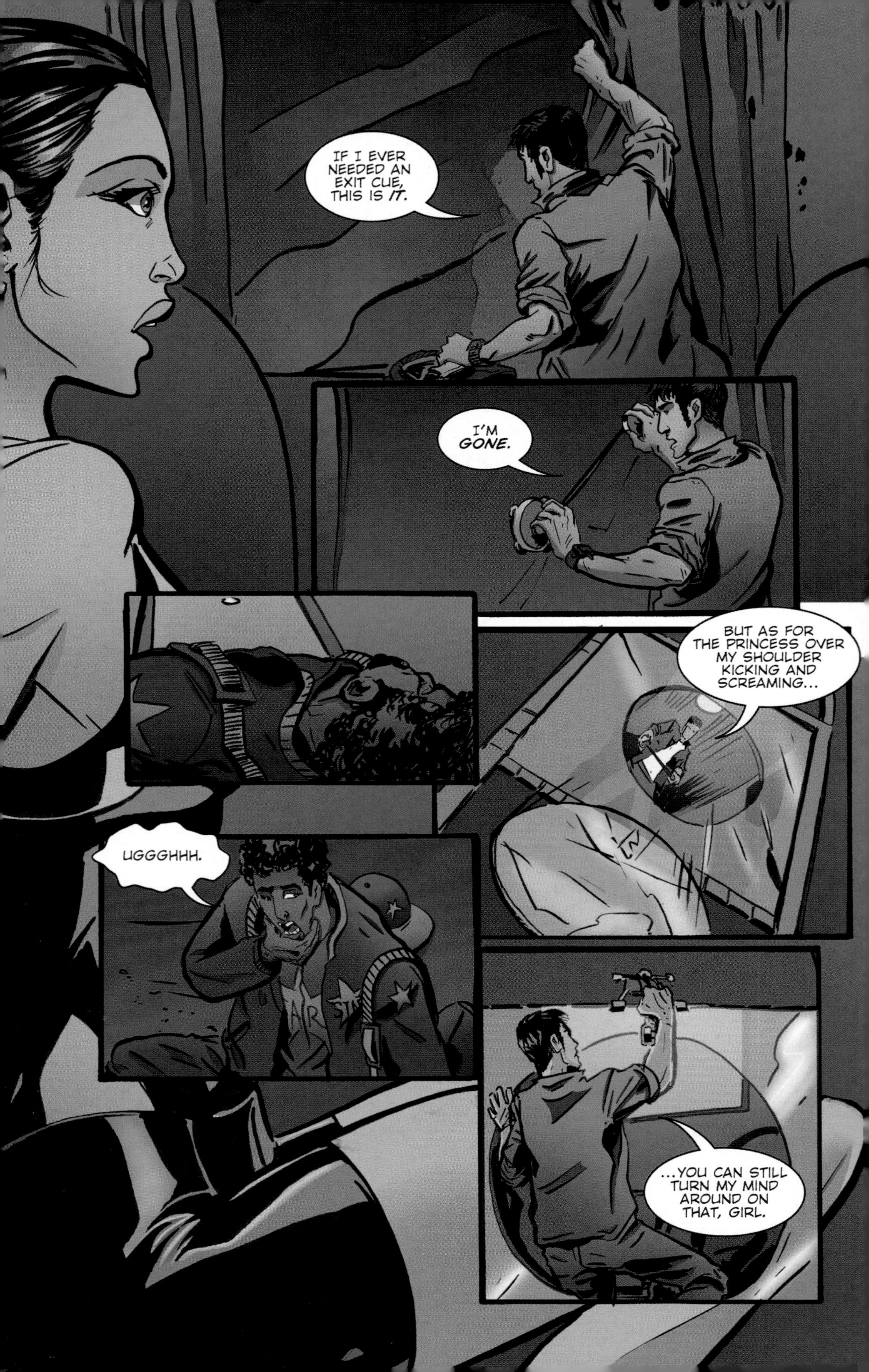
IF I EVER NEEDED AN EXIT CUE, THIS IS *IT*.
I'M *GONE*.
BUT AS FOR THE PRINCESS OVER MY SHOULDER KICKING AND SCREAMING...
UGGGHHH.
...YOU CAN STILL TURN MY MIND AROUND ON THAT, GIRL.

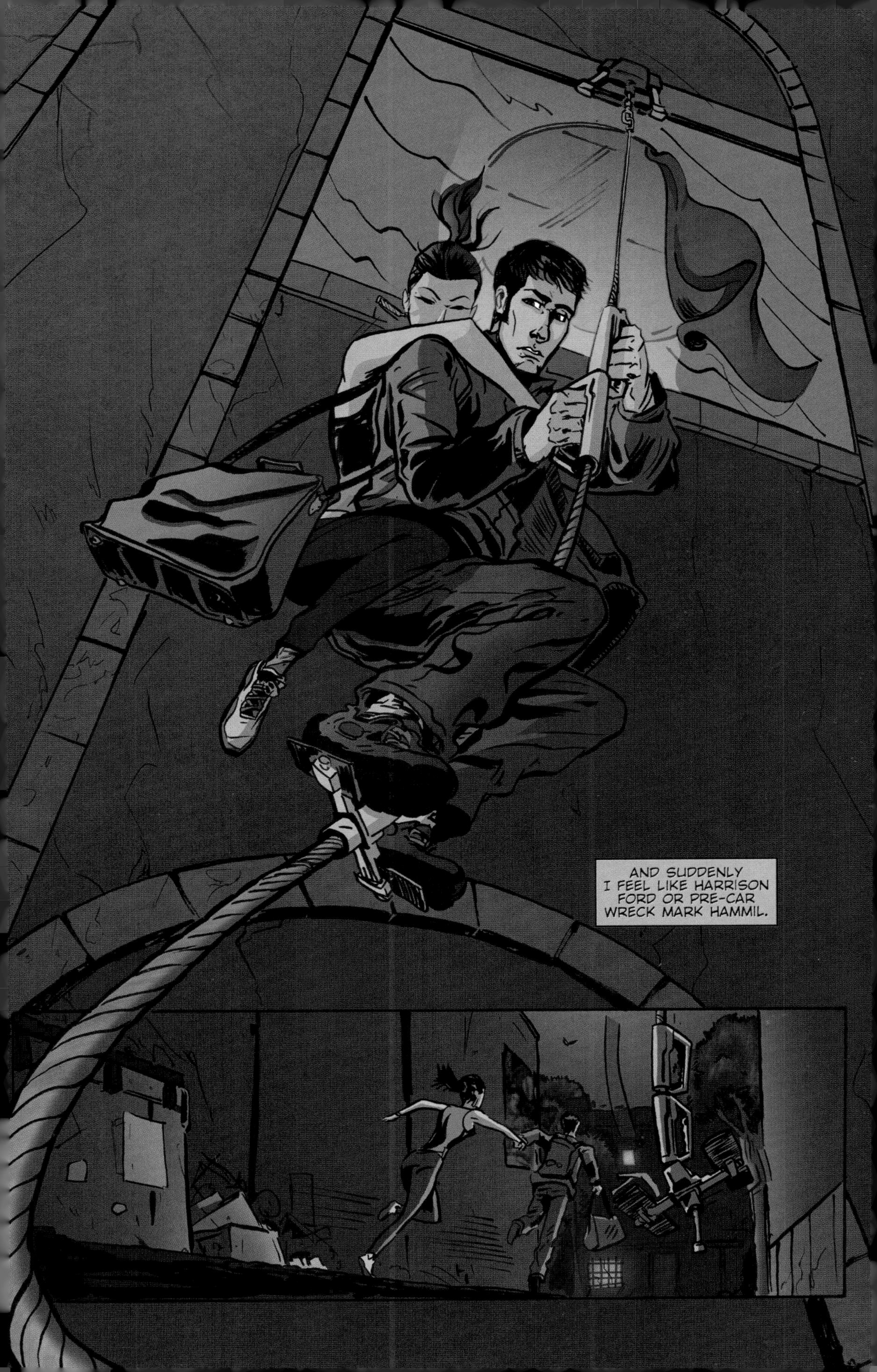
AND SUDDENLY I FEEL LIKE HARRISON FORD OR PRE-CAR WRECK MARK HAMMIL.

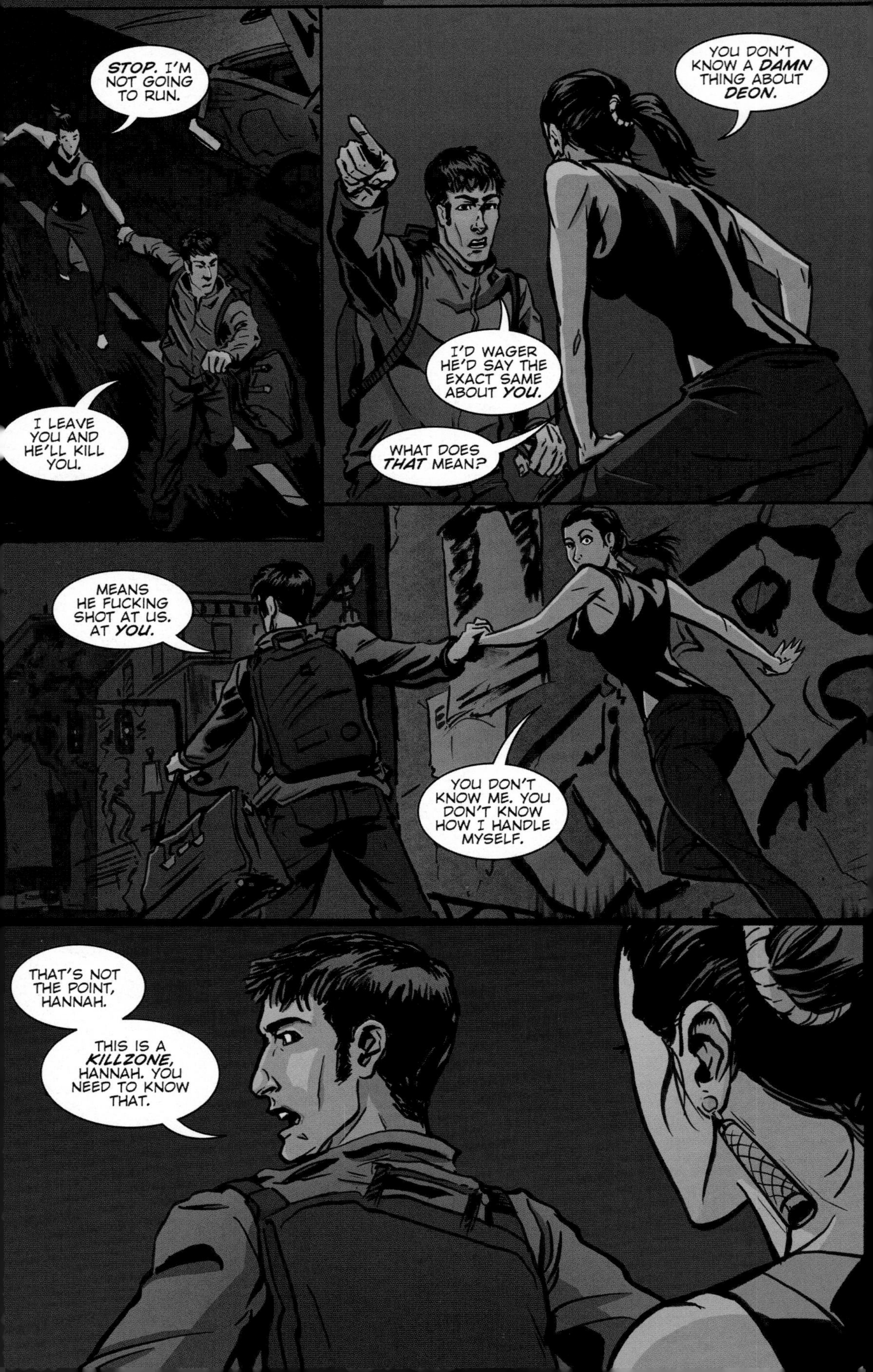
STOP. I'M NOT GOING TO RUN.
I LEAVE YOU AND HE'LL KILL YOU.
YOU DON'T KNOW A DAMN THING ABOUT DEON.
I'D WAGER HE'D SAY THE EXACT SAME ABOUT YOU.
WHAT DOES THAT MEAN?
MEANS HE FUCKING SHOT AT US. AT YOU.
YOU DON'T KNOW ME. YOU DON'T KNOW HOW I HANDLE MYSELF.
THAT'S NOT THE POINT, HANNAH.
THIS IS A KILLZONE, HANNAH. YOU NEED TO KNOW THAT.

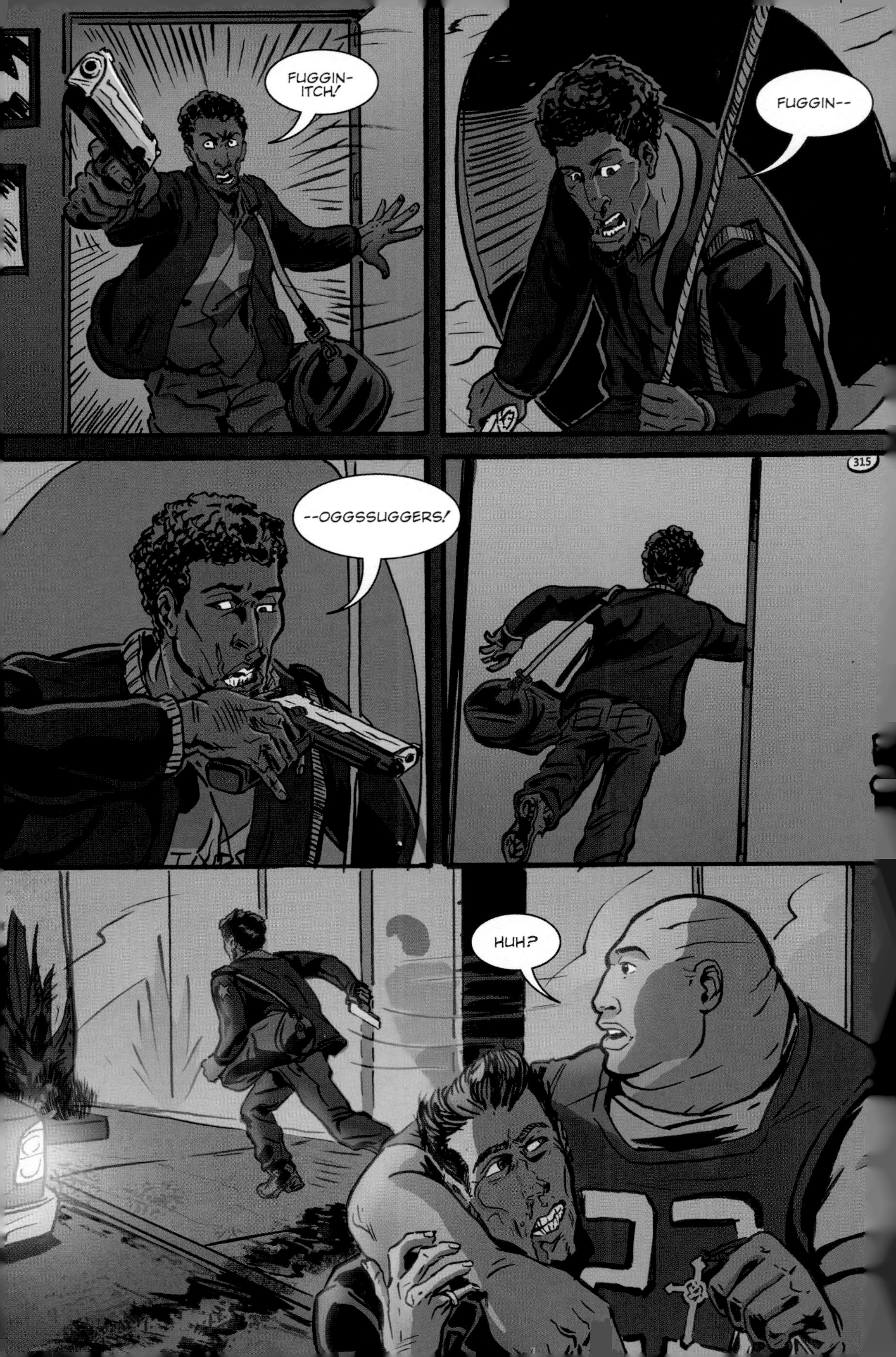

FUGGIN-ITCH!
FUGGIN--
--OGGSSUGGERS!
HUH?

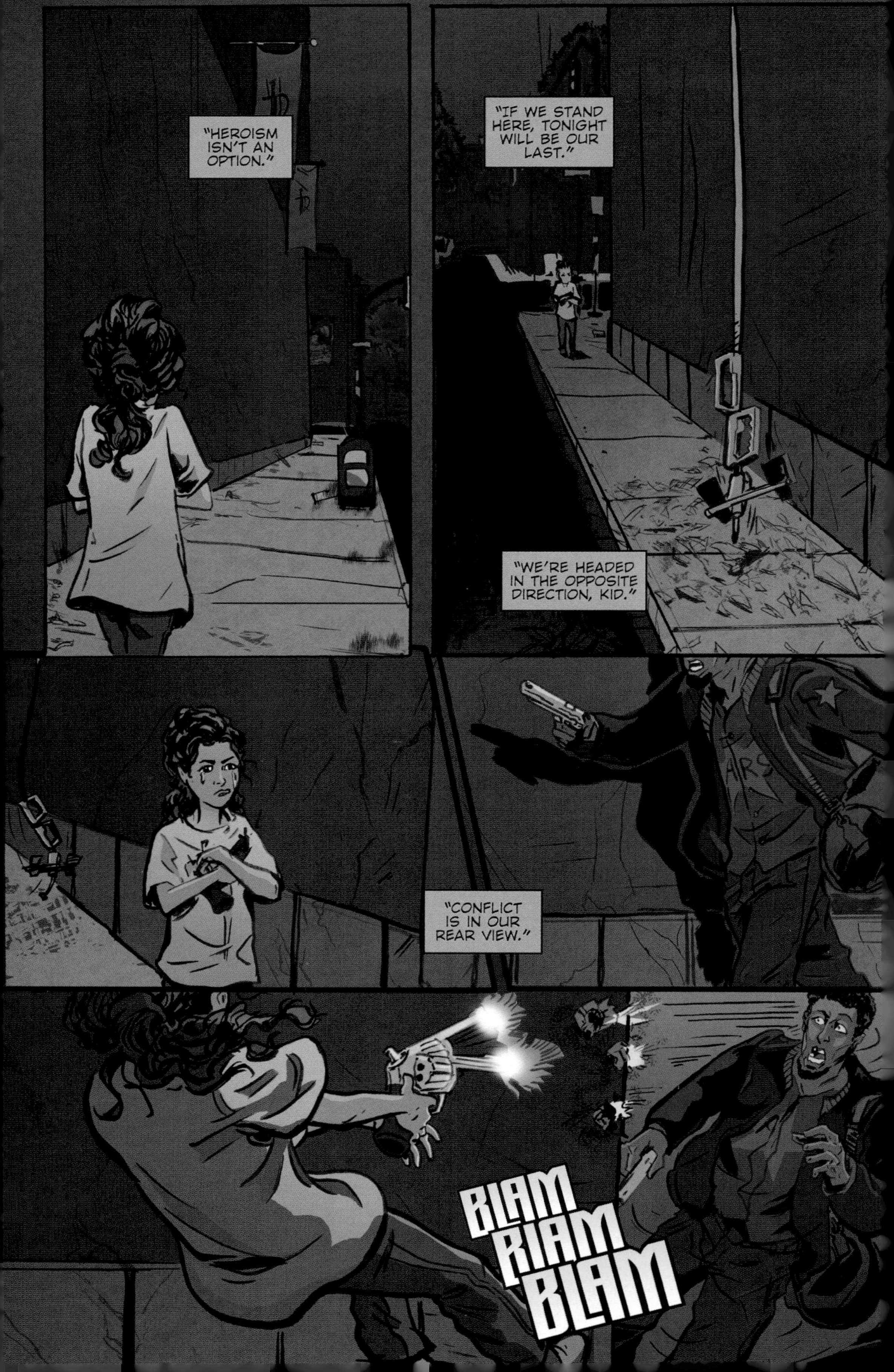
"HEROISM ISN'T AN OPTION."
"IF WE STAND HERE, TONIGHT WILL BE OUR LAST."
"WE'RE HEADED IN THE OPPOSITE DIRECTION, KID."
"CONFLICT IS IN OUR REAR VIEW."
BLAM
BLAM
BLAM

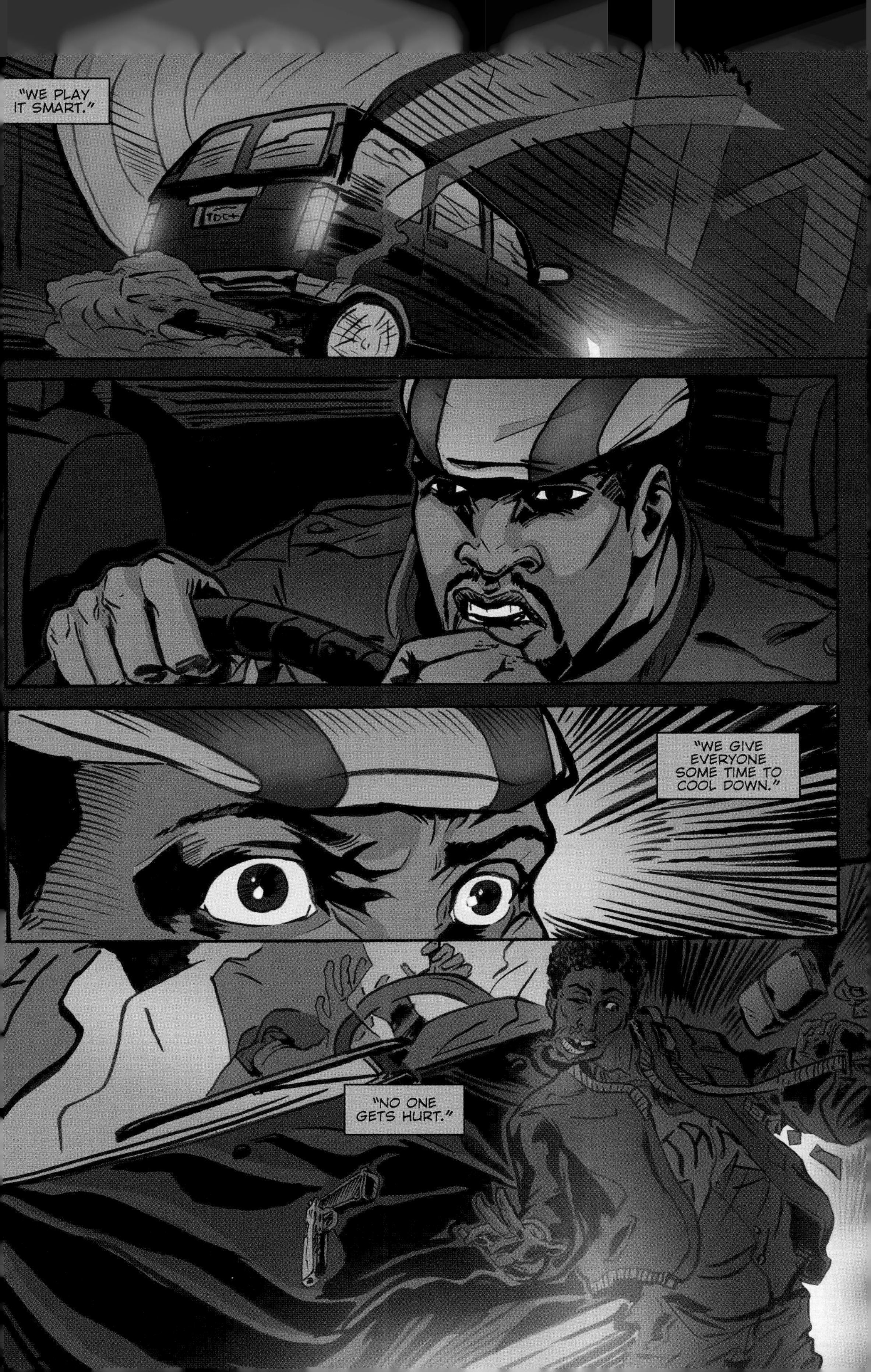
"WE PLAY IT SMART."
"WE GIVE EVERYONE SOME TIME TO COOL DOWN."
"NO ONE GETS HURT."

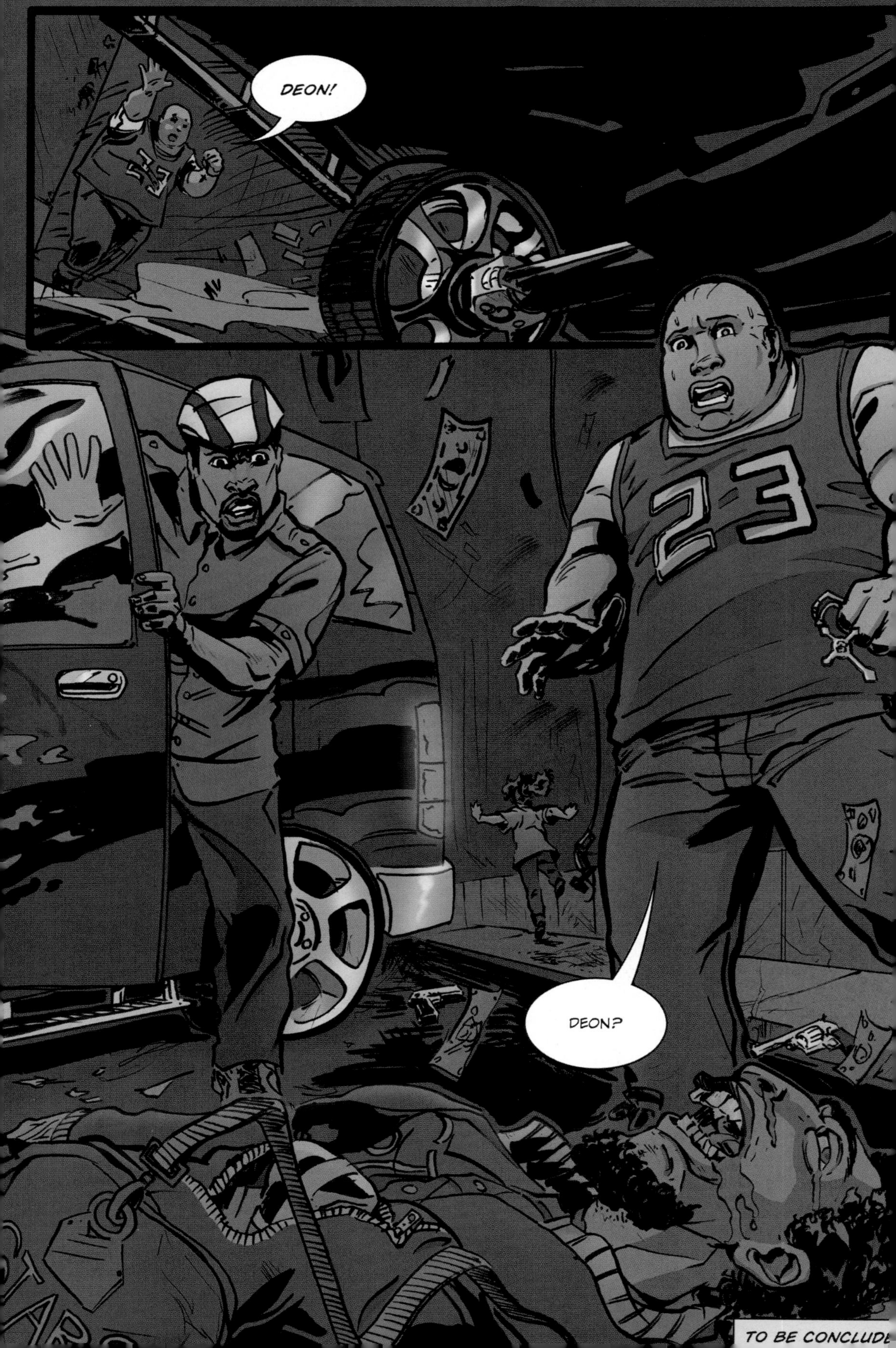
DEON!
DEON?
TO BE CONCLUDE

GHOSTWRITTEN

This time our GHOSTWRITTEN section features some words from GHOST TOWN co-creator Rob Ruddell.

I have always loved time travel stories. Throughout my life, I always fantasized about playing with time. I still recall the first time I watched the episode of *The Twilight Zone* called "A Little Peace and Quiet" where the main character 'Penny' yells, "Shut up" and freezes time. At the end, she freezes time during a nuclear attack and looks up at Soviet missiles which hover, about to explode. Inspired by The Twilight Zone, movies like '*The Girl, The Gold Watch and Everything,*' (another story about stopping time), '*Back to the Future,*' the Terminator films, I often jotted down story ideas about messing around with time. I especially loved science fiction stories that were grounded in a reality that gave the story a truth and realism. That's where *Ghost Town* came from; it doesn't seem possible scientifically to go back in time but it does seem theoretically possible to send things forward. What if we sent something horrible, like a devastating bomb, forward in time? Sending a bomb forward in time isn't a story though. Who would choose to stay in a city where a catastrophic bomb will eventually go off? Who are these people and what are their stories? What about the people who left in such a hurry that they abandoned everything they worked so hard to provide for their families? What dark secrets are hidden in the Nation's Capital that needs to be rescued? That's where Nate came from. He's the guy that we follow into 'The Rad.' Nate is the ultimate thrill seeker, but his race with destiny has a dark secret. Why would anyone risk their life day in and day out? Nate's dark and secret past drives him into the deadly blast radius that is Washington D.C.

Back in 2007, when I met Dave Dwonch at Wondercon in San Francisco, I never would have guessed that we would be collaborating on a comic book together only five years later. After listening to an interview on the *Comic Geek Speak* podcast, I sought Dave out so I could pick up one of his books. We hit it off and a couple of years later we were having dinner (with Justin Greenwood, the artist on Ghost Town Issue #1) and I mentioned that I had a story rattling around in my head about terrorists sending bombs forward in time. It still took several years of conversations and planning, but I couldn't be more proud when I held that first issue of the book in my hand.

If you are reading these words, it means you have picked up the third issue of Ghost Town. For this I would like to profoundly thank you. These books were an absolute pleasure to be involved with. As a lifelong comic book fan, it has been a huge gift to be able to help create the framework for the story, develop character designs, approve scripts, and then get early glimpses of artwork. I truly hope you have enjoyed the story so far and will continue to be drawn forward to the eventual cataclysmic ending of the tale. I would like to thank Dave Dwonch, Justin Greenwood, Ryan Lindsay, Daniel Logan and Brian Dyck for their amazing work bringing this book to life. I'd also like to thank Action Lab Comics for assisting me with getting this story out of my head and onto the spinner rack.

-Rob

THE STREET WALKING DEAD
ZOMBIE TRAMP
THE CULT HIT SERIES NOW IN THE DANGER ZONE!
ACTIONLABCOMICS.COM/DANGER-ZONE

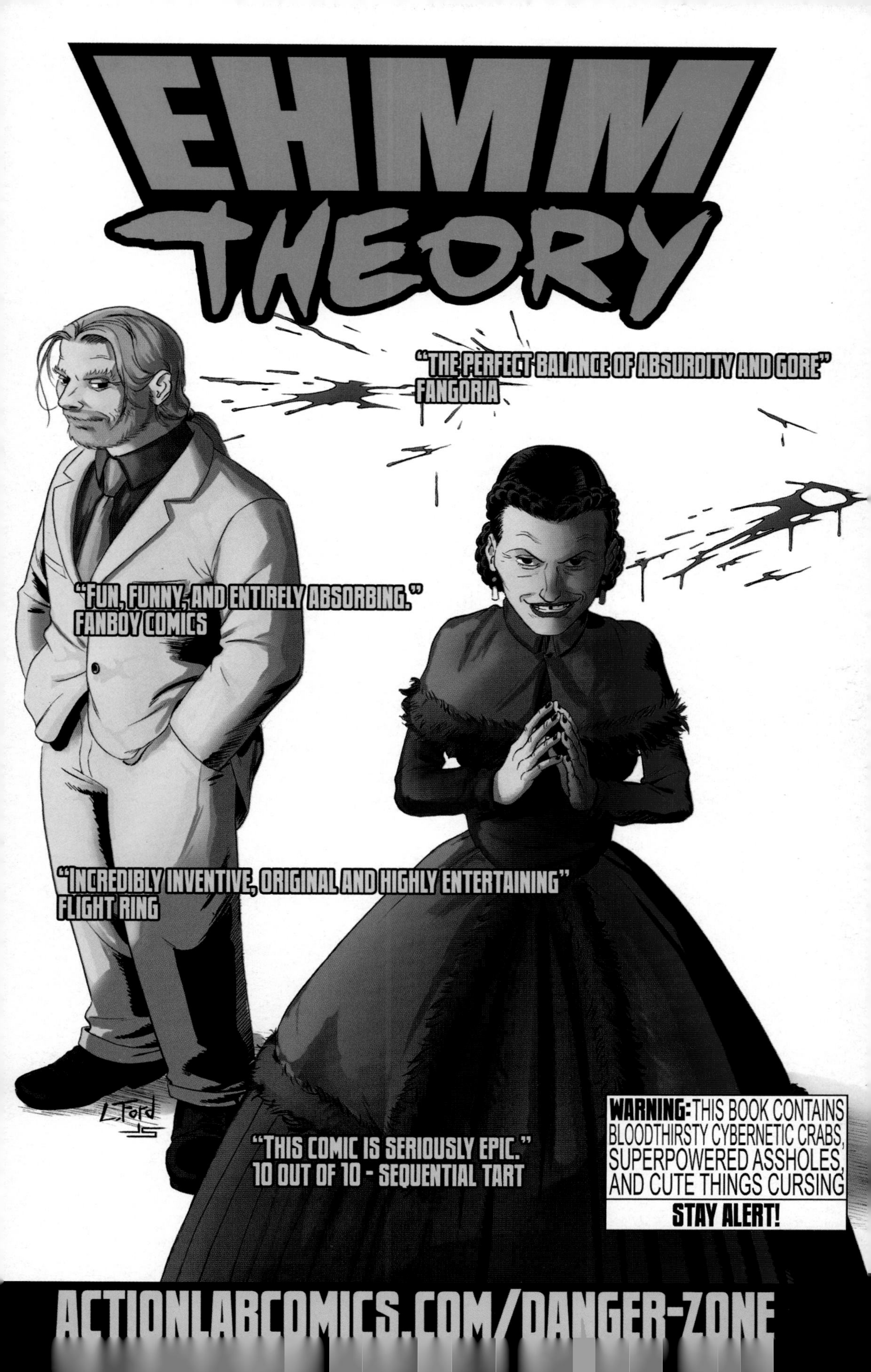

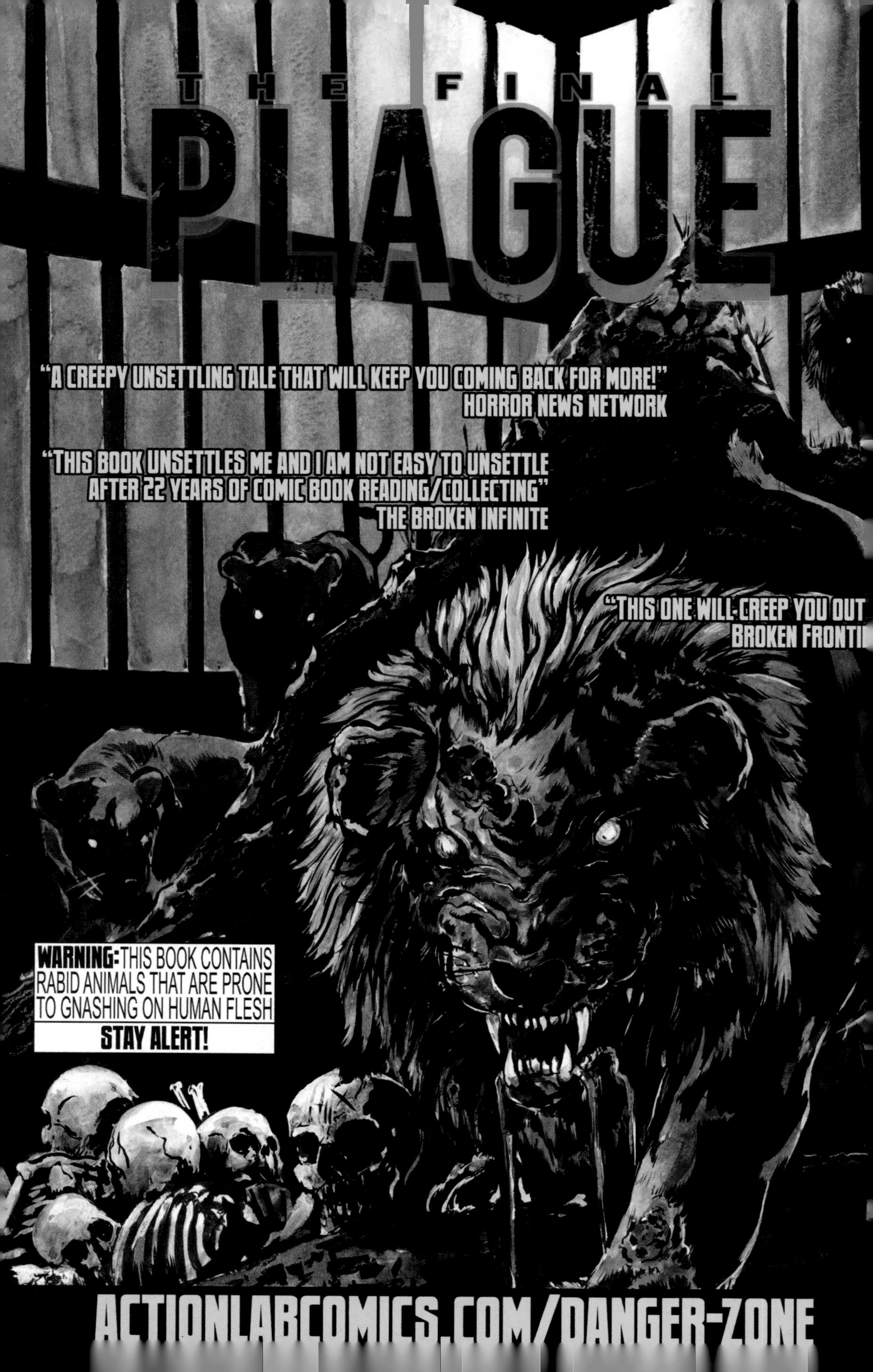
THE FINAL
PLAGUE
"A CREEPY UNSETTLING TALE THAT WILL KEEP YOU COMING BACK FOR MORE!"
HORROR NEWS NETWORK
"THIS BOOK UNSETTLES ME AND I AM NOT EASY TO UNSETTLE AFTER 22 YEARS OF COMIC BOOK READING/COLLECTING"
THE BROKEN INFINITE
"THIS ONE WILL CREEP YOU OUT
BROKEN FRONTI
WARNING: THIS BOOK CONTAINS RABID ANIMALS THAT ARE PRONE TO GNASHING ON HUMAN FLESH
STAY ALERT!
ACTIONLABCOMICS.COM/DANGER-ZONE

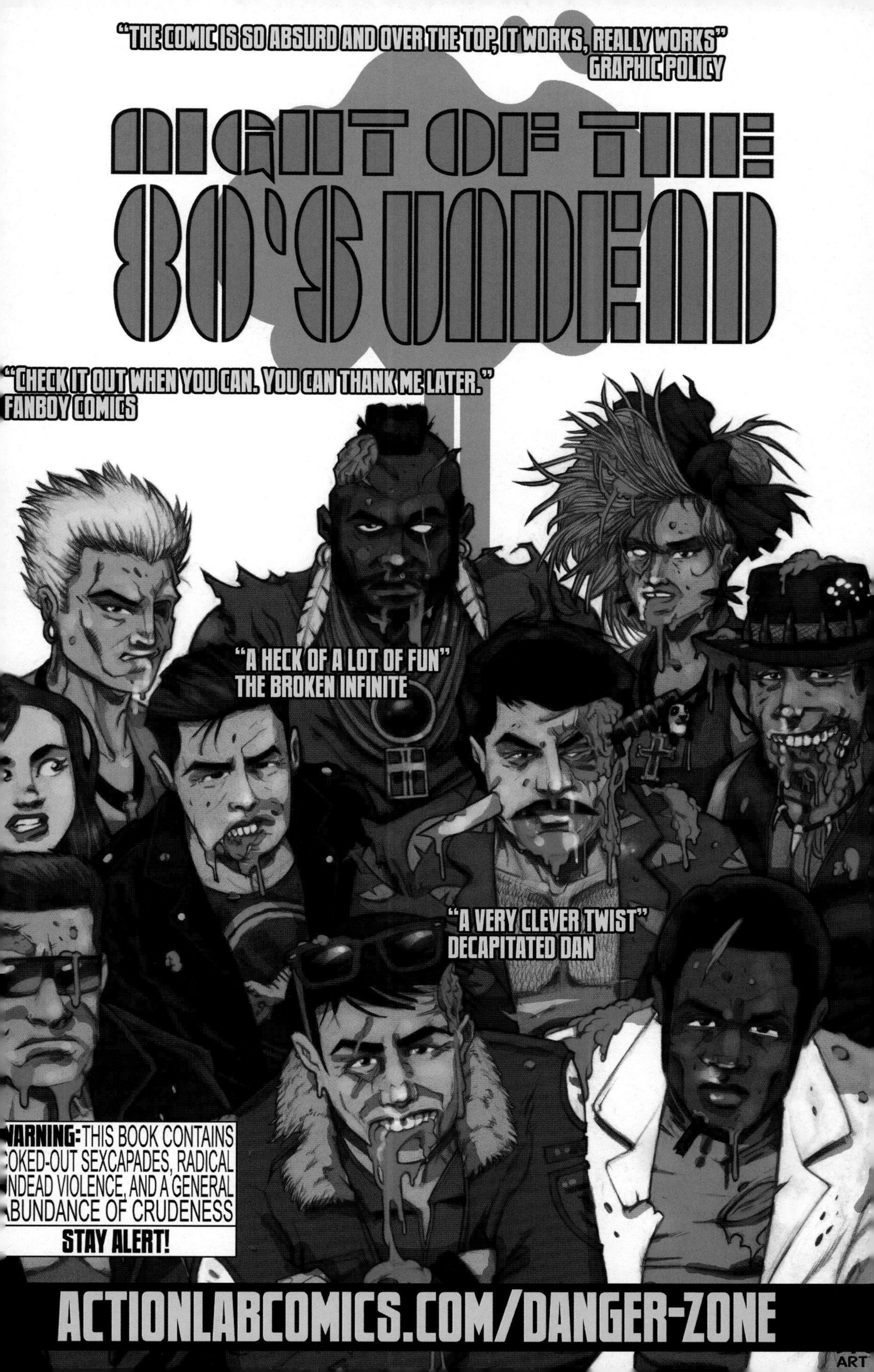
"THE COMIC IS SO ABSURD AND OVER THE TOP, IT WORKS, REALLY WORKS"
GRAPHIC POLICY
NIGHT OF THE 80'S UNDEAD
"CHECK IT OUT WHEN YOU CAN. YOU CAN THANK ME LATER."
FANBOY COMICS
"A HECK OF A LOT OF FUN"
THE BROKEN INFINITE
"A VERY CLEVER TWIST"
DECAPITATED DAN
ARNING: THIS BOOK CONTAINS
OKED-OUT SEXCAPADES, RADICAL
NDEAD VIOLENCE, AND A GENERAL
BUNDANCE OF CRUDENESS
STAY ALERT!
ACTIONLABCOMICS.COM/DANGER-ZONE
ART

STAY ALERT!

SHIPPING SOON!

WARNING: THESE BOOKS MAY CONTAIN SUPER-COOL CONTENT THAT COULD BLOW YOUR MIND!

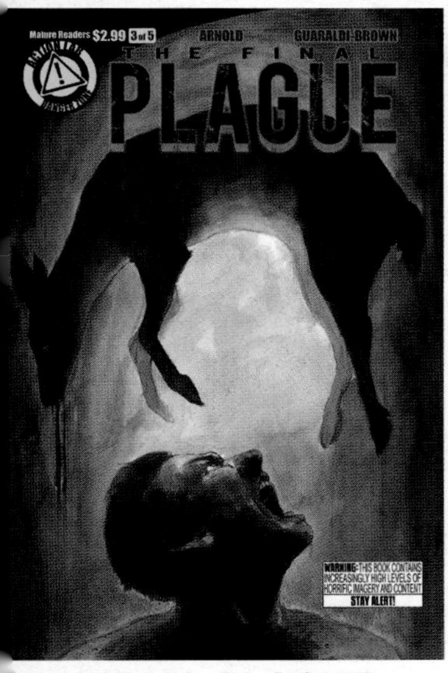

Mature Readers $2.99 3 of 5
ARNOLD
GUARALDI-BROWN
THE FINAL
PLAGUE
WARNING: THIS BOOK CONTAINS INCREASINGLY HIGH LEVELS OF HORRIFIC IMAGERY AND CONTENT
STAY ALERT!

'HE FINAL PLAGUE
·3 (OF 5) $2.99

'RITER: **JD ARNOLD**
.RTIST: **TONY GUARALDI-BROWN**

›wa, New Jersey, and now... the ʼorld! The scope of The Final Plague egins to take shape, and no one, owhere, is safe. Is this really umanity's final hours?!?

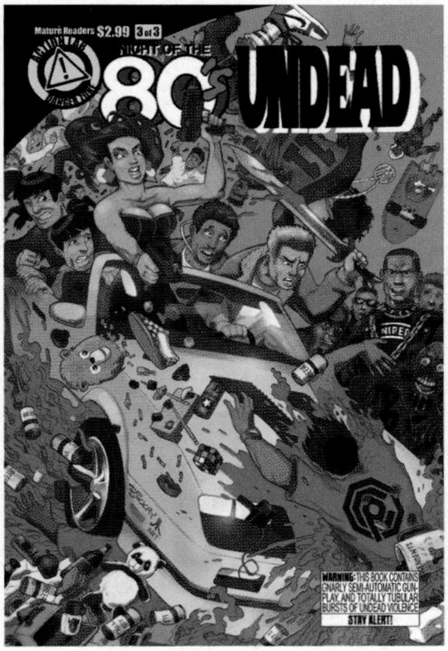

Mature Readers $2.99 3 of 3
NIGHT OF THE
80's UNDEAD
WARNING: THIS BOOK CONTAINS GNARLY SEMI-AUTOMATIC GUN-PLAY, AND TOTALLY TUBULAR BURSTS OF UNDEAD VIOLENCE
STAY ALERT!

NIGHT OF THE 80'S UNDEAD
#3 (OF 3) $2.99

WRITER: **JASON MARTIN**
ARTIST: **BILL McKAY**

Our gang of 80's Hollywood teens make their last ditch effort at escaping the escalating commie zombie cocaine virus that's rapidly spread to engulf their fellow tinsel-town residents!

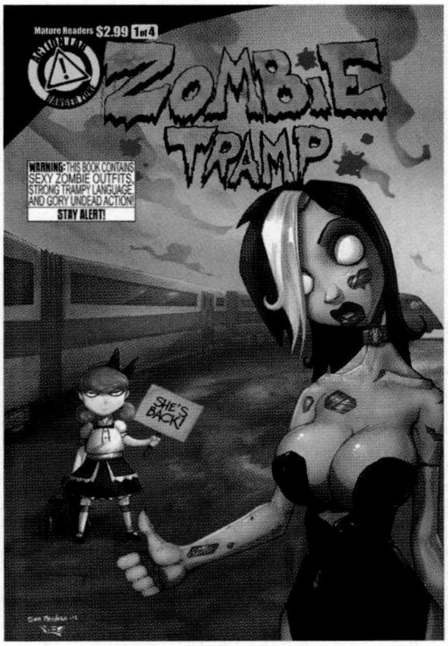

Mature Readers $2.99 1 of 4
ZOMBIE
TRAMP
WARNING: THIS BOOK CONTAINS SEXY ZOMBIE OUTFITS, STRONG TRAMPY LANGUAGE AND GORY UNDEAD ACTION!
STAY ALERT!
SHE'S BACK!

ZOMBIE TRAMP Vol.2
#1 (OF 4) $2.99

WRITER/ARTIST: **DAN MENDOZA**

Where does our former Hollywood call girl turned undead heroine go after the events of volume one? And more importantly, what fetish fashion will she wear?? All aboard *The Taint Train of Terror* to find out!

'ROM THE ZONE

ake note adventurous readers - and yes, that's you, you're in the Danger 'one after all - next month marks the first transition from what we've lubbed (internally at least)... PHASE ONE of our mature readers imprint, vith the end of one of our first mini-series, *The Night of the 80's Undead*, nd the start of the first of more new series that are planned, *Zombie 'ramp*! You may have noticed the *Zombie Tramp* volume one graphic ovel last month (check the store shelves and have a look, there should till be some copies in finer retail outlets), and now, two months later the ll new sequel series is set to make it's debut in the Danger Zone, eralding the beginning of... yep, DZ PHASE TWO! So if you yearn for ore zombies with tongue firmly planted in decaying flesh-like cheek, ke you found in *80's Undead*, then you can't go wrong with *Zombie 'ramp*, she's a cartoon grindhouse zombie hooker with an undead heart hat's cold! But unlike all the other mindless undead killing machines, ombie Tramp only takes to violently lethal measures on those who have coming (hey, she must have a heart of gold or something), and she's lways sure to look real good while doing it! Be sure to take a closer look ourself at this title that's already become a fan favorite.

his is just the first of many super cool new creator owned concepts ned up to expand our line with DZ phase two (and your minds, man, and our minds), with the brand of inventive genre blurring comic fiction that ou've quickly come to expect from us with our phase one books. We uly hope you'll find Danger Zone to be a name you can trust for ntertaining comics that tease and challenge your eyes and (in-between e)-ears!

e sure to visit us on the web (see the links below) for a closer look at our urrent and upcoming titles, and you can also visit us at New York Comic on next month (and score some exclusive con merchandise)!

TAY ALERT!

ason Martin - President, Action Lab: Danger Zone

OUT NOW!

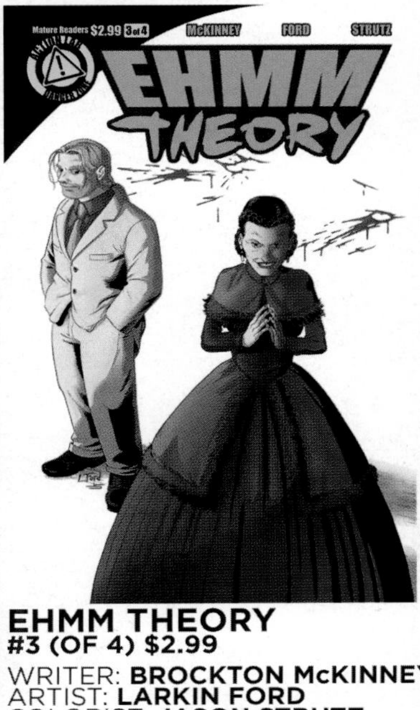

Mature Readers $2.99 3 of 4
McKINNEY
FORD
STRUTZ
EHMM
THEORY

EHMM THEORY
#3 (OF 4) $2.99

WRITER: **BROCKTON McKINNEY**
ARTIST: **LARKIN FORD**
COLORIST: **JASON STRUTZ**

You demanded answers, and you get 'em! Who is pulling Saint Peters strings? What is Gabriel's final task? Who is the mysterious Tym?

Facebook.com/ActionLabDangerZone Twitter.com/ActionLabDanger

ACTIONLABCOMICS.COM/DANGER-ZONE

READ MORE NOW

ACTIONLABCOMICS.COM

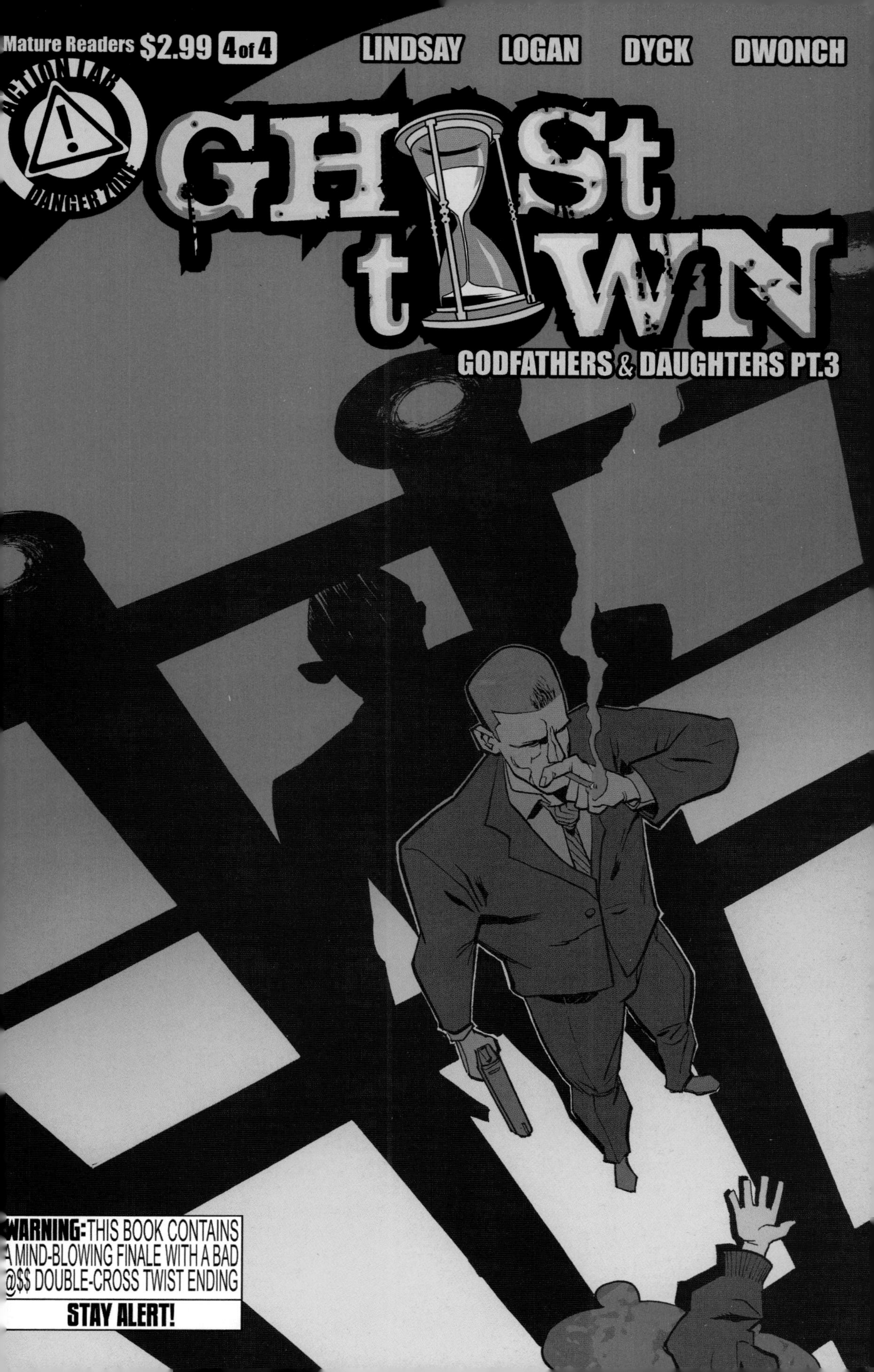

Mature Readers $2.99 4 of 4
LINDSAY LOGAN DYCK DWONCH
ACTION LAB DANGER ZONE
GHOSt tOWN
GODFATHERS & DAUGHTERS PT.3
WARNING: THIS BOOK CONTAINS A MIND-BLOWING FINALE WITH A BAD @$$ DOUBLE-CROSS TWIST ENDING
STAY ALERT!

GODFATHERS & DAUGHTERS
PART 3

GHOST TOWN CREATED BY ROB RUDDELL & DAVE DWONCH
EDITED BY SHAWN GABBORIN
COVER BY JUSTIN GREENWOOD & JORDIE BELLAIRE

RYAN K LINDSAY
WORDS
DANIEL LOGAN
PICTURES
BRIAN DYCK
COLORS
DAVE DWONCH
LETTERS

JASON MARTIN - PUBLISHER
KEVIN FREEMAN - PRESIDENT
SHAWN PRYOR - VP DIGITAL MEDIA
DAVE DWONCH - CREATIVE DIRECTOR
SHAWN GABBORIN - EDITOR IN CHIEF
JEREMY WHITLEY - MARKETING DIRECTOR
CHAD CICCONI - ASSOCIATE EDITOR
COLLEEN BOYD - ASSOCIATE EDITOR

ACTIONLABCOMICS.COM/DANGER-ZONE

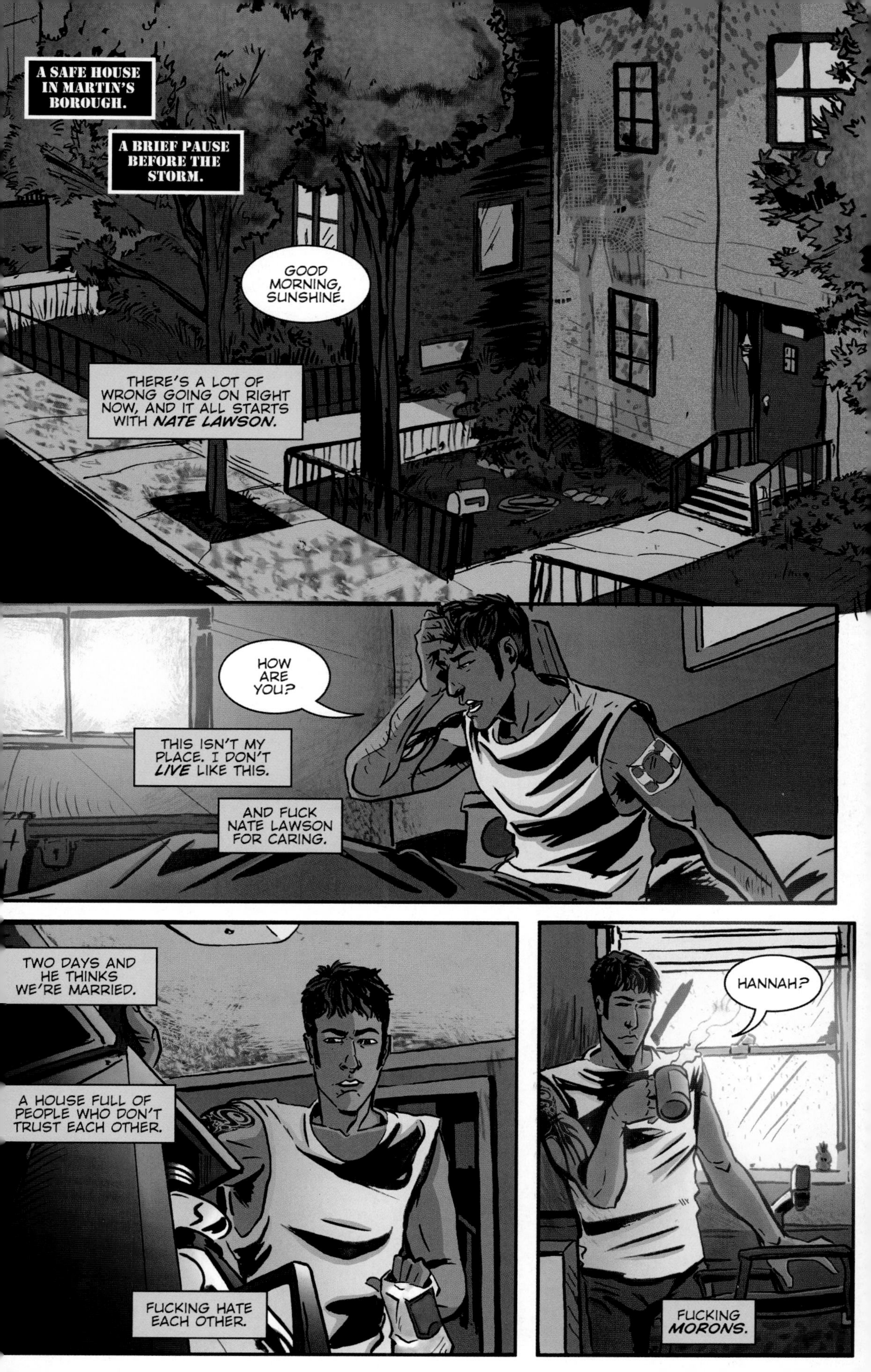
A SAFE HOUSE IN MARTIN'S BOROUGH.
A BRIEF PAUSE BEFORE THE STORM.
GOOD MORNING, SUNSHINE.
THERE'S A LOT OF WRONG GOING ON RIGHT NOW, AND IT ALL STARTS WITH NATE LAWSON.
HOW ARE YOU?
THIS ISN'T MY PLACE. I DON'T LIVE LIKE THIS.
AND FUCK NATE LAWSON FOR CARING.
TWO DAYS AND HE THINKS WE'RE MARRIED.
A HOUSE FULL OF PEOPLE WHO DON'T TRUST EACH OTHER.
FUCKING HATE EACH OTHER.
HANNAH?
FUCKING MORONS.

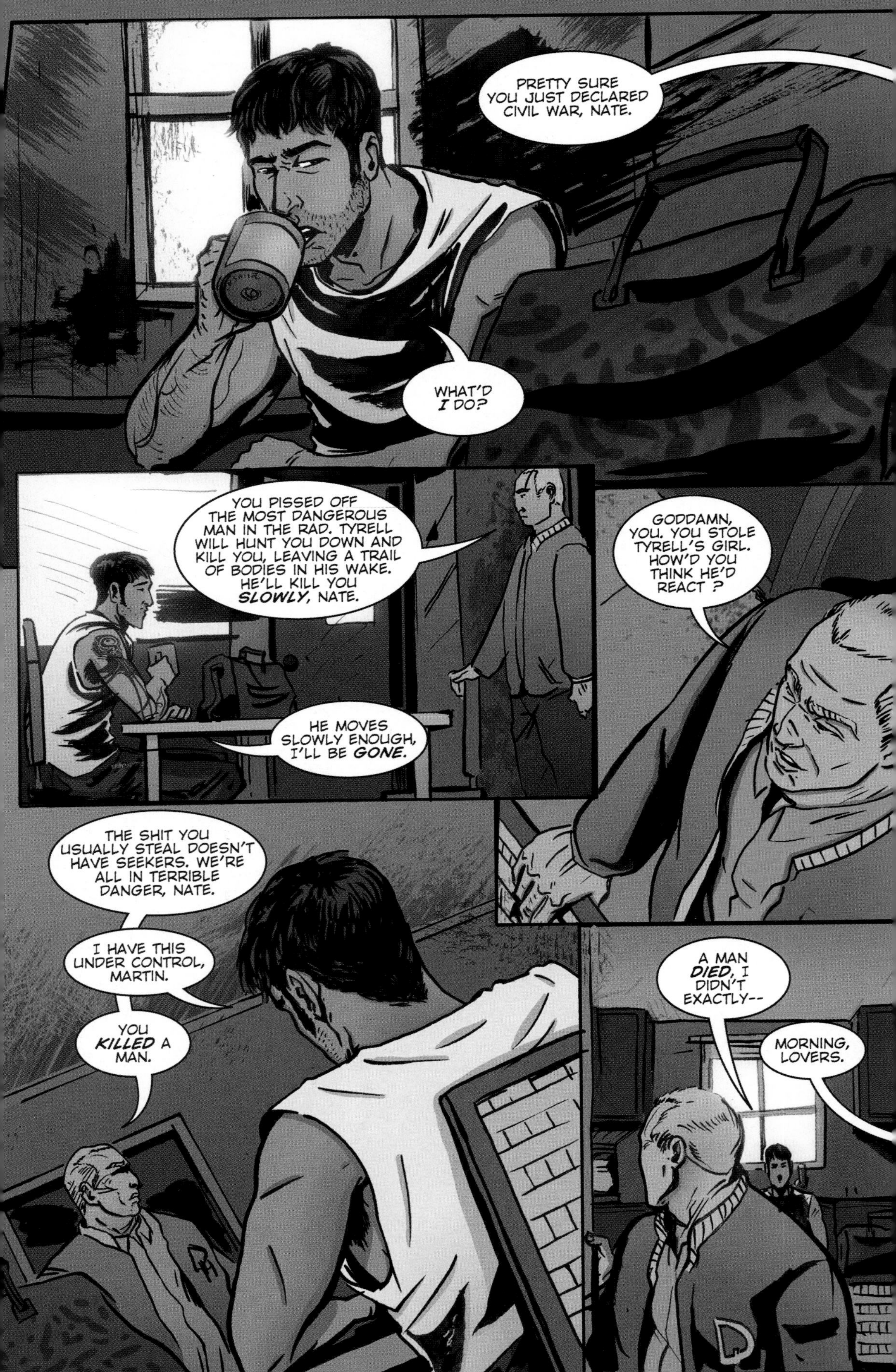
PRETTY SURE YOU JUST DECLARED CIVIL WAR, NATE.
WHAT'D *I* DO?
YOU PISSED OFF THE MOST DANGEROUS MAN IN THE RAD. TYRELL WILL HUNT YOU DOWN AND KILL YOU, LEAVING A TRAIL OF BODIES IN HIS WAKE. HE'LL KILL YOU ***SLOWLY***, NATE.
HE MOVES SLOWLY ENOUGH, I'LL BE ***GONE***.
GODDAMN, YOU. YOU STOLE TYRELL'S GIRL. HOW'D YOU THINK HE'D REACT ?
THE SHIT YOU USUALLY STEAL DOESN'T HAVE SEEKERS. WE'RE ALL IN TERRIBLE DANGER, NATE.
I HAVE THIS UNDER CONTROL, MARTIN.
YOU ***KILLED*** A MAN.
A MAN ***DIED***, I DIDN'T EXACTLY--
MORNING, LOVERS.

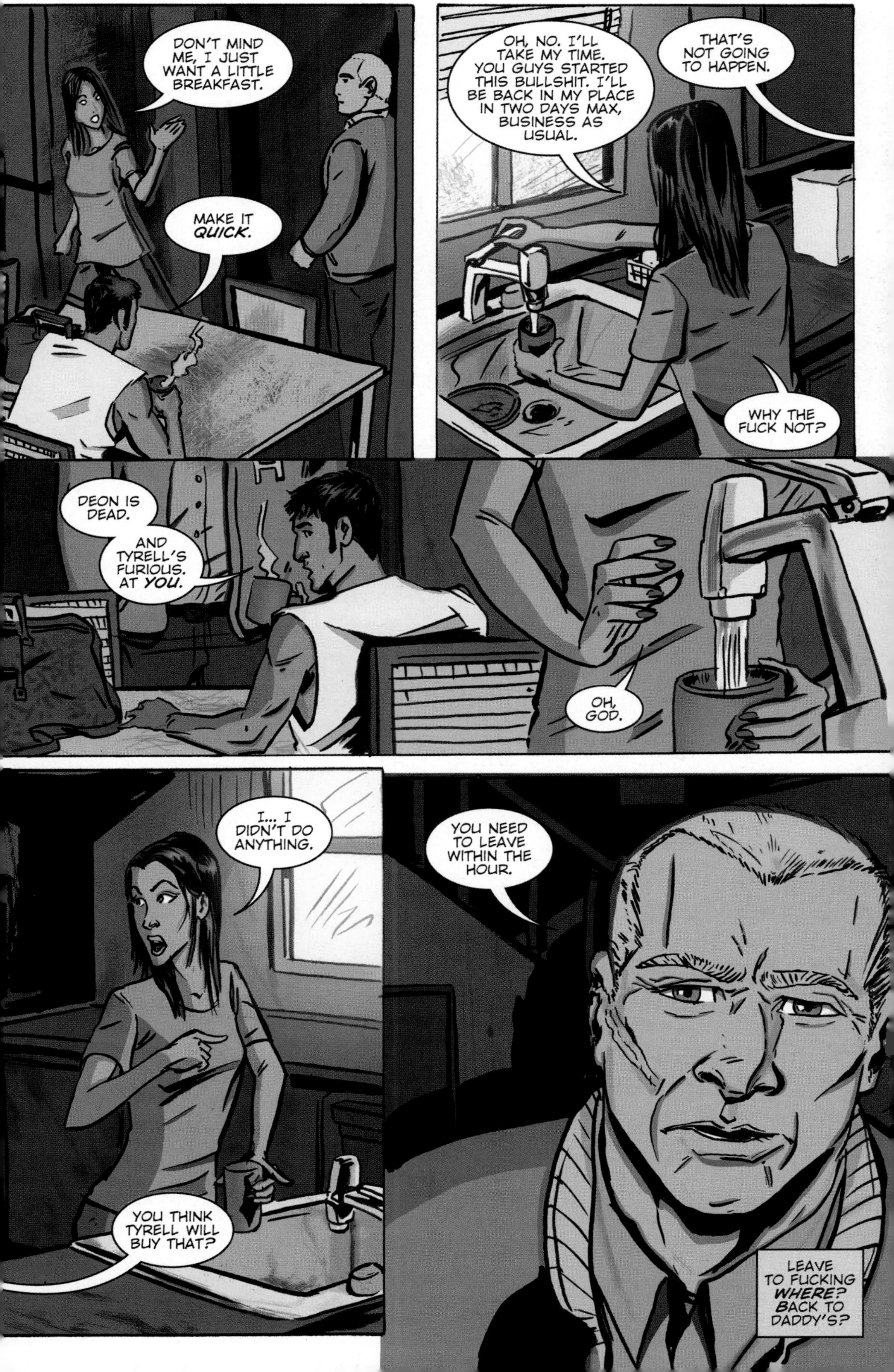
DON'T MIND ME, I JUST WANT A LITTLE BREAKFAST.
MAKE IT *QUICK.*
OH, NO. I'LL TAKE MY TIME. YOU GUYS STARTED THIS BULLSHIT. I'LL BE BACK IN MY PLACE IN TWO DAYS MAX, BUSINESS AS USUAL.
THAT'S NOT GOING TO HAPPEN.
WHY THE FUCK NOT?
DEON IS DEAD.
AND TYRELL'S FURIOUS. AT *YOU.*
OH, GOD.
I... I DIDN'T DO ANYTHING.
YOU THINK TYRELL WILL BUY THAT?
YOU NEED TO LEAVE WITHIN THE HOUR.
LEAVE TO FUCKING *WHERE?* BACK TO DADDY'S?

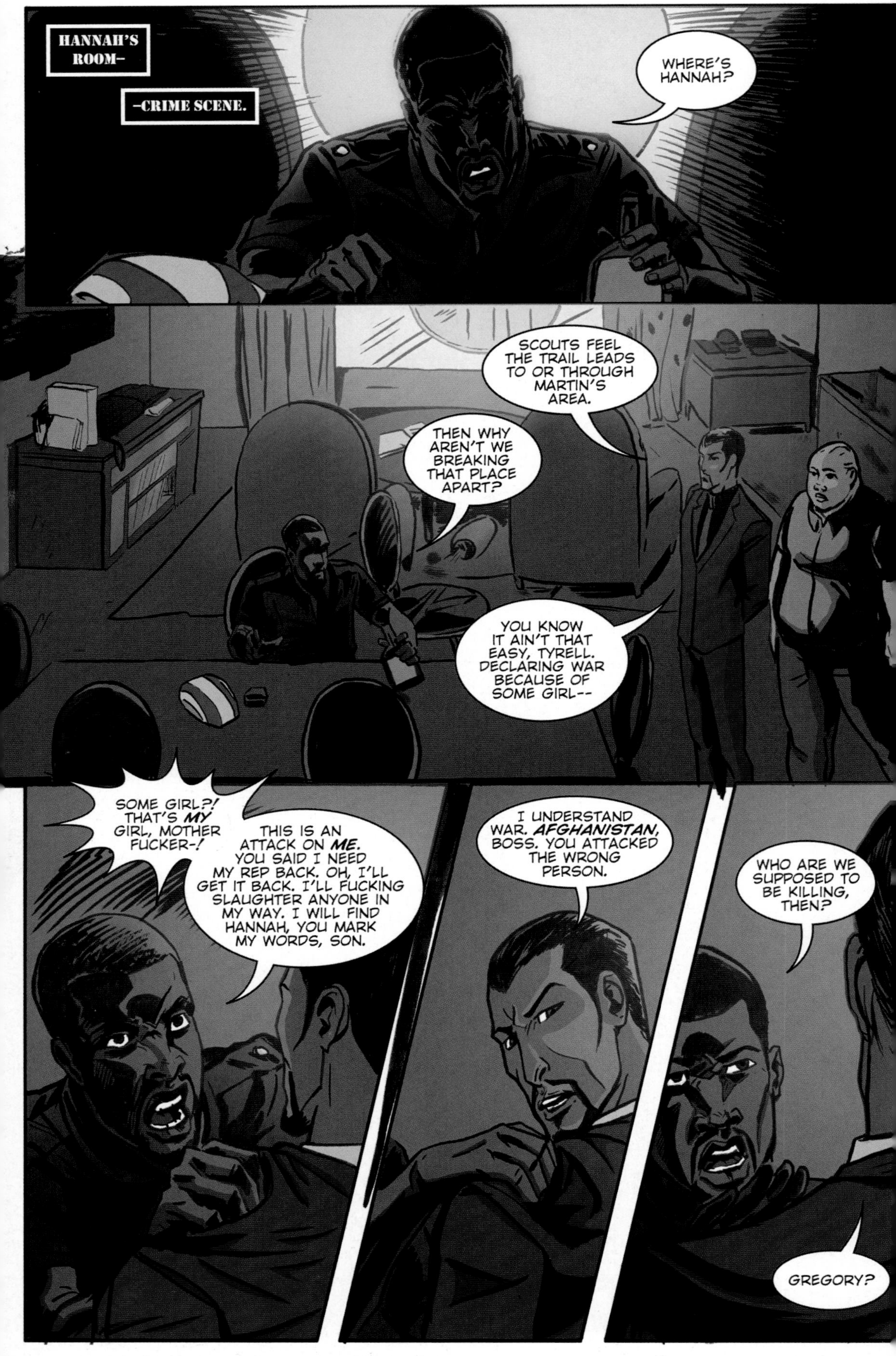
HANNAH'S ROOM-
-CRIME SCENE.
WHERE'S HANNAH?
SCOUTS FEEL THE TRAIL LEADS TO OR THROUGH MARTIN'S AREA.
THEN WHY AREN'T WE BREAKING THAT PLACE APART?
YOU KNOW IT AIN'T THAT EASY, TYRELL. DECLARING WAR BECAUSE OF SOME GIRL--
SOME GIRL?! THAT'S MY GIRL, MOTHER FUCKER-!
THIS IS AN ATTACK ON ME. YOU SAID I NEED MY REP BACK. OH, I'LL GET IT BACK. I'LL FUCKING SLAUGHTER ANYONE IN MY WAY. I WILL FIND HANNAH, YOU MARK MY WORDS, SON.
I UNDERSTAND WAR. AFGHANISTAN, BOSS. YOU ATTACKED THE WRONG PERSON.
WHO ARE WE SUPPOSED TO BE KILLING, THEN?
GREGORY?

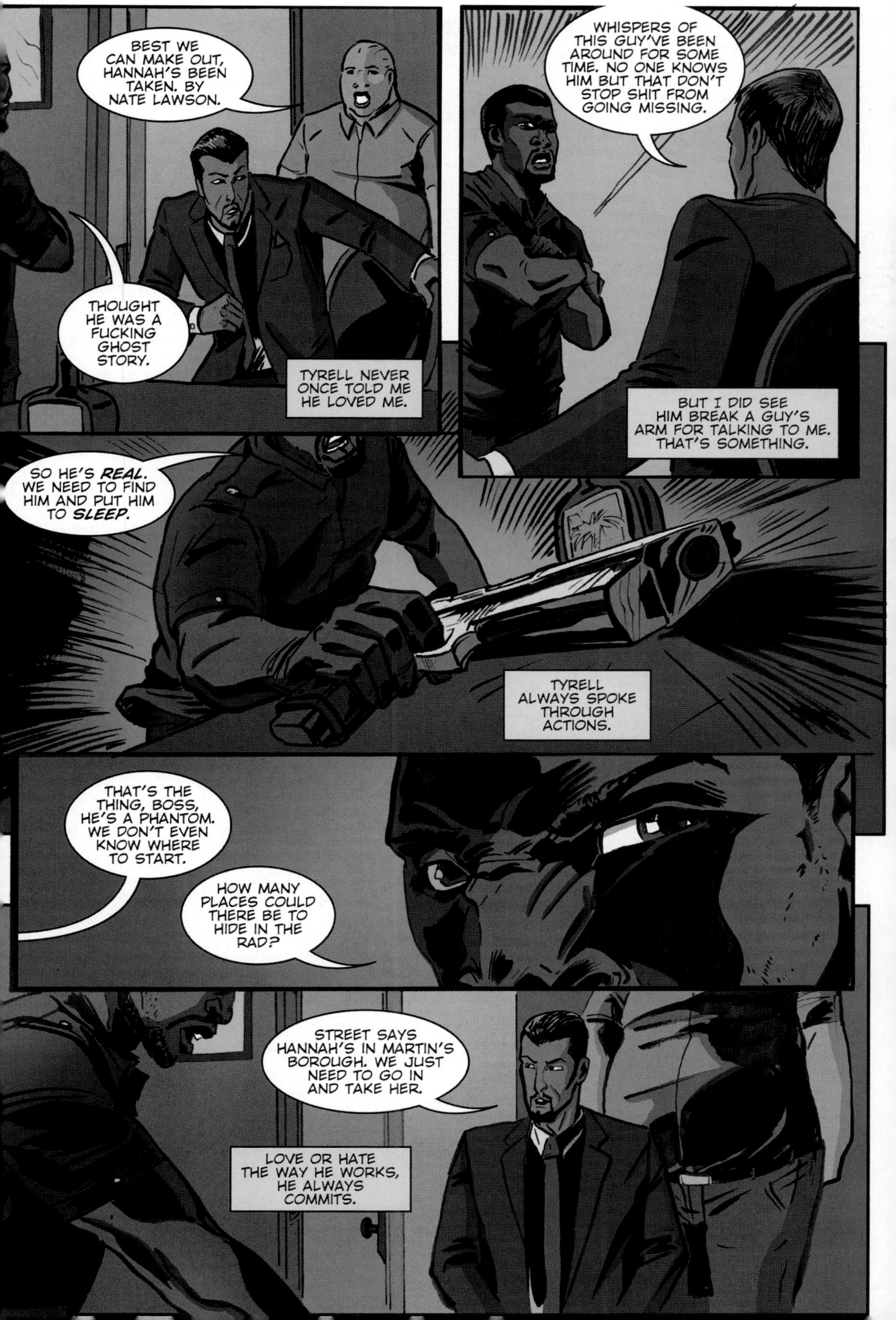
BEST WE CAN MAKE OUT, HANNAH'S BEEN TAKEN. BY NATE LAWSON.
THOUGHT HE WAS A FUCKING GHOST STORY.
TYRELL NEVER ONCE TOLD ME HE LOVED ME.
WHISPERS OF THIS GUY'VE BEEN AROUND FOR SOME TIME. NO ONE KNOWS HIM BUT THAT DON'T STOP SHIT FROM GOING MISSING.
BUT I DID SEE HIM BREAK A GUY'S ARM FOR TALKING TO ME. THAT'S SOMETHING.
SO HE'S ***REAL***. WE NEED TO FIND HIM AND PUT HIM TO ***SLEEP***.
TYRELL ALWAYS SPOKE THROUGH ACTIONS.
THAT'S THE THING, BOSS, HE'S A PHANTOM. WE DON'T EVEN KNOW WHERE TO START.
HOW MANY PLACES COULD THERE BE TO HIDE IN THE RAD?
STREET SAYS HANNAH'S IN MARTIN'S BOROUGH. WE JUST NEED TO GO IN AND TAKE HER.
LOVE OR HATE THE WAY HE WORKS, HE ALWAYS COMMITS.

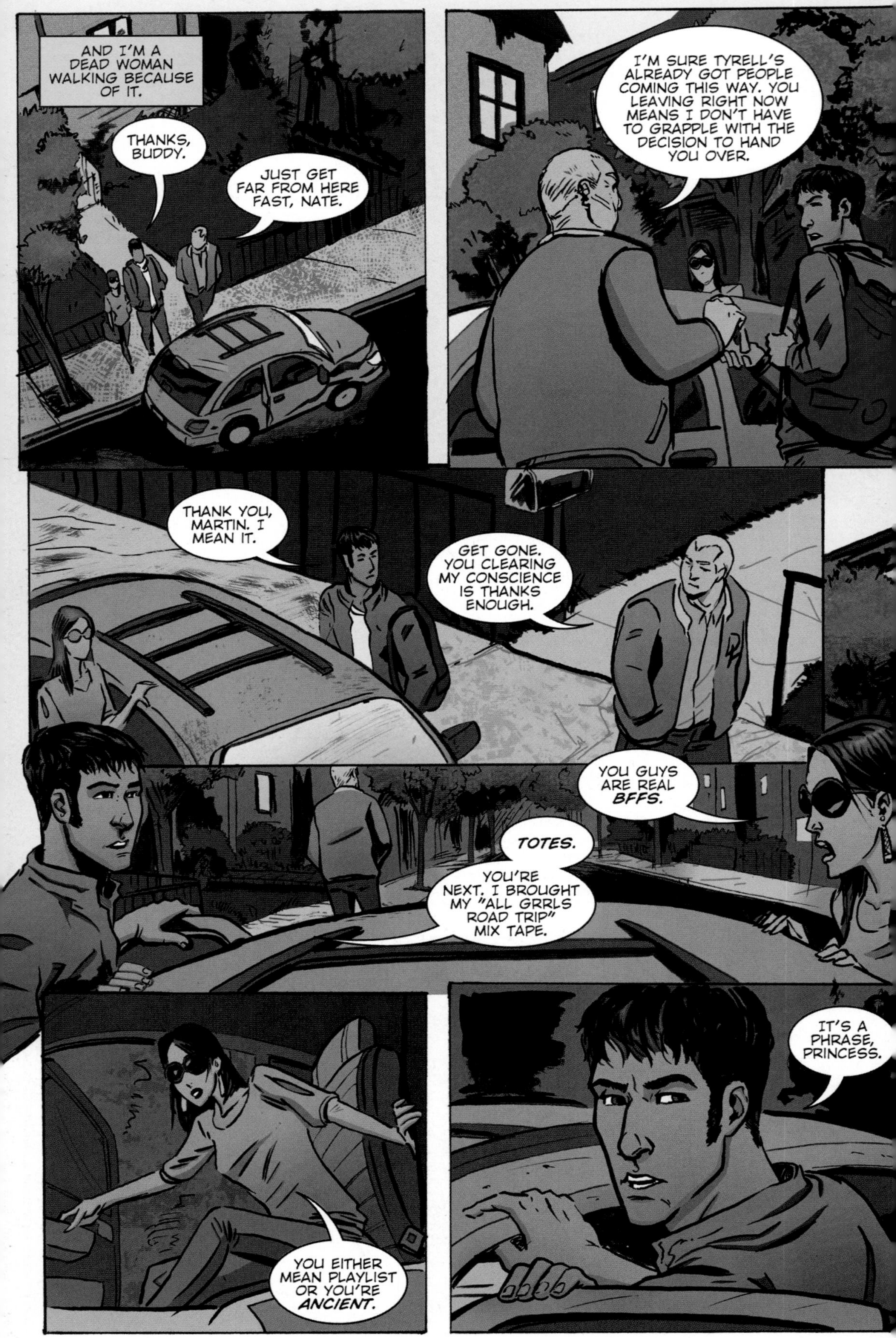
AND I'M A DEAD WOMAN WALKING BECAUSE OF IT.
THANKS, BUDDY.
JUST GET FAR FROM HERE FAST, NATE.
I'M SURE TYRELL'S ALREADY GOT PEOPLE COMING THIS WAY. YOU LEAVING RIGHT NOW MEANS I DON'T HAVE TO GRAPPLE WITH THE DECISION TO HAND YOU OVER.
THANK YOU, MARTIN. I MEAN IT.
GET GONE. YOU CLEARING MY CONSCIENCE IS THANKS ENOUGH.
YOU GUYS ARE REAL *BFFS*.
TOTES.
YOU'RE NEXT. I BROUGHT MY "ALL GRRLS ROAD TRIP" MIX TAPE.
YOU EITHER MEAN PLAYLIST OR YOU'RE *ANCIENT*.
IT'S A PHRASE, PRINCESS.

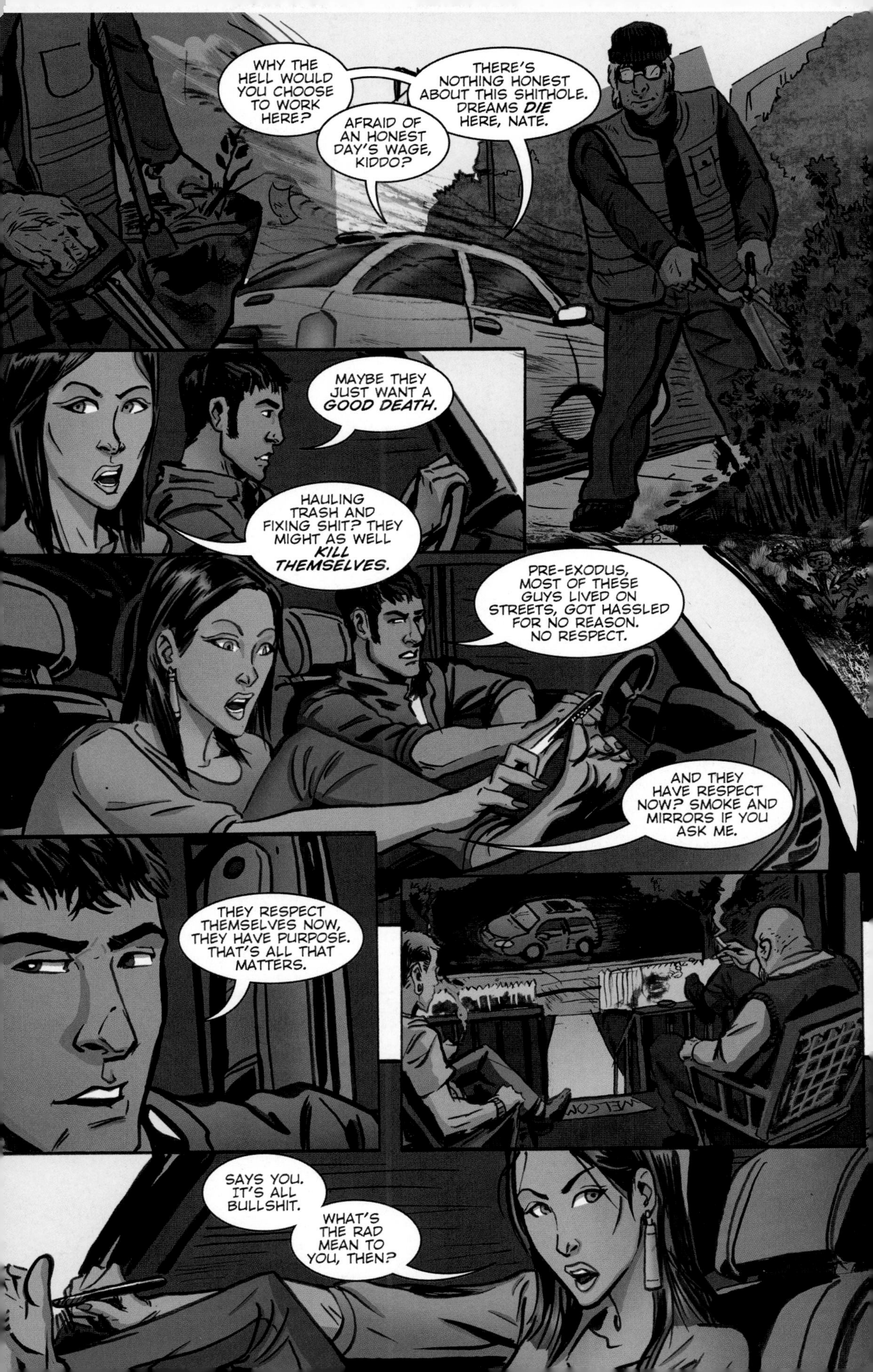
WHY THE HELL WOULD YOU CHOOSE TO WORK HERE?
AFRAID OF AN HONEST DAY'S WAGE, KIDDO?
THERE'S NOTHING HONEST ABOUT THIS SHITHOLE. DREAMS DIE HERE, NATE.
MAYBE THEY JUST WANT A GOOD DEATH.
HAULING TRASH AND FIXING SHIT? THEY MIGHT AS WELL KILL THEMSELVES.
PRE-EXODUS, MOST OF THESE GUYS LIVED ON STREETS, GOT HASSLED FOR NO REASON. NO RESPECT.
AND THEY HAVE RESPECT NOW? SMOKE AND MIRRORS IF YOU ASK ME.
THEY RESPECT THEMSELVES NOW, THEY HAVE PURPOSE. THAT'S ALL THAT MATTERS.
SAYS YOU. IT'S ALL BULLSHIT.
WHAT'S THE RAD MEAN TO YOU, THEN?

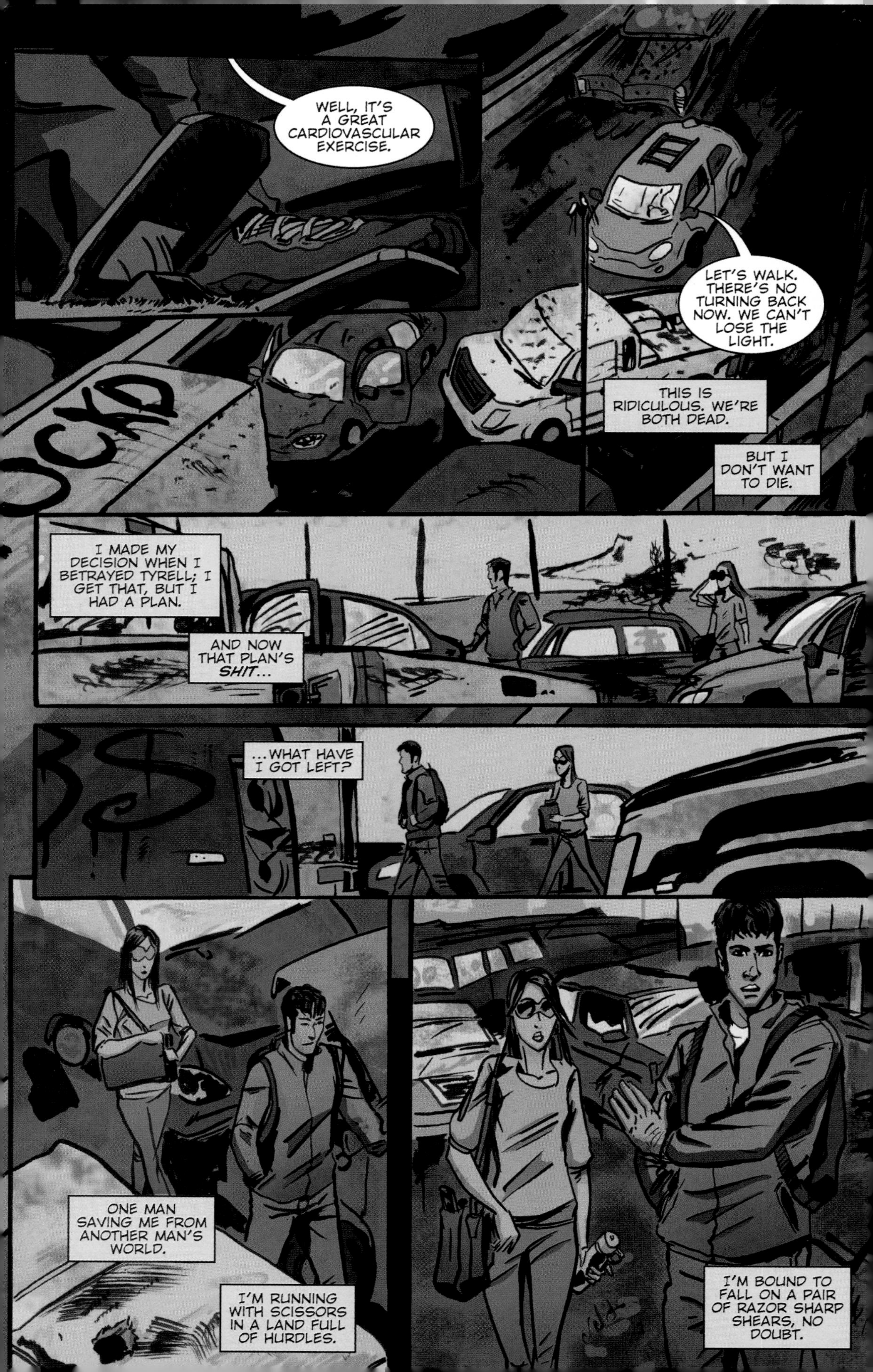
WELL, IT'S A GREAT CARDIOVASCULAR EXERCISE.
LET'S WALK. THERE'S NO TURNING BACK NOW. WE CAN'T LOSE THE LIGHT.
THIS IS RIDICULOUS. WE'RE BOTH DEAD.
BUT I DON'T WANT TO DIE.
I MADE MY DECISION WHEN I BETRAYED TYRELL; I GET THAT, BUT I HAD A PLAN.
AND NOW THAT PLAN'S *SHIT*...
...WHAT HAVE I GOT LEFT?
ONE MAN SAVING ME FROM ANOTHER MAN'S WORLD.
I'M RUNNING WITH SCISSORS IN A LAND FULL OF HURDLES.
I'M BOUND TO FALL ON A PAIR OF RAZOR SHARP SHEARS, NO DOUBT.

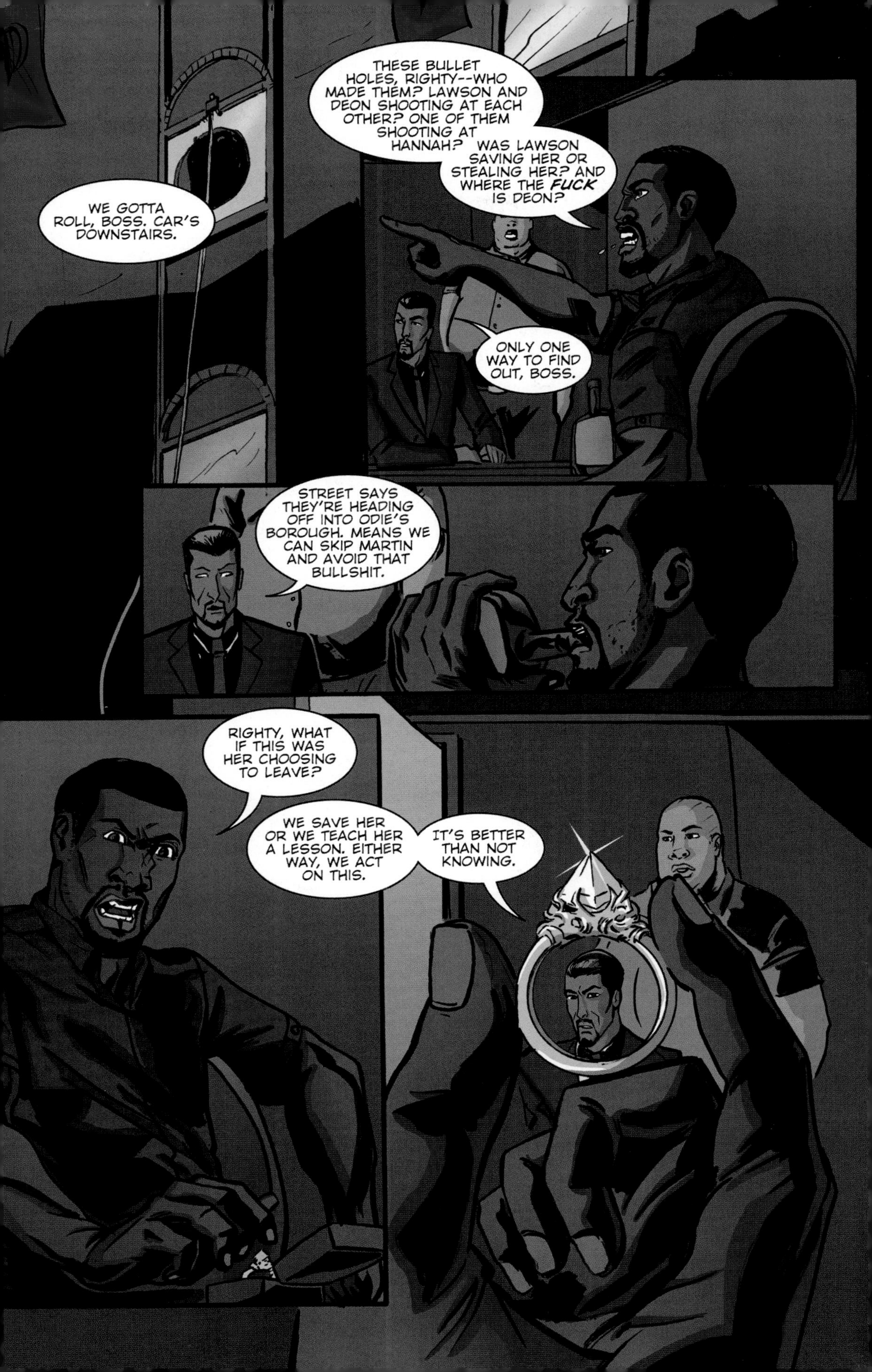
THESE BULLET HOLES, RIGHTY--WHO MADE THEM? LAWSON AND DEON SHOOTING AT EACH OTHER? ONE OF THEM SHOOTING AT HANNAH?
WAS LAWSON SAVING HER OR STEALING HER? AND WHERE THE *FUCK* IS DEON?
WE GOTTA ROLL, BOSS. CAR'S DOWNSTAIRS.
ONLY ONE WAY TO FIND OUT, BOSS.
STREET SAYS THEY'RE HEADING OFF INTO ODIE'S BOROUGH. MEANS WE CAN SKIP MARTIN AND AVOID THAT BULLSHIT.
RIGHTY, WHAT IF THIS WAS HER CHOOSING TO LEAVE?
WE SAVE HER OR WE TEACH HER A LESSON. EITHER WAY, WE ACT ON THIS.
IT'S BETTER THAN NOT KNOWING.

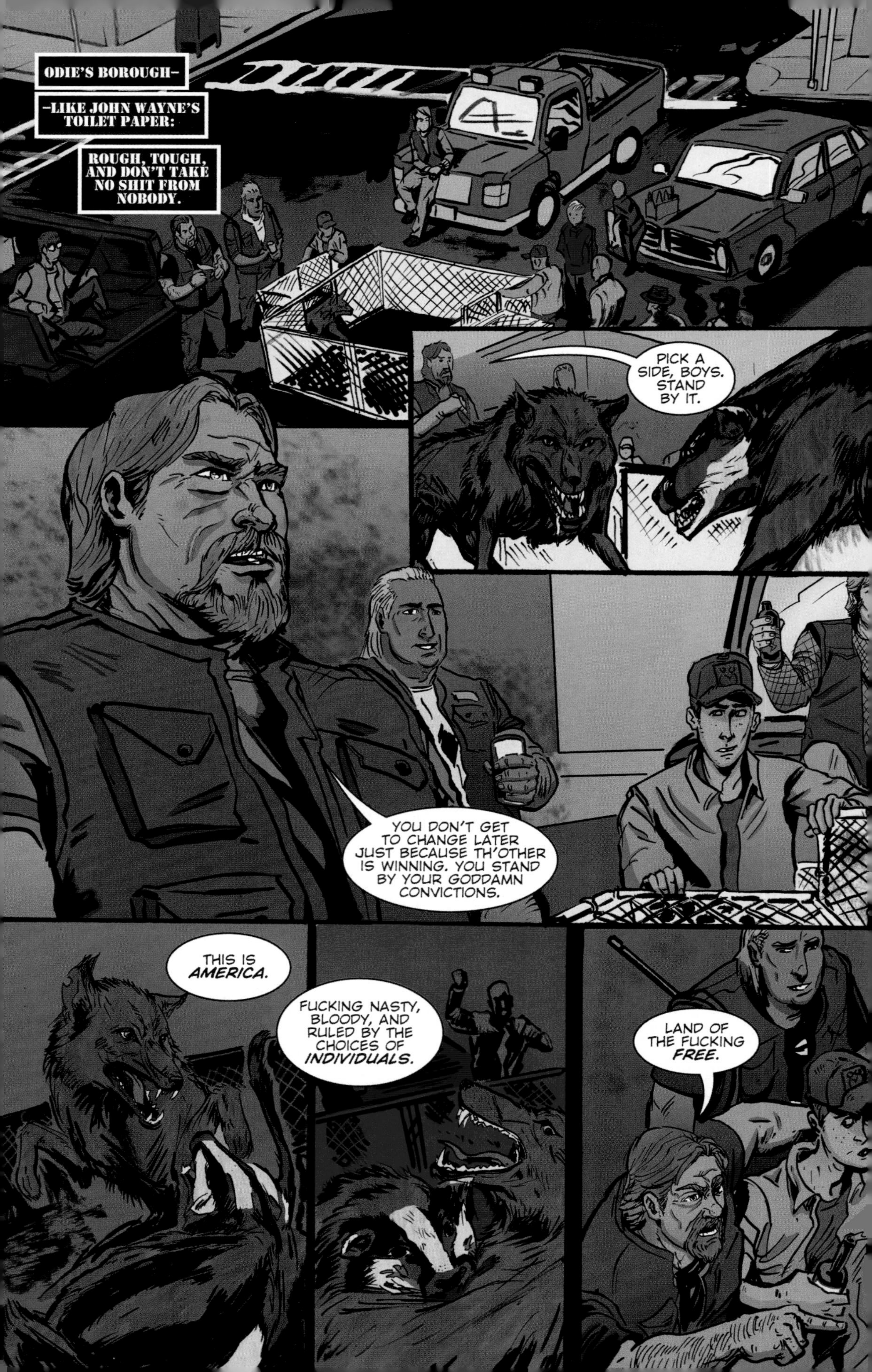
ODIE'S BOROUGH–
–LIKE JOHN WAYNE'S TOILET PAPER:
ROUGH, TOUGH, AND DON'T TAKE NO SHIT FROM NOBODY.
PICK A SIDE, BOYS. STAND BY IT.
YOU DON'T GET TO CHANGE LATER JUST BECAUSE TH'OTHER IS WINNING. YOU STAND BY YOUR GODDAMN CONVICTIONS.
THIS IS *AMERICA*.
FUCKING NASTY, BLOODY, AND RULED BY THE CHOICES OF *INDIVIDUALS*.
LAND OF THE FUCKING *FREE*.

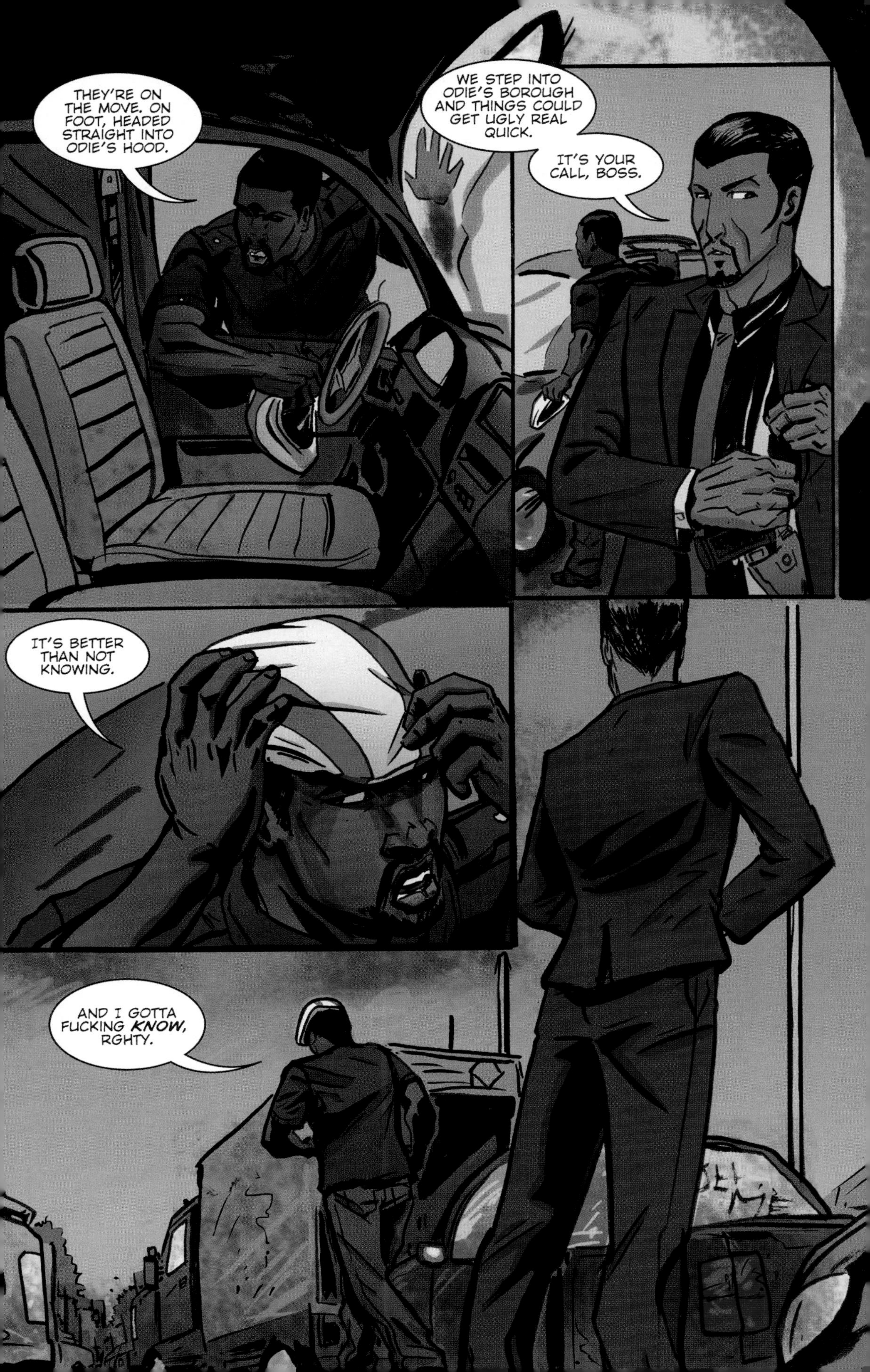
THEY'RE ON THE MOVE. ON FOOT, HEADED STRAIGHT INTO ODIE'S HOOD.
WE STEP INTO ODIE'S BOROUGH AND THINGS COULD GET UGLY REAL QUICK.
IT'S YOUR CALL, BOSS.
IT'S BETTER THAN NOT KNOWING.
AND I GOTTA FUCKING *KNOW*, RGHTY.

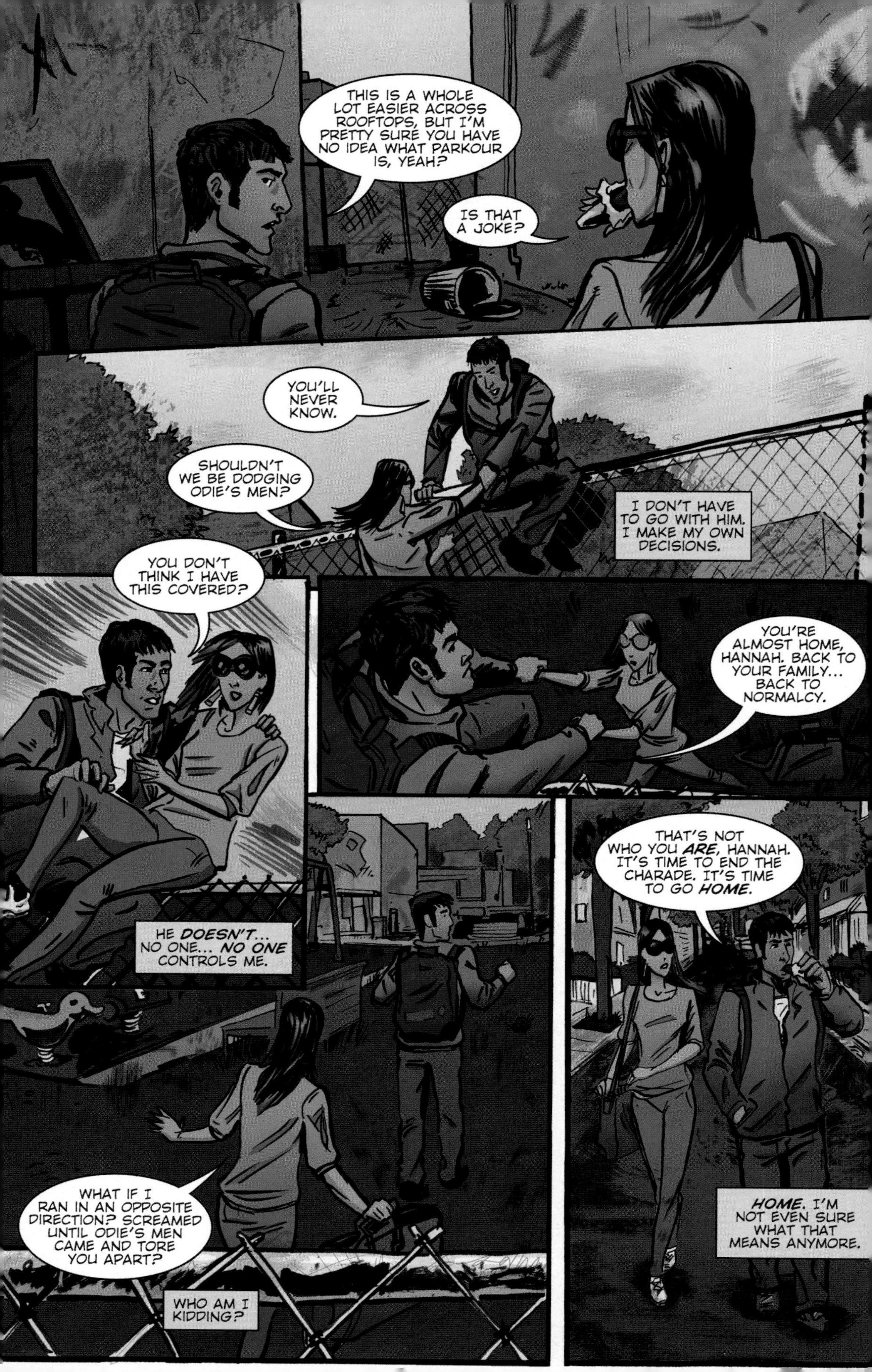

THIS IS A WHOLE LOT EASIER ACROSS ROOFTOPS, BUT I'M PRETTY SURE YOU HAVE NO IDEA WHAT PARKOUR IS, YEAH?
IS THAT A JOKE?
YOU'LL NEVER KNOW.
SHOULDN'T WE BE DODGING ODIE'S MEN?
I DON'T HAVE TO GO WITH HIM. I MAKE MY OWN DECISIONS.
YOU DON'T THINK I HAVE THIS COVERED?
HE *DOESN'T*... NO ONE... *NO ONE* CONTROLS ME.
YOU'RE ALMOST HOME, HANNAH. BACK TO YOUR FAMILY... BACK TO NORMALCY.
WHAT IF I RAN IN AN OPPOSITE DIRECTION? SCREAMED UNTIL ODIE'S MEN CAME AND TORE YOU APART?
WHO AM I KIDDING?
THAT'S NOT WHO YOU *ARE*, HANNAH. IT'S TIME TO END THE CHARADE. IT'S TIME TO GO *HOME*.
HOME. I'M NOT EVEN SURE WHAT THAT MEANS ANYMORE.

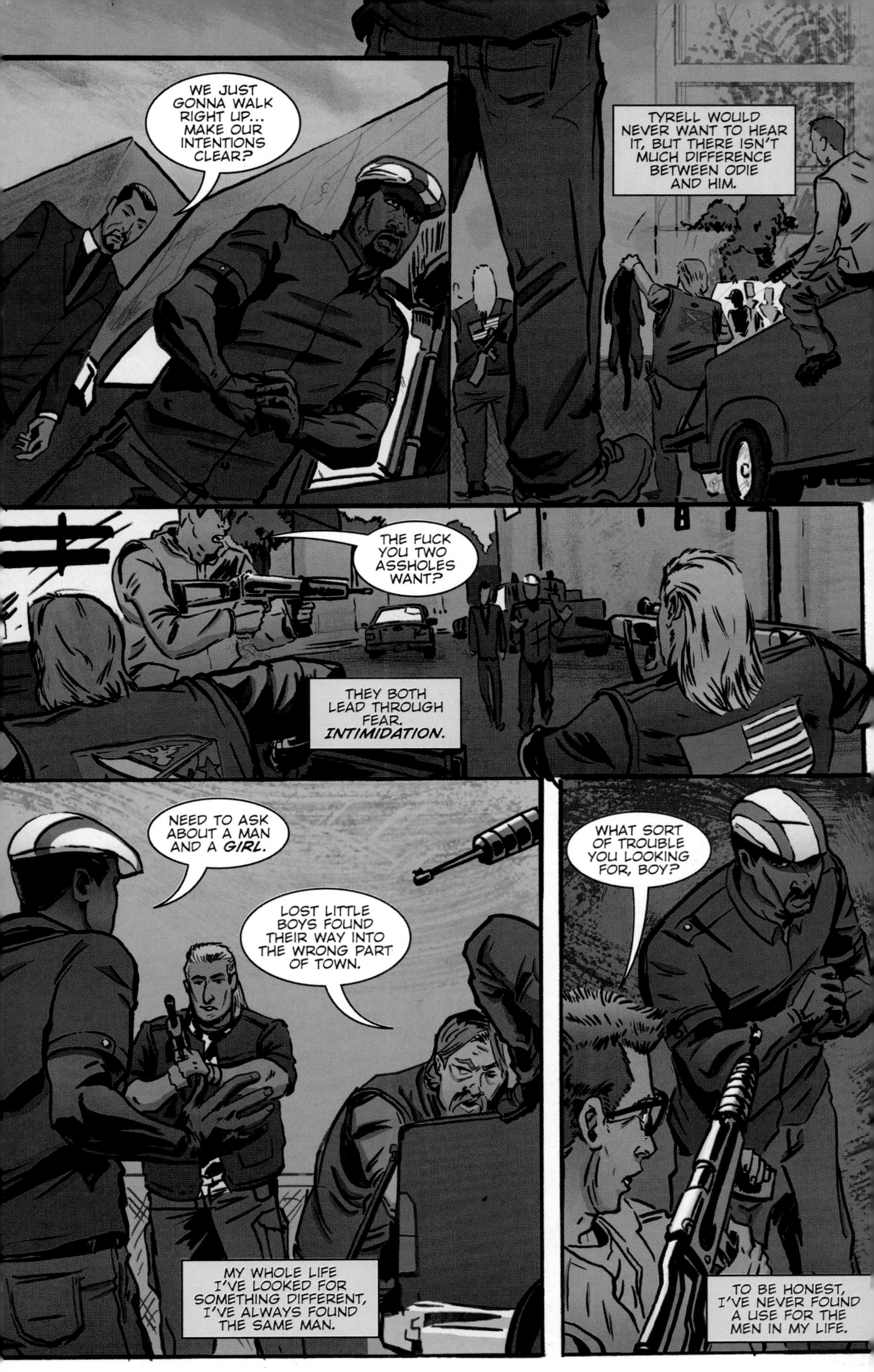
WE JUST GONNA WALK RIGHT UP... MAKE OUR INTENTIONS CLEAR?
TYRELL WOULD NEVER WANT TO HEAR IT, BUT THERE ISN'T MUCH DIFFERENCE BETWEEN ODIE AND HIM.
THE FUCK YOU TWO ASSHOLES WANT?
THEY BOTH LEAD THROUGH FEAR. INTIMIDATION.
NEED TO ASK ABOUT A MAN AND A GIRL.
LOST LITTLE BOYS FOUND THEIR WAY INTO THE WRONG PART OF TOWN.
MY WHOLE LIFE I'VE LOOKED FOR SOMETHING DIFFERENT, I'VE ALWAYS FOUND THE SAME MAN.
WHAT SORT OF TROUBLE YOU LOOKING FOR, BOY?
TO BE HONEST, I'VE NEVER FOUND A USE FOR THE MEN IN MY LIFE.

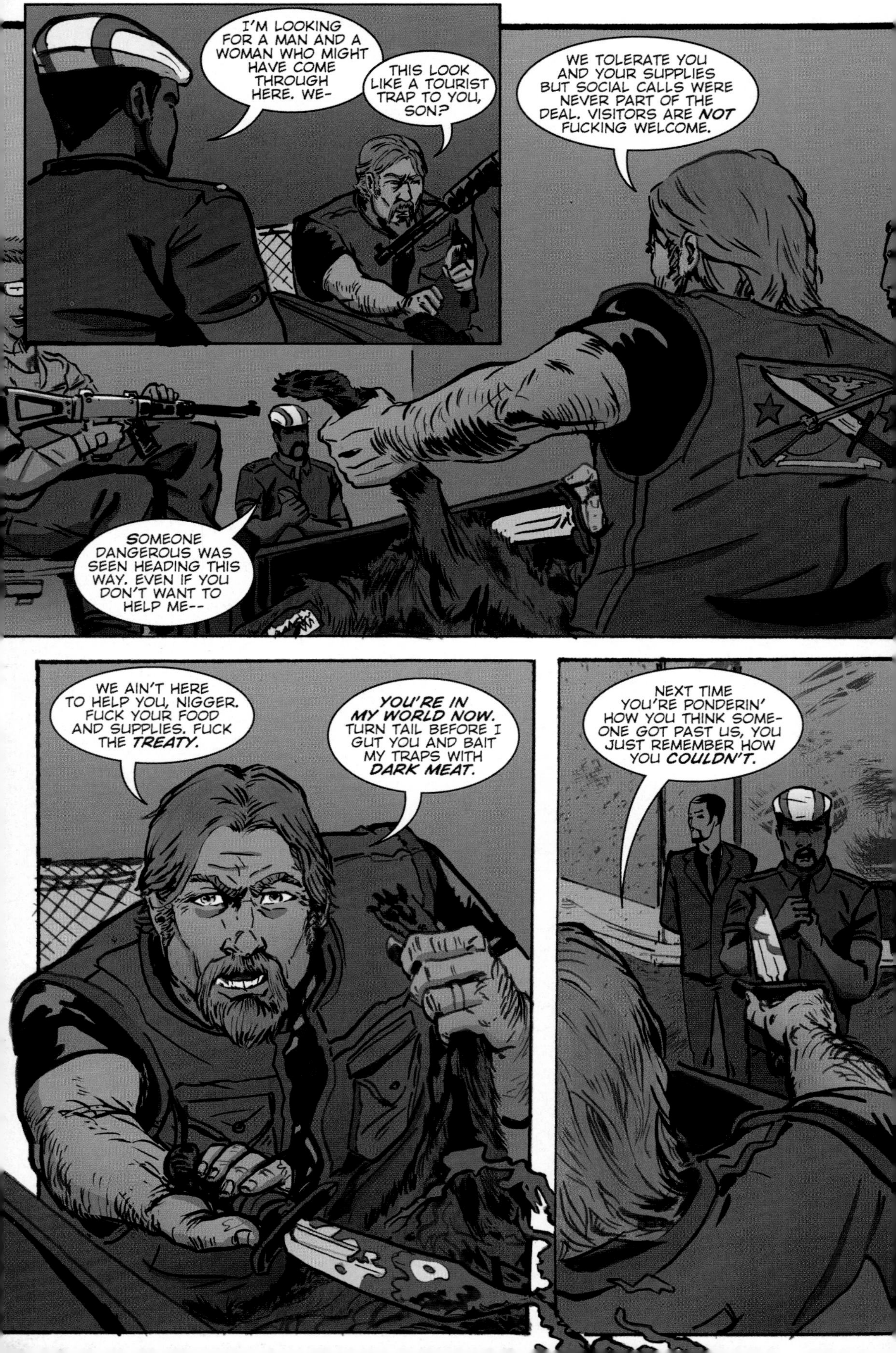
I'M LOOKING FOR A MAN AND A WOMAN WHO MIGHT HAVE COME THROUGH HERE. WE-
THIS LOOK LIKE A TOURIST TRAP TO YOU, SON?
WE TOLERATE YOU AND YOUR SUPPLIES BUT SOCIAL CALLS WERE NEVER PART OF THE DEAL. VISITORS ARE *NOT* FUCKING WELCOME.
SOMEONE DANGEROUS WAS SEEN HEADING THIS WAY. EVEN IF YOU DON'T WANT TO HELP ME--
WE AIN'T HERE TO HELP YOU, NIGGER. FUCK YOUR FOOD AND SUPPLIES. FUCK THE *TREATY*.
YOU'RE IN MY WORLD NOW. TURN TAIL BEFORE I GUT YOU AND BAIT MY TRAPS WITH *DARK MEAT*.
NEXT TIME YOU'RE PONDERIN' HOW YOU THINK SOME-ONE GOT PAST US, YOU JUST REMEMBER HOW YOU *COULDN'T*.

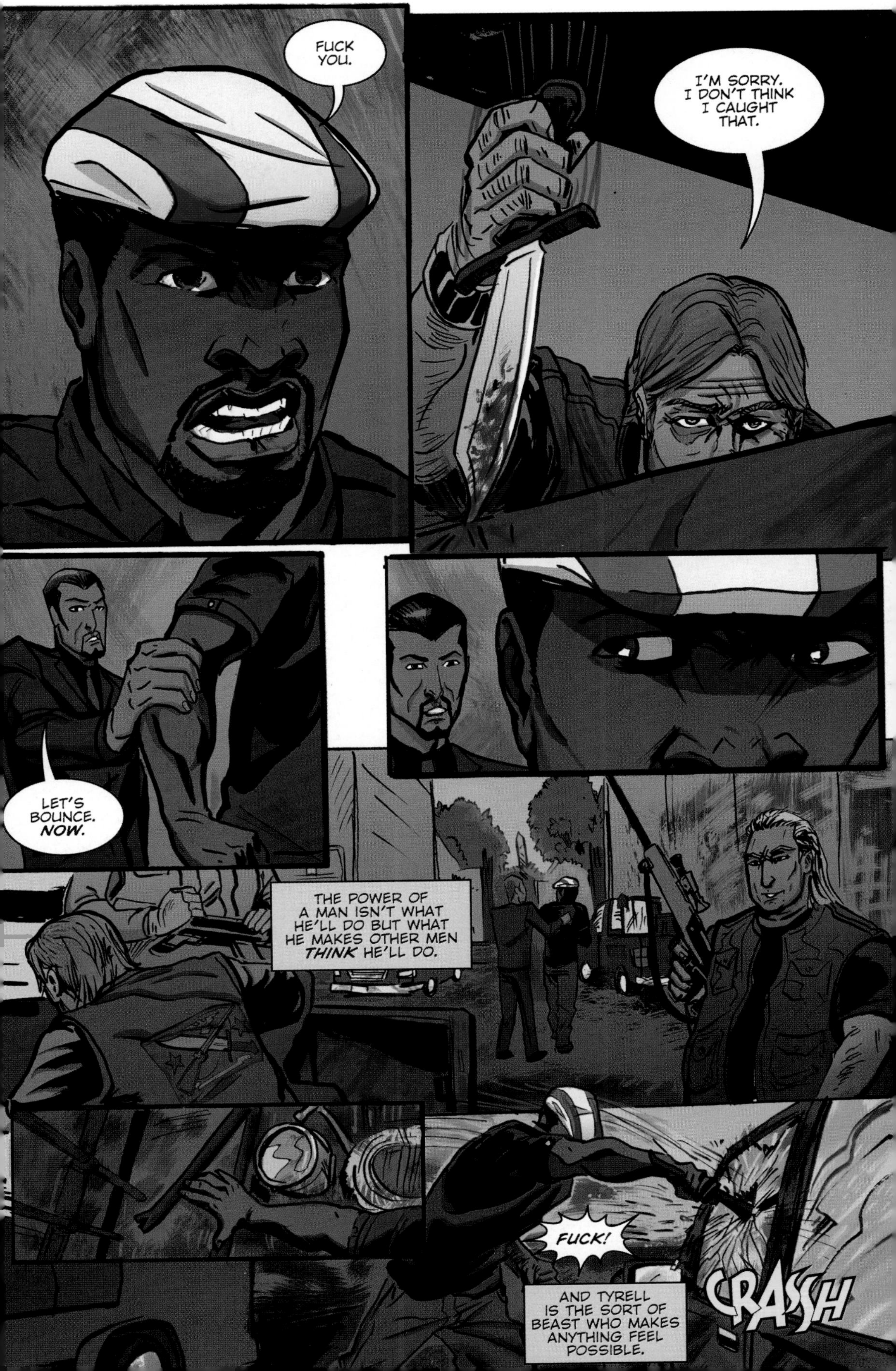
FUCK YOU.
I'M SORRY. I DON'T THINK I CAUGHT THAT.
LET'S BOUNCE. *NOW.*
THE POWER OF A MAN ISN'T WHAT HE'LL DO BUT WHAT HE MAKES OTHER MEN *THINK* HE'LL DO.
FUCK!
CRASH
AND TYRELL IS THE SORT OF BEAST WHO MAKES ANYTHING FEEL POSSIBLE.

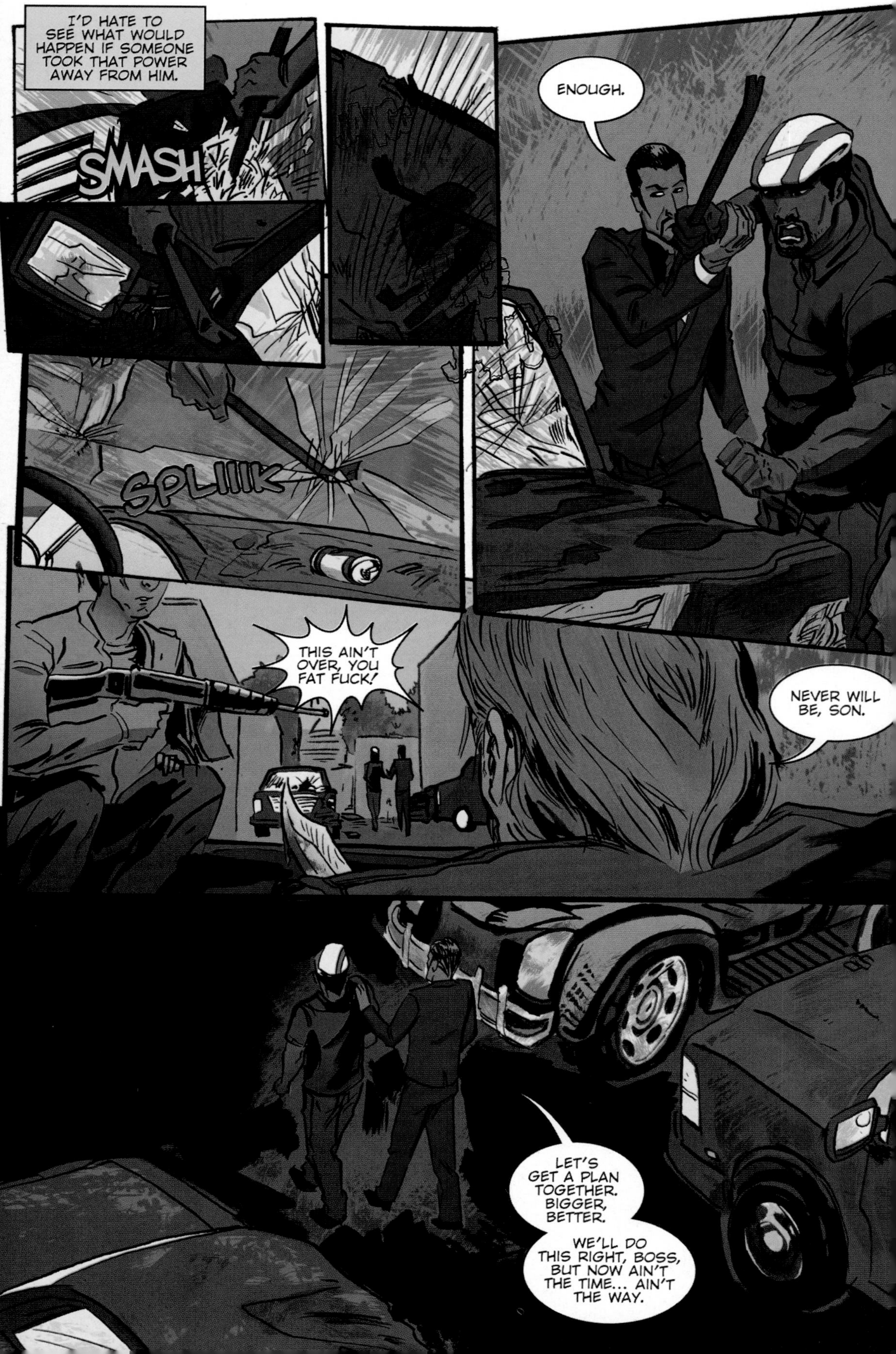
I'D HATE TO SEE WHAT WOULD HAPPEN IF SOMEONE TOOK THAT POWER AWAY FROM HIM.
SMASH
ENOUGH.
SPLIIIK
THIS AIN'T OVER, YOU FAT FUCK!
NEVER WILL BE, SON.
LET'S GET A PLAN TOGETHER. BIGGER, BETTER.
WE'LL DO THIS RIGHT, BOSS, BUT NOW AIN'T THE TIME... AIN'T THE WAY.

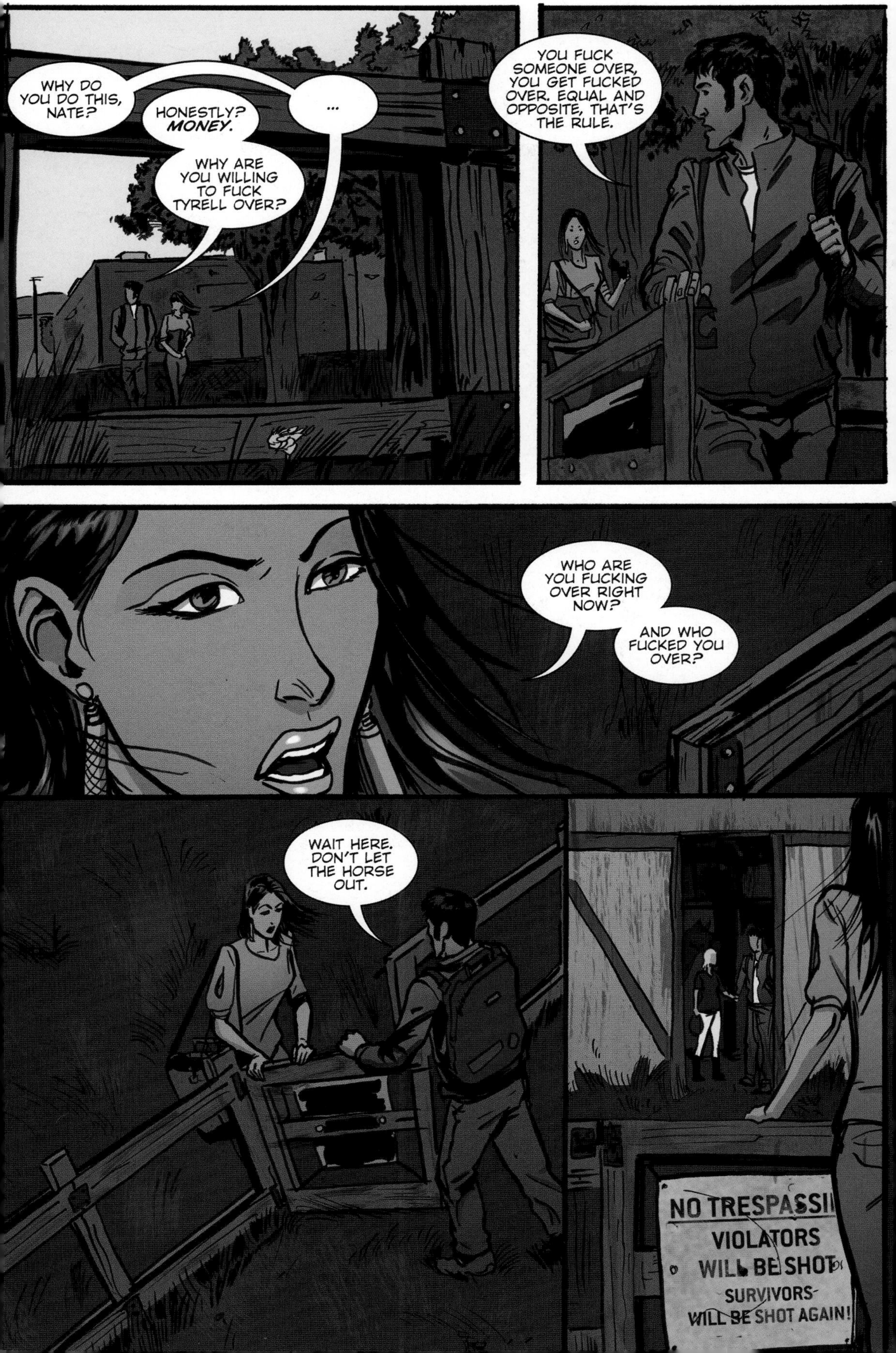
WHY DO YOU DO THIS, NATE?
HONESTLY? *MONEY*.
...
WHY ARE YOU WILLING TO FUCK TYRELL OVER?
YOU FUCK SOMEONE OVER, YOU GET FUCKED OVER. EQUAL AND OPPOSITE, THAT'S THE RULE.
WHO ARE YOU FUCKING OVER RIGHT NOW?
AND WHO FUCKED YOU OVER?
WAIT HERE. DON'T LET THE HORSE OUT.
NO TRESPASSI
VIOLATORS WILL BE SHOT
SURVIVORS WILL BE SHOT AGAIN!

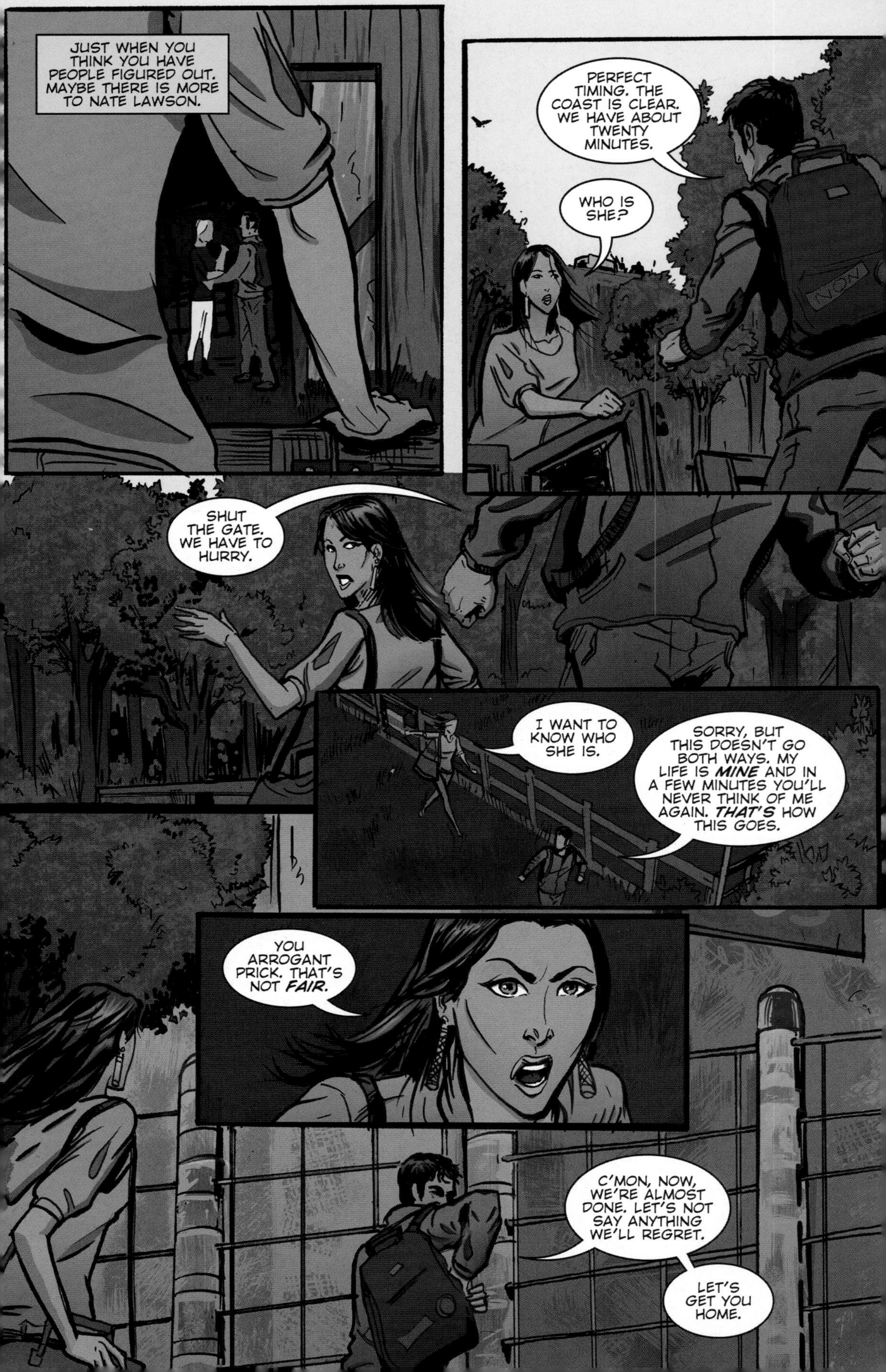
JUST WHEN YOU THINK YOU HAVE PEOPLE FIGURED OUT. MAYBE THERE IS MORE TO NATE LAWSON.
PERFECT TIMING. THE COAST IS CLEAR. WE HAVE ABOUT TWENTY MINUTES.
WHO IS SHE?
SHUT THE GATE. WE HAVE TO HURRY.
I WANT TO KNOW WHO SHE IS.
SORRY, BUT THIS DOESN'T GO BOTH WAYS. MY LIFE IS ***MINE*** AND IN A FEW MINUTES YOU'LL NEVER THINK OF ME AGAIN. ***THAT'S*** HOW THIS GOES.
YOU ARROGANT PRICK. THAT'S NOT ***FAIR.***
C'MON, NOW, WE'RE ALMOST DONE. LET'S NOT SAY ANYTHING WE'LL REGRET.
LET'S GET YOU HOME.

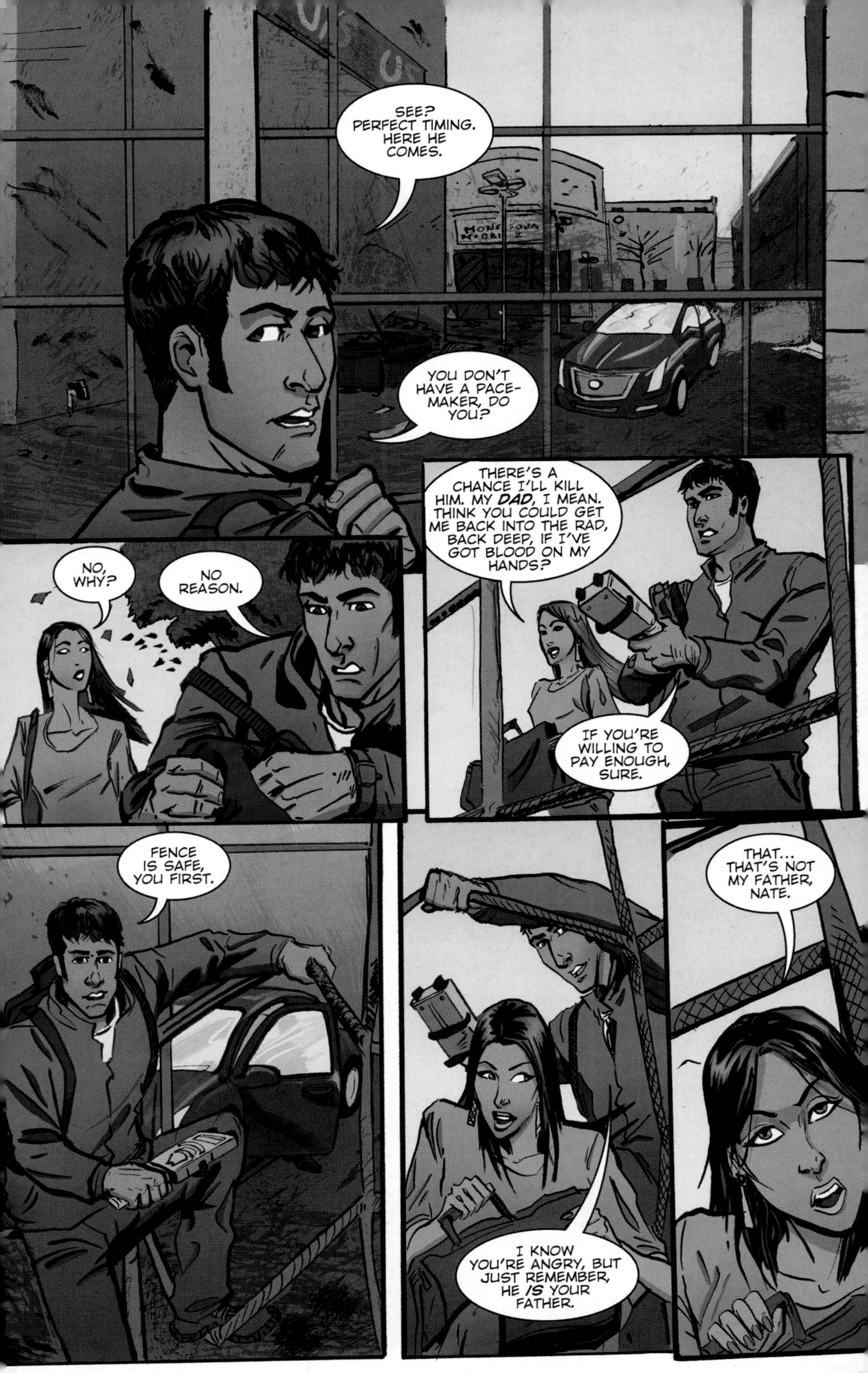
SEE? PERFECT TIMING. HERE HE COMES.
YOU DON'T HAVE A PACE-MAKER, DO YOU?
NO, WHY?
NO REASON.
THERE'S A CHANCE I'LL KILL HIM. MY DAD, I MEAN. THINK YOU COULD GET ME BACK INTO THE RAD, BACK DEEP, IF I'VE GOT BLOOD ON MY HANDS?
IF YOU'RE WILLING TO PAY ENOUGH, SURE.
FENCE IS SAFE, YOU FIRST.
I KNOW YOU'RE ANGRY, BUT JUST REMEMBER, HE IS YOUR FATHER.
THAT... THAT'S NOT MY FATHER, NATE.

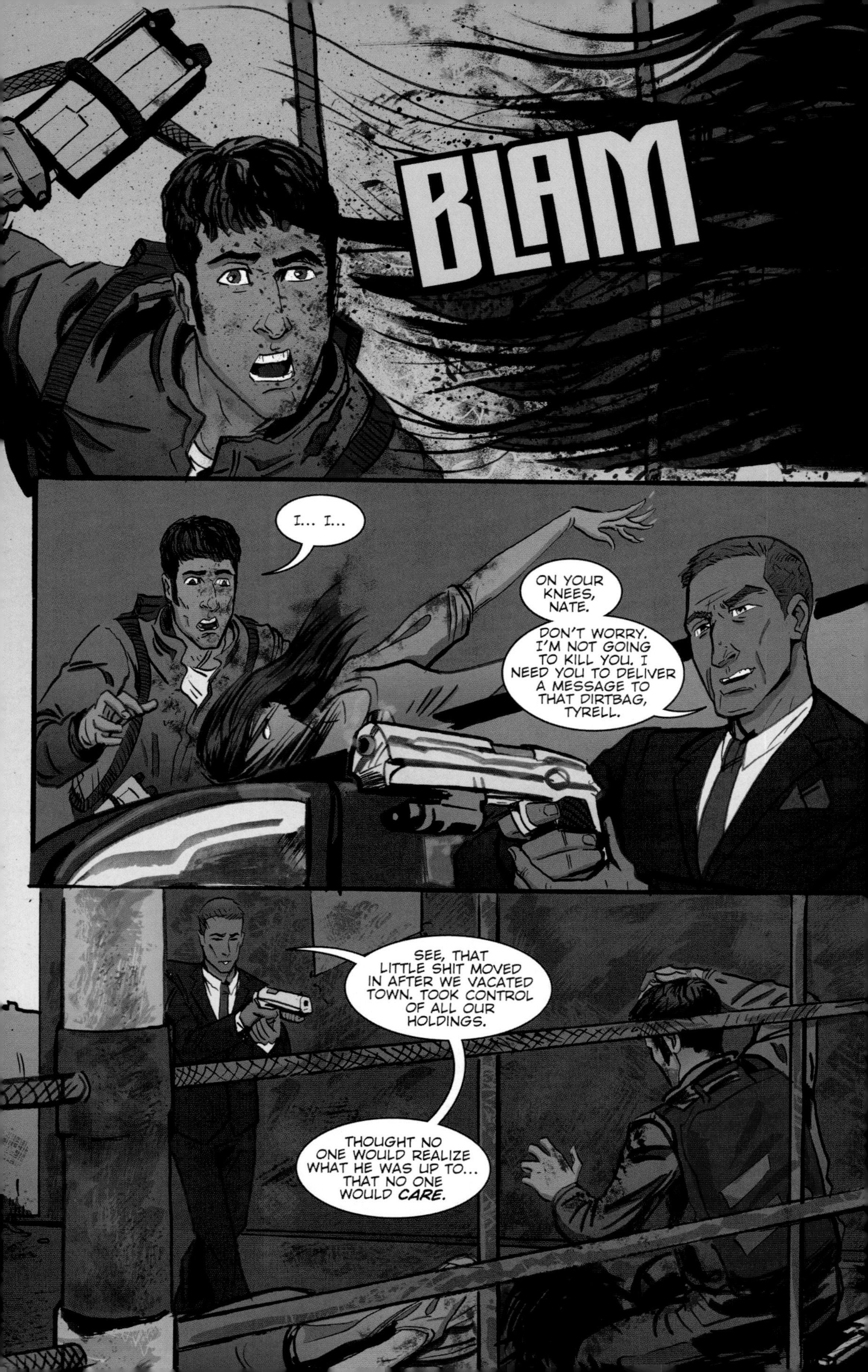
BLAM
I... I...
ON YOUR KNEES, NATE.
DON'T WORRY. I'M NOT GOING TO KILL YOU. I NEED YOU TO DELIVER A MESSAGE TO THAT DIRTBAG, TYRELL.
SEE, THAT LITTLE SHIT MOVED IN AFTER WE VACATED TOWN. TOOK CONTROL OF ALL OUR HOLDINGS.
THOUGHT NO ONE WOULD REALIZE WHAT HE WAS UP TO... THAT NO ONE WOULD *CARE*.

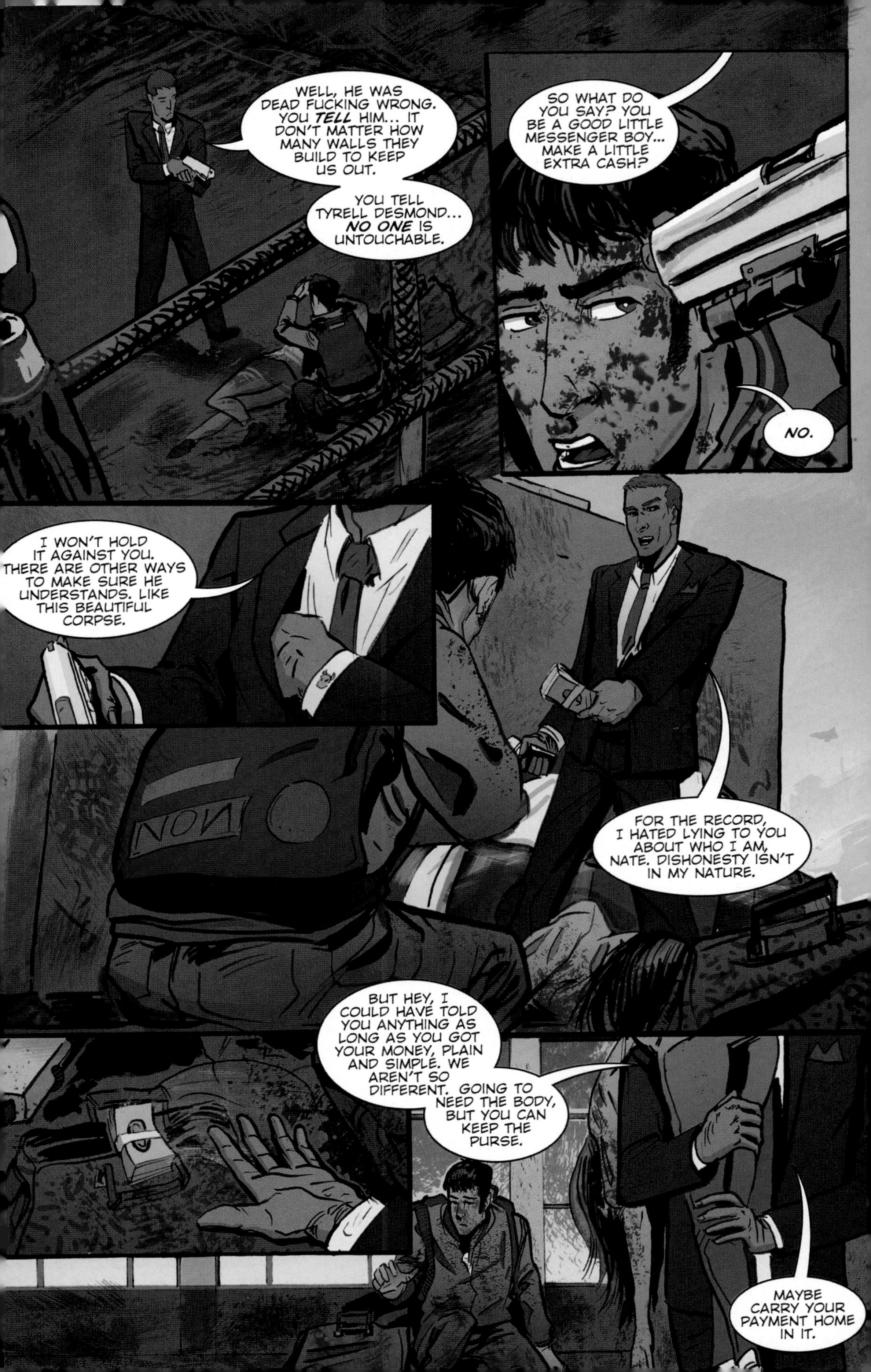
WELL, HE WAS DEAD FUCKING WRONG. YOU *TELL* HIM... IT DON'T MATTER HOW MANY WALLS THEY BUILD TO KEEP US OUT.
YOU TELL TYRELL DESMOND... *NO ONE* IS UNTOUCHABLE.
SO WHAT DO YOU SAY? YOU BE A GOOD LITTLE MESSENGER BOY... MAKE A LITTLE EXTRA CASH?
NO.
I WON'T HOLD IT AGAINST YOU. THERE ARE OTHER WAYS TO MAKE SURE HE UNDERSTANDS. LIKE THIS BEAUTIFUL CORPSE.
FOR THE RECORD, I HATED LYING TO YOU ABOUT WHO I AM, NATE. DISHONESTY ISN'T IN MY NATURE.
BUT HEY, I COULD HAVE TOLD YOU ANYTHING AS LONG AS YOU GOT YOUR MONEY, PLAIN AND SIMPLE. WE AREN'T SO DIFFERENT. GOING TO NEED THE BODY, BUT YOU CAN KEEP THE PURSE.
MAYBE CARRY YOUR PAYMENT HOME IN IT.

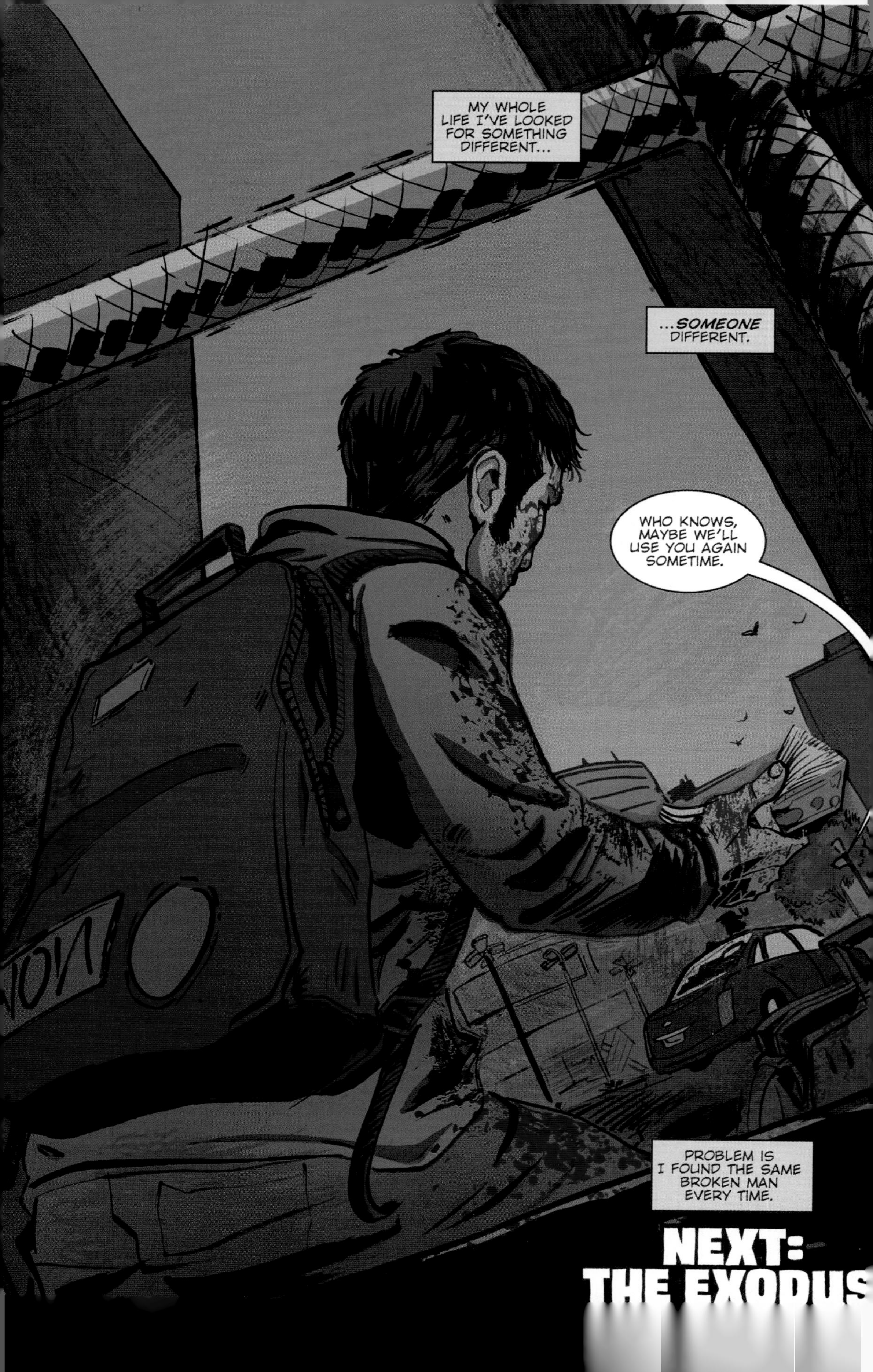
MY WHOLE LIFE I'VE LOOKED FOR SOMETHING DIFFERENT...
...SOMEONE DIFFERENT.
WHO KNOWS, MAYBE WE'LL USE YOU AGAIN SOMETIME.
PROBLEM IS I FOUND THE SAME BROKEN MAN EVERY TIME.
NEXT: THE EXODUS

GHOSTWRITTEN

And so ends the first arc of Ghost Town. Pre-Apocalyptic Washington DC is a rough place, eh?

For those of you that aren't familiar with my work, I guess introductions are in order. I'm Dave Dwonch, Action Lab's Creative Director, and writer of Vamplets, Double Jumpers, and the co-creator of Ghost Town. Rob Ruddell and I have been great friends for several years now, and when he came to me with the initial concept, I knew he had something special. We began mulling over what we'd do in this brave new world, and came up with a gaggle of really strong ideas. Justin Greenwood and I had pitched a series to ONI a while back and they hired him out from under my nose for Resurrection (which he parlayed into a gig on Wasteland). I have wanted to work with him for as long as I can remember , and it was kismet that his schedule opened briefly for the first issue of Ghost Town. I knew he had to get back to his day job at ONI after Ghost Town #1, but I didn't have to look far to find someone he could pass the torch to.

I have known Daniel Logan forever—we basically cut our teeth together at an indie publisher years ago, and our graphic novella, "Back in the Day," was the first book out of the gate for Action Lab. He came on board and we hit the ground running on designs for the primary cast. Then… I got busy. Really busy. Work at Action Lab increased, and I couldn't keep up with the book.

Daniel suggested Ryan Lindsay as scripter. Not only did he take the gig, he took an active role in expanding the universe, creating Etana Roche and tightening up the random ideas and locations within The Rad. He and Daniel truly carried us through this first series, and I cannot thank them enough for the blood, sweat and tears they've given to making this book a reality.

And now, Ghost Town is calling me back into it.

The five of us have worked really hard in crafting the book you hold in your hands, and I've been missing writing these characters. Next year you'll be seeing Ghost Town: The Exodus, which will be written by me and will bring us back to the beginning and the darkest time in American History: The evacuation of the country's capital. You'll see the "origins" of some of the characters Ryan and Daniel gave us in Godfathers and Daughters, and we'll be digging deeper into the microcosm of The Rad. It'll be a bold new beginning that will unsettle, entertain, and hopefully inspire.

See you in 2014.

--Dave

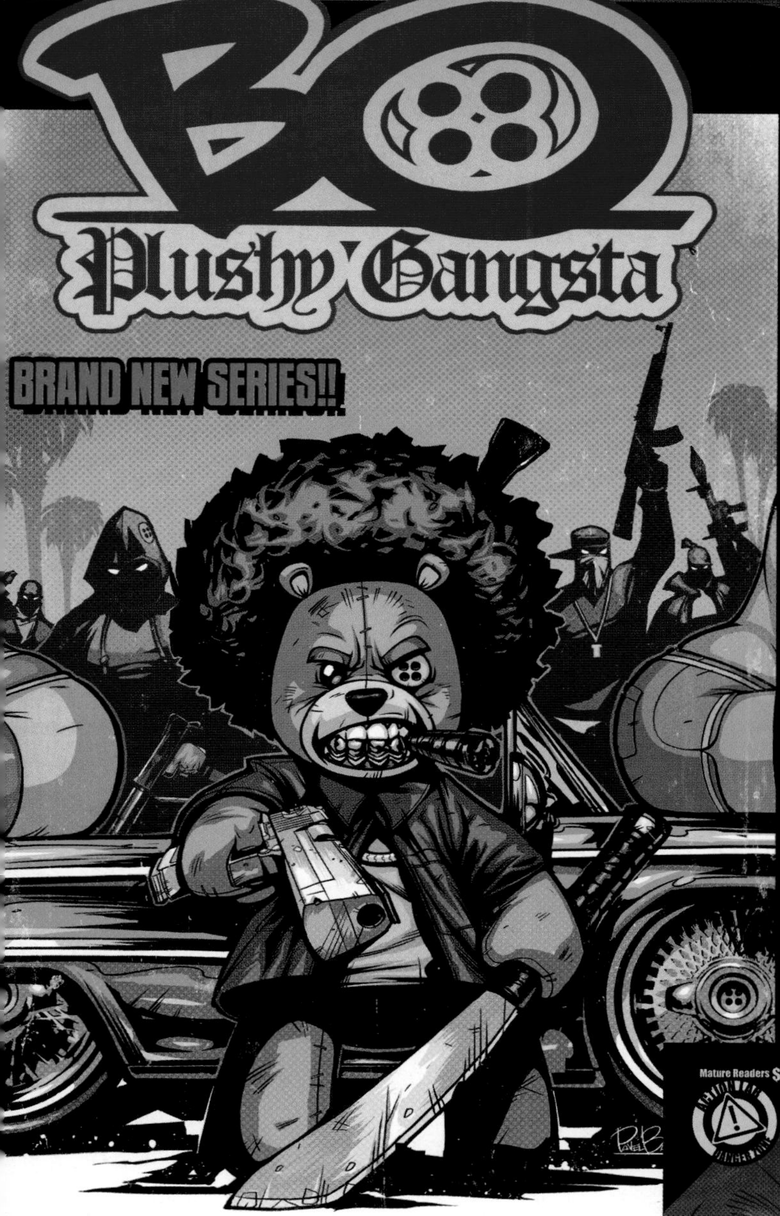
BO
Plushy Gangsta
BRAND NEW SERIES!!

JANUARY 2014
ISSUE 1 - $3.99
MATURE READERS
SHIPS WITH 2 COVERS!

FROM RUSSIAN VIDEO GAME ARTIST PAVEL BALABANOV

Are the legends of Bo, the "teddy bear" gangsta, true? And, did we just say teddy bear gangsta?!?

You're about to find out-- when Bo's girls get nabbed by a rival gang boss, the mysterious and fearsome plushy gangsta is forced into action!

PERFECT FOR FANS OF BODY BAGS OR THE RIDE!

WARNING: THIS BOOK CONTAINS PLUSHY GANG VIOLENCE, TEDDY BEAR CURSING, AND DRUG USE

STAY ALERT!

SCARFACE MEETS TED IN VIDEO GAME STYLE!

1 IN 5 VARIANT COVER

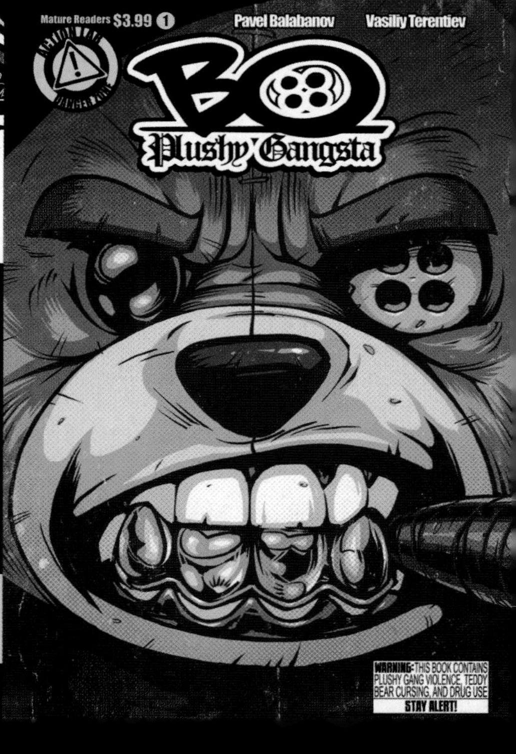
Mature Readers $3.99 1
Pavel Balabanov
Vasiliy Terentiev
BO
Plushy Gangsta
WARNING: THIS BOOK CONTAINS PLUSHY GANG VIOLENCE, TEDDY BEAR CURSING, AND DRUG USE
STAY ALERT!

DIAMOND ORDER CODE NOV130741

ACTIONLABCOMICS.COM/DANGER-ZONE

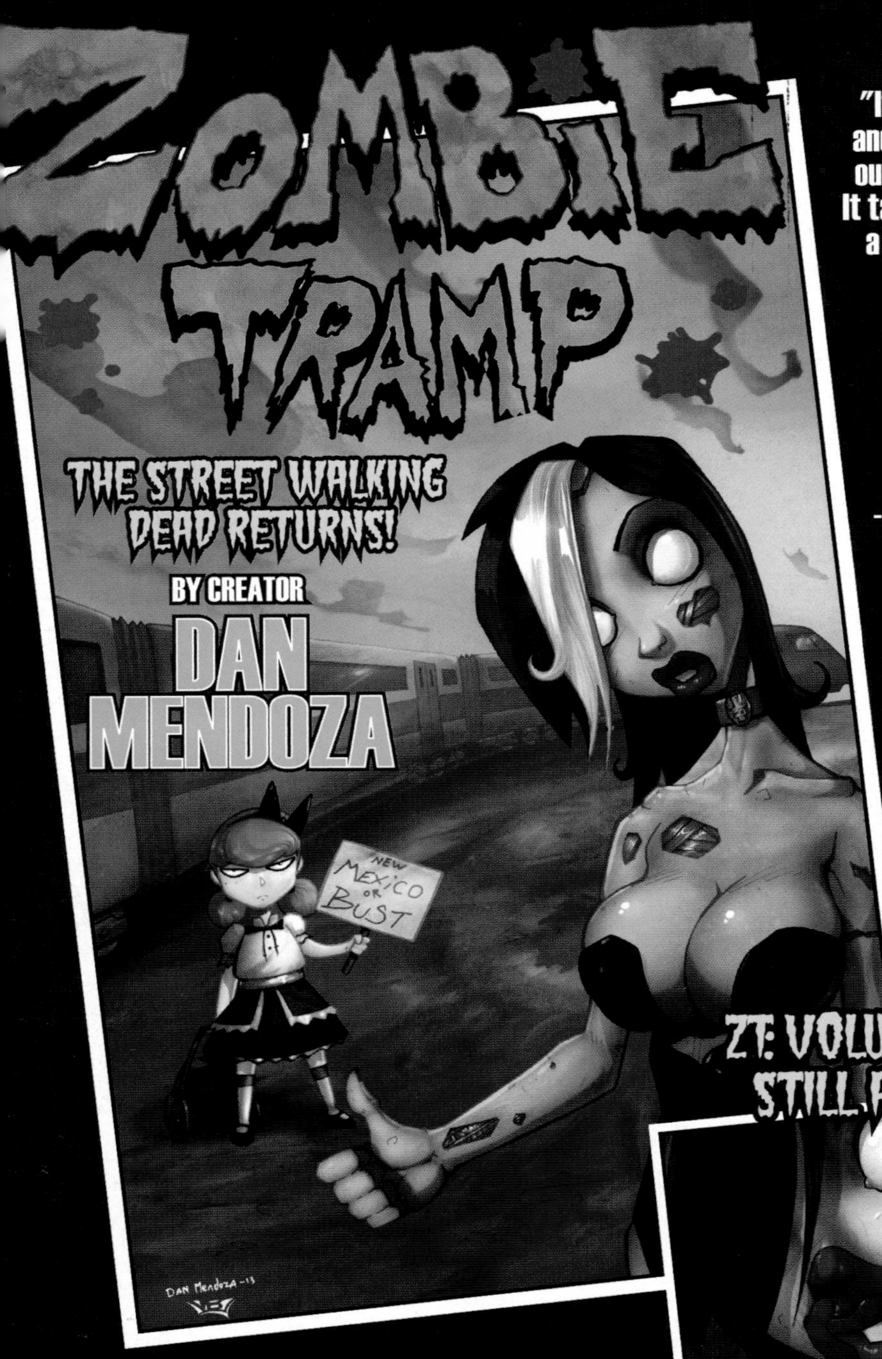
ZOMBIE TRAMP
THE STREET WALKING DEAD RETURNS!
BY CREATOR
DAN MENDOZA
NEW MEXICO OR BUST
DAN Mendoza -13

"It's one of the most origi
and fun zombie books to co
out in the past several yea
It takes a genre that's beco
a bit stale of late and adds
crazy sexy twist to
--AintItCoolNews.c

"This is one indy co
you do not want to mis
--shockhorrormagazine.c

"This was a rea
wonderfully fun co
with nice art an
very shocking endi
I really enjoyed
--ComicsBulletin.c

ZT: VOLUME ONE TPB
STILL AVAILABLE!

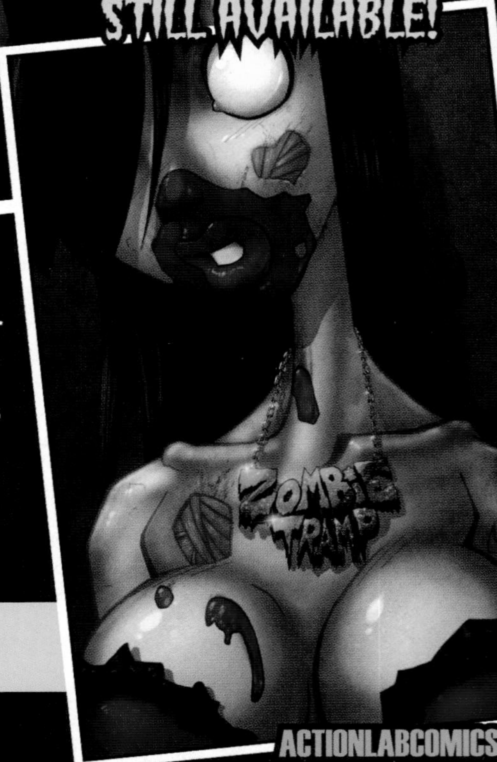
ZOMBIE TRAMP

We're back for volume two, and picking up right where we left off, where does Janey, our former Hollywood call girl turned undead heroine, go from here? What fetish fashion will she wear?? And more importantly, why is it called the Taint Train of Terror? All aboard to find out!

FANS OF TRUE BLOOD AND
GRINDHOUSE CINEMA
WILL LOVE ZOMBIE TRAMP!

ACTION LAB DANGER ZONE

PICK UP VOLUME TWO NOW!

ACTIONLABCOMICS.C

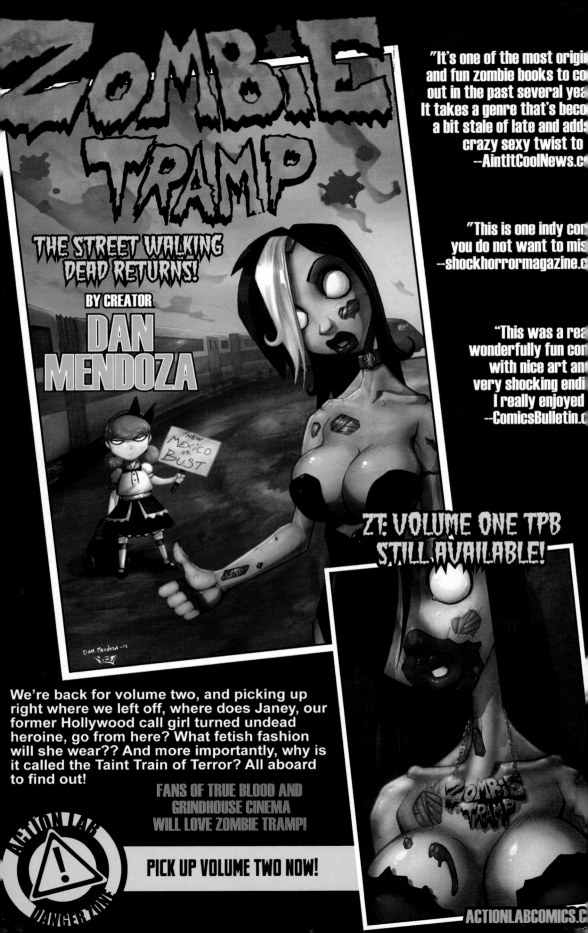

ACTION LAB DANGER ZONE
DANGER ZONE
THE BRAND NEW MATURE READERS LINE OF CREATOR OWNED TITLES FROM ACTION LAB ENTERTAINMENT!
Mature Readers
Pavel Balabanov
Vasiliy Terentiev
BO Plushy Gangsta
Mature Readers
McKinney
Ford
Strutz
EHMM THEORY
DOUBLE JUMPERS
CHOOSE YOUR CHARACTER!
Mature Readers
THE FINAL PLAGUE
Mature Readers
Dwonch
Greenwood
GHOST TOWN
VEGAS
Mature Readers
Martin
McKay
NIGHT OF THE 80's UNDEAD
FRANKIE SAYS RELAX
SubCulture
Merlin's Outhouse
OMNIBUS
THE TRIP
Mature Readers
Dan Mendoza
ZOMBIE TRAMP
SHE'S BACK!
ACTIONLABCOMICS.COM/DANGER-ZONE
WARNING: THESE BOOKS MAY CONTAIN SUPER COOL CONTENT THAT COULD BLOW YOUR MIND!
STAY ALERT

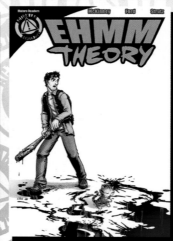

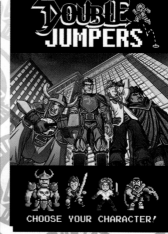

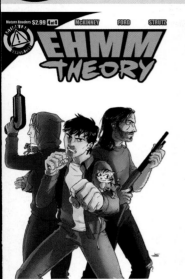

ACTION LAB
DANGER ZONE
READ MORE NOW

Ghost Town - Action Lab

00411

7 99975 19465 3

ACTIONLABCOMICS.COM